I0652703

CRIMINAL ROGUES

CRIMINAL ROGUES

VOLUME I

THE EXPLOITS OF DANBY CROKER

R. Austin Freeman

A PRINCE OF SWINDLERS

Guy Boothby

Coachwhip Publications
Landisville, Pennsylvania

Criminal Rogues, Volume 1
Copyright © 2012 Coachwhip Publications
The Exploits of Danby Croker, by R. Austin Freeman, first published 1916
The Viceroy's Protegé, or A Prince of Swindlers, by Guy Boothby, first
   published 1900
No claims made on public domain material.

ISBN 1-61646-140-3
ISBN-13 978-1-61646-140-9

CoachwhipBooks.com

All Rights Reserved. No part of this publication may be reproduced,
stored in a retrieval system or transmitted in any form or by any
means—electronic, mechanical, photocopy, recording or any other—
except for brief quotations in printed reviews, without the prior permission of the author or publisher.

CONTENTS

The Exploits of Danby Croker

A Prince of Swindlers

THE EXPLOITS OF DANBY CROKER

BEING EXPLOITS FROM A SOMEWHAT
DISREPUTABLE AUTOBIOGRAPHY

R. AUSTIN FREEMAN

PREFACE

ELSEWHERE I HAVE observed that the primary and only legitimate function of a work of fiction is to furnish entertainment to the reader; but that if this function is duly discharged there can be no harm in an author's artfully and unostentatiously insinuating into his work a certain amount of matter having a more serious purpose. Even a book written in so light a vein as is the present "disreputable autobiography" may have a serious message for the sufficiently thoughtful reader; and it is of the subject of that message that I should like to speak.

Those who are familiar with the practice of the Court of Criminal Appeal may find in chapter XII something reminiscent of an actual case that was once heard in it. More than this, I suppose I had better not say; but I may be permitted to express the hope that those who are concerned in the administration of the law will subject to the most jealous and searching scrutiny all fingerprint evidence that is not fully corroborated. The wild and dangerous statement made many years ago by Galton that a fingerprint furnishes "evidence requiring no corroboration" seems to have been accepted even in high legal quarters. But it is utterly untrue. A fingerprint, duly attested by the evidence of a witness, has an evidential value equal to that of the testimony of the particular witness. An unwitnessed fingerprint has no value at all until it has been proved that it really is a fingerprint and not a fraudulent imitation; which can be done only by the evidence of some person who witnessed its production. A fraud that is so easy calls for safeguards at least

equal to those set up against the more difficult fraud of a false signature.

That is all I have to say. Now I will "holde my pees" and let the
reader get on with the story.

R.A.F.

Halton Camp West, Bucks,
July, 1916.

I
THE CHANGELING

"Methinks you are my glass, and not my brother,
I see by you I am a sweet-fac'd youth."
Comedy of Errors.

WHAT A WORLD of trouble would be saved if people would only be honest!

The thought—a little obvious, perhaps—occurs to me again and again as I sit in leisured retirement, compiling (with a certain retrospective satisfaction) these records of an ill-spent life; and I reflect with increasing wonder on the tolerance of mankind for those social vermin who batten on the industry of their fellows.

What a simple and pleasant life it would be if there were none but honest men! The costly machinery of the law would be unnecessary, the labourer would reap the harvest of his effort, commerce would thrive unhindered—and, incidentally, these chronicles would never have been written.

For the whole disastrous train of events herein set forth arose out of the dishonesty of Tom Nagget. But for Tom, my life might—mind, I don't say it would, but it might—have been one of productive industry, laborious, uneventful, and probably devilish dull.

A rather mysterious person was Tom Nagget. By his own account he was connected with *Scrubb's Handbook*, a guide to the hotels and hydros of the United Kingdom. But no one had ever seen this work of reference; and this fact, together with the singular fluctuations in Tom's financial condition, formed the subject of curious comment among the little coterie that used to gather round the fire in Joe Dalby's studio.

That was in Tom's absence, of course. When he was present the company was regaled with accounts of gay doings at fashionable hotels and seaside resorts not entirely unconnected with the feminine denizens thereof. To all of which we were accustomed to listen with outward scorn and secret envy.

The crucial event of my life occurred soon after the Enesdale Motor Company had dispensed with my services. Being then without employment, and uncommonly short of funds, the natural thing appeared to be to take a few days at the seaside; and thus, following the dictates of Nature, I had just taken a ticket for Hunsgate-on-Sea, when who should come pushing through the crowd but Tom Nagget, figged out in a smart grey suit, exactly similar to my own, and carrying a brand-new suitcase marked with the initials D.B.

Now, I did not wish to travel with Tom. I am a rather solitary man, and, besides, I was traveling first class. When one is hard up it is agreeable and reassuring to travel first class; and really it is a quite inexpensive luxury if one is content to make shift with a third-class ticket. So I allowed Tom to push through to the platform, and, when I had seen him safely bestowed (in a "third" forward), I waited for the train to start, and then hopped into a first smoker.

But though absent, Tom was not forgotten. In the solitude of my compartment I ruminated upon the cryptic characters that I had read on his suitcase. "D.B." were the letters, and obviously they had no connection with his lawful name; for even a Scotchman could hardly contrive to wriggle a D into Thomas, or a B into Nagget. And, seeing that the suitcase was new, and the lettering freshly painted, there could be little doubt that the falsification was deliberate. Thomas was up to something.

As to the similarity of his clothes to mine, there was nothing in that. It is true that he wore a straw "boater," a grey flannel suit, and brown boots, and so did I; but then so, also, did fifty per cent of the young men who had entered the train. This is a machine-made age.

But the similarity in dress reminded me of another much more curious resemblance. The fact is that Tom and I were as like as two peas, and yet, oddly enough, no one but Joe Dalby had ever noticed the likeness. But Joe was a sculptor, accustomed to dissociate form from colour, and he viewed us with an unbiased, monochromatic eye.

"If I were to model a bust of you, and one of Tom," he said, when he revealed to me this *lusus naturæ*, "you couldn't tell one from t'other. You are like a couple of chessmen or billiard-balls, only distinguishable by your respective colours."

And Joe was right. I realised it at once when he pointed it out. In the shape of head, in features, even in our light-grey eyes, we were identical. But whereas my head-covering was of the golden or flaxen type, poor Tom's cranium was disfigured by a crop of jet-black hair, with heavy eyebrows to match. It was a thousand pities, for otherwise he would have been a really good-looking fellow. But it was not only our heads that were similar: in height, in build, and in carriage we were singularly alike; and though I bear Thomas no special goodwill, I will do him the justice to say that a better set-up, smarter, or more elegant young man you wouldn't wish to see.

Reflection on this natural phenomenon led to speculation. Since the difference between us was mainly of colour, and colour is mutable, it could be removed. Black hair can be bleached by peroxide to the semblance of golden; golden hair can be dyed black. Supposing I were to dye my hair black, where would be the difference between us? There would be none. By the casual stranger, at least, we should be indistinguishable.

Suppose, for instance, that I presented myself, thus transformed, at Thomas's boarding-house, and engaged a room. What a to-do there would be! And what a mighty frustration of the schemes of the secretive Thomas! I leaned back on the cushion, and shouted with laughter. Dromio of Camden Town and Dromio of Bloomsbury! The possibilities were really excruciating.

And, after all, why not? Hair-dye is cheap, and there is no law against using it. Why not convert this brilliant possibility into an actuality?

The more I turned over the idea the better I liked it. I am not an inquisitive man, but I must admit that the mysterious doings of

Tom Nagget piqued my curiosity. He was so secret about himself, and such a boastful bounder, too.

"I'll do it!" I decided, at length. "Yes; by Jove, I will!" And, the momentous resolution formed, I fell to making my plans.

The boarding-house scheme I rejected on consideration, for the cat would be out of the bag at once, and Tom would be on his guard. It would be better to watch him from a safe distance, and keep him unaware of his dual personality. Then, when the chance presented itself, I could wade in and make things hum.

As the train slowed down in Hunsgate Station, I grasped my rug and holdall and sprang out, shutting the door after me—a wise precaution when one has a third-class ticket. Then I plunged into the crowd and kept a wary eye on Tom until he bustled out of the station, when I, too, emerged and strolled down the High Street in search of a tea-shop. There was no scarcity of these establishments, but I am somewhat fastidious in the matter of tea, and the rather fly-blown aspect of those that I encountered repelled me. Suddenly my attention was arrested by a shop- window from which a wax bust looked out inanely on the street. The bust represented a gentleman of a suety complexion with glossy black hair (which reminded me strongly of Tom Nagget), and was guarded by a battalion of bottles, each of which bore on its label the mystic word "Snatcho" above the portrait of a person resembling a hairy Ainu.

I made a mental note of the shop, and, when I had consumed a substantial tea, I returned and entered boldly. The presiding genius of the place, an elderly man whose head suggested a billiardball which had been the subject of unsuccessful experiments with Snatcho, leered at me inquiringly.

"Have you got any black hair-dye?" I asked.

"Yes, sir," he replied with a glance of, not unnatural, surprise at my golden locks.

"I want to dye my hair black," I said, "but only temporarily. I want some stuff that I can clean off without difficulty when I've done with it."

"Ah! Then the 'Balm of Ethiopia' will suit you, sir. It resists soap and water perfectly, but can be removed in a few minutes with a little methylated spirit."

"Is it difficult to put on?" I asked.

"The application of a dye," he answered, "requires skill and experience. The hair must be coloured to the roots, but the skin must not be stained. Perhaps," he added, "as you only require a single application, you would be wiser to entrust the operation to me."

With this suggestion I at once fell in. The birdresser conducted me to a secret chamber behind the shop, whence I emerged a quarter of an hour later, hideously and wonderfully transformed. As I stood opposite a pier-glass waiting for my change, I seemed to be the subject of some horrible enchantment, for the figure that stared out at me from the mirror bore no resemblance to me, but was beyond all question that of Tom Nagget. Even my eyebrows had spread out into the semblance of small moustaches, and only Providence preserved my cheeks and lip intact. For I am what is described as clean-shaven, though, as a matter of fact, I do not shave. There is no need. Nature, satisfied with her handiwork, has forborne to disfigure my countenance with bristles.

As I staggered out into the street it seemed to me that all eyes were fixed on me. Of course they were not. It was merely my natural self-consciousness, though a good many people did look at me—especially the women and girls—more so than usual, I thought, though this must have been a delusion. Still, they did look, and with obvious approval, strange to say; and though I despised their lack of taste, I did not repulse them. A good-looking shop girl at a draper's door ogled me as I passed, and I winked in response; a buxom housemaid who was cleaning a window smiled down at me engagingly, and I kissed my hand. It was shockingly bad form, I admit, and very different from my usual modest and gentlemanly behavior. But, of course, good or bad form was no concern of mine; it was entirely Tom Nagget's affair.

After the crowded High Street, it was a relief to come down to the sea-front, though that was pretty crowded, too, for the tide was up, and the population of the sands had overflowed on to the esplanade. However, there remained a slip of uncovered sand between the margin of the surf and the row of bathing-machines that had been hauled up for the day, and here I strolled up and down

for a while, considering my plan of action. Suddenly, I noticed the
people, with one accord, scuttling like rabbits towards the town, a
phenomenon that was easily explained by a smart patter of rain-
drops. It was only a summer shower, but it would be well to get
under cover. I tried the back door of a bathing-machine but, as I
had expected, it was locked. However, I knew something about
locks, and I knew that the lock of a bathing-machine was not likely
to be a Chubb. With a glance at the keyhole, I drew out my bunch
of keys, and, selecting the one that appertained to my own back
door, I inserted it and gave a tentative turn. The lock clicked, the
door yielded, and I entered, bolting myself in to avoid discovery.

The benches at the side of the machine being unreposefully
narrow, I spread my rug on the dry though sandy floor, and,
placing my holdall for a pillow, lay down at my ease, and, as the
rain drummed on the wooden roof, I lit my pipe and cogitated.

Not a bad shelter, this; better than crouching in a doorway or
standing under a dripping shop-blind. I was glad I had found it,
and made a mental note of it in case of a rainy day. Rainy day?
Why not night, too? Yes, by Jingo! Why should I go to a beastly
boarding-house or flea-bitten lodgings when I could have this for
the mere turning of a key? I looked about me. Not so bad, this, for
a bachelor's chamber; clean, airy, quiet, select, and cheap. "Man
wants but little here below," and if he can get that little for nothing, why, so much the better for him. When, on the clearing-up of
the shower, I stepped out once more into the open, I had already
constituted myself the tenant of "all that messuage and premises
known as and being number 73," for the term of my stay, at a pep-
percorn rent.

I saw nothing of Tom Nagget that day. I walked about the streets
and haunted the esplanade, but the two Dromios remained asun-
der. I dined luxuriously—I could afford to, having no rent to pay—
and spent the evening at the Marine Amphitheatre, where, I fear, I
conducted myself (or should I say himself?) with reprehensible
levity. A moonlight ramble along the shore—not entirely solitary—
finished up the day in a highly agreeable manner, and, when I rolled
home to number 73, the harbour bell was chiming half-past twelve.

I was aroused in the morning by what I, at first, took to be the shock of an earthquake. The clink of a chain, however, impinging on my awakening consciousness, informed me that the machine was being towed down to the sea. Clearly it was time for me to make myself scarce before I was beset by the murmuring waves. Accordingly, I grabbed up my rug and holdall, and, softly unlocking the landward door, dropped down on the sand. And none too soon; for as I turned away, my commodious seaside residence plunged into the breakers.

But I was back again presently with a couple of towels and a ridiculous combination garment, in which I disported myself for half an hour among the waves in the brilliant morning sunshine. I was an enthusiastic swimmer, and, besides, one must wash somehow.

After the bath, I took a brisk walk along the shore, revisiting the scene of my midnight ramble, until raging hunger drove me to the excellent restaurant where I had dined on the previous evening; and here, having trifled with a couple of eggs, a gammon-rasher, half a lobster, and the best part of a cottage-loaf, I sat smoking a contemplative pipe and reading the papers until the morning was well advanced. Then, leaving my rug and holdall to be called for in the evening, I went forth to look for Tom Nagget.

Better had it been for me and for my fellowmen had I left Tom Nagget alone. For, like that earliest *faux pas* that, banishing peace and innocence,

"Brought death into the world and all our woe,"

this act was the unconsidered antecedent of consequences incalculable and without end.

But let me not anticipate.

My wanderings through the town had brought me to a little square—Hougoumont Square, I think it was called—when I became aware of the clamour of many voices, and above the confused uproar I distinctly made out the cry of "Stop thief!" I halted to listen. The place where I stood was at the junction of two converging streets, and I commanded a view down both. Suddenly I saw a

couple of policeman with an attendant crowd dart across the farther end of the one to the right, and almost at the same moment a
man shot across the left-hand one and vanished into a narrow by-
street.

The hunter's instinct is born in us all, the heritage from skin-
clad, palæolithic ancestors. As the man disappeared, I uttered a
cheerful view-halloo! and started in pursuit.

I reached the by-street in time to see the fugitive dart round
the farther corner, and, as I weathered the corner, a leg twinkled
for an instant at the entrance to a court, and was gone. I put my
hands to my mouth and shouted "Yoicks!" and my call was echoed
in a chorus of answering howls from behind.

When I arrived at the mouth of the court, the fugitive had vanished, but at the farther end I could see a narrow alley, which I
immediately made for, hallooing joyously. The alley, however,
turned out to be a cul de sac, and as soon as I realised this I turned
and raced back; and, as I reached the entrance, I ran full tilt into
an advancing constable.

"He isn't here!" I exclaimed, struggling to extricate myself from
the constabulary embrace. "He must have gone down the next turning. D'you hear? Don't stand clawing me about, man; you're letting the fellow escape."

"Oh no I'm not!" said the constable, taking a more secure hold
of my collar.

"You confounded idiot!" I shouted, wriggling frantically as the
crowd closed round and the second constable grabbed me by the
arm. "You don't suppose I'm the man, do you?"

"I don't suppose," answered the constable; "I know. I saw you
mizzle over the garden wall, and I followed you, and I've been following you, and now I've got you, and you'd better come along
quiet."

"Yes; it's no good wriggling, you know," said the second constable.

I burst into a torrent of expostulation, but it was of no use. The
two constabulary lunatics hustled me along at a brisk walk, and
whenever I tried to speak they shook me violently from side to side

until my head waggled like that of a china mandarin; an imbecile proceeding, and offensive too, which rendered articulate speech difficult and eloquence impossible.

Once inside the station, however, I made myself heard. The constables were obviously half-witted, so I addressed myself to a grey-haired sergeant who sat at a desk with a large ledger-like volume open before him.

"Look here, sergeant!" I exclaimed haughtily. "What is the meaning of this ridiculous outrage?"

"If you'll just keep quiet a minute, you'll hear," said the sergeant, dipping his pen in the ink and looking inquiringly at the constables.

"I don't know what the charge is, sir," said the first constable, "but I was on duty in Augusta Road when this lady, Mrs. Gammet, called me into the side-gate and told me that a robbery had just been committed, and that the thief had run out of the back door. I went into the garden and saw this man climbing over the wall. I climbed over after him, and followed him up the alley into the street, blowing my whistle. Constable Cox, hearing my whistle, joined in the chase, and we pursued the man until he ran into Dove's Court, which is a blind alley; and then, when he found there was no entrance out—"

"Exit, you mean," corrected the sergeant.

"No exit out of the court, he had to come back to the exit in—"

"Entrance, you mean?" said the sergeant.

"To the entrance in, where we met him, and I took him into custody."

The sergeant entered this idiotic statement in his ledger, and then asked:

"Who charges him?"

"These three ladies, sir," replied the constable; and I then became aware of three well-dressed women who were standing apart and regarding me with looks of concentrated hatred.

"I charge him with stealing my purse," said a sharp-featured woman of about thirty, coming forward and glaring at me. "I left it on my dressing-table when I went down to breakfast—"

"Stupid thing to do," said the sergeant. "Yes?"

"Well, when I came up again, it was gone."

"What makes you think the prisoner took it?" asked the sergeant.

"How else could it have gone?" demanded the lady. "Do you think it flew away of its own accord?"

"What makes you think the prisoner took it?" repeated the sergeant.

"I don't think," replied the lady; "I know."

"How do you know?"

"Because he's a thief!" was the crushing reply.

The sergeant, motioning me to keep silent, regarded the lady critically, as if he would have pursued his inquiries, but, apparently, deciding to reserve this tit-bit for the magistrate, he turned to the other two, and asked: "Anything else?"

A stout, middle-aged woman stepped forward, and, casting a look of defiance at me, said:

"I charge him with stealing my gold watch and chain. I saw him standing by my dressing-table, putting something in his pocket, and my watch and chain had disappeared. When he saw me, he ran out of the room and down the stairs, and I saw him run out into the garden and climb over the wall."

"How did he get into your bedroom?" asked the sergeant.

"Walked in, I suppose!" was the reply.

"He was boarding at my house," interposed the third lady. "He came and engaged a room yesterday afternoon. This morning, after breakfast, Miss Crabbe came down and said that somebody had stolen her purse. Then Miss Walker and I went upstairs, and she found this man in her room. I saw him come out and run downstairs, and then I called the constable; who happened to be passing. The man ran out of the back door into the garden, and I saw him climb over the wall and the constable after him."

The sergeant noted down these misstatements, and then turned to me.

"You have heard the charges," he said. "It is my duty to warn you that anything you may say will be used in evidence against you. Now, then. What have you got to say?"

"I have to say," I replied wrathfully, "that the whole thing is a ridiculous mistake! The constable has arrested the wrong man!"

"Oh, here, I say!" protested the constable, "dror it mild, young man! When I saw you skedaddling over the wall!"

"What about the watch that Miss Walker says she saw you take?" asked the sergeant.

"She is mistaking me for someone else," I replied. "I have never seen these three ladies before in my life, and I have never been inside the house they refer to. I don't even know where it is."

"Well," exclaimed Miss Crabbe, "of all the barefaced, impudent, shameless—"

"Are you quite sure he is the man, Mrs. Gammet?" asked the sergeant.

"Am I sure?" repeated Mrs. Gammet. "Considering that he sat at my dinner-table last night, devouring my food as if he was famishing, and then sat in my drawing-room swilling tea fit to burst, and playing penny nap, and winning four-and-sixpence off me, to say nothing of—"

"What name did he give?" inquired the sergeant.

"Barrett—Daniel Barrett," replied the landlady.

"Is that your name?" the sergeant asked, turning to me.

"No, of course it isn't!" I answered scornfully.

"What is your name, then?"

I was about to blurt out my full name and description, when some protective instinct restrained me. After all, I was not a bishop or a Lord Mayor, whose name would convey a guarantee of respectability.

"I decline to give my name," I answered.

"Very well," rejoined the sergeant, "then we'll put you down as Daniel Barrett. The case will come on this afternoon," he added, turning to my accusers, "so you had better be in court by two-thirty, and bring some additional witnesses to swear to his identity. Good-morning."

He dismissed the ladies with a curt bow, and once more addressed himself to me.

"Now, Barrett, let's see what you've got in your pockets."

It was ignominious, but yet it was a relief to reach some solid ground in this nightmare of unrealities. I turned out my pockets one after the other, and laid the contents on the table, when the sergeant, having satisfied himself that I had nothing more concealed about me, examined them in detail.

"Well," he concluded, when he had gone through the collection, "there's no lady's watch here, and no purse. We must have a look at the garden, and see if he has dropped them there. What luggage have you got, Barrett?"

"A rug and a holdall," I answered. "I left them at Giglioli's restaurant, where I had breakfast this morning."

"Oh, at Giglioli's, eh? We'll call there and have a look at them. That'll do. Put him in No. 3."

As the constable conducted me to the cell, he asked confidentially:

"Where did you drop the swag, Barrett? You may as well tell us, you know."

"I never had the swag, as you call it," I answered angrily. "The other man is clear off with it by now, thanks to your thick-headedness!"

"Oh, chuck it!" exclaimed the officer. "What's the good? Didn't I see you get over the wall?"

"No, you did not," I replied. "The man that you saw—"

"Here, in you go!"

With an unceremonious shove he introduced me to the interior of No. 3, and, banging the massive door, left me to my reflections.

That those reflections were none of the most cheerful it is unnecessary for me to say. Indeed, the more I considered my situation, the less I liked the look of it. No proof that I might bring forward as to my real identity furnished any answer to the statement of the woman Walker that she saw me steal the watch, or that of the landlady or the constable. My only hope was in Giglioli. If I could prove that, while the thief was at breakfast in Augusta Road, I was breakfasting at the restaurant, that would be an unquestionable alibi. But I foresaw that it would be a perilous business.

When I had been pacing up and down the cell for about an hour, I heard footsteps approaching; a key was thrust into the lock, and, as the door swung open, the sergeant confronted me.

"Come out, Barrett," said he, "and let the recognising officer have a look at you."

I obeyed eagerly enough, for even an hour's imprisonment had made me yearn for a glimpse of the outer world, though with some uneasiness too; for my late experiences made me somewhat distrustful of the recognising officer, whoever he might be.

"This is a bit of luck for you, Barrett," said the sergeant, as he walked me along the corridor. "The officer happens to have come here to look at another man, so he can see you at the same time. It will save you the delay of a remand."

I expressed my gratification at this good fortune, and was then led out into a yard, where I was directed to stand at "attention" while a burly, red-faced man in plain clothes inspected me as if I were a doubtful work of art and he the prospective purchaser. We stared at one another with mutual curiosity as he tried me full-face, three-quarter, and profile, and then directed me to walk across the yard that he might observe my gait.

"D'ye know him, Mr. Sharpe?" the sergeant inquired when the inspection was finished.

"No," replied the officer. "Never saw him before. Seems to be a new hand. I shall see him again, though, I expect!"

And with this he turned on his heel, and strolled away, whistling cheerfully. I breathed more freely. Here, at last, was one sane man among this Bedlamite crew.

When the sergeant had conducted me back to my cell, he stood for a few moments holding the door open and looking at me, not unkindly.

"Look here, Barrett," said he, "I'll give you a word of advice. Drop this mistaken-identity balderdash. It won't wash. You were taken red-handed, and you've got no defence. Now, the magistrate who'll hear your case is a lenient man, and if you plead guilty and throw yourself on the mercy of the court, he may deal with you as a first offender and let you off with a light sentence. Otherwise, you may get sent for trial at the Assizes and catch it hot, to say nothing of the delay. You think about it." With this friendly and really useful hint, he slammed the door, and I resumed my melancholy perambulations.

It must have been about three o'clock when I was led out of my cell and taken to the adjoining courthouse. As I took my place in the dock, I looked earnestly at the magistrate, and, catching his benevolent, spectacled eye, felt my spirits revive. I would explain to him about Giglioli, and he would see that there had been some mistake; for, after all, a man cannot be in two places at once.

Despite the sergeant's advice, I entered a plea of "not guilty" with considerable confidence, relying on my alibi; but the evidence of the first witness swept away my last hope, and I knew that I was lost. That witness was the landlady, who, having been sworn, informed the Court that her name was Sarah Gammet.

"Do you recognise the prisoner?" the magistrate inquired.

"Yes," was the reply. "He came to my house yesterday afternoon and engaged a room for a week. He dined at my table, and spent part of the evening in my drawing-room playing cards with me and some of the boarders. He went out about nine and came home at half-past eleven. This morning he went out early and came back just as we had finished breakfast, saying that he had breakfasted at a restaurant." The witness paused, and as I leaned helplessly on the dock-rail the court seemed to swim around me. My alibi was worthless. Malignant fate had headed me off from the only avenue of escape. The rest of the evidence I listened to as one in a dream, and even the statement that "the prisoner's suitcase had been searched in the presence of the constable and found to contain a purse identified by Miss Crabbe as her property," failed to rouse me. It was only when the magistrate, turning his spectacled eyes on me (less benevolently this time), addressed me by name, that my attention revived.

"You have heard the evidence, Barrett," he said. "You were seen to take the watch, the stolen purse was found in your suitcase, and you have been identified by the landlady, four of the boarders, the servant, and the constable. Have you anything to say?"

I murmured wearily that the constable had arrested the wrong man.

"How long have you been in Hunsgate?" the magistrate asked.

"I came down yesterday afternoon."

"And where did you spend the night?"

"In a bathing-machine."

An incredulous titter arose from the spectators, the sergeant frowned impatiently, the constables grinned, and the magistrate shook his head. "You can't expect me to believe that in the face of the evidence," he said.

"I don't," I replied. "I see that appearances are hopelessly against me, and I only ask you to deal with me as leniently as you can."

"Are there any previous convictions against him?" the magistrate asked.

"Apparently not, your worship," answered the sergeant. "This seems to be his first offence."

"Then I hope it will be his last," said the magistrate. And, addressing me, he continued: "I can't deal with your case under the First Offenders Act, Barrett. The robbery was too deliberate. But I will treat you as leniently as I can. You must go to hard labour for twelve months, and I trust that, when you come out of prison, you will endeavour to live an honest life."

I followed the sergeant out of the court with a certain dull relief. The ordeal was over, and I knew the worst, though as yet I could not realise my amazing position. I still had a vague expectation that I should wake presently and find that all this horror was nothing but a dream.

"You've had a let-off, Barrett," said the sergeant, as he ushered me back to my cell, "though you'd better have taken my advice. However, you're in for it now, but still, if you take your gruel like a man, the time will soon pass; and when you come out, bear in mind what the magistrate said. You can take it from me that there are no fortunes to be made on the cross. A crook's life is a dog's life, and don't you forget it."

The rest of the swiftly ensuing events of that day of wrath flit across my memory like the shifting scenes of some dismal phantasmagoria: the railway journey, brief and ignominious, with the chilly manacles encircling my wrists; the smiling country seen through closed windows and passing away like a lost paradise; the gay passengers, pausing in their gaiety to watch me with looks of horrified pity; the frowning prison looming up ahead; the yawning gateway, the dry-faced janitor, the vision of men clad in shapeless buff suits hideous and grotesque, like a group of horrible pierrots from some underworld burlesque; and then the curtain fell with a clang of iron on the first scene of a life-long tragedy.

Ye must be born again. Yea, verily; and herein is the place of the new birth.

2
THE PRISON-BREAKER

NIGHT! NIGHT IN the prison, with the dismal bell in the clock-tower telling out the slowly passing hours. My second night in gaol. The end of the first day, for I had been brought to the prison on the preceding evening. Yesterday morning I was free, a blithe holiday-maker, roaming happily by the summer sea, all unsuspicious of impending disaster. And now—

I glanced around the bare, unlovely cell, with its pitiful furniture: the comfortless stool and fixed table, the tin bucket and basin, the little sweeping-brush and dustpan, the "pint," the plate, the wooden spoon—wooden because a metal one might aid the inmate to shuffle off the burden of undesirable existence—the slate with its attached scrap of pencil; wretched appurtenances of a state neither civilised nor barbaric, that hovered insecurely on the very outside edge of humanity; the state of the social pariah.

I could see them all distinctly by the light that filtered through a square of ground glass from the gas-jet outside—for the indulgence of darkness is withheld from the prisoner—and dimly, too, I could see the "judas," the little glazed spyhole in the door that served to remind me of the loss of all civil rights, including that of decent privacy. Once already I had seen the judas blink for a moment, and I had known that I was being inspected by the passing warder.

I had thrown myself down on the plank bed without undressing—for I was too restless to "turn in" deliberately—and now lay with my eyes fixed dreamily on the illuminated square of glass, meditating on the past and the probable future. As to the silly masquerade that had landed me here in the place of some unknown criminal, I had not patience to think of it; rather did my memory occupy itself with the events that had befallen since I arrived at the prison.

All too clearly they passed before me, these first scenes of my prison life. The "reception-room," the matter-of-fact doctor, the not ungrateful bath, the induction into the hideous, buff prison suit, the official photographer who forbore to ask me to "smile pleasantly," but objected to a temporary squint that I had assumed, and the taking of my "particulars," or personal description. At the recollection of this last ceremony, indeed, I smiled grimly, for, to my profound amazement, the disguise that had been the cause of my undoing had passed undetected.

As I had listened to the officer dictating to the scribe, "Eyes light grey, complexion medium, *hair black*," I had chuckled inwardly thinking of the surprise that was in store for them at the next haircutting. Only one thing had been left undone. My fingerprints had not been taken. The officer to whom this duty appertained was absent. But I gathered that he would be back on the following day, and that this finishing touch would then be added. My sign-manual would be taken, to be duly filed at the Habitual Criminals' Registry, and I should be turned out a finished criminal.

My reflections were by no means undisturbed. A few cells away, a restive prisoner was enlivening his vigil with snatches of song, and ringing his bell continuously. Already the warder had paid him several visits, each followed by an angry colloquy in which, although it was muffled by the thick door of my cell, I could make out the words, "report for punishment in the morning." But the prisoner refused to be pacified. He could not sleep, and he did not intend that anyone else should.

These sounds from without presently started a new train of thought. During the afternoon, I had been permitted to work, with a small gang, at a new ventilating shaft which was under construction, and which passed through the gallery above by way of a disused cell, the door of which had been removed. The work had necessitated the making of an opening in the roof, and, through this, I had obtained a brief glance at the outer world. The hubbub from the neighbouring cell and the tramping to and fro of the warder started, as I have said, a new train of thought in which these details came back to me. And as I considered them, they suggested a very curious possibility, which, in turn, generated a rash and daring resolution.

The bell-ringing and discordant caroling continued, and I listened expectantly. Presently the warder approached down the gallery, his footsteps ringing with a sharp staccato, eloquent of suppressed irritation. He passed my cell; I heard the jarring of a lock, a brief but angry altercation, and then the resounding bang of the closing door. As his returning footsteps became audible, I sprang to my feet and vigorously pressed the bell-push.

Here let me explain, for the benefit of those fortunate persons who are unacquainted with the internal arrangements of a prison, that the pressing of the bell-push not only rings the bell at the end of the corridor, but also pushes down a small semaphore-arm or indicator outside the cell, which ends in a disc bearing the number of the cell. Thus, the officer can see, by looking along the gallery, which prisoner has rung.

I pressed the bell-push, then, as the warder was approaching. The next moment a key was rammed into the lock, the door swung open, and an angry face looked in on me.

"Well! And what's the matter with you?"

"I am extremely sorry to trouble you," I said suavely, "but I really think there must be something wrong with this window. There's such an awful draught, and, besides, the frame seems to be coming away from the brickwork. I am afraid it will fall in on me."

That fetched him! An insecure cell-window is a serious matter. He stepped into the cell with his eye on the window, and, as he passed me, I gave his advancing ankle a gentle push with my foot, jiujitsu fashion, and stepped back quickly. As he staggered sideways I gave him a vigorous shove in the back, and he alighted on all fours on the plank bed. He was up again with astonishing quickness, and yet not quickly enough; for in a moment I had sprung outside and slammed the door on him.

A cell-door, I need hardly say, has no keyhole on the inside, and the lock is of the snap variety. Consequently our positions were for the moment reversed. He was now the prisoner.

A single wrench at the indicator disabled it, and I poked it up out of sight. Then, running down the gallery, I bent back the clapper of the bell—which was once more ringing furiously—and threw it out of action; when, to the uproar, succeeded a silence broken only by the caroling of the prisoner, and a muffled thumping from my late apartment.

But I did not linger to enjoy the quiet. Lightly and silently I ran up the little iron staircase to the gallery above, and stole along it to the empty cell through which the new shaft passed. Everything was as we had left it. Even the ladder, leading to the loft above, was still in position, to my surprise and gratification; and, reflecting on the curious lack of precaution thus displayed, I mounted it gleefully, and pulled it up after me.

The tools and materials were still scattered about the floor of the loft, and I was tempted to furnish myself with an outfit; but reflecting that it was unwise to burden myself with things for which I had no immediate use, I contented myself with a combined wire-cutter and flat-nosed pliers and a length of stout wire which I cut from a coil. The appliances for picking a lock were almost certain to be of use.

Twisting the wire round my neck, collarwise, I set the ladder against the opening that we had made in the roof, and mounted. It was a slate roof of a low pitch on which one could walk without much difficulty. I crept up to the ridge, and, without exposing myself unduly—though it was a dark night, and I was not likely to be seen—looked around. The boundary wall was at some distance from the building on which I stood, excepting at one corner, where it approached within a few feet, and here the summit of the wall was not more than eight feet below the level of the eaves. Looking at it, I judged that the ladder would span the interval. As to the wall itself, which was not less than twenty-five feet high, I should have to drop down and take my chance of a broken limb.

Creeping back to the opening in the roof, I hauled up the ladder as noiselessly as I could, and set off with it towards the corner that approached the wall. It was an excellent ladder for the purpose, being furnished with iron hooks at one end, which would engage securely with the gutter. The only doubtful point was its length. It was only ten or eleven feet long, and there would certainly be nothing to spare.

Arrived at the fateful corner, I sat down on the slates at the edge of the roof, and, fixing my heels firmly in the iron gutter, began cautiously to slide the ladder across the space. It was an anxious time. If the ladder should prove too short, I should have to make my way, somehow, down to the yard, and my chances of escape would be infinitesimal.

Foot by foot the ladder advanced until more than half of it projected, and it began to be difficult to hold by reason of the increasing leverage. I saw that I must let it go with a run, and chance making a noise, or I might find myself levered off the roof by its weight. Accordingly, I gave it a brisk shove forward, and held my breath until my fate should be decided. With a grinding rattle it slid swiftly out until the hooks approached the gutter, when I checked it at the risk of being pulled over. The hooks fairly engaged in the gutter, and the lower end, describing a short arc, struck the top of the wall with only an inch or two to spare.

I drew a deep breath. At least, I should get outside the prison wall, though in what condition remained to be seen. Rolling over on my face, I stuck my legs over the edge of the roof, and felt for the top rung of the ladder, and a mighty nervous moment it was until my foot touched it. Then all was plain sailing, and I backed carefully down, averting my eyes from the gulf beneath until I reached the foot of the ladder, and, stepping off, seated myself astride on the top of the wall. So far it was well enough. The wall was quite comfortable to sit upon, being rounded at the top, but the ground looked a prodigious long way down; so far down, indeed, that a sheer drop from it was almost certain to involve a broken leg. And, with a broken leg, what chance would there be of escape?

The wall, as I have said, was rounded at the top, but at each side there was a projecting fillet not more than an inch and a half wide. Narrow as it was, however, I seemed to see in that fillet the bare chance of safety. At any rate, I would try it.

Unhooking the ladder from the gutter, at the imminent risk of upsetting my balance, I slid it down past me, across the top of the wall, until it hung down on the outer side, when I hitched the hooks on to the fillet. It was a precarious hold, which a breath might dislodge, but it was better than dropping the entire height. With infinite care, I set my foot on the ladder, and let myself down rung by rung, hardly daring to breathe. I had nearly reached the bottom— beyond which was an unavoidable drop of some fifteen feet—when the hooks slipped from the fillet. There was a grinding noise, followed by a tremendous shock, and I found myself lying on my back, half stunned, with the ladder on top of me.

Shaken though I was, I was on my feet in an instant, and with my course of action clearly marked out. Half a mile away the lights of the town of Ashbury twinkled alluringly, and I had made up my mind to seek the sanctuary of the town. The country was all very well at night, but, when daylight came, an escaped convict in a prison suit would be a too conspicuous object. A change of clothes was the most urgent need, and clothes were most plentiful in a town. Without a moment's hesitation, I headed across the fields for the lights.

Nevertheless, when I entered the quiet streets of the sleepy little town, I walked with uncommon wariness. The lamps were unpleasantly numerous, and my distinctive costume was calculated to attract notice. Hence, I zigzagged, crabwise, along the streets, *obliquis gressibus*, dodging the lampposts, and keeping a sharp look-out for dark entries and casual foot passengers, especially those of the constabulary variety.

I was creeping along a narrow street in the deep shadow cast by the projecting storeys of a row of ancient houses—and commending the wisdom of our ancestors as shown by this sensible mode of construction—when the sound of noisy and rather irregular footsteps became audible from behind. Someone was approaching from that direction.

I hurried forward, and, near the corner, came suddenly on what I took to be a deep doorway, but which, when I entered it, turned out to be the entrance to a little close or yard. It was extremely dark, and when I had sneaked up a short distance from the entrance I felt so secure that I returned to look out at the disturber of my peace.

He was not a policeman, obviously, for, as he passed a lamp, I could see that he wore a billycock hat, and the irregularity of his gait hinted at recent conviviality. It really seemed as if Providence were offering me the means of rehabilitating myself. Here was a man, apparently about my own height, dressed in a decent suit of clothes, and so far under the influence of the flowing bowl as to be a pretty easy victim. What could be more simple than to knock him on the head, drag him into the entry, and exchange garments with him?

But there is a vast interval between conceiving a plan and executing it. To knock down a drunken man at the risk of killing him outright required a degree of callous brutality that I realised was beyond what I had at present attained to. I knew that I was not going to knock the man down, and with this knowledge, as the staggering steps drew nearer, I withdrew farther up the entry.

And fortunate it was that I did so, for, when he arrived at the entrance, instead of passing, he upset my calculations completely by entering the passage and groping his way along one side.

Utterly taken by surprise, there was nothing for me to do but to retire farther up into the darkness; which I did as noiselessly as I could, but yet not so silently as to escape unperceived, for, as he halted at a door that gave on to the passage, he challenged me in thick, uncertain accents:

"Who zat?"

"Stevens!" I replied promptly.

"Stevensh? Who's Stevensh?"

"I am," I answered.

He paused to consider this statement, and I watched him anxiously; for, although I was invisible to him, his figure stood out in distinct silhouette against the faint light of the street. Again, the project of knocking him on the head presented itself as a theoretical possibility, and I turned it over impartially in my mind as he produced his latchkey and began to make ineffectual prods at the vicinity of the keyhole.

"Wah'sh you doing, Stevensh?" he asked, still jabbing at the elusive orifice.

"Resting," I replied.

"Resting, eh?" said he, describing a few irregular figures on the door with the key. "I don't believe you. I tell you what 'tis—you're drunk! Thass whass matter with you."

He wiped the key up and down the door, chuckling softly until, the full humour of the situation bursting upon him, he broke into a peal of jovial but idiotic laughter.

The position was becoming serious. If he kept up this hullabaloo, he would certainly attract someone to the spot. That would not do at all, and I was beginning to consider my original scheme in a more businesslike spirit, when the Providence that watches over men in his condition intervened. The opportunity was gone, the temptation had passed, for the key miraculously entered the keyhole, the lock clicked, the wassailer dived in like a disreputable harlequin, and the door closed with a loud bang.

I listened eagerly for the shooting of bolts, but no such sound came to my ears. Instead, I heard the clatter of uncertain feet upon the stairs, with an occasional thud, as if a step had been missed, and, presently, the noisy shutting of a door. Then all was still.

I stole out of the entry and looked at the outside of the house. The ground floor was occupied by a shop, the fascia of which bore the name "Minikin Brothers." Pursuing my investigations, I discovered the same name above the adjoining shop, and, turning the corner into the main street, I perceived a large, modern shop also adorned with the brotherly superscription.

Searching for a spyhole in the steel blind, I was about to examine the wares of the Brothers Minikin, when my investigations were brought summarily to an end; for there hove into sight a silently moving figure, unmistakable even in the distance and the dim light; the figure of an approaching policeman.

Quick as thought, I slipped round the corner into the entry, and, bringing my eye close to the keyhole of the door, examined it anxiously. Now, I know something about locks, for I once spent a few dreary but useful months as a draughtsman to a lock manufacturer, and I at once recognised the article before me as a common builder's night-latch, an artless affair that a skilfully wielded hairpin might deal with quite efficiently.

But there was the policeman. If he should come prying up the entry before I could finish, then, indeed, was I lost. Still, I must keep cool, and act deliberately—there is no greater waste of time than hurry.

Slipping the coil of wire from my neck, I rapidly measured the keyhole, and, turning up the end of the wire to a suitable length with the invaluable pliers, cut off about six inches, and fashioned a rough bow in the reverse end. A careful trial of this showed that it was well enough as far as it went, but insufficient by itself to open the lock. Deliberately, but with a rather shaky hand, I cut off another length of wire, and quickly bent it up with the pliers into a second skeleton.

The combination seemed to be what was needed, but the manipulation was not easy in the dark, and, in the midst of my struggles to work calmly, a hollow rattle, proceeding faintly from the street, told me that the constable had reached the corner and was testing the security of the steel blind.

My hands began to tremble violently, and I felt the sweat trickling down my face, but still I strove to concentrate my attention on the lock. It was my only chance.

Suddenly I felt one of the levers yield. Holding it back, I worked on with the other key, and then that yielded too. The door opened with a soft creak, and I slipped into the hall; and even as I turned with my hand on the knob, a bright light flashed on the opposite wall of the entry. Very softly and silently I pushed the door to, and noiselessly eased the latch back into its box. Then I stood like a statue, and waited.

It had been a near thing. The latch was hardly released, and my thumb was still on the knob, when the door trembled to a heavy push, and a beam of light shot in through the large keyhole below. But I was saved. The soft tread of the guardian of the peace passed on up to the close, and then back again to the street. He little recked, good, worthy man, when he tried the door, of the buff-clad, grotesque figure that was standing within a foot of his constabulary nose.

The danger passed, I wiped my clammy face with my sleeve, and proceeded to explore. The hall was absolutely dark, but, groping with my hands, I soon discovered a door on the side nearest the street and presumably leading to the shop. It was locked, but, since the key had not been removed, the precaution was not of much use, and, with infinite care to avoid making any sound, I opened it and passed through, closing it after me.

I was now in the end shop, as I could see plainly enough, for the cimmerian darkness of the hall had given place to a dim twilight—produced by the little by-pass jets of the gas-burners—in which the surrounding objects were clearly visible. And when my eyes encountered those objects, I could have shouted for joy. Oh, thrice-blessed Minikins! What benedictions did I not call down upon your brotherly heads, and upon that of the intoxicated angel who had led me to your abode of bliss!

For the Brothers Minikin were general outfitters—nay, more; they were universal providers! The fact was set forth in mere white paint on a common blackboard. It should have been written in letters of gold on a ground of Tyrian purple. Universal providers! And who so universally unprovided as I?

I wandered from department to department with ecstasy in my heart, and my prison shoes in my hand. What a stock it was! Hats, suits, collars, neckties, umbrellas; shirts enough to clothe the nakedness of an archipelago of cannibal islands; and, as to the boots, there seemed enough to furnish footgear for an army of centipedes.

But I did not waste time in mere gloating. I commenced critically, and with care—since expense was no object—to select an outfit in accordance with my somewhat fastidious taste, replacing the rejected articles tidily in the drawers when I had made my selection, and leaving everything as I had found it.

A fancy-striped shirt, a white collar, a quiet but sumptuous necktie, a tweed hat—a straw "boater" is so apt to fly off if one is hurried—a pair of smart brown boots with red rubber soles, and tan socks to match; these articles I accumulated in my passage through the emporium, and then I proceeded to the tailoring department to choose a suit. This was a weighty matter, for I am particular as to the cut of my clothes, and I rather distrusted Minikins in the matter of style. A number of wax-headed effigies stood about in stiff attitudes, displaying selections from the repertoire, and persuasive tickets hooked on them expounded the virtues of the garments in such comments as "Latest fashion," "Very smart," "As worn," and so forth.

I glanced from one to another of these silent exponents of fashion, and finally directed my attention to a goggle-eyed image, attired in a lavender-striped suit of surpassing hideousness which, if one was to believe the ticket, was "All the go." The effigy was about my height and girth, though, I need not say, not at all my figure. However, I ventured to divest him of his jacket and try it on myself, when, finding that it fitted to a nicety, I took it off, and searched it for some distinguishing mark. Such a mark I found in the form of a label, stitched to the inside, and inscribed "Fitting 6.2A."

With this clue I now turned out several of the drawers, until I lighted on a neat suit of dark-grey flannel bearing these mystic numbers. Then I proceeded tidily to put back the rejected ones, but first I stripped the effigy of the lavender suit, and, folding it carefully, placed it at the bottom of the drawer.

Then I retired with my booty to the trying-on room to exchange the livery of dishonour for the habiliments proper to my station. The light was inconveniently dim, but, as far as I could judge, the effect was quite satisfactory; and, when I had surveyed myself in the long mirror, and regretted afresh the disfigurement of my dyed hair, I stepped out into the shop with new-born self-respect. Here the aspect of the despoiled effigy jarred on my sensibilities. The fellow was positively indecent. Not only had he no clothes; he hadn't even a figure. He was a mere naked, dichotomously branching pasteboard cylinder. I could not find it in my heart to leave him thus.

Stepping back to the trying-on room, I fetched my discarded exuvium, and proceeded to induct him into such a suit of clothes as I will warrant he had never worn before. His rigid feet I thrust into the prison shoes and socks, his cylindrical legs into the baggy buff trousers, and when I had covered his shapeless nudity with a prison shirt and jacket, and set the convict cap rakishly on his idiotic head, I picked up the fallen ticket and hooked it on his breast; for it seemed to me that the playful colloquialism "All the go" was not entirely irrelevant to the present transaction.

Before leaving, I cast a wistful eye on the till. A little cash would be exceedingly useful. But I refrained. Selecting, as a final keepsake, a neat partridge cane, I walked softly, in my rubber-soled shoes, back to the door by which I had entered, passed out, and turned the key.

In the dark hall I waited a few moments, and listened. There was no sound from without, and none from within save a distant, rhythmical snore. I opened the outer door, and listened again, and, as all was silent, I stepped outside and, easing the latch with my picklocks, which I had been careful to bring away with me, quietly closed the door.

The illuminated clock in the High Street showed a quarter to one as I strode along the silent pavement. My purpose was to make my way through the by-streets to the high-road to Eastgate-on-Sea.

But now Fortune, hitherto so kind, played me a scurvy trick, for in the first side-street into which I turned I saw a police officer in earnest conversation with a couple of prison-warders. They were standing under a lamp some distance away, and all might have been well if I had kept my head. But I did not. At the sudden apparition, I halted and turned back. The officer challenged. I shot round the corner, and, darting across the road, dived into a narrow street; and a chorus of whistles from the rear told me that my enemies were in full cry after me.

I had run silently on my rubber soles up several courts and by-streets, with the whistles sounding dismally behind, when suddenly there loomed straight ahead a level-crossing, flanked by a signal-box. Turning off to the right to avoid the crossing I came to a foot-path that ran just outside the railway fence; and along this I raced at the top of my speed, while the whistles screamed from the neighbourhood of the crossing. Shortly I came abreast of a siding on which stood a row of empty trucks, and at this moment I became aware of the rumble of an approaching goods-train. I climbed over the fence, and crouched behind one of the trucks, intending to dodge in front of the train if my pursuers came along the path, and so put it between them and me.

But the whistles now sounded from across the line, and, as the train approached, a sudden, loud clank of colliding trucks told me that the engine had slowed down. Looking back, I perceived the crimson eye of the signal barring the way. Then the engine crawled past my hiding-place, and I saw the driver gazing in the direction whence the whistles were sounding. A few moments later a familiar rattle caused me to look back again.

The red light had turned to green, and already the engine was snorting afresh. As the renewed clank of the couplings told of increasing strain, I sprang forward, and, grasping the top edge of a passing truck, set my foot on the grease-box and hauled myself up, and the next moment was lying full length on the bottom of the truck close to the side nearest the signal-box.

The train rumbled on with gradually accelerating speed. The light from the signal-box fell into the truck, just missing me as I hugged the side, and I knew that the level crossing was passed. In another five minutes we were clear of the town, and all immediate danger was at an end. It had been a narrow shave, but I had scraped through, and now the problem of my future proceedings—disregarded while the danger was immediate—called urgently for consideration. Whither was I being carried? And what was to be my next move? I was some sixty miles from London, and had not a farthing in my pocket. Now, I could walk sixty miles in a couple of days—but not without food. And already I was both thirsty and hungry. Something would have to be done.

As to the first question—that of my present destination—that was soon settled. In about a quarter of an hour the train began to slow down, and, peering over the edge of the truck, I saw that we were entering a large goods-yard. Probably our train consisted of empty trucks, and, if this was so, it was time for me to shift my quarters.

As we entered the siding, we drew alongside another train, not an empty one, certainly, for the waggons were mostly furnished with tarpaulin covers. It was starting shortly, too, for steam hissed loudly from the engine, and the side-light twinkled on the distant guard's van. When we came to rest, my truck halted opposite a covered waggon on which I could dimly perceive a paper ticket. I scrambled down from the truck and put my face close to the ticket. With some difficulty I made out the words "Bricklayers' Arms," whereupon, without more ado, I pushed aside the tarpaulin cover and climbed up into the waggon.

I was none too soon. For hardly had I taken my place on the barrels with which the waggon was filled when a quick succession of clanks was followed by a horrible jerk and a furious joggling to and fro. Then, with a monotonous rumble, the train moved out of the siding. My new conveyance was a distinct improvement on the other, for it rattled along at such speed that in about ten minutes we were back at Ashbury. A convenient chink under the tarpaulin allowed me to look out with safety, and, as we entered the town, I peeped forth in an agony of suspense lest the train should be stopped and searched. But still it rumbled on. I saw the dark, deserted station glide by, and, as we passed the crossing, I had a fleeting vision of a constable and a warder on guard at the gates. From my dark hiding-place, I waved them a silent farewell, and rumbled on through the sleeping town Westward Ho! To freedom and safety!

The first problem, then, was solved. I should not have to walk that sixty miles. And very soon I found the solution of the second; found it in the open tops of the very uncomfortable barrels on which I was reclining, which, on examination proved to be filled with apples. Now, I am rather partial to apples. Moreover, an eminent authority assures us that they are not only nutritious and digestible, but are entirely free from the objectionable purin bodies. I do not, in general, trouble myself about purins or xanthins, but one may as well adopt the purin-free diet when one can—and there is nothing else. I fell to upon those apples with avidity, and, when I had eaten a dozen or so, I hankered no more for the succulent gruel or the good, brown prison bread. But I grew most uncommonly sleepy, and, though the waggon-springs were of the stiffest, and the apples were abominably knobbly, I presently fell into a deep and delicious sleep.

From this sweet and dreamless slumber I was aroused by a most infernal jolting. Peering out under the tarpaulin, I perceived that it was still dark, but a faint flush in the eastern sky marked the passage of the hours, and warned me to begone. The train appeared to be stopping on a low embankment, for I could dimly discern the shapes of roofs and chimney-stacks against the murky sky.

As the train continued to slow down, I thrust my head out and looked round. The line made a sharp curve here, and I saw at once that this was the place to alight, for if I climbed down on the convex side of the curve I should be hidden by the train both from the guard and the engine-driver. The train was now barely moving; my opportunity had come. Picking up my cane, I lifted the tarpaulin, scrambled out, and, flinging myself clear of the train, fell sprawling full length upon the ballast.

I was up again in a moment, and, without pausing to look round, I ran across the line, descended the rough slope of the embankment, and, climbing over the high boundary fence, dropped down into a bed of weeds. I was now, apparently, on a small patch of waste land, but houses rose on both sides, and, reflecting cheerfully that where there are houses there are roads, I struck across the rough field and soon came out into a half-finished suburban street.

The light of the dawn was growing in the east, but it was an unchristian hour to be abroad, and it behoved me to go warily, for, respectable as my appearance was, I might nevertheless be stopped, and then what account of myself could I give? It would never do.

Accordingly I kept, as far as possible, to open spaces, maintaining a careful watch with eye and ear, and avoiding the few policemen that I saw while they were still afar off. But still I worked my way steadily westward, until, as the grey light of dawn merged into actual daylight, I suddenly realised my whereabouts. I was on the outskirts of Lewisham; far away enough from home, it was true, but farther still from Ashbury and the dismal gaol. With a sigh of infinite relief, I turned at length into Lewisham High Road, and, swinging my cane and whistling gleefully, set forth briskly on the ten-mile walk that was to bring me to home and final safety.

New Cross, the Old Kent Road, and the Borough are not among the loveliest spots on earth, but as I strode through them I breathed the airs of paradise. Blackfriars Bridge in the gay morning light was a dream of beauty, and the policemen, dear, honest souls, no longer to be feared now that the town was astir, glanced at me benevolently, and even wished me "Good morning!" For my description was not yet out, or, if it was, it referred to a pitiful, buff-clad "zany of sorrow" in a ridiculous Scotch cap. Minikins' had not yet spoken.

So, with a gaiety of heart that scorned mere bodily fatigue, the long miles of pavement were conquered one by one—though, to be sure, it was a weary tramp from Lewisham to Regent's Park—until half-past six found me within hail of my goal, girding up my loins for the final effort. It would require nice management and a fair allowance of luck. The mere picking of the lock of my back door was intrinsically simple. But it had to be done in daylight, and done quickly, too, and I must not be seen doing it. For my golden hair was still dyed an unlovely black, my person still disguised under the similitude of Tom Nagget. If I were seen, I should certainly be mistaken for Tom, and might well be asked how I came to be breaking into Danby Croker's studio. That would involve explanations, and the cat would be out of the bag, with possible consequences of the most disastrous kind. No; I must not be seen. It would be sad indeed if, after weathering the storm, I should wreck my craft on the harbour bar.

As I approached the vicinity of the studio, I visualised my absent latchkey, and inspected the two picklocks. As a matter of fact, one would do, for the wards of the key were dummies, and I ought to get the bolt back at the first try. Thus reflecting, I turned into the mews that formed the rather undistinguished approach to my residence, and looked along it anxiously. All was quiet, with a single exasperating exception, a premature milkman, driven abroad, no doubt, by insomnia, and waking the echoes with discordant yelps. I pushed my hat to the back of my head, and turned down the brim to hide my blackened hair, and then, walking quickly past him with averted face, I made straight for my back door with the picklock in my hand.

It was an anxious moment. I inserted the wire in as keylike a fashion as I could, and carefully probed until I felt it engage. The latch shot back at the first trial, and the door yielded to the push of my hand. I entered; I closed the door; I shot the rarely used bolts at the top and bottom. I was at home, and safe at last from pursuit.

Only one thing remained to be done to close the episode for ever. And I did it forthwith. Tired, footsore, hungry, thirsty, I went straight to the workshop to seek out a big, stoppered bottle labeled "Methylated Spirit." Hugging the bottle, I proceeded to my bedroom, and there, with my head over the washhand-basin, I poured the precious spirit on my hair, rubbing it in with my hands, and dabbing it on again and again with my sponge. It was a dirty business, and it took time, but the reward was great. When, after a quarter of an hour's strenuous exertion, I desisted, my hair and eyebrows glittered as of yore like threads of spun gold, and the only witnesses that remained to testify to that tragedy of errors was a blackened sponge, two soiled towels, and a pool of inky fluid in the basin.

The spell was broken; the enchantment was removed. The mirror prevaricated no longer, but once more rendered faithfully the familiar visage of Danby Croker.

3
THE BRAZEN SERPENT

I WONDER HOW long it took the hermit-crab to learn to stick his soft tail into a protecting whelk-shell? Generations, no doubt; and many a painful nip he must have got in the interval. How much more ready is the response of man to external changes! Clothe a rowdy undergraduate in the clerical garb, and forthwith his mien is sober, even into smugness. Trick him out in the motley of the Army, and he will bounce and swagger like a very Bobadil. Clap a tall hat on him, and dub him "doctor," and, behold! respectability envelops him as a garment. Dress him in the horrible livery of the gaol, and he shall walk the crooked way henceforth and for ever. Man is a very adaptable animal.

On the morning after my escape from prison I awoke in my own familiar bedroom, but with the sense of a new personality. I was an escaped convict. It is true that I was an innocent man, that my whole prison life was less than forty-eight hours, and that my description in the register was so inaccurate that I was fairly safe from identification. The fact remained that I was an escaped convict, "wanted" by the police. Hereafter must I walk abroad warily, must slip past "the man in blue" with averted face, and scan the feet of every tall civilian for the tell-tale constabulary boot.

The subtle change appeared in my very first action. I had received a letter from old Mr. Parmenter, the famous collector, asking me to call on him. Now, I had often called on old Parmenter, for we had a strong bond of sympathy: we both loved the beautiful productions of the goldsmith. With this difference, however—that he delighted in possession; I in production. Artistic metalwork was the passion of my life, and the irony of Fate had led me to the machine-shop and the drawing-office. A Cellini by instinct, I was, in actual fact, an engineer.

I have hinted at a departure from my customary conduct. It was a small matter, but significant of the change. When I set forth for Parmenter's house my pocket contained a fat cigar-case, and the cigar-case contained two metal plates, each coated with a thick slab of moulding-wax. I had nothing definite in my mind, only I might get a chance of taking a "squeeze" of something, and that squeeze might be useful hereafter.

I found old Parmenter seated on the floor, or rather on a cushion—he was too stout to kneel with comfort—arranging a new haul in the bottom drawer of his coin-cabinet.

"Morning, Danby," he chirped, holding out his hand. "I can't get up to shake hands. Too fat, to tell the brutal truth, so you must excuse me. Obesity knows no law!"

He was a genial old fellow, was Parmenter. "You are wondering what I want you for, I expect," he continued.

"I supposed you had got something new that you wanted me to look at," I replied.

"No; it's not that this time, though I am always glad to have your opinion of a new find, for there's no judge like the actual craftsman. No; I've got a little project, Danby. You're out of a job just now, aren't you?"

"Well, just at the moment."

"Well, now, do you remember old Jacob Lyon, the curio-dealer? But of course you do. Well, old Lyon is dead. Died quite suddenly. And I have bought the stock and goodwill from his daughter, Judith, and taken over the lease."

"What on earth did you do that for?" I exclaimed.

"I had an idea that I might put some responsible person in to carry it on— There, it's no use beating about the bush. I thought I'd put you in if you cared to take it on."

I was thunderstruck. In fact, I thought old Parmenter was going "balmy."

"Don't refuse it hastily, old fellow," he went on persuasively; "it's a really good thing."

"Why don't you run the show yourself?" I asked.

"No time. Besides, my dear Danby, I am an incurable collector. I shouldn't buy anything that I didn't like, and, if I liked the things, I'd see everybody hanged before I'd part with them. I should never sell anything. It wouldn't suit me at all, whereas it would suit you down to the ground. You are fond of works of art, but you don't want to possess them. You could have the handling of things of beauty, and then make a profit on them."

I wandered round the cabinet which stood in the middle of the room, reflecting on the proposition. It undoubtedly had its attractions. To live amidst the things that I loved would be a pleasant life, and possibly profitable, too. I looked down absently at the medals exhibited in the cabinet. The glazed top had been removed, and I could get a better view than usual. Suddenly my attention was arrested by a splendid bronze medallion, and I stooped to examine it.

"What a lovely thing this is!" I exclaimed. "This oval medallion, I mean. It looks like a genuine Cellini, too!"

"Genuine!" exclaimed Parmenter, craning up so that I could just see the top of his head over the cabinet. "It's more than genuine—it's nearly unique. That is the famous 'Brazen Serpent' medallion. It was made by Cellini for Pope Clement VII, but his Holiness did not like the reverse, and ordered Cellini to design a fresh one, which he did, and struck three impressions, one in gold, one in silver, and one in bronze. But just then the Pope died, and Cellini had the three medallions left on his hands, and, as he did not care for the new reverses he destroyed the die. So only three impressions with the new reverse were ever struck. This is the bronze one, and it is worth about five thousand pounds."

"And where are the other two?"

"The gold copy is at the Uffizzi. As to the silver one, some fool has probably melted it down. At any rate, no one has ever seen it. It would be worth a fortune if it ever turned up. But to come back to my little plan, Danby; don't you think it might suit you? And doesn't it occur to you that your skill as a metal-worker might come in uncommonly useful?"

As a matter of fact, it had, but I dissembled. And, meanwhile, I drew out the cigar-case, and opened it silently.

"How do you mean?" I asked. "I am only an amateur as far as goldsmith's work is concerned; and besides, you blooming collectors won't look at anything new."

"Not if we know that it's new," chuckled old Parmenter; "but sometimes we don't."

I was really shocked at the old reprobate.

"You mean to say," said I, delicately lifting the medallion out of its recess, and laying it noiselessly on the smooth mahogany, "that I might do a little in the forgery line."

"Forgery is an unnecessarily strong expression," said Parmenter. "Let us say you make a faithful copy of one of the delightful productions of an old master, and offer it for sale without comment. You don't compel anyone to buy; you merely offer it. It's just a case of *caveat emptor*. It's the connoisseur's business to know. I don't complain if someone sells me a copy. Only he doesn't. I don't let him."

I took out one of my plates of moulding-wax, and laid it softly on the medallion, standing on tiptoe to look over at Parmenter. "That's mere sophistry," said I, making firm pressure on the wax, and feeling the medallion sink into it. "But you know perfectly well that if I sell you a copy, and allow you to believe you are buying an original, I am practicing a fraud on you." I lifted the wax, and, carefully picking off the adherent medallion, laid the latter down, reverse side up.

"There is no fraud if there is no misrepresentation," said Parmenter.

I replaced the wax, which, as I could see, bore a perfect impression of the medallion, in the cigar-case.

"I am afraid you are a very wicked old gentleman," said I, taking out the second plate, and laying the wax carefully on the reverse of the medallion.

Parmenter chuckled gleefully, but made no reply.

"You see," I continued, keeping a steady pressure on the wax, "it is not merely a question of morality. It is a matter of policy. Big profits are made, no doubt, on forgeries, but who gets those profits? Not the forger. It is the dealer who rakes in the shekels."

"Exactly!" exclaimed Parmenter, as I once more picked the medallion out of the wax in which it was embedded; "that is just the point. I am proposing that you shall become a dealer."

I silently replaced the bronze oval, obverse upwards, in its recess, and slipped the wax mould into the cigar-case. And, as I pocketed the case, I said reproachfully:

"You are holding out a great temptation to me, Mr. Parmenter." And I spoke the truth. He was. But he little suspected the nature of the temptation.

"Nonsense!" said the old gentleman. "Here, come and help me up, and we'll go and have a look at the place. I think you'll see an opening in it." I went round and hoisted him to his feet—no small matter, for he weighed fully eighteen stone—and when we had replaced the glazed top of the cabinet, and made all secure, he toddled off to get ready.

"I should like to hear your scheme in a little more detail," I said, as we trudged along side by side. "You know that I've got no capital, of course?"

"I guessed it," said Parmenter. "But you won't want any. I've bought the stock and goodwill, and taken over the lease, and I propose to transfer them to you by a deed. The goods will be absolutely yours, and you will repay me ten per cent. of the profits until the purchase-money is repaid. Then you will be free; and, meanwhile, I take the entire risk if the concern turns out a failure."

It was a very generous proposal—absurdly generous. So generous, in fact, that it made me a little suspicious. Absolute altruism is a somewhat rare product.

"But, look here, Mr. Parmenter," said I: "where do you come in? What are you going to get out of this?"

Old Parmenter chuckled.

"So young and so suspicious!" said he. "But I should have thought it would be obvious; however, if it isn't, I will explain. You know that the lamented Jacob had an excellent connection—as a buyer, I mean. I have had some very good things from him from time to time, and more will come to you, no doubt. Now, all I want is the first refusal of anything that is likely to suit me. That is all. I will pay the full market price—I am a rich man, and not niggardly— but I want the first chance. I want to get to windward of Jacobi; he's my chief rival, and Lyon used to favour him. I lost that Brandenburg snuff-box through Jacobi getting in first. Now I shall want you to promise me the first pick of all new stock that comes in, and if you do that I shall have made an excellent investment."

This was intelligible enough. I knew Jacobi as a rich and eager collector, who, however, unlike Parmenter, combined profit with pleasure by doing an occasional deal. And I knew that the two men were deadly rivals, perpetually tripping one another up in the auction-rooms, and generally adding to the gaiety of nations and the auctioneer's commissions.

The premises of the late Mr. Lyon engendered certain suspicions in my mind, they were so uncommonly convenient. They formed the ground floor of a small, old-fashioned private house in a by-street off High Street, Camden Town, the door of which bore a brass plate inscribed "J. Lyon, Dealer in Works of Art." The house stood at the corner of a paved court, and had a deeply recessed side-door opening on the court; an ideal arrangement for visitors of a diffident and retiring habit of mind.

"The business premises," said Parmenter, ringing the bell, "are bigger than they look. The shop, if we may call it by that name, consists of the ground-floor rooms, but all the rest of the house is used for storage excepting the second floor, which is occupied by Judith Lyon, and she wants to keep it. I suppose you don't mind."

He cocked a roguish eye on me, and I looked down my nose. Women are all very well, and I had a sneaking admiration for Jewesses of a certain type, but I would have preferred the fair Judith a little farther away. Women are kittle cattle.

"It depends on what she is like," I said airily. And at this moment the question was solved by the opening of the door.

Now, for sheer, repulsive ugliness, commend me to an ugly Jew. On the other hand, there are Jews who to the best-favoured Gentile are as a gold brocade to a faded wall-paper.

Judith Lyon was what Mr. Pater would have called "opulent"; tall, shapely, gorgeous, red-haired, with a face and figure that would have sent Solomon flying to the nearest registry-office.

I walked into the hall with a graceful bow and an unctuous smirk; and I regret to say that, as old Parmenter passed me, he positively winked.

On the collection of lumber that filled the house, I could form no sane judgment. When Judith Lyon sat down on a worm-eaten chair, that chair creaked with ecstasy, and its whispers of Wardour Street were hushed. When she looked in a Venetian mirror, its bumpy surface showed me the face of an angel—with a toothache. When she tinkled a rickety harpsichord, I heard the sound of the timbrel mingling with the clamour of the "jumping chariots." It was of no use. Of course, I signed the deed; Judith witnessed it, and we sealed it with a Tassi gem out of the stock. When I shook hands with old Parmenter opposite the Cobden Statue, and turned homewards, I carried the duplicate deed and inventory in my pocket, and the image of Judith Lyon in my heart.

But, business is business, and the day was still young. Parmenter's subtle hints, reacting on my natural ingenuity, had suggested quite a pretty little scheme, and that scheme must be pushed forward, for on the next day but one I entered into occupation of my business premises. Meanwhile, Judith was acting as caretaker, and the Lord only knew what bedevilments she was up to.

The wax moulds were perfect. I viewed them through a lens, and marveled at my own dexterity. The next thing was to blacklead them, which I did with the utmost care, using the graphite from a 6 B Kohinoor pencil, and the softest of camel-hair brushes. Then I fitted up a little tank and a Daniell battery, for I proposed to make electrotypes in silver from the moulds; and the silver was the difficulty. The process that I had in mind would use up more than ten shillings' worth, and I had to go out and change my last sovereign but one to obtain the material. For I had dropped three pounds odd in the escapade at Hunsgate.

The whole of that day I tended the battery, keeping up a gentle current and a regular deposit, and it was late at night before a sufficient thickness of metal had grown on to the moulds; by which time I had fed no less than eighteen shillings into the tank. At last I ventured to take the moulds out of the tank. It was an anxious time, for I could not hope to pick off the electros without damaging the moulds, and if I had failed I had failed finally.

But I had not failed. The thick shells of metal separated cleanly from the moulds, and as I looked at them through a watchmaker's lens I could have shouted with triumph. Each was a replica, absolutely sharp and perfect, of one side of the medallion, but in bright silver instead of bronze. It only remained to join them together, and a perfect medallion would be the result.

So great was my delight and enthusiasm that I set to work without delay. The backs of the electros had to be filed flat and true, and each one brought to exactly half the thickness of the medallion. I had not been able to measure the original, of course, but I had looked at it, and an engineer's eye can be trusted to the hundredth of an inch.

I worked until past one in the morning, and then turned in, but I was up again at seven, as keen on my copy as the divine Benvenuto had been on the original. It was a delicate and difficult task, since the faces and edges must not be rubbed, and it was past noon before I had filed the two halves to the exact thickness, and finished them up dead true with scraper and surface-plate.

The actual joining of the two halves I had to effect with soft solder, since I dared not use much heat; and then I had to deposit some fresh silver on the edge to cover the join, and burnish this new deposit. But, when I had done this, and cleaned off the stopping varnish, there lay before me a perfect medallion in silver. Of course, it was bright and new, an obvious electro that could not deceive a baby—if the baby was on his guard. But would he be? That remained to be seen.

A little cautious treatment with hydrogen peroxide took off the blatant newness and clothed it with a bluish film of oxide that made it look quite venerable; in which state I wrapped it carefully in tissue-paper, and, putting it in my pocket, set forth gleefully for my place of business. I was not expected, but that was all the better.

On arriving at 8, Poplar Grove—that was my business address— I let myself in at the side-door with my latchkey, and, passing through a little lobby, entered the back room, where I sat down on a worm-eaten monks' seat and took the inventory from my pocket.

There were several medallions in cases of various periods, but none of these was likely to agree in shape with my oval master-piece. Presently, my eye caught an item that seemed more likely: "Cinquecento trinket-box of carved pearwood with relief—'Jacob personating Esau.'"

A certain appropriateness in the subject attracted me. I smiled grimly, and, noting the number, I went in search of the box, which I presently found in the drawer of a Japanese cabinet. It was a small, flat casket, like a slab of inferior soap, and bore a crudely carved relief on the lid, from which I gathered that, if the person-ation was successful, Esau must have been uncommonly like a monkey. However, the box seemed to answer the purpose perfectly; it was lined with faded crimson velvet, which imparted to the me-dallion that I laid in it an air of quite respectable antiquity.

I placed the box—open—in a glazed cabinet opposite the win-dow. No one could fail to see it there. Then, having locked the glass door and put the key on my bunch, I opened old Lyon's desk and took out the ledger. A curious and cryptic volume it was, but I was not, just now, concerned with its subtleties. I wanted the address of Mr. Jacobi, and, when I had found it, I put away the book, and, taking a sheet of headed letter-paper, proceeded to indite a little note to my prospective customer. I informed him that I had taken over the business of the late Mr. Lyon, and that I had found among the stock certain trifles of antique art which I thought would be of interest to him, and which I should like to show him before they were inspected by another client whom I expected to-morrow evening. That ought to fetch him, I reflected, as I sealed up my letter. The chance of being beforehand with some other collector was one that Jacobi was not likely to miss.

I was about to leave, when I was assailed by a pang of sudden uneasiness. Suppose the house should be broken into in the night, and the precious medallion stolen? Or suppose the fair Judith should play me false? No; I would not risk it. Unlocking the cabinet, I returned the medallion to its tissue-paper and pocketed it. Then, with my mind at ease, I sneaked out silently and dropped my letter into the pillar-box.

The train was laid. The trap was baited. With the promise of a golden haul before my mental optics, I strolled off to Soho, dined handsomely, and spent a jovial evening in Joe Dalby's studio.

About four o'clock on the following day I sat down in an oaken Elizabethan chair—a palpable "fake"—for a few minutes' rest. I had arrived betimes at Poplar Grove, and, after replacing the medallion in the cabinet, had spent a busy morning raking together a collection of ivories, netsuke, medals, caskets, stibium-cases, and other portable trash for the entertainment of Jacobi. Judith Lyon had looked in for a few minutes, gorgeous, debonair, and friendly in a business-like, matter-of-fact way, and had then taken herself off. The way in which the house was left to take care of itself was really alarming. I should have to give the police a hint. And yet perhaps that would hardly do. I must have a word with Judith on the subject. She knew the ropes.

Suddenly a bell jangled. I went out and opened the front door. It was Jacobi.

"So you've taken over this show, have you?" said he, looking at me disparagingly. "Know anything about the business?"

"Very little," I replied. "But I shall pick it up."

"I expect you will," said Jacobi, with a grin. "And you'll drop a little capital in the process. What stuff is this that you wrote to me about?"

I led him into the room where, on a small table in front of the cabinet, I had set out part of the collection of trash.

"These are some of the things," I said.

He glanced at the collection superciliously, looked curiously round the room, and then his eye lighted on the medallion, which displayed the reverse. He looked at it fixedly for a moment, and then, picking up a Roman stibium-case, pretended to examine it minutely. But his glance continually wandered to the medallion, and his face wore a distinctly startled expression.

"These things are no use to me," he said, laying down the stibium-case. "Besides, I've seen 'em all before. Didn't you say you had some other things?"

"Yes, there are a few more upstairs."

"Run up and fetch them down, will you?" said Jacobi. And the note of eagerness in his voice made my heart leap.

I went out, shutting the door after me, and stamped noisily upstairs. Then, hastily grabbing up a handful of small "antiques," I stole down on tiptoe. Now my astute predecessor had bored one or two holes in the door, ostensibly for ventilation, but, from their position at the eye-level, obviously for the inspection of doubtful clients. To one of these holes I applied my eye, and the spectacle that I beheld filled me with rapture.

Jacobi was staring into the cabinet like a hungry cat before a meat-safe, and frantically trying the various keys from his bunch on the keyhole. After watching him for a few moments I tiptoed quickly up a few stairs, and then, descending noisily, entered the room, to find my client with his back to the cabinet, gazing dreamily out of the window.

Jacobi examined the trash that I had brought down, and, as he lifted the pieces, I noticed that his hands were shaking with a fine tremor. Of course, the things were of no use to him. I knew that. But I waited anxiously for his next move.

"What's that medallion in the cabinet there?" he asked carelessly.

"I don't know," I answered vacantly. "I found it locked up in the safe, though why old Lyon should have been so careful of it I can't imagine. It's only a copy—at least, so I understand."

"Who says so?" demanded Jacobi.

"A client of mine who knows a lot about medals had a look at it. He thought it was a good copy, but he wanted to refer to the original, which he says he has access to. If it's a correct copy, he's going to take it, and he has paid a deposit of ten pounds."

"Who's your client?"

"He didn't want his name mentioned," I replied.

"May I just have a look at the thing?" said Jacobi.

I could not very well refuse; and besides, Jacobi was no great judge, and the light was none too good. But I should have been sorry to let Parmenter have my masterpiece in his hand.

Jacobi examined the medallion closely, especially at the edge, turned it over, weighed it in his hand, and finally looked up at me with an eagerness that he strove vainly to conceal.

"I'll give you twenty pounds for it," said he.

"Why," I exclaimed, "Mr. Par—I mean my client—is ready to give thirty if it's all right; that is, if it's a true copy."

"Look here," said Jacobi: "I'll give you fifty. I'd like to have it, and that's the truth."

"If old Par—my client—won't give more than that, you shall have it," I said. "I can't go back on my promise, you know."

He didn't know anything of the kind. He was furious with disappointment, and positively sweating with eagerness; and it took me close on half an hour to get the medallion out of his hands. When he finally departed, cursing audibly, he left me outwardly apologetic, but inwardly triumphant. For he had gorged the bait, and was fairly on the hook.

I was so pleased with myself that, when Judith came in about six o'clock, accompanied by an elderly woman, I proposed a little supper to celebrate my accession to office. She accepted gladly, for she had a proposition to make in connection with the elderly lady, whom she wished to engage as housekeeper, and whose services to me she proposed to exchange for the use of the kitchen. This arrangement suited me exactly. It solved the difficulty of leaving the house empty, and provided a chaperon for Judith—a rather necessary thing for both of us. And it was particularly opportune just now, since I had decided not to leave the house for a moment until the medallion was disposed of.

Accordingly, I handed Judith a sovereign. It was the "last of the flock," as a matter of fact, but I disbursed it with a light heart—there were plenty more in Jacobi's bank—and bade her go forth and purchase the materials for the feast. And while she was gone I studied her lamented papa's very remarkable ledger; and Rachel, the new housekeeper, laid the cloth in the front room.

I look back on that supper with retrospective relish. It was a
simple affair—and Judith did it uncommonly cheaply, too—just a
matter of a few oysters, a galantine, pâté-de-foie-gras, a few sweet
trifles, a scrap of Roquefort, and a bottle of inexpensive champagne. But youth and high spirits are better than costly dishes, wit
and gaiety than rare vintages. And we did it in style, too. The flowers were stuck in antique silver vases, the viands set out on Sèvres
porcelain and Sheffield plate. We quaffed the foaming wine from
Venetian tazze, we drank our coffee out of priceless Nankin cups,
and Judith licked up the last drop of Chartreuse, with daintly pro-
truded tongue, from the bottom of an exquisite Bohemian glass.

The supper went off with great éclat, and the time sped apace
with joyous babble and harmless mirth. Badinage and swift repar-
tee flew back and forth across the little table—it was a Cromwellian
"gate-leg" and nearly dislocated my kneecap with one of its incalculable legs—and Judith enriched the entertainment with one or
two anecdotes that threw a curious sidelight on the business methods of her late papa, and incidentally proved that the lady herself
was "not born yesterday," as the saying has it. Indeed, Miss Lyon
was a decidedly downy bird, but an excellent comrade too; gay,
sensible, as witty as she was handsome, totally free from coquetry,
and gifted with that indispensable spice of gluttony that turns a
mere repast into a banquet.

The lantern clock, that dangled its weight from a bracket on
the wall, struck twelve; I had set it going in the morning. Judith
rose and shook the crumbs froth her lap.

"Time's up," said she, in her business-like way. "I've had a jolly
evening, and, if I put you on to a good deal, you must give me another. I'll wash up the things in the morning."

I was about to make one of my suave and tactful rejoinders when
the interruption came. I had been half expecting it; had, in fact,
been on the qui vive all the evening. And now it had come.

"Listen!" I exclaimed; and then I turned out the gas.

A stealthy sound came from the lobby by the side-entrance; the
click of a cautiously opened latch, and the soft creak of door-hinges.
I stole out by the hall to the door of the back room, with Judith

close to my side. She was not particularly nervous, she only wanted to hold my hand, and I didn't mind that. As the opposite door of the room opened stealthily, we each applied an eye to one of the spyholes.

"Goodness gracious!" whispered Judith. "It's Mr. Jacobi!"

It was. I had half expected him to come; in fact, I had left the side-door unbolted on the chance. And here he was with an electric lantern in one hand and a small bunch of keys in the other, stealing on tiptoe towards the cabinet.

His face was haggard with eagerness and terror—a very devil of a face—and the hand that carried the lantern shook so that the light danced up and down the wall. He made for the cabinet without a sound, and forthwith fell to trying his keys one after the other. It must have been a poor lock, for the fourth key opened it. The glazed door swung back with an audible creak, and a shaking hand reached in and clutched the medallion.

As Jacobi shut the cabinet, I sprang into the room. He turned like lightning, with a shrill, whinnying scream of terror, but I had him by the throat in an instant, and Judith, who had followed me, snatched the medallion from his hand and laid it on the table.

"Will you please light the gas, Miss Lyon?" I said. "And then perhaps you wouldn't mind fetching a constable."

"Oh, don't do that!" bleated Jacobi, who had sunk, half fainting, on a most uncomfortable Queen Anne chair. "Don't go away, Miss Lyon. I am sure we can—er—arrange this—ha—this little affair."

"Little affair, eh!" I exclaimed. "You won't find it a very little affair at the Old Bailey. And you are proposing that I shall compound a felony. No, Mr. Jacobi, that won't do."

"Now, don't be hasty, Mr. Croker," gasped Jacobi. "Don't, sir, I beg you. You know I was anxious to purchase this—this excellent forgery. That was all I wished, I assure you."

"Do you generally do your shopping after midnight, with the aid of a dark-lantern and a jemmy?" I inquired.

"Yes, I know," said Jacobi, mopping his pale face with his handkerchief; "it does look irregular, I admit it. But, if you will overlook the—er—the—informality, so to speak, and allow me to treat for the purchase—it would—er—in fact, I should—"

As his speech petered out into a tremulous mumble, Judith whispered in my ear: "Let him buy the thing, and put the screw on—hard."

Oh, woman, woman!

"What do you offer?" I demanded judicially.

"I'll give you a hundred pounds—down," said Jacobi eagerly. "I've got a blank cheque in my pocket."

"A hundred!" I exclaimed scornfully. "Why, my other client has already offered two! And I have refused him. I think of sending the thing to Christie's."

Jacobi arose in sudden wrath.

"Old Parmenter is a thief!" he exclaimed. "And a liar too! I left him at the club only half an hour ago, and the old villain swore he knew nothing about it."

"Neither did he," said I, rather taken aback. "Parmenter's not my client. Did you tell him what medallion it was?"

"Not me," replied Jacobi. "He pretended not to know, so I didn't tell him. But look here, Mr. Croker: what will you take? Will you close if I spring two-fifty? That's a large sum, and more than the thing is worth; but I want it, and I'm willing to pay. Come, now, two-fifty, cash down." He made as if to take out his pocket-book, and I wavered. It certainly was a large sum, and still more certainly was more than the thing was worth. But—

The side-door banged (Jacobi must have left it ajar); the house trembled to elephantine footsteps in the lobby, the door flew open, and disclosed a fresh visitor.

It was old Parmenter.

My patron stared from one to another like a man in a dream, then walked slowly into the room, the picture of astonishment and suspicion. Suddenly he observed the medallion lying on the table; and when he saw what it was I thought his eyes would have dropped out on to the floor.

"Lord save us!" he gasped. "It's the lost medallion—or rather a copy of it," he added quickly with the collector's instinctive caution. "Where did you get it, Danby?"

"Out of the stock," I answered calmly.

"The stock!" he shouted. "Then it's mine!"

"No; I'm hanged if it is," said I. "The stock is mine, absolutely."

"Of course it is," said Jacobi; "and you have just accepted my offer."

"No, I haven't," I replied. "I was considering—"

"But I'm entitled to the first refusal," said Parmenter. "Didn't you—"

"No, he didn't!" bawled Jacobi. "I was here first, and I—"

"Now, you know, you can't both have it," Judith interposed. "Be reasonable. I'll tell you what," she added, turning to me: "we'll sell it by auction."

It was a stroke of genius—an inspiration. I picked up the medallion, and, as Judith clapped a spinning-stool on top of the harpsichord, with a little buhl cabinet before it for a desk, I snatched up a steel mace and climbed on to the "rostrum."

"Now, gentlemen," said I, tapping the top of the cabinet with the handle of the mace, "take your seats, if you please."

The two collectors sank gloomily into a pair of corkscrew-legged chairs, and glared at me silently. I passed the medallion down to Judith, and when she had exhibited it tantalisingly before the eyes of the "bidders," I opened the proceedings.

"Lot 1, gentlemen. A remarkably fine and well-preserved copy of the famous 'Brazen Serpent' medallion of that immortal master-craftsman and moral expositor Benvenuto Cellini, exquisitely wrought by an unknown artist in the very finest silver imported for the purpose direct from the mines of Peru. What shall we say for this fine work of art, gentlemen? This unique and beautiful reproduction of the master's handiwork? Shall we say a thousand pounds?"

I named this sum in a spirit of facetiousness. Imagine my astonishment when Parmenter rapped out:

"Eleven hundred!"

"Twelve!" said Jacobi promptly.

"Thirteen!"

"Fourteen!"

My head swam. My senses reeled. I could hardly believe my ears. The room seemed to float about before my eyes. And still the

monotonous voices told out the incredible sums, growing moment
by moment more fabulous; and still the two collectors sat like
graven images with "practicable" jaws, and Judith, in a flush of
ecstasy, stalked to and fro, flourishing the medallion and chirping
triumphantly, "Lot 1, gentlemen!"

It was beyond belief. I felt myself on the verge of hysterics. I
wanted to shout with laughter. It was only when the price had
mounted well over two thousand pounds that I suddenly came to
my senses. For I realised, in an instant of reflection, that I must
not knock the masterpiece down to Parmenter. I could not let him in.
And the bids were coming more slowly now. I must be on my guard.

"Two thousand four hundred!" said Parmenter.

There was a pause. Had I lost the chance, after all? A cold chill
ran down my back at the dreadful thought. I raised the mace, and
looked steadily at Jacobi.

"Two thousand four hundred bid, gentlemen," said I. "Going at—"

"Two thousand five hundred!" exclaimed Jacobi, leaning forward with starting eyeballs.

Parmenter's mouth opened; but before he could utter a sound
I brought down the mace on the little cabinet with a crash that
ruined it for ever.

Parmenter leaped to his feet.

"This is a conspiracy!" he shouted. "The lot was not sold fairly;
you knew I was about to bid. I demand that the lot shall be put up
again."

"I can't do that, Mr. Parmenter," I said. "The lot is knocked
down to Mr. Jacobi, and when I have his receipt for it and his
cheque, the property will be handed to him."

The cheque was already drawn as I spoke; and I myself wrote
out, on a sheet of headed paper, a receipt for "a copy, in silver, of
Cellini's 'Brazen Serpent' medallion," mentioning the price paid.
Meanwhile, old Parmenter stamped up and down the room like an
infuriated mammoth, to an infernal accompaniment of china dogs,
shepherdesses, Venetian glass and pottery, which rattled down
from the shelves like the thunderbolts of Sodom and Gomorrah.
He continued his destructive perambulations even after Jacobi,

having signed the receipt, and delivered up the cheque, had snatched the medallion from Judith's hand and hurried away. Suddenly he halted, and shook his fist in my face.

"You are an ungrateful, treacherous scoundrel!" he exclaimed. "You have broken your solemn promise, and conspired against me with a stranger!"

"I think you'd better be off home now, both of you," said Judith, "or there won't be a breakable thing left in the place."

This seemed eminently sound advice, and, in pursuance of it, I led old Parmenter out at the side-door, and we walked up the street together in silence.

Suddenly he halted, and looked me straight in the face.

"There's something queer about this business, Danby," said he. "Tell me honestly why you knocked that medallion down to Jacobi in that pointed way."

"If you go and have a look at it by daylight you'll know!" said I.

"What do you mean?" he demanded eagerly. "Do you know the history of that copy—if it is a copy?"

"I know an electro when I see one!" I replied.

He looked at me curiously for some moments; then, in a low voice that was almost a whisper, he said:

"Danby, I believe you've been considering those few words of advice that I gave you yesterday morning."

That was the end of my first definite transgression (except that, a few days later, Judith appeared, most unseasonably, as I thought, in a new sealskin coat). It was not a warning to sinners. Rather was it an encouragement to further misdeeds. And it marked out my course finally upon the chart of the future.

Facilis descensus Averni.

4
THE CONSTABLE'S HELPMATE

IT IS AN accepted belief that the burnt child dreads the fire, and no doubt he does. But does his dread deter him from further meddling with it? I think not. Rather, I imagine, does that very dread invest the phenomena of combustion with a new interest, and induce a fearful pleasure in incurring fresh risks. An element of danger is the very pith and marrow of adventure.

I may be wrong. Perhaps I am only reading into other folk's minds the accidents of my own temperament. At any rate, I am certain that I was lured into the risky adventure which I am about to relate by previous experience of its danger.

I have mentioned the very curious resemblance between me and Tom Nagget: curious, because it was so complete and yet so absolutely disguised by our difference in colour. Tom's hair and broad eyebrows were jet-black; mine were golden—or, as the feeble expression has it, "flaxen." And that was all the difference. When I had dyed my hair and eyebrows black—that was when I was staying at Hunsgate-on-Sea—I had personated Tom perfectly. Too perfectly; for I was actually mistaken for him by a policeman (Tom had been doing something naughty), and was incontinently clapped into gaol.

Now, seeing that I had managed to escape from prison, one would have thought that thenceforward I should shun black hair-dye as the devil shuns holy water. But did I? Not a bit of it. Though my liberty depended on my avoidance of the sinister colour, I must needs try the personation trick a second time; must thrust my head again into the trap out of which I had wriggled, just for the pleasure of hearing it snap.

About a fortnight after I had taken over the curio business of the late Jacob Lyon, I received a very singular letter. It was actually addressed to Jacob Lyon himself, but since his present whereabouts were uncertain, and were undoubtedly outside the jurisdiction even of the Dead Letter Office, I ventured to open it; and was forthwith confirmed in certain suspicions as to the business methods of my worthy predecessor.

> "Sir," it began,—"I have got some stuff of the rite sort, and will call at your plaice this evening about nine leave the side-door on the jar.—Your obedient servant,
>
> Milkey.
>
> "P.S.—Same old lay."

"Milkey"! Was such name ever borne by mortal "on the night's Plutonian shore"? No! Certainly not. An obvious *nom de guerre*. And then "the same old lay"! What lay? It was not very difficult to guess. "Milkey! Milkey!" I apostrophised the absent tradesman, "I am afraid you're a wrong 'un." And a "wrong 'un" he subsequently turned out to be.

I had some thought of consulting old Lyon's daughter, Judith, on the subject. But I am a cautious man—at times—and cautious men do not make confidences to the ladies. Besides, it would be hardly fair to Milkey.

At ten minutes to nine that evening I set the side-door ajar, and waited in the back room. At five minutes past nine the door creaked and closed softly, a stealthy step was audible in the lobby, and then a man entered the room. He was not a prepossessing person. His hair was about a quarter of an inch long, his beard of a similar length, and his bullet-head had a general prickliness of aspect suggesting a disreputable horse-chestnut. He seemed to like my appearance as little as I liked his, for he stood for some moments staring at me in disapproving silence.

"Where's old Lyon?" he inquired eventually.

"Ah, Milkey, there you have me," said I. "Abraham's bosom has been mentioned, but the accommodation must be getting limited."

"What d'yer mean?" demanded Milkey.

"I mean that Jacob Lyon has been gathered to his fathers. He vacated the throne about a month since, and Esar-haddon reigns in his stead. I am Esar-haddon."

"Never heard of you before," said Milkey; "but if you've took over the business, I suppose you're willing to pick up a bargain and not ask no questions, ain't you?"

"I am not inquisitive by nature," I replied.

"That's all right," said Milkey, producing a small parcel and untying the string; "and look here, Mr. Haddon: don't you go for to put on the screw, same as what old Lyon used to!"

I promised to refrain from this objectionable practice, and Milkey laid the parcel open on the table. Its contents were rather surprising, for they included an opal pendant, a handsome diamond bracelet, several diamond and ruby rings, and a shapeless lump of silver weighing about a pound.

"A queer collection this, Milkey," said I. "Very queer. I trust you came by these things honestly."

He looked at me with a startled expression, and then broke into a slow grin.

"Rather," said he. "They was left me by my wife's grandmother."

This being the case, there could, of course, be no harm in making him an offer. I did so, and saw at a glance that I had offered too much. However, a man's wife's grandmother doesn't die every day, and, after all, forty-five pounds was not so very excessive. I paid him in cash, of course—Judith Lyon had advised me to keep a hundred pounds in the safe, and now I understood why—and he pocketed the notes and gold with undissembled joy.

"Well, so long, sir," said he, buttoning up his coat. "You'll hear from me again before long"—were his other ancestors ailing, then?—"S. R. Haddon, I think you said?"

"Exactly, Milkey," said I, letting him out.

"S. R. Haddon." I smiled at his ridiculous mistake, which, nevertheless, offered a useful suggestion. For I had been unwilling to put my name on the door; I still had a few decent friends, and was not without hopes of a social rehabilitation. S. R. Haddon it should be. I would have the name put on the door above old Lyon's plate. Milkey should be my godfather.

The question that now arose was what to do with my newly acquired property. I was not disposed to offer the articles to my not very numerous clients, for, really, on consideration, I was inclined to doubt the authenticity of Milkey's grandmother; to regard her, in fact, as an illegal fiction, a sort of feminine John Doe. Finally I decided to pick the stones out of their settings, and sell them separately to a dealer, reserving the metal for use as raw material; a discreet decision, no doubt, though it nearly led to disaster.

The choice of a suitable dealer presented no difficulty. I had heard, through Judith Lyon, of a certain Mr. McKeggie, with whom her father did an occasional deal, and who, Judith roundly asserted, was nothing more or less than a "fence," or receiver. He would buy the stones without doubt, and ask no questions.

But I must go carefully, for a receiver is commonly an informer (or "nark," as Milkey would probably have expressed it). And, thus reflecting, I suddenly remembered my strange resemblance to Tom Nagget. By the mere application of a little black dye to hair and eyebrows I could exchange my personality for his. And it would be quite fair, too; I owed him one for that Hunsgate business.

On the very next evening there emerged from my residence, with some rapidity and a great deal of caution, a black-haired, black-browed individual, having the outward and visible aspect of Tom Nagget. An application of the invaluable "Balm of Ethiopia" had transformed the gold of my ambrosial locks to ebony, and temporarily abolished my sense of personal responsibility. I had put on my evening clothes, for I had an order for the stalls at the Olympus, where I proposed to finish up the evening when I had dispatched my business.

The interview I will pass over lightly, since it was but the pre-
lude to the real events of the evening. Mr. McKeggie—who, for a
Scotchman, had a curiously Asiatic type of countenance—greeted
me as an old acquaintance by the name of Jackson. That put me at
my ease instantly. I accepted the style and title of Jackson without
comment; I accepted his playful allusions to "that Pimlico job" with
a modest smirk; I accepted the paltry sum that he offered for the
trial sample of half a dozen stones that I had brought; and I left
with the firm resolution to find some better and safer market for
"mineral specimens."

On leaving the theatre I made my way to the vicinity of Wardour
Street, where I consumed a modest supper, undisturbed by the
waiter's manifest disapproval of my solitary state. Thereafter I lingered a while in the haunts of frivolity, my borrowed personality
inclining me to get into some sort of mischief; but Satan not being
ready with the usual suggestion, I sauntered homewards, enjoying
the unwonted quiet of the deserted streets. London, after midnight,
has a special charm of its own, a charm that appeals particularly
to the town-dweller, familiar with the diurnal noise and bustle of
the streets.

But I had misjudged the Father of Lies. He had not failed me,
after all. I had walked barely a quarter of a mile up the Hampstead
Road when I became aware of a hurrying figure on the opposite
pavement; a figure that I could nowise mistake, especially under
the present circumstances. It was Tom Nagget

I could have shouted with laughter. It was really too farcical. I
felt an insane impulse to rush across the road and link my arm in
his; to exhibit to the astonished foot-passengers the amazing spectacle of Tweedledum and Tweedledee. But I refrained. Instead, I
watched him furtively—and speculated on his possible movements.

It was past midnight, and yet he was walking directly away from
his lodgings, which were in Camden Road. Moreover, he carried a
handbag, and seemed to be full of business.

My curiosity was aroused. Here was my *alter ego* clearly bound
for some nocturnal tryst. I must look into this. It was, in a manner,

my affair. I stood watching him until he had passed some hundred yards to the south; then I turned and followed.

At the bottom of Hampstead Road he turned westward, and I followed at a respectful distance, until, near the end of the Euston Road, he suddenly diverged into Cleveland Street. Then I mended my pace, and, even thus, only reached the corner of the street in time to see him whisk round into a side-turning. I now broke into a run. My dress shoes were fortunately fitted with rubber-tipped heels, which enabled me to close up the distance without betraying myself by the sound of my footsteps. But in the narrow, empty streets through which my quarry zigzagged, I had much ado to keep him in sight without exposing myself; and, with all my caution, I nearly overran him in a street at the back of Middlesex Hospital, for, when I peeped round the corner before emerging, he was only about twenty yards away.

I lurked in my hiding-place to watch him; and certainly his movements were peculiar and rather suspicious. He had halted opposite a corner house, and, after looking up and down both streets, turned his face towards the second-floor windows of the house, and then taking off his hat, stood bareheaded. This I suspected to be a signal to someone in the house, and my suspicion was shortly confirmed, for, in less than a minute, the private door at the side of the shop opened slightly, whereupon Thomas crossed the road, entered the house and quietly closed the door.

It was a most brazen proceeding.

But what could it portend? An assignation of some kind, obviously. But at a shop in a seedy back street! Of course, Tom Nagget was an utter bounder, but still—

Suddenly my eye caught a mystic shape against the dim sky; three small globes, suspended in a triangle from the corner of the house, the device of the princely house of the Medici; in short, a pawnbroker's sign.

And had it come to this? Was I playing Tweedledee to a ruffian who could descend to an intrigue with a pawnbroker's slavey? A mercenary intrigue, too, involving the use of a black bag? Alas!

Eheu! Alackaday! Sorrowfully and with deep humiliation I crossed the road, taking out a little bunch of skeleton keys, which had somehow found its way into my overcoat-pocket, and examined the door. As I expected, it had a common night-latch; the pawnbroker trusted, no doubt, to bolts and chains. But had this unfaithful stewardess rebolted the door? I feared not; and my fears were justified, for when, having looked carefully up and down the street, I tested the latch with my simple wire skeletons, behold, the door opened!

I stepped into the hall, and, meditating on this woeful lack of precaution, closed the door silently, and listened. A faint jingle, as of keys, came from the back shop, and then a sound like the trying of a lock in an iron door. I stole on tiptoe along the hall, feeling my way—for it was pitch dark—until I came to an open door. This, I found, led into a narrow passage, one side of which was formed by a row of small doors, evidently belonging to a set of those cubicles or compartments which pawnbrokers delicately provide for their clients to screen them from impertinent observation.

The third door was unfastened, and I gently pushed it open until I could peep into the shop. Then my darkest and most hideous suspicions were confirmed; for there, before my very eyes, was my base counterfeit, Tom Nagget, industriously trying a false key in the lock of a large iron safe. The key was evidently home-made, produced, doubtless, from a wax "squeeze" taken by the faithless Abigail, and it refused to perform its office; whereupon Tom cursed softly, but with unction, and, withdrawing it, fell to work on it with a file by the light of a stinking, little lantern. I took advantage of the slight noise to creep into the cubicle and crouch behind the counter, from which position, hidden completely by the darkness, I watched the nefarious proceedings.

It took Tom nearly a quarter of an hour to shape the key completely; I could have done it myself in five minutes, and I itched to rush out and wrest it from his muddling fingers. But at last it was finished. At the sixth trial the lock snapped; a turn of the brass handle shot the bolts back noisily, and the massive door rumbled outward with a loud squeak. It was a clumsy performance, and, to make it worse, at the very moment that the door opened, Tom knocked down his case of tools with an appalling clatter, and then swore furiously, as if that was of any use.

However, now that the safe was open he lost no time, but began to hand out the most curious samples of miscellaneous property. Silver teapots, candlesticks, bundles of spoons and forks, card-cases, cruet-stands, and shapeless ingots came out one after the other—a highly suspicious-looking collection. The spoons, forks, and small articles Tom bundled into his bag, standing the others on the counter; but evidently he was in search of something else, for he rummaged frantically in the interior of the safe, pulling out the drawers, and thrusting his hand deep into the pigeon-holes. Clearly he had not come here only for a few oddments of silver.

Suddenly he emitted a grunt of deep satisfaction, and drew out his hand. It grasped a small paper parcel, carefully tied up with string, and secured with a large seal.

This seemed to be the object of his quest, and he wasted an appreciable amount of time gloating over it. He even fumbled with the string, as if inclined to untie it, but eventually thought better of the matter, and dropped the little parcel into his bag to keep the spoons and forks company; a proceeding that I viewed with regret, for I was eaten up with curiosity respecting the contents of that parcel. Evidently it was something of value.

The next article that he brought out of the safe was a large cashbox, which he tried to unlock with a key from his bunch, but without success. Then he had recourse, once more, to the file; and so preoccupied did he become with his labours that he rested the key on the counter as he filed it, and made no end of a noise.

I must admit that this rather alarmed me, for he was endangering my liberty as well as his own; and my uneasiness was further increased when, in one of the intervals of silence when he paused to try the key, my quick ear detected the sound of a stealthy push at the street-door.

As soon as the grating of the file recommenced, I crept silently out into the hall. Now, I omitted to mention that there projected from the corner of the hall—which was also the corner of the house—a small bay window, from which one could look along both the streets on which the house abutted. It was fitted with ground glass, with a pattern of round, clear spots, through which one could peep out without being seen.

To one of these clear spaces I applied my eye, and looked straight into the open mouth of a police-sergeant. That zealous officer leaned, helmet in hand, against the door, with his ear pressed to the letter-box; and his mouth gaped like that of a newly caught fish, no doubt to catch any stray sound-waves that might miss his auditory meatus. Moreover, he was not alone. Beside him an attendant constable stood in a listening attitude, and positively grinning with expectant glee.

Here was a pretty mess! That idiot Nagget was still filing away like a saw-setter. I could hear him where I stood. If I could not manage to clear out quickly, the police would enter presently, and there we should be—Tweedledum and Tweedledee with a vengeance! It was a ridiculous idea, but I didn't find it very amusing.

As I crept back to the cubicle, I considered the situation. There was that donkey Tom still working away with his file, as if there were no such things as policemen in the world. He had moved down to the farther end of the counter with his preposterous little glim of a lantern, and had pushed the bag and cashbox up to my end. I could just see them silhouetted against his lighted face. And, critical as the position was, I could not resist the temptation.

The bag was only about three feet away from my cubicle. I could reach it easily by leaning over. And reach it I did. Rising slowly, and leaning on the counter, I stretched out my arm and just managed to get my hand into the open bag. The parcel lay on top of the other contents, my fingers closed on it, and, daintily lifting it out, I conveyed it to the tail-pocket of my dress coat. Then I crouched down again and resumed my cogitations.

At the next trial, the key turned in the cash-box, and the lid came open. Peeping round the partition, I saw Tom take out a bundle of bank-notes and stow them in his bag. Then he seemed to notice the absence of the parcel, for he groped frantically among the forks and spoons, and, snatching up his lantern, examined every corner of the interior.

I shall never forget his face. It was the *bonne-bouche* of the entertainment. I had to cram my fist into my mouth to avoid screeching aloud. And all the time, as he searched, he kept up a running soliloquy that was a positive disgrace to an educated man.

Suddenly a door creaked behind us. It gave Tom a terrible start—and me, too, for that matter. Then a voice—apparently a woman's—exclaimed in a loud whisper:

"Fred! Fred! There's two policemen listening at the front! You'd better go out at the side-door while the coast is clear!"

Tom's soliloquy recommenced, but in the midst of a string of nonsensical expletives the silence was shattered by the loud jangling of the street-door bell.

At the first crash of the bell, Tom jumped about three feet, and then began to curse and whimper and dance about like an imbecile, while a muffled scream from the invisible woman was followed by the quick patter of bare feet on the stairs, and then the closing of a distant door.

Again the bell clanged loudly and went on jangling continuously in a truly horrible manner. But Tom, who was fairly out of his senses with panic, merely clutched at his hair and hopped about like an absolute fool.

This wouldn't do. If there was a side-door, that was the way of escape, but perhaps it would be wise to send Tom first as an advance guard. Yes; undoubtedly it would.

I waited for a brief spell of silence, and, as the clamour of the bell ceased for a moment, I exclaimed in a hoarse whisper:

"Look out! He'll be off!"

As Tom staggered back with a squawk of terror, I leaped up, stamped my feet, thumped at the partition, and ran from one cubicle to another, banging at the doors as I went. That started him. Snatching at the lantern as he went, he blundered away down the shop and out at a door, and I vaulted over the counter, kicking the cashbox down with a hideous crash, and groped my way noisily after him, making no great efforts, however, to overtake him.

Nevertheless, I nearly came up with him at the side-door, the bolts of which he was shooting back with unnecessary noise; but fortunately I was some paces away when he got it unfastened, for, as he lifted the latch, it flew open with a bang, and the two police-men tumbled in like a couple of bullocks.

I saw their shapes, for one horrid instant, black against the dim light of the street; then I turned, and, running lightly along the passage, darted up the stairs. But I had hardly reached the first-floor landing when a loud trampling from behind told me that Tom was still at large, and was taking the same route.

The light from a street-lamp showed me that there were four rooms on the landing, and a recess covered by a curtain. I slipped behind the curtain, and had barely concealed myself when Tom came up the stairs, three at a time, and darted into the room next to my hiding-place. A moment later, the two policemen came thun-dering up and charged into the room opposite to me. Now, I had noticed that the door of this room was, for some reason, fitted with substantial brass bolts on the outside—an absurd arrangement, but providential under the circumstances.

Without a moment's hesitation, I sprang across the landing and seized the door-handle. The officers saw me, and made a simulta-neous rush, but before they could reach the door, I had slammed it to and shot the top bolt. For greater security, I shot the other bolt before leaving. Then I tripped lightly down the stairs.

Tom Nagget must have become aware that the policemen were imprisoned—indeed, they made no secret of the matter—for, just as I reached the front door, he came bounding down the stairs into the hall. This was a nuisance. I wanted him to escape, but I did not want him to see me. Wherefore, I demanded, in a stern, official voice: "Is that you, Sergeant?" And Tom turned and fled in the direction of the side-door.

But it was indeed time to go. The officers upstairs were making the most infernal din, rattling the door, ringing the bell, and, worst of all, blowing their whistles out of the window. I took a precau-tionary peep from my former observatory, the little bay window, and, finding the coast apparently clear, opened the street-door, stepped out, and very softly closed it after me.

I was about to cross the road when, round a corner a couple of hundred yards away, a policeman appeared, advancing at a brisk double. My heart sank, and, for an instant, I was tempted to make a bolt for the next turning. But a moment's reflection showed me the folly of this, and suggested the bolder and safer plan.

Sauntering quietly round the corner, with my opera-hat well back on my head, I surveyed the long, straight street. Just ahead, Tom Nagget was giving a little exhibition of really high-class sprinting, while, from a first-floor window, two frantic policemen leaned forth and made night hideous with the discordant shrieks of their whistles. I halted under the window, and, looking foolishly up at the two officers, inquired:

"Wass matter? Watcher makin' that noise for?"

The Sergeant pointed to Tom's rapidly diminishing figure.

"Run after that man and stop him!" he shouted.

"Whaffor?" I asked. "Whass he done?"

"He's a burglar!" bawled the Sergeant. "Don't stand there gaping like a fool! Can't you see he's running away?"

"Does cer'nly look like it," I admitted.

And it certainly did.

"D'ye hear?" screeched the Sergeant. "Why don't you run after him, you idiot?"

"Why dontcher come down and run after him yourself?" I retorted.

The Sergeant's language was positively coarse. He was worse than Tom Nagget, though more amusing, for, his vocabulary being richer, he was not reduced to vain and senseless repetitions. But I was not going to chase Tom Nagget. I had learned the danger of that on a previous occasion. The other constable would arrive anon, and he might collar me by mistake; and mistakes would be awkward just now.

The other constable did, in fact, arrive in time to enjoy the Sergeant's lurid peroration, and uncommonly blown he was. But his superior did not mind that.

"Here, Smith," he roared, "run and stop that man! He's broken in here! And shove that idiot into the side-door to let us out!"

The panting constable bustled me in at the side-door, and then went off in pursuit at a laboured double. I watched him from the door, and grinned. It was a ludicrous sight—like a steam-roller pursuing a motor-bicycle.

Having groped my way through into the shop, I lit the gas, and, just lingering to transfer the bundle of bank-notes from Tom's bag to the inside of the open safe, I ascended the stairs to the first-floor landing, and sang out:

"Where 'bouts are you?"

"In here," responded a voice, accompanied by a hurricane of thumps on the door. "Come, look sharp!"

I withdrew the bolts, and the two officers rushed out on to the landing.

"What jer bolt yourselves in for?" I asked.

By way of reply, the Sergeant grabbed me by the collar and ran me down the stairs into the shop.

"Now, Larkins," said he, "you stay here while I go and see if that chap has been stopped. Or, rather," he corrected himself, as his eye lighted on the overturned cashbox, "I'll stay here while you go and see after the man."

"Man's off by this time," I remarked. "Day after the fair, doncherknow."

"Here, you get outside," said the Sergeant. "We've had enough of you!" He seized me by the collar, and hustled me along the passage to the side-door. "Now, then, Johnnie, out you go!"

In effect, I went out as if discharged from a catapult.

"Look here, Sergeant!" I remonstrated, as Constable Larkins emerged and started off up the street at a brisk trot. "Who are you calling 'Johnnie'? That isn't t'way to speak to a gentleman!"

The door slammed in my face. I turned away with a deep breath of relief, and, sauntering round the corner, crossed the road and entered the street by which I had arrived. Once out of sight of the house, however, I mended my pace considerably, for reflection on the Sergeant's part might engender suspicion; but I still maintained a slightly serpentine mode of progression, and bore away westward, in the opposite direction to that taken by Tom Nagget. Crossing Great Titchfield Street, I proceeded swiftly along Ridinghouse Street, and swung round by All Souls' Church into Portland Place. Here I paused to light a cigar and unbutton my overcoat to display my shirt-front; then, tucking my stick under my arm, I stuck my hands into my trousers-pockets, and advanced up the broad pavement with a raffish straddle.

About half-way up Portland Place I encountered a constable who, I thought, inspected me with undesirable attention. I accordingly halted, as I approached him, to relight my cigar, swaying gently and regarding him with a stern expression and a slight squint; which so abashed him that he hurriedly wished me "Good night!" and moved away.

Albany Street, with its nocturnal population, was plain sailing; an intoxicated man in a dress-suit was one of the *feræ naturæ* proper to the locality; and, after a brief spell of anxiety in the immediate approaches to my residence, I let myself into the studio as the clock of an adjacent church was striking three.

It had been a sporting evening, and, on the whole, satisfactory. I had enjoyed it prodigiously, and had acquired valuable experience. As I sat by the washstand, sponging the repulsive black hair-dye from my golden locks with the aid of a bowl of methylated spirit, I entertained myself with what the novelists call "psychological analysis."

The little parcel lay open on the dressing-table, displaying a really magnificent pearl necklace; and the question that I debated was, Could I honestly retain it? Strictly speaking, the necklace did not belong to me. But, then, neither did it belong to the pawnbroker, who was a palpable fence; and as to Tom, why, he had no claim on it at all.

It was a difficult problem. Much too difficult to be solved at three o'clock in the morning. So difficult, in fact, that the solution came only after the lapse of months, when the whirligig of time had brought wisdom as well as experience. As will appear in due course.

5
A VOTIVE CANDLE

THE PROCESS COMMONLY known as "turning the tables" is, by universal consent, admitted to be an excessively disconcerting one. To pursue a bull buffalo across the grassy plains is well enough, despite the physical exertion. The sensations produced thereby are entirely pleasurable. But when the buffalo so far forgets himself as to turn right-about face and pursue *us*, why, that is an entirely different matter. It is, in fact, an unwarrantable departure from the programme.

This is what I felt when I entered Joe Dalby's studio on a certain Saturday evening, and was saluted by a peal of ribald laughter. The tables were being turned on me. I saw it at a glance.

Joe Dalby is a sculptor; and his studio—the big one in which he works in the clay—looks like the anteroom to a cement factory. On the present occasion there were three persons in it, to wit: Joe himself, in his linen smock; an obscure but clever portrait painter named Morton, and Tom Nagget. It was at Tom that I looked more particularly as I entered, for he occupied the model's chair, a revolving contrivance on a low platform; and if there could have been any doubt as to the nefarious object of his presence, "confirmation strong as holy writ" was to be found in the roughly set-up head on the modeling-stand. The rascal was sitting for a portrait bust.

"What's the joke?" asked Tom, looking round uneasily.

Morton leaned back in his chair shouting with laughter. Joe reached up another handful of clay from the bin and, rolling it between his hands into a repulsive grey sausage, sniggered softly.

"I don't see what you fellows are laughing at," said Tom, with an evident suspicion that they were laughing at him. I did, of course, though I pretended not to, and grinned inanely while Joe pinched a pellet off the sausage and spread it on the effigy's chin with a dexterous twirl of his thumb.

"Don't sit there laughing like a silly hyaena!" exclaimed Tom; whereupon Morton became hysterical, and Joe nearly dropped the sausage. "Do you see what the joke is?" he added, turning to me.

Of course, I said I did not, and then Joe proceeded to explain.

"The joke is," said he, "that Danby has been having his portrait done by proxy."

"What the deuce do you mean?" demanded Tom.

"If you will come out of that chair and let Danby take your place, you'll see," said Joe.

Tom sprang off the throne, and invited me to take the vacant chair. There was no escape. The cat was fairly out of the bag now. Stifling a desire to punch Joseph's dear old thick head, I stepped up and seated myself in the model's chair.

"Well, I'm hanged!" exclaimed Tom—prophetically, as I suspected—staring round-eyed first at the clay head and then at me. "The likeness is perfect. But you said just now that it was a good likeness of *me!*"

"So it is," said Morton. "It is an equally excellent likeness of either of you."

Tom pondered for some moments and then, obtuse idiot as he was, gave utterance to the inevitable conclusion. "But if that head is exactly like both of us, we must be exactly like one another!"

"Precisely," said Morton. "You have not studied your Euclid in vain."

"But we're not!" persisted Tom.

"Yes, you are," said Morton. "In shape of head and features, you two are as like as two bally peas. If it were not for the striking difference in your colour, it would be hardly possible to distinguish one from t'other. As it is, with your strongly contrasting hair, you don't appear much alike at a casual glance. I never noticed the resemblance until Joe pointed it out; and I must say that, as a portrait painter, I find it most surprising and instructive; I had no idea that colour played such an important part in a likeness."

Joe Dalby grinned, and I knew that the dear old ass was going to say something silly. And he did; to wit: "It *is* a rum go! Just think of the possibilities! Suppose Danby were to dye his hair and eyebrows black—"

"Yes," interrupted Morton, "or if Tom were to bleach his hair and eyebrows with peroxide or chlorine, or something—"

"Gad! I never thought of that!" exclaimed Joe. "So he could! Why, it's a regular comedy of errors. Talk about a *doppelganger!*"— and the amiable old idiot laughed until I wanted to bang his dear old fat head against the wall.

"But Danby would have the best of it," he continued, rolling the clay sausage between his hands. I yearned to cram it in his mouth and stop his confounded babbling. "He could wash the hair-dye off when he'd had enough, but Tom would be done for. When once his hair was bleached, he'd have to wait for it to grow again. He couldn't unbleach it."

"No; but he could dye it black," said Morton.

"My scissors! So he could!" Joe was so overcome that he flung himself, with a yell of laughter, into a ragged armchair—and rose again hastily to examine a projecting gimp pin.

So the cat was out of the bag, and the fat was in the fire. I glanced at Tom with a sickly smile—for one had to look amused— and the foxy expression that was stealing over his face told me all, and a good deal more than all, I wanted to know,

Tom Nagget was not a clever man, but he was a downy bird. The terms are by no means convertible. Your sharp practitioner is usually a man with a third-rate brain. But none but an arrant donkey could fail to grasp the possibilities of the case after the demonstration that had been given; and Tom had plenty of low cunning.

I left the studio early to think over the position; and a mighty queer position it was. Tom, as I knew, was a "crook," a professional criminal. I had actually seen him commit a burglary. And his intention—I had read it in his face—was to use me as a stalking horse; to adopt my personality as a disguise when "on the lay."

Here was a pretty state of affairs! If he should happen to be spotted passing forged cheques, or picking pockets, or "doing a crack," it would be my description that would be sent to Scotland Yard and posted outside police-stations. Of course, I might have retaliated on Tom by dyeing my hair black, but then there was that unfortunate affair at Hunsgate-on-Sea. I had been arrested—an innocent man of unblemished character—*with my hair dyed black*, and actually clapped in Ashbury Gaol, whence I had escaped the following night. It would never do for me, an escaped convict, to resume the incriminating disguise. I was "wanted," with black hair. But neither would it do for me to be arrested at all. If once I fell into the hands of the police, I should be thoroughly examined by my old friend the "recognising officer"; and whether my hair was dyed black, or was of its natural golden lustre, the beggar would spot me, I felt sure.

Suddenly another quaint possibility occurred to me, and I chortled aloud. Supposing Tom should get nabbed? The recognising officer would have a look at *him!* And Tom would be a gone coon. The prison people had not spotted my dyed hair, but bleached hair, at close quarters, hits you in the face. Black or bleached, it would be all the same: if Tom was once nobbled, he would certainly be recognised as the dark-haired gent from Ashbury Gaol, and back he would go to my vacant apartments. And I should be free for ever

When I realised this, I began almost to hope that Tom would try the personation trick. It would be a contest of wits between him and me, and I was a move ahead; for Tom did not know about that Hunsgate and Ashbury affair.

I tried very hard to keep an eye on friend Thomas after this, but didn't succeed very well, for it was more than a week before I met him again. Then, one night about ten o'clock, I ran up against him in the Hampstead Road.

"Hallo, Tom!" I exclaimed jovially. "What a stroke of luck to meet you here! I was just strolling down to the Oxford. Care to come? I'll pay."

He looked at me furtively, and mumbled something about being tired.

"Tired, are you?" said I. "Well, then, come and split a bottle of fizz with me. That'll buck you up."

Again he looked at me uneasily.

"No, thanks, ol' man," he murmured. "I've had a glass 'lready. Going home."

This looked bad. He certainly *had* had a glass. Just enough to take the sharp edge off his consonants, but that was all. And never, in the memory of man, had Tom Nagget been known to decline eleemosynary refreshment. Champagne, too! There could be only one explanation—he was afraid to be seen with me in a public place.

I examined him attentively, though without ostentation. There was something queer about his usually sleek hair. It had a wiry look—it "stared," as horsey men say—and when I moved, so as to bring his head between me and an electric street lamp, there was a curious purple tinge at the edges. All this was highly suspicious.

"Going home, eh?" I said. "Then I suppose I shall have to do likewise, though I feel more inclined for mild conviviality. We may as well walk together as far as my turning."

He received the suggestion without enthusiasm, but he couldn't very well refuse, so we set forth together; but I noticed that he looked about him uneasily as we walked, and that he showed a marked preference for back streets. I cudgeled my brains, as we trudged along rather silently, for some plan to get a really good look at Tom in a proper light, and it was only when we were approaching the vicinity of the disused studio that I rented, and occupied as a bachelor's flat, that I hit on one.

"Are you any judge of port, Tom?" I asked suddenly.

I knew that he had a very special weakness for this pernicious liquid, and claimed to be somewhat of a connoisseur.

"I think so. Why?"

His awakened interest encouraged me.

"Because I've got some stuff that was sold to me as ''sixty-three.' I wish you'd come in and give me your opinion of it."

Tom licked his lips, hesitated, swallowed, and finally agreed.

"But it isn't likely to be ''sixty-three,'" said he.

It was not "'sixty-three," in fact. You don't get that vintage for thirty-six shillings a dozen. But it was a good, strong, full-bodied wine; and when I had filled a big claret-glass to the brim, and handed it to Tom, I felt that things were progressing. I poked up the fire, and laid myself out for conversation and anecdote, while Tom lay back in my low, folding chair. It was so low that he was almost recumbent, and had to raise himself to drink.

It was distasteful to me thus familiarly to entertain this mean rascal, but I did it, and did it thoroughly, never losing sight of my purpose. My conversation was carefully adjusted to the needs of the moment. I began in my funniest vein. Personal reminiscences— extemporised on the spur of the moment—and uproarious anec- dotes formed the initial treatment, and, under cover of his idiotic laughter, I kept his glass replenished and roused up the blazing fire.

By the time he had swallowed the third glass his maudlin hilarity had passed the zenith, and his attention began to wander. Then I changed my tactics, and from facetiæ turned to metaphysics. His efforts to follow me were really pathetic, and the more so inas- much as my remarks were mostly quite devoid of meaning. He blinked at me owlishly, and, when I put a direct question, begged me to "Say that again, ol' f'ler; didn't quite follow y' there." I said it again at wearisome length, and his eyelids drooped. I droned on in a monotonous singsong, and they drooped more. At length an unmistakable snore put a term to my labours. The wine, the fire, and the metaphysics had done their work. Thomas had sunk into a dead sleep.

And now for the inquest. Now we should see what we should see.

I stepped over lightly, and touched his hair. It felt like oakum. Quite so, but I am a man of method. With my pocket scissors I snipped off a small wispy and having poured some methylated spirit into a wineglass dropped it in. The wisp of black hair sank to the bottom, and immediately a purple cloud formed round it. Pres- ently I fished the hair out with a pair of tweezers, and, behold I it was black no longer, but a golden-straw colour, very like that of my own.

That settled it. It was a clear case. But the question was, what was his game? I stepped back to him, and, having slipped a pillow under his head to moderate his snores—for he might wake himself, which would be a nuisance—I looked him over. A folded newspaper, peeping from his inside breast-pocket, attracted my attention. One doesn't usually carry a newspaper in that way. Very carefully I drew it out, and noiselessly opened it. It was the *Evening News*, and on the very front page enlightenment stared me in the face:

> "THE ENTERPRISING BURGLAR
>
> "An unrehearsed comedy was enacted last night in the rural village of Hornsey. It appears that Mrs. Walker, an elderly widow lady, hearing suspicious sounds from the dining-room beneath her bedroom, rose, and boldly proceeded to investigate. On entering the dining-room, she found herself confronted by a golden-haired young man who was busily turning out the plate-drawer. The two regarded one another for a while with mutual surprise. Then the burglar retired hastily, taking a harlequin leap through the back window by which he had entered. Mrs. Walker summoned the police, who found that nothing had been taken, but, on the contrary, something had been left behind, to wit: a small letter-case. To their regret, it contained no letters, but what it did contain was a packet of newly taken photographs which Mrs. Walker instantly recognised as excellent portraits of her uninvited guest. The police are much obliged."

There! What did I say about downy birds? Obviously this cunning donkey who was now snorting and snuffling in my chair, had had these photographs taken after having bleached his hair; and he hadn't had the sense to remember how little a photograph discriminates between fair hair and dark. For fair hair is yellow, and yellow photographs nearly black. Of course, the photographs would do for me, but they would equally well do for him with his dark hair. All that he had done was to make the town unsafe for either of us. And it was all so unnecessary; for the old woman had seen *him*, and would be ready to swear to *me*.

I refolded the paper, and stowed it in his pocket. You can't hit a drunken man, or I would have hammered him then and there. But I shook my fist in his unconscious, bloated face, and swore he should pay the uttermost farthing.

There he sat, puffing out his cheeks and dangling his purple hands over the arms of the chair, a bestial spectacle. There was his wine-glass, with a sticky heeltap in the bottom, and the marks of his greasy paw on the clear glass, from which I should have to wash them. I looked at them with a certain distasteful interest, and then—

Hey! What? An illuminating gleam had flashed into my mind. "The marks of his greasy paw!" His fingerprints, in short. Yes; by Jove!

The great Fingerprint Superstition has always delighted me. There is something deliciously artless in the awe with which detectives, judges, and other unsophisticated persons seem to regard these simple markings. For, after all, what is a fingerprint? It is just the impression of an elastic body with a relief pattern on its surface. That is all. Like an indiarubber stamp.

Now, no one attaches any special significance to the mark of a rubber stamp. People take their signatures to the stamp-maker, and he turns them out a stamp in facsimile. But it never occurs to them that if they took their fingerprints (or some other person's) he could equally well make a stamp in facsimile of *them*. But he could. And what is more, the stamp would be a true facsimile, because the fingerprint is itself a stamped impression. Very well, then. Why shouldn't I reproduce Thomas's fingerprints? That would be a really juicy joke.

But if it was to be done, now was the time. The obvious preliminary was to get a model to work from, and here was Tom with the ten purple originals dangling over the arms of the chair. It was a chance in a million.

I tiptoed into my little cupboard of a kitchen, and put the egg-saucepan, full of water, on the gas-stove. Then, while it was heating, I went in search of those cakes of dentists'-wax that I had bought a few days ago. Ah, here they were, twelve of them, but I only wanted two. I picked out a couple of the round cakes, and, fitting each into a circular canister-lid, dropped them into the saucepan.

Tom gurgled on, all unconscious of my proceedings.

As soon as the water was hot, I fished out the cakes of wax in their canister-lids, with a spoon, drained the water from them, and tested their temperature. Mustn't have them too hot. That would wake up the patient.

When they had cooled down sufficiently, I approached Tom with one, and, very gently taking hold of his dangling right hand, let the tips of the fingers rest lightly on the wax, and slowly increased the pressure. After a few moments I raised the fingers, and, just glancing at the four beautifully clear impressions, repeated the operation with the thumb. Then I went round, and treated the left hand in like manner. It was a perfectly simple proceeding, and barely took ten minutes. But the result! When I looked at those sunk impressions through my pocket-lens, I could have hugged myself with delight.

I took the moulds into my bedroom, and laid them on the wash-stand to cool; and as I had now no further use for Thomas, I filled my bath-sponge with cold water, and, carrying it out into the studio, slapped it on his face, hard. My word! What a hubbub he made! How he leaped into the air and spluttered and bubbled and swore! It was "fair ridicklus," as my friend Mr. Scroggie would say. But I had no time really to enjoy this "turn." I just bundled him down the stairs, shot him out into the mews—and shut the door.

I don't suppose the reader wants to be bored with details of "industrial processes." Of course, when the moulds were hard, I blackleaded them, and took copper electros. This gave me a complete set of copper fingertips, exact reproductions, even to the microscopic markings and pores of the skin. The rest was easy. I had experimented in the processes of rubber manufacture—there aren't many chemical or mechanical arts that I have not experimented in—and from the copper "models" I easily managed to make a set of thin rubber stamps, each of which was a facsimile of a finger-tip or thumb-tip. When I had cemented these false finger-tips on the finger-ends of a pair of thin kid gloves—turned inside out, for reasons which will appear later—my apparatus was complete.

It was a screaming farce. Never shall I forget the delight with which I first tried those gloves on. How I danced round the room in an ecstasy, sweeping my gloved hands over dusty surfaces, and dabbing them on clean plates and sheets of paper, which I left covered with Tom Nagget's dirty fingermarks. Jiminy! How I laughed!

But a truce to untimely levity. There was business on hand. Here was the apparatus of a very pretty adventure, and the question was, what was I going to do with it? Tom had led off, so to speak, with an old woman and a packet of photographs. What was my reply to be? The natural and sporting thing seemed to be to follow suit. But could I? Let me just look through my hand.

I did so. I was not rich in old women, for the fact is that I usually give a rather wide berth to the obsolete human female. Of course there was Rachel—Judith Lyon's chaperon—but she was no good; much too downy; and, besides, I should have to enter my own premises, which would be ridiculous and unsafe. The only other old woman whom I could think of was—yes, of course! ha, ha!—was Joe Dalby's Aunt Jemima. She met the case perfectly.

Joe had often told us about her: a grim old lady who lived at Lavender Hill with a solitary domestic as old as herself, and stone deaf. And she was dogless, too—a rare and precious virtue in an elderly woman. As to the five cats and the cockatoo, I didn't mind them. Cats don't bark, and they only miaul for purely personal reasons, and so occasion no comment beyond a stray boot or a lump of coal.

I decided accordingly on Aunt Jemima.

Next day I journeyed to Lavender Hill, and had a look at the house, a small detached villa in Camomile Grove. It was perfectly practicable either from front or rear; in fact, its only protection was the certainty that there was nothing in it to steal. I examined more particularly the back, which looked on a narrow lane. The garden was enclosed by a six-foot wall, and there was a gate, unbolted at the moment, and thus affording a cautious peep at the back of the house. I noted a flimsy back door and a ridiculous little window about four-feet-six from the ground, apparently placed there by a considerate builder for the convenience of burglars, and then I closed the gate and retired.

It looked a simple enough affair, just a matter of pushing back a catch and sliding the window up. And, with all those photographs in circulation, the sooner it was done the better, for there was no knowing what Tom might be up to next. In fact, there was no reason why I should not do it this very night, and there were very good reasons why I should. To-night it should therefore be.

About nine o'clock in the evening I began my simple preparations by getting into my dress-clothes; for on a nocturnal expedition an evening-dress suit is a better protection than a suit of plate armour, besides being less conspicuous. It accounts plausibly (though quite insufficiently, if you come to think of it) for one's being abroad at that ungodly hour. But I put on a black silk tie instead of the regulation white, so that, when my overcoat was buttoned, I should not appear to be in evening-dress.

The other appliances that I required were a strong pocket-knife, a small jemmy, the magic gloves, and a candle. The last two were of the essence of the enterprise, and I began with the candle—a short six of the kind known to the vulgar as "compo-sight." I warmed it gently at the fire until it was slightly soft on the surface, then I put on the left glove, and, picking up the candle by the wick with my right hand, seized it firmly with the fingers and thumb of the left. Thus I held it for a minute, and then, carefully releasing it, carried it by the wick into the bedroom, and, having dipped it in cold water, examined it.

The impressions on it of Tom Nagget's fingers were surprisingly distinct. I could hardly myself believe they were a fake. When it was quite hard I tenderly wrapped it in tissue-paper, and stowed it in my overcoat-pocket. I next turned the magic gloves right side out, when they looked like ordinary kid gloves, the false linger-tips being now inside; and, having put them in my pocket with the clasp-knife, and secreted the jemmy inside my dress-coat, I clapped on my opera-hat, buttoned my overcoat, tucked a cheap pheasant cane under my arm, and went forth.

It had turned half-past eleven when I entered the lane after a cautious look round. It was a dark night, and the place seemed quiet and peaceful.

No confounded dogs or fowls, and, as for the cats, as I said before, no one minds them. I scrambled up the wall with some difficulty, and immediately dropped down on the other side, for a man on a wall is a conspicuous object against the sky. My descent introduced me into a symposium of several cats, who exploded violently and dispersed like non-luminous rockets.

When I had noted that the back of the house, like the front, which I had already inspected, was all dark, I softly unbolted the gate, in case a hasty retreat should be necessary, crept forward in the shadow of the party-wall, and approached the little window.

It was a perfect disgrace to the builder, was that window. I had hardly begun to press with my knife on the trumpery catch when it snapped back, and quite startled me. I slid the window up slowly without difficulty or noise, climbed through the opening, and was inside the house. It was a flat affair. A common tramp could have done it easily. I hadn't even had to put down my walking-stick.

The place that I had entered appeared, by the light of a wax match, to be a kind of lobby or back hall, into which the garden door opened. This I unbolted, and released from its chain, and then cautiously opened another door and entered what was evidently the dining-room. Through this I groped with the aid of another match, and, passing out by a door at the farther end, found myself in the hall.

I stayed here only long enough to unbolt and unchain the front door (thus securing a choice of exits in case of an emergency) and place my stick in the umbrella-stand, and then I returned to the dining-room, where, finding that the window was shuttered and covered with a thick curtain, I thought it safe to light the gas. The chandelier was over the table, on which I knelt to apply the match; and as the cheerful light burst forth a hoarse voice close behind me exclaimed:

"Keep your 'air on, Billy!"

I did nothing of the kind. In fact, I nearly fell off the table. Never in my life have I got such an awful turn. And all through a beastly cockatoo!

Of course I proceeded at once to silence him by covering his cage with a tablecloth, but not before he had let off a couple of bugle-calls, a jubilant whistle, and a peal of idiotic laughter; and even when I had got him covered up I could hear him muttering and cursing obscurely inside.

This regrettable incident hurried me somewhat. Hastily I unwrapped the precious candle from its enshrouding tissue-paper, stood it on the mantelpiece, lighted it, turned the magic gloves inside out and put them on, carefully adjusting the finger-tips, buttoned up my overcoat, and blew out the candle. Now I was ready.

The first object of my solicitude was the cellaret. It contained a beer-bottle (half empty) and several clear glass tumblers. I passed my hands through my hair, to impart a slight greasiness to my fingertips, and reached out the bottle and a tumbler, leaving on the glass a set of Tom Nagget's right-hand fingerprints that might have served for a frontispiece to Galton's immortal treatise.

I was just setting down the glass when a sound as of an insane muffin-man smote my ear. Some fool was ringing a hand-bell out of a back window. Here was a pretty kettle of fish! If this row went on I should have to bolt without showing myself, and then of what use would the fingerprints be? Hang that cockatoo!

However, the row didn't go on. It ceased, and, shortly after, my charmed ear detected a sedate and elderly creak on the stairs. I whipped off my gloves, stuffed them in my pocket, and listened.

The sound continued to approach; the glimmer of a candle showed through the crack of the door; the door itself opened a few inches, and a head was cautiously thrust in—an old woman's head, stern-faced, forbidding—clearly the head of Aunt Jemima.

The old lady regarded me fixedly, as if committing my features to memory, though not without some signs of alarm. But she was a plucky old cat—I'll say that for her—and I bowed graciously.

"Howdy-do?" said I. "May I ask what you are doing in my dining-room?"

"Hey? What?" Aunt Jemima came in, candle and all. "What did you say?"

I repeated my question and she slapped her candlestick down and faced me.

"Well, I'm sure!" said she.

"Quite so, madam; but that doesn't answer my question."

"Your question!" She turned pale with wrath.

"Well, of all the outrageous, unconscionable, impudent, bare-faced—"

"Hush!" I interrupted. "Pray moderate your language. Consider the cockatoo!"

She considered him, or, at least, as much of him as was visible through a large hole that he had torn in the plush tablecover, and her anger rose. She snatched off the tablecover—whereupon he whistled joyfully for a hypothetical cab—and turned to me furiously.

"May I ask, sir," she said, "if you are a burglar or an escaped lunatic?"

"Really, madam! Really!" I protested. "This is not courteous. I fear I shall have to leave you."

In fact, it was time to go, with that infernal bird blowing coach-horns and shouting for pots of beer. I turned to retire with dignity, but, stumbling over a cat, I staggered precipitately out into the lobby.

Quickly letting myself out of the back door, I strode down the garden, softly opened the gate, and looked out. The devil! Here was a constable coming up the lane, flashing his beastly lantern like a toy heliograph.

The beggar saw me at once, so there was no escape. I beckoned mysteriously, and he approached.

"Was that you ringing that muffin-bell?" he demanded.

"Yes. There is someone in the house," I replied; and returned up the garden, calling out to the constable to wipe his shoes as he came in. Entering the back door, I raced through the lobby and burst into the dining-room, glaring wildly, and gnashing my teeth.

Aunt Jemima was inspecting the candle with a satisfied grin—another victim of the fingerprint superstition—but the grin faded when she saw me; at least I think it did, for she didn't wait, but as I dashed at the fire-place, and snatched up the poker, she left the room. Which is stating the case inadequately, but you understand.

I turned out the gas, picked up her candlestick, and followed, heading her off the upper stairs and shepherding her along the hall to the kitchen-stairs, down which she bolted like a rabbit. I had no idea old ladies were so active.

Meanwhile, the constable was blundering through the dark dining-room. I heard a familiar hoarse voice say "Hallo!" and then another voice say something that I won't repeat, but I gathered that the constable and the cockatoo had met. A moment later the officer appeared lighted by Aunt Jemima's candle, that I had put down on the hall-table. I held up my hand and said, in a warning tone:

"Be careful. It's a female, *and she is armed!*"

The constable was distinctly ruffled. Also his finger was bleeding.

"Armed be blowed!" he exclaimed, with a scornful glance at the poker that I still held. "Here, let me come!"

I let him come, and he began to descend the kitchen-stairs just as a massive door slammed in the basement, and a key turned in a large and rusty lock. I turned away and, tip-toeing along the hall, softly opened the front door.

Great Jeroboam! Was there ever such infernal luck? At the moment that I opened the door, behold! a police inspector, supported by a sergeant, in the very act of raising his hand to the bell-pull. You could have knocked me down with a feather!

"Anything wrong here?" the inspector asked briskly.

"Wrong!" I exclaimed in indignant tones. "I should jolly well think there is! One of your men has broken into the house, and the Lord only knows what he is doing to my cook in the cellar. Just listen to that!"

Opportunely enough the sound of heavy blows upon a door arose from the basement, mingled with feminine squawks of "Murder!" The two officers looked at one another and frowned; the inspector demanded "what the deuce was up," and the pair marched in and headed swiftly for the kitchen-stairs.

It was really time for me to tear myself away. Taking my stick from the umbrella-stand, I stepped out to the gate, looked right and left, and then sped away up Camomile Grove on the wings of the wind.

Once fairly round the corner, I dragged my hat from beneath my waistcoat, punched it out, and clapped it on my head, and, as I sprinted out into Lavender Sweep, I unbuttoned my overcoat to display my shirt-front. For here a hansom was just setting down a lady and a gentleman. I hailed the cabby, and sprang on the footboard.

"I'm going home," said the cabby. "Off to the stables, I am."

"Where are the stables?" I asked.

"Pancras Road," he answered.

"That'll do," I said. "Put me down there."

I took my seat and drew the doors to in an agony of impatience, for the bobbies must have been already on the warpath. But then the trap opened, and the cabby's face appeared.

"It'll be three 'ogs and a tanner, mister," was the trivial observation that he delayed to make.

"Oh, all right!" I shouted. "Off you go!"

The trap fell, the cab turned right about, and the horse, smelling the stables afar off, broke into a canter. But he didn't say "Ha, ha!" as did the Jobian horse, or if he did, the remark didn't reach me, for my attention was occupied by a concerto of police-whistles proceeding from Aunt Jemima's.

The *Evening News* is an amusing little half-pennyworth. I made the remark to Joe Dalby on the following evening, and he cordially agreed with me. The fact was that, as I entered the studio, I found him reading aloud from the latest edition to a select audience of two—Morton the portrait painter and Tom Nagget. And this is what he read:

"The golden-haired disciple of the late W. Sikes, who distinguished himself a few nights ago by leaving his photograph at the house he had broken into, has made another appearance in public. But this time he left no photographs, nor even a lock of his hair—only a very complete set of fingerprints. Miss Jemima Dalby, the owner of the house into which he broke, has been shown the photographs, and recognised them instantly as those of her midnight visitor. It is unfortunate that this gentleman forgot to leave his name and address, but doubtless he will shortly repair the omission."

As Joe finished, he and Morton and I shouted with laughter. I suppose they were laughing at Aunt Jemima, but I wasn't. It was Tom Nagget's face that doubled me up. Never have I seen a human being look so much like a stuck pig.

Well, well, I had played my card, and taken the trick. It was Tom's turn now. I apostrophised him silently as he sat there: "Your play, Tommy dear."

But Tom only scratched his head.

6
THE EMPEROR'S KEEPSAKE

THE PROPOSITION, "'TIS distance lends enchantment to the view," yields, on conversion, the cognate truth that things which look well enough when seen afar off are apt, on closer inspection, to develop unexpected ugliness. I realised this when I began critically to consider my present mode of life. Viewed from afar, the curio business of the late Jacob Lyon, which I had taken over, had suggested certain sporting possibilities that attracted me; but more intimate acquaintance had brought into view sordid elements that I had not bargained for and that grated on my refined sensibilities.

Milkey was one of these. I have no wish to disparage Milkey. Compared with other burglars—for such was Milkey's professional status—he was a favourable specimen. Nor would I heedlessly condemn his vocation. An uncle of mine, a retired Army officer, had a very fine collection of curios which he had "obtained" from sundry temples and joss-houses, towns and villages (inhabited by "niggers, by gum, sir"), in the course of his campaigns; and I could not discover that his methods of acquirement differed materially from Milkey's, or that they had entailed any public reprobation. My uncle called his things "loot," Milkey called his products "swag"; but "swag" and "loot" are, *mutato nomine*, one and the same thing. So, until our ethical notions clarify, and we cease to abrogate the Ten Commandments by "accepted custom" or Act of Parliament, we mustn't be too hard on Milkey.

Nevertheless, as I watched that industrious tradesman untying a small parcel in the back room, his presence grated on me. I am not quarrelling with his personal appearance, which had improved markedly; his hair had grown to a full half-inch, and, this being only Tuesday night, traces of the Saturday morning shave still lingered on his chin. It was the contents of the parcel that disturbed my equanimity. They were stolen goods, and I was a common receiver. That was what I jibbed at. A common fence like old Jacob Lyon. Not the sort of position, I am sure you will agree, for a gentleman of culture and lofty moral ideals.

"Well, that's my little lot," said Milkey, laying open the parcel. "Twelve 'postle spoons, two salts, snuff-box, hammerthist brooch, gamp'andle, and pair of pearl lug-weights."

I raked over the collection distastefully. Excepting the pearl earrings there was nothing of any value, and the deal was soon concluded and the "swag" lodged in the safe. Milkey pocketed the wages of sin, and then, instead of departing, proceeded to extract from his overcoat-pocket an elongated object wrapped in green baize.

"This here," he said as he removed the wrapping, "is another property, as the auctioneer blokes say. It's a blimy candlestick. 'Tain't mine—leastways, I didn't collect it. I swopped a teapot for it along of Little Mo—him what calls hisself Alfred Johnson; you know him, I expect."

"I have not that honour, Milkey," I answered stiffly, holding out my hand for the candlestick (the adjective "blimy," it will be understood, was merely an embellishment of speech, a sort of verbal appoggiatura).

"Yus," said Milkey, handing me the candlestick; "it's a fair licker to me what Mo was up to. Fly little blighter he is ordinary, but that blooming teapot wasn't no class; thin as paper it were, whereas there might be a dozen ounces in that there candlestick, allowin' for the lead in the foot."

I examined the "property" closely under the gaslight.

"A dozen ounces of what?" I asked.

"'Ard stuff, o' course," he replied.

"What is hard stuff?"

"Well, silver, then, if yer don't understand English."

It was not respectful of him, but I let that pass. "You've been done, Milkey," I said. "Little Mo has done you in the eye."

"I'll do him on the nose if he has," said Milkey, with a ferocious glare. "But he ain't. What d'yer mean?"

I pointed to a spot on the candlestick. It was a square "Adam" pattern, and on one of the projecting angles a tell-tale rosy gleam showed through the silver.

Milkey stared at it incredulously. His keen eye caught the rosy gleam, and he made appropriate comments, which I will not report verbatim, but which were to the effect that the candlestick was composed of copper, and that Little Mo was a person of defective moral character.

"And the little blighter's waltzed off with my teapot!" he concluded plaintively. "But wait till I come acrost him! I'll teapot him!"

On the exact nature of this operation I can only speculate; the verb "to teapot" has been omitted from my dictionary. Besides, it was no business of mine. Little Mo was really the interested party.

I dealt fairly and even liberally with Milkey. The current price of copper being about tenpence a pound, five shillings seemed a good price for the candlestick, and he departed with this additional sum in his pocket and a thirst for vengeance in his heart.

My own feelings on the transaction were somewhat mixed. The candlestick was an object that lay within my own specialty, and I had seen at a glance that it was a splendid specimen of Sheffield plate, an unusually rich and delicately wrought example of late "Adam" design, and I dated it somewhere between 1795 and 1800. But, dearly as I love good Sheffield plate, the thing was of no use to me, for it had been "pinched"—it was stolen property. I could neither sell it nor keep it for my own use, and, as for melting it down, even if I had been capable of the baseness of melting a charming work of art, there was barely a shilling's worth of metal in it.

I wrapped it in its baize covering, and when I went home I took it with me, and stood it on a small table that I might look at it as I smoked my final pipe by the studio fire. And as my meditative eye roamed over its delightful details, from the graceful, urn-shaped

socket to the exquisitely chased ram's heads and festooned
garlands on its flat sides, somehow it seemed to stir some chord
of memory, to suggest some recent event that I strove in vain to
recall.

It was only when I got up to refill my pipe from the tobacco-jar
that I found the clue. The new number of the "Connoisseur" was
lying on the table. Of course! There had been something about a
candlestick which I had just glanced at, but had not had time to
finish. I hunted up the paragraph, and, having found it, sat down
to read.

"The subject of Sheffield plate," it ran, "reminds us of the
candlestick that was stolen from Lord Barmington's house last
week by a burglar, who evidently mistook it for a silver piece. It
was a fine example of copper rolled plate, of the 'Adam' pattern,
but its special value lay in its history and associations. It was one
of a pair that belonged to Napoleon during his exile, and used to
stand on his writing-table at Longwood. General Power, Lord
Barmington's grandfather, was one of the officers who had charge
of the Imperial captive, and on his departure from St. Helena he
received these two candlesticks as a keepsake from the Emperor,
who then wrote on the foot of each with the point of his penknife,
'Napoleon I.' 'The initial I,' he said drily, as he made the gift, 'might
be interpreted "Imperator" or "Infelix," at the choice of the reader.'
One of the candlesticks was stolen before General Power left the
island, and has never been heard of since. And now the other has
gone, to the profound vexation of its owner, who, naturally, set
great store by it."

I laid down the magazine and took up the candlestick. The signature would be on the bottom of the base, of course. I turned it
up, and, sure enough, there it was, "Napoleon I," scribbled across
one corner, with the letters "A. J. P." scrawled underneath—the
initials of the ancestral General clearly. He didn't mean to lose the
second one. This was the lost sheep, then. I was glad to know it,
for it solved the difficulty at once. All I had to do was to hand it
back to its owner. The thing was of no use to me. I couldn't sell it,

and even if I could I wouldn't. These personal touches are the heart and soul of the antique. If the thing had been of solid gold, encrusted with gems, it should still have gone back to Lord Barmington. I am not a collector—I have no hankering to possess—but I flatter myself that I am a real lover of antiques.

But this solution had a further advantage. I had fallen in love with this piece for its mere beauty and charm. But as I am not a collector, a perfect facsimile is as good for me as the original. It is the beauty that I want, not the authenticity. And if I restored the original, there was no reason why I should not keep a copy for my own use.

I sprang from my chair and began to rummage in my store boxes. Ah! Here was what I wanted—a big tin of elastic moulding composition, a compound of glue and treacle. I would take a mould in this convenient material, and then I could make an electrotype at my leisure.

I set to work with my customary energy, heating up the composition in my largest saucepan. The whole business took little more than an hour, for I have had a good deal of practice at electro work, and am pretty expert. But, of course, I could only make half the mould, for it was a big mass, and would take some hours to cool thoroughly.

I was up betimes on the following morning, and, after an early breakfast, made the other half of the mould, and took separate impressions of the nozzle and drip-pan. Then, having weighed the candlestick and ascertained the position of its centre of gravity, to enable me to calculate the quantity of lead in the foot, I looked up his lordship in the directory, and wrote him a short note. It was not a discreet thing to do. I had better have sent the candlestick to him by post, and given no name or address. But I had some vague idea of making a useful friend, and, of course, it is easy to be wise after the event.

I wrote, on headed paper, from Poplar Grove, to the following effect: In the course of my business as a dealer in works of art, there had come into my possession a candlestick which I suspected to be the one stolen from his lordship's house. If he would care to call on me, I should be happy to show it to him. Meanwhile, I begged him to consider my communication as strictly confidential.

That evening I shelled the candlestick out of the mould, which was in two halves, and, as far as I could see, an absolutely perfect impression. Then I wrapped the original in its baize cover, and when I went to my business premises next day I took it with me.

Early as I was, I found a telegram from his lordship awaiting me, and close on the heels of the telegram came Lord Barmington himself. Judith Lyon let him in, and when he entered and saw me standing at the desk, he stared in utter amazement. And well he might. When you go to interview the proprietor of a suburban curio-shop, you don't expect to find a man of my appearance and presence. It was perfectly natural.

My visitor saluted me stiffly, and turned to watch Judith out of the shop—if I may so describe the ground-floor rooms—and a deuce of a time she was in going, by the way. Then he produced my letter, and thanked me drily for sending it.

"I hope, Lord Barmington, that you have not mentioned this matter to anybody?" I said, a little anxiously.

"I have not," said he.

Thereupon I proceeded to unlock the safe, quite glad to turn my back on him for a moment, for his admiring regard, though flattering, was almost embarrassing. I took out the candlestick, removed its wrappings, and handed it to him.

"Yes; this is the one," he said, after looking it over, and examining the base.

"You are quite sure it is not the one that was lost at St. Helena?"

"Quite. Here are my grandfather's initials. He only wrote them after the fellow-one was stolen."

"Then I am most happy to restore it to you, and, if you are going to carry it in your bag, I had better wrap it up."

So saying, I swathed the piece in its baize covering, and, meanwhile, his lordship devoured me with his eyes until I turned quite red. Damme! It really wasn't quite the ticket! Of course, I could sympathise with his feelings. I like to look at good-looking people myself, especially girls, but there was no need to stare like that!

I wrapped the thing up under his eyes, tied a wisp of string round it, and handed him the green bundle. He took it from me ungraciously, and asked, in a gruffish voice:

"How much?"

"I beg your pardon!" said I. "How much what?"

"How much have I got to pay?" he said impatiently.

"Really, Lord Barmington," I protested, "I understood you to say that this candlestick was your property!"

"So it is," said he.

"Then, as it is now in your possession, it seems to me that the transaction is finished. I merely stipulate that my name shall not be mentioned in connection with the affair."

"Oh, very well! But may I ask how you came by the piece?"

"It was brought to me by a man who had obtained it from a person whom I suspect to be a receiver of stolen property. Where the receiver got it I have no idea. My client, of course, supposed it to be silver."

"And you don't feel disposed to give your—ah—clients away?"

"I don't want to be mixed up with stolen property."

"No; I suppose not. Police inquiries and that sort of thing; wouldn't suit you at all. But you'll allow me to refund what you paid the other Johnnie?"

"Certainly not. I wash my hands of the affair altogether. But I may tell you that I shall be only a few shillings out of pocket. The thing is of no intrinsic value."

"No; I suppose it isn't when you come to think of it." This seemed to be a new idea to his lordship, and the look of comprehension that stole into his face made me sorry that I had been so explicit. Slowly and thoughtfully he deposited the little bundle in his bag, and then, looking at me with a rather puzzled expression, asked: "Is that all?"

"That is all, my lord," I replied stiffly, preceding him to open the door.

"Then I must thank you for the trouble you have taken, and wish you good-morning."

I walked out into the hall and opened the street door. He passed me with a cool nod, and I heard him mutter to himself as he went out that it was "a deuced queer business!"

It was. And highly unsatisfactory. His lordship's attitude had not been what they call in diplomatic circles "correct." It had been distinctly ungracious. He had taken my altruistic conduct for granted, and had barely thanked me. I wished, now, that I had sent the confounded thing by post.

But I had one consolation: the moulds. I could indemnify myself by making a really fine copy for my own use; and, as I went about my scanty business that day, I planned out my methods. At first I had proposed merely to make a copper electro. But now my ambition soared higher. I would have a silver surface as well. Of course, electro-plating was out of the question. That dainty ornamentation would be ruined by having a layer of silver spread over it. It would be like putting a thick coat of paint over a delicate wood-carving. No; I would reproduce the actual Sheffield character or leave it in the plain copper.

Let me explain, for the benefit of the uninitiated, the difference between the two kinds of plate. In ordinary electro-plate, the piece is made in copper or white metal, and, when it is finished, is coated with a layer of silver, electrically deposited, which, of course, covers the surface impartially and obliterates all sharp and delicate work. The old Sheffield plate, on the other hand, was made from rolled copper already covered with a fairly thick layer of silver, so that the chasing and silversmith's work was executed on the actual surface of the silver. Hence its incomparable superiority.

Now my scheme was this: I would first deposit a layer of silver on the inside of my mould and then cover that with a thick deposit of copper. Thus the silver surface would take the sharp impression of the mould, and the copy would be identical in appearance with the original. I decided to retain the Emperor's autograph, but the worthy General's initials were of no interest to me. Those I would erase from the mould before beginning.

It seemed an excellent plan, and its execution occupied me through many delightful evenings. For there was a good deal of finishing work to be done after the candlestick had been taken from the moulds. There were the seams, left by the joins of the moulds, to be removed; there were the nozzle and drip-pan to be finished and fitted, and finally, after careful weighing, there was a measured quantity of lead to be introduced into the foot. This was quite a ticklish business, but I did it eventually by pouring the melted metal through a hole that I had made in the socket, having previously heated the candlestick to a little over the melting-point of lead. Finally I closed up the hole in the socket and the little puncture that I had made to let out the air, and the piece was finished— a perfect replica of the original save for the absence of the General's initials and of the rubbed edge that had disclosed the underlying copper to Milkey's astonished and disapproving eye.

Temperaments differ strangely. On some men, like old Mr. Parmenter, for instance, the effect of works of art is to excite a desire for possession. They are primarily collectors. Now I am not a collector: I am a craftsman. Creation, not possession, is what really gives me pleasure. I had enjoyed the making of this candlestick exceedingly, but now that it stood before me, a glittering reality, my interest in it waned. I found that I did not want it particularly, after all.

It was about this time that I received a note from old Parmenter. He was making one of his periodical clearances of duplicates, and he wanted the collection conveyed to the sale-rooms. It appeared that he couldn't take them himself, as he was confined to the house by an attack of gout; not a severe attack, but Parmenter was of a somewhat "full habit," as he expressed it, and eighteen stone on a tender big toe is no joke. So he asked me to take the things for him.

Now this request suggested an idea. Why should I not pop my candlestick in as a sort of appendix to Parmenter's collection? The auctioneer would detect the fake, no doubt, but it was not his business to give his clients away. The thing would be sure to fetch a pound or two from some confiding collector and might furnish some sport into the bargain. I decided to do it.

Accordingly, when I had fetched the parcel from old Parmenter's, I rewrote his list and added to it: "One plated candlestick, 'Adam' style," without further comment. Then I thoroughly greased my hair—it is a sin to put grease on hair like mine: utterly destroys the splendid golden lustre, and makes it look like ordinary brown hair—plastered it well down at the sides, darkened my eyebrows, and put on a pair of weak spectacles, and having thus ruined my personal appearance, I set off for the well-known salerooms of Messrs. Moore and Burgess, just as the shades of evening were gathering in the streets.

A pasty-faced person of bilious aspect attended to me in a small anteroom. He opened the parcel containing old Parmenter's "little lot," as Milkey would have said, and ran through the contents disdainfully, checking each article from the list. Apparently he didn't care much for coins or medals. But when he disinterred my "property" from its abundant wrappings, his countenance brightened visibly.

"This is a bit off Mr. Parmenter's special line," he remarked, weighing the piece in his hand, and turning it over curiously. "What is it supposed to be, now?"

"A candlestick," I replied. "Plated, it says in the list."

"I can see that," he said testily; "but I mean what sort of plated candlestick is it supposed to be? Because I can tell you what it is. It's a very fine piece of Sheffield. Well preserved, too, though it badly wants cleaning." (I may mention that I had darkened it slightly with sulphur, and then rubbed the projections bright with a touch of tripoli.)

"Now, how ever can you tell where it was made?" I asked. "Is there a mark on it?"

Of course, I knew there was, and I had seen him look at it.

"There may be. I haven't looked. It is my business to know these things."

"Yes; but how do you know?" I persisted.

He placed the tip of his forefinger on a rather bumpy forehead, and reflected.

"Now, how do I know?" He pondered on the question for some moments, and then, looking at me impressively, replied: "I can't tell you. The mind of the expert works subconsciously. The experience of years develops a sort of sixth sense—an instinctive—ha—hum—do you understand what the French express by the word 'flair'?"

"'Flare'?" I repeated vacantly. "Isn't that the stuff they make lard from?"

"Oh, you're thinking of pig's flare." He shut his big account-book with a bang, and turned his back on me. "Those things will go into next Thursday's sale," he said shortly. He was quite huffy.

As a dealer in works of art, I generally received catalogues of any sales that were taking place, and I duly received one from Messrs. Moore and Burgess. I ran my eye down it until I came to the description of my masterpiece:

"Lot 163. Candlestick, Sheffield plate, square shaft. Adam period. Mark, crossed keys and escutcheon. Inscription, 'Napoleon I' scratched on foot."

I laid down the catalogue and grinned. That my humble electro should have passed muster, not merely with a common collector, but with a regular, brass-bound, flairy expert, was a triumph that I had not anticipated. I was flattered.

But if that was the way the cat was jumping, there was more than flattery to be got out of it. There was profit, and a little entertainment into the bargain. All that was necessary to set the ball fairly rolling was to underline Lot 163 in red ink, and post the catalogue off to Lord Barmington. Which I accordingly did.

Now the entertainment that I promised myself out of this little affair was obviously conditional on my being present at the sale. Otherwise, I should miss all the fun. But could I be present? That was the question. I am not a nervous man, but it was a ticklish business for me to be seen just now in a place like Burgess's. Consider the circumstances.

Here was that rascal Tom Nagget, a professional criminal with the whole police force yapping at his heels, masquerading as *me*. Tom was as like me as a twin-brother, and he had actually made up designedly to render the likeness complete. More than that, the police were in possession of photographs of him in the make-up—

virtually photographs of me. It would be midsummer madness for me to appear in a public saleroom until Tom should be nobbled and the bubble of our identity burst.

Yet I wanted to go; in fact, there was no use in foolishly trying to deceive myself. I meant to go. And there was only one safe method of doing it. I must disguise myself.

Now I hate disguises. One reads in novels of amateur detectives, smart, handsome, well-set-up young fellows—like myself, for instance—just clapping on a white wig, tying on a false beard like a chest-protector, drawing a sort of railway-map of wrinkles on their faces, and gaily mingling with the populace or jostling the elbows of unsuspecting detectives. But that is all rubbish. If a fellow were to do that in real life, he would be hauled up by the police for obstructing the traffic.

Real daylight disguise is a tedious and troublesome affair, and horribly uncomfortable.

However, it had to be done, unless I was willing to give up the sale—which I wasn't—and accordingly, when the day of adventure arrived, I proceeded to make my toilet.

I greased my hair and darkened my eyebrows, as before. That made a considerable change in my appearance, and then I fixed on a false moustache—not the sort of thing that you stick on for private theatricals, and hold on with one hand while you flourish your rapier with the other. This was the correct article (never mind where I got it), and it had to be put on properly.

First, it had to be fixed on securely with spirit gum; then, with the same beastly adhesive, a quantity of loose hairs had to be cemented on the skin round the edges to hide the join; and finally, it had to be trimmed up neatly with scissors until it looked exactly like the natural disfigurement.

The transformation that it effected was complete. I looked in the glass and shuddered. To think that Nature might actually have grown a thing like that on my upper lip, and condemned me to the miserable alternative of scraping it off daily, or looking like a walrus! A beardless man—with a suitable face—has much to be thankful for.

I didn't trouble to get to the rooms prematurely; in fact, I arrived just as the first of old Parmenter's coins was being put up. I looked about me cautiously. Jacobi, the omnivorous collector and dealer, was there, and I recognised several other well-known members of the profession. There seemed, too, to be a good sprinkling of amateurs, but I noted with anxiety that Lord Barmington was not among them. It would be a nuisance if he didn't turn up after all. I had looked to him to supply the fun of the fair.

The last of old Parmenter's trash had passed into the possession of the assorted idiots who were ready to swop new coins for old, and still there was no sign of his lordship. It was getting serious.

"Lot one hundred and sixty-three!" The singsong announcement came from the rostrum (which, by the way, was occupied by my flairy acquaintance of the other evening), and an assistant handed up my *chef d'œuvre*. "A Sheffield candlestick bearing the mark of that famous maker Henry Wilkinson. A handsome piece this, gentlemen, and in faultless preservation. What shall we say for this fine candlestick?"

Someone murmured "A guinea!" and the piece was handed round for inspection. I watched its progress anxiously, and noted that when it came to Jacobi, that wily connoisseur turned it up, glanced carelessly at the bottom of the foot, and passed it on.

"One guinea is bid for this fine piece of Sheffield plate!" the auctioneer chanted. "One guinea only—"

"And a half!" This was from Jacobi, who was trying to look as if he hadn't spoken.

"One guinea and a half. This is ridiculous, gentlemen, for this fine—"

"Two!" This from Jacobi's unseen rival, who, I somehow suspected, was bidding on behalf of the flairy one himself.

The piece had crawled up reluctantly to three and a half guineas, when I was aware of a commotion in the crowd behind me, and of a voice inquiring who the deuce you were shoving, sir. The movement communicated itself to me; a hand grasped my arm, and a breathless voice asked which lot was being sold. Something familiar in the

tone made me look round quickly. The speaker was Lord Barmington.

"Going at three and a half guineas—it's against you, Mr. Jacobi—
three and a half—"

"May I see the lot, please?"

The eagerness of his lordship's demand caused Jacobi to look
round quickly, and methought his jaw dropped considerably. But
not Jacobi alone. Bidders and onlookers alike, scenting an "incident," looked curiously at my late client as the piece was handed
to him. His scrutiny was not a long one. He just glanced at the
mark, turned the foot up, and examined the signature intently for
a moment, and then returned the candlestick to the attendant.

"Five guineas!" said he.

Now this was foolish. It gave the show away at once, and people
who had never given the piece a thought now reached out for it,
and scrutinised it eagerly.

Among them was a tall man on my left, who had certainly been
watching with interest, but who now became so anxious for a closer
inspection that he trod heavily on my foot. I mentioned the circumstance to him, and instinctively glanced down at the clumsy
hoof that had been set down on my delicate extremity. Imagine my
feelings when I found the hoof encased in a regulation constabulary boot!

Jacobi glared savagely at his lordship, and grunted sulkily "And
a half." Evidently his little plans were upset by the new arrival. He
had spotted the piece, and had meant to buy it to retail to his lordship at a profit. But he was going to make a fight for it.

"Six," said Lord Barmington.

"And a half," replied Jacobi.

And so the bidding went on until one or two excitable amateurs, impulsive asses, who were not fit to be trusted alone at an
auction, caught the infection, and "waded in."

"Twenty-one guineas in four places," said the auctioneer, who
seemed to have abandoned his personal interest in the piece.

I saw the detective draw near to Lord Barmington and touch
him on the arm, but his lordship shook him off, and shouted:

"Twenty-two!"

"May I have a word with your lordship?" said the officer.

"Presently, presently!" was the reply. "Twenty four!"

"I wish to point out to your lordship—"

"Not now," Lord Barmington interrupted impatiently. "I can't talk to you now! Twenty-six! Can't you see I'm busy?"

"But I wish to point out—"

Lord Barmington shook his head angrily, and shouted "Thirty!" And the detective, with a despairing shrug of his shoulders, subsided into watchful inaction.

The excitement waxed apace. The bidding grew wilder and more wild. Lord Barmington meant to have the piece, at all costs. Jacobi, who was running a sort of one-man knock-out, meant him to pay through the nose, and, as to the amateurs, they lost their heads completely, as amateurs will. The word "Half!" ceased to be heard, and the price hopped up at first by whole guineas and then by twos, threes, and ultimately by fives.

It was only when three hundred had been reached and passed that the bidding began to slacken. Jacobi was the first to drop out, and soon the others, observing the fact, gave up one by one. I regretted their faint-heartedness. It had been like a dream—a golden dream—for the guineas that were rolling in in this preposterous fashion were my guineas! Still, I hadn't done badly.

"Three hundred and fifteen guineas, gentlemen! This splendid candlestick, with its romantic associations, is going for the absurdly inadequate sum of three hundred and fifteen guineas! It is against you, sir. Is there really no advance on this trifling sum?"

Apparently there was not; and the auctioneer, having looked round the room with an expression of pained surprise, brought down the hammer with a protesting whack, and said to his clerk: "Lord Barmington."

His lordship thrust his hand into his breast-pocket, and was in the act of drawing out a cheque-book, when the detective once more bespoke his attention.

"Well, *what* is it?" his lordship demanded testily.

"You mustn't pay for that candlestick, my lord!"

"What?"

Astonishment overcame habitual politeness.

"I am Detective-Sergeant Burbler, my lord," the officer explained, in a low tone. (But I heard him all the same. I made it my business to.) "That is your own candlestick, the one that was stolen, I mean."

"Oh, no, it isn't!"

"I beg your pardon, my lord, but I have the description, and it tallies exactly."

"Ah! But I've got the other candlestick. It was—ah—er—returned to me—by post—anonymously!"

Lord Barmington gave these particulars jerkily, and with a very red face. Of course, the sergeant didn't believe him, and didn't pretend to. But there was nothing more to be said; and a couple of minutes later I saw his lordship go forth from Burgess's with a springy tread and an elongated parcel under his arm.

I went forth also.

Old Parmenter was very pleased with the prices that his raffle had fetched—so pleased that he offered me a small commission on the transaction.

"No, thanks," said I. "Fact is, I've made a bit myself. Took the liberty of putting in a piece of my own with your little lot—a plated candlestick!"

Parmenter's face clouded.

"Oh, that was *your* candlestick, was it? What did it fetch?"

"Three hundred and fifteen guineas!"

"Hey?" said Parmenter.

"It was an antique, you know," I hastened to explain.

Parmenter smiled sourly.

"So I see," he said, glancing at the catalogue. "Adam period. Can't get much farther back than that. But look here, Danby: if you've been up to any chickery-pokery, I'm not going to have it put on to me! Understand that!"

"Oh, it's all square," said I. "It was put in by me as a plated candlestick—which it certainly was. They called it Sheffield plate.

I didn't. And as to the chappie who bought it, I suppose he knew what he was about!"

Parmenter chuckled. His silly joke had mollified him.

A couple of days later, I received his cheque, and paid it into my account in person. On my way home from the bank I ran up against Joe Dalby. He saluted me with effusion and a broad grin.

"So Aunt Jemima's young man has been at it again!" he remarked, when we had exchanged greetings.

I veiled my anxiety, and merely replied: "Has he?"

"Rather! Do you mean to say you haven't read about the Barmington affair?"

That Barmington affair!

"No," I answered as coolly as I could. "What was it?"

"Why, he broke in and nipped off with a plated candlestick—plated, you understand—and left a set of fingerprints on a silver beaker! He must be a silly guffin!"

"They identified him by the fingerprints, I suppose?"

"Afterwards, yes. But Lord Barmington saw him, and identified him by the photographs that the Police have. What's the matter, old chap?"

"It's as good as a play!" I said, grinning mirthlessly, like a death's-head on a clay pipe.

Ye gods and little fishes! Lord Barmington! Now I understood that unmannerly stare!

"Talking of Lord Barmington and his candlestick," pursued Joe, "that's a queer start about the one that was lost at St. Helena. Have you seen the evening paper?"

"No!" I gasped. "What about it?"

"Why, it has turned up, in the Crumford Museum. Been there over eighty years, and no one spotted it until yesterday. Rum go, isn't it?"

Rum go, indeed! I should think it was! The fat was in the fire now, and no mistake!

7
WOMAN AND SUPERWOMAN

SOME PEOPLE HAVE no imagination, and not even an instinctive perception of fitness. I throw off this psychological aphorism in connection with a concrete instance which introduces the present episode: an oaken chair of the time of the sixth Edward—a time-blackened, battered, round-angled venerable survivor, from the dim past, which would have been a perfect example of the period but for the lack of imagination on the part of the mediæval donkey who made it. The fellow had actually forgotten the worm-holes! Of course, the omission was fatal from a collector's point of view. There was nothing for it but to make good the deficiencies with a "worm-eater's" drill—a tedious and monotonous task, for when you have drilled the holes, you must put a drop of walnut stain in each, or else they "grin"; and you don't want a Tudor chair to look as if it had just recovered from smallpox.

I had just bored the two hundred and fifty-third hole, and was resolving to give that mediæval craftsman a bit of my mind the next time he called for orders, when the door opened softly, and Judith Lyon entered. Her appearance struck me dumb with amazement. I had always regarded Judith as an eminently capable, matter-of-fact young woman; in fact, "leary"—were it permissible to apply such an adjective to a lady; but, of course, it is not. However, here was the sober Judith tricked out in the glaring colours of that most militant society, the Gadfly League.

"Well, I didn't expect this of you, Judith," I said, gaping at her open-mouthed.

"Oh, you needn't distress yourself, Danby," she chuckled. "It's only a fancy dress. There's a carnival at the Camden Hippodrome to-morrow night, and Sol Cohen has given me a ticket. This was the cheapest fancy dress I could think of; you see, it's just an ordinary frock and hat trimmed up with a yard or two of green and white ribbon. Costs next to nothing. How do you like it?"

"Oh, of course you look charming; but then you always do!"

"I know," sniffed Judith. "But you want to see me in my skates to judge of the effect. I'll put them on."

"Not here!" I exclaimed. "Think of the china, Judith."

She gave a look of haughty disdain, and seated herself on an oaken coffer.

"Do you suppose I should go to a carnival if I couldn't manage my skates?" she demanded, dexterously clamping the little trucks to the soles of her shoes. Then she added, with a smile, "To think of your taking me for a real militant!"

The skates being duly adjusted, she rose cautiously from the coffer, looking surprisingly tall

"Now you can judge of the effect better," she said, standing very erect and majestic; and at that very moment the two little four-wheeled carts darted away in opposite directions. There was a confused din of metallic stamping; the house shook to a heavy concussion; two Japanese jars bounded from a shelf; and Judith ejaculated "Oo-er!"

Now, when a young lady, under stress of bodily suffering, makes use of the exclamation "Oo-er!"—especially with an accent on the "er"—it is possible to form certain surmises as to her social antecedents. It is, for instance—but this is callous, to say nothing of the beastly snobbery. Here is the fair Judith sitting on the floor, rubbing an already swollen ankle and executing rapid variations of facial expression, which, under less distressing circumstances, would have been quite amusing, and I am actually commenting unchivalrously on a mere verbal atavism. I am shocked at myself.

But my callousness was not apparent. In a twinkling I had her shoe unlaced and had hoisted her on to the coffer, and a pretty burden she was to lilt, for these Israelitish maidens run to weight.

Then I escorted her upstairs, and, having delivered her into the hands of the faithful Rachel, returned to my "worm-eating." But a little later I visited her, and found her lying with a wet rag on her ankle, free from pain, though uncommonly glum.

"This puts an end to the carnival jaunt!" she remarked gloomily. "One-and-ninepence for ribbon clean thrown away, and a five-shilling ticket wasted, too—unless I can sell it to somebody," she added, with awakening hope.

I waited for the inevitable proposition, and hadn't to wait long.

"Wouldn't you like to go, Danby?" she asked persuasively. "You can have the ticket half-price."

"No costume," I said.

"It won't cost much to hire one; or you can have the loan of mine," she added flippantly.

I smiled feebly; but she resumed with more animation.

"Seriously, though, Danby, there's no reason why you shouldn't; and it would be a joke."

"They wouldn't let me in," I said. "They'd say the dress was improper for a man."

"But," exclaimed Judith, "they'd never spot you. Don't you see? Your face is as smooth as mine is, and, with that squeaky voice of yours, you'd pass easily for a girl."

The crudeness of her expressions jarred on me. "Squeaky voice indeed!" As if—but there! What can you expect of a person who says "Oo-er!" And it was undoubtedly true that my countenance was completely free from those too-common traces of a simian ancestry, and that my voice had a melodious, flute-like quality unusual in the human male.

"Why not, Danby?" said Judith, with an anxious eye on the prospective half-crown; "you're just about my height, the things would fit you perfectly with a little management."

And, after all, why not? Masquerade, with its attendant adventures, was my special weakness, as the reader must have observed; and it would be more amusing to masquerade as a suffragette than as a clown or a jockey, or any nonsense of that kind. The end of it was that I compounded with Judith for seven-and-sixpence, which sum was to include the price of the ticket and the hire of the costume. Her skates were useless for me, but I could easily hire a pair at the Hippodrome.

Thus was started a train of circumstance fortunate in the end, though not without its moments of peril and misgiving; by which I passed amidst shoals and quicksands into a haven of security.

But I anticipate—very considerably.

On the following evening, when the dusk had fallen, I emerged tremulously from the side door of Poplar Grove. A preposterous hat was pinned on my flaxen wig, and, though the whole contrivance was secured with a motor-veil, I hardly dared to wink for fear it should drop off. As a matter of fact, I had tested it, and found it quite secure, but still I distrusted it, and this, with the bewildering conduct of my unaccustomed garments, made me dreadfully self-conscious.

Instinctively I made for the quieter thoroughfares, and crept nervously by the wall, until, presently; finding that I attracted no notice, I became more confident. My disguise was really excellent. The wig was so perfect a match that I was able to brush my own hair from my forehead over it and so conceal the edge; in fact, the motor-veil was a needless concession to my own nervousness.

I was tripping demurely with mincing step along a quiet by-street, when suddenly there appeared round a corner two figures whose aspect brought my heart into my mouth. For their costume was the replica of my own.

There was no escape. They had seen me instantly, and were even now bearing down on me with expectant smiles. I smirked in return—there was nothing else to do—and then we met. The taller of the two, a buxom, round-faced girl, halted and barred the way.

"Hallo!" said she. "Where are you off to?"

"Carnival," I replied. "Camden Hippodrome."

"Oh, tosh!" she exclaimed. "Why aren't you coming to the meet?"

Now the wise man—and such, I trust, am I, in a small way—shuns the practice of untruth, especially when he is not likely to be believed. Morality and discretion alike called for strict veracity in the present instance.

"The fact is," I said humbly, "I am an impostor. This is a fancy dress."

My round-faced friend was disappointed, and expressed her feelings in the current idiom.

"Oh, what a beastly, rotten shame! And you're just the sort of girl we want."

Perhaps there was more truth in the latter statement than the fair speaker realised. But I made no reply, and she continued, "I say, can't you chuck that silly carnival and come with us? It'll be a frightful spree—we're going to old McCarker's house—he's away in Scotland, you know, and his caretaker goes out on Thursday evenings and leaves Mrs. Caretaker all aloney. That's why we're going to-night."

"But what are you going to do? And who is McCarker?" I asked.

"Oh, he's the Secretary of State for something or other, and we're going to call and do a little house-decoration. It will be *awful* fun. You will come, won't you?"

Without waiting for a reply, she passed her arm through mine and rotated me on my vertical axis until I faced right about. Of course, I ought not to have gone. To risk an encounter with the police in my present circumstances, and in female clothing too, was sheer insanity. But—well, the possibilities were stupendous ; and besides, the round-faced girl wouldn't listen to a refusal.

"What's your name?" she asked, as we set forth arm-in-arm. I replied modestly that I answered to the name of Lydia Tarkington.

"What a gaudy name for a police report," she said enviously, adding, "I'm Susannah Larkin, and my friend here is Miss Aspasia Diggle."

Miss Diggle bowed—rather frostily, I thought. She was a diminutive suffragette of the earnest and neurotic type, clearly disapproving of the irresponsible Susannah, and a little suspicious of me. In fact, I fancied that I caught her once or twice glancing inquisitively at my feet; but that may have been mere self-consciousness.

On the top of the omnibus that bore us southward, Susannah explained to me the plan of campaign, which I need not repeat, since it will appear in due course. At present we were bound for "headquarters," where we should pick up the rest of the raiders and listen to a brief address from the vice-president, a Miss Beedlestone.

The hoarse voice of Big Ben was proclaiming eight o'clock as we turned into Adam and Eve Court, Westminster, and were duly admitted by a stolid porter to a tall new building. The prospect of entering a room filled with women was somewhat alarming, and I think my manner must have betrayed some trepidation, for, as we ascended the stairs, Susannah fixed a constabulary grip on my arm and adjured me not to be nervous. Nervous I was, nevertheless, and strongly inclined to make my escape before it was too late; but even as I hesitated I was lost. Miss Diggle pushed open a door on the first floor, and Susannah bundled me in neck and crop.

I sank into a chair by the door and surveyed the scene with guilty fascination and a good deal of alarm. The members were ranged around a long table, at the head of which sat a small, eager woman, who grasped an ivory hammer and beamed admiringly on a lady who stood beside her addressing the meeting.

"The little woman with the hammer is our president, Miss Munker," Susannah whispered; "the other is Miss Beedlestone. I wish she'd shut up and let us get to work."

The vice-president was a large, gelatinous woman, with a heavy jowl and an indelible smile. She appeared to have an unusual number of teeth (which, of course, was an optical illusion), and her role was that of the candid and playful cynic. Spreading a pair of large hands starfish-wise on the table, she leaned forward and grinned confidentially at her audience.

"I was remarking," she said, "when I was interrupted, that all our methods converge upon a single point—publicity. To be seen, to be heard, to be talked about. Those are our vital necessities. The daily Press is our sword of conquest. Through the newspaper columns we march to victory. In a word, ladies, we have to recognise that this great movement is, in the last resort, conducted by the newspaper reporter."

"I object to that," interposed one of the members.

Miss Beedlestone's smile broadened even unto her second molars. "You may object—"

"I do!" said the first lady.

"So you have said."

"And I say it again."

"But it's true, you know, after all," asserted another lady.

"It isn't!"

"It is!"

"It isn't!" Here the other members, becoming involved in the vortex of dissension, the proceedings became, for the moment, reminiscent of the jungle market or the game of pit.

"Ladies! Ladies!" remonstrated Miss Munker, bringing the chairman's hammer down smartly on Miss Beedlestone's little finger. "Order, if you please! Your turn will come in due course, Miss Sibbeth."

"It has come now if I choose to speak," said Miss Sibbeth doggedly.

"But, you know," said Miss Munker, in persuasive tones, "we can't all speak at once."

"Yes, we can," retorted Miss Sibbeth; "we're doing it."

Miss Munker groaned.

"Perhaps," she suggested, "we had better waive the contentious clause."

"Very well, madam," assented the vice-president, surreptitiously licking her little finger, "then I will proceed to demonstrate some of what we may call the 'minor modes of political warfare.' Here, for example, we have a few foolish trifles, sent to us by our friend and sympathiser, Mr. Addleston Bobbs; crude and childish emanations from the male mind, for which we shall make allowances, seeing that they are eminently suited to their purposes, the purpose of maintaining a living interest in our Cause. Number one is a cigarette-box, intended to be sent by post to Cabinet Ministers. It purports to contain cigarettes, but I need not say that it does not. It is in the nature of a surprise packet." Amidst laughter and applause she held up a small cubical box, on the front of which was a press-button and the inscription "cigarettes."

"I shall press the button, and you will see what happens." She held the box at arm's length before the smiling, expectant faces, and pressed her thumb firmly on the button; then she flung the box on the table, and stuck her thumb into her mouth.

"Idiotic jokes! No patience!" she exclaimed angrily, wiping her thumb with her handkerchief. But the other ladies—whose thumbs had not been pricked—callously handed the box round with titters of enjoyment.

"Perhaps," said Miss Munker, cautiously picking up the box, "the concealed pin-point is a mistake. Let us see." She pressed the button with the handle of her hammer, whereupon the lid flew open and a little figure, in the dress of a female convict, sprang up and displayed a tiny label bearing the inscription "Votes for Women."

The vociferous applause that greeted this apparition was interrupted by the brusque entry of a very small and very fierce-looking woman, dressed in the uniform of the league, who announced in impressive tones that "the caretaker had just left the house, and that the artificer was ready to begin." The statement was received with a volley of laughter that somewhat puzzled me at the moment; but, as the company rose *en masse*, I rose too, and forthwith made my way out of the room, still closely guarded by Susannah.

"You will come with me, Lydia," said the latter as we emerged into the street; "we won't go with the crowd, I know the way."

She linked her arm in mine, and, somewhat to my discomfort, insisted on holding my hand; a harmless enough proceeding, but yet it made me feel that I was playing it rather low on poor, innocent Susannah.

"But what are we going to do?" I asked.

"Listen, dear, and I'll tell you." At that "dear" I again squirmed guiltily, and she went on: "The caretaker has gone out for the evening, and Mrs. C. is alone. Very well. A party of Gadflies will ring at the front door. Mrs. C. won't let them in, but she is sure to come to the window to see who they are. Then, while they are keeping her attention occupied, the rest of us will enter the house from the back."

"But how?"

"Oh, we've taken the ground-floor of a house that backs on old McCarker's. All we have to do is to climb over the wall of the back yard into McCarker's, and then the artificer will let us in."

"The artificer! Who's he?"

Susannah giggled luxuriously.

"That's the cream of the joke. He's a burglar. Miss Munker found him. Before she went in for the suffrage she used to go in for philanthropy and theosophy and chiropody, and all that sort of thing, you know. That's how she came to know about him."

"But, my dear girl," I exclaimed, aghast, "do you know that it is a felony to break into a dwelling-house at this time of night?"

Susannah was quite undisturbed.

"Oh, that's all right," she said airily. "It may be a felony for ordinary people, but we are different."

I was horrified. Also I was considerably alarmed. Burglary, in my present costume, was a good deal more than I had bargained for. And even as I was gloomily considering the position we arrived at our destination—a small stationer's shop in a small side-street. I looked despairingly at the private door, standing ajar, and longed to escape; and yet curiosity lured me on. Besides, I could not leave Susannah with no sane person to look after her.

Very reluctantly I pushed open the door, and passed with my companion along a narrow, dark passage to a good-sized room at the back, where the entire contingent was assembled—for Susannah and I had lagged behind the rest. It was a queer spectacle. Never have I seen women so excited. They seemed to be on wires, and the noise was deafening. But I had little attention to bestow on the ladies. The "artificer" took up all I had to give. Amidst the crowd, I did not observe him when I first entered the room; but when I did see him I nearly fainted.

It was Milkey.

He was standing, with his cap in his hand, scowlingly attentive and evidently fast losing his temper. For the fact is that, of the fifteen women present, every one but Susannah was giving him minute and voluble instructions as to how to break into the house, and a man can't attend to fourteen sets of directions at one and the same time. At last Milkey could stand it no longer. Flinging his cap on the table, he fetched the latter a whack with his fist that shook the room, and caused each of the overstrung women to jump about eighteen inches clear of the floor. Then, in the silence that ensued, he opened his mouth and spake.

"Look 'ere; there's too much bloomin' chin-waggin' in this 'ere show. Blimy! It's like a-arguin' with a boiled sheep's 'ed; nothin' but joar, joar, joar!"

"You mustn't speak to us in that impertinent manner," said Miss Munker.

"Ho, mustn't I?" retorted Milkey. "Well, you let me know when it's time to begin, and until that time you be good enough to keep yer heads shut."

It was extremely impolite of Milkey, though I admit the provocation, and might have led to regrettable discord but for the timely arrival of an excited young lady who was acting as Miss Munker's aide-de-camp, and who burst into the room like a green and white whirlwind.

"It's all clear!" she exclaimed. "The caretaker woman is talking to Miss Sibbeth from the dining-room window. She's a horrid woman—Irish, and most abusive."

The announcement was the signal for a tumultuous rush for the door. Milkey was hustled forward with the crowd, and, as the room emptied, I could hear him protesting in the passage, not meekly, nor in delicately-chosen phrases. Susannah would have gone with them, but I restrained her; I didn't want to be brought into too close contact with Milkey.

"It'll take him some time to break in," I said, especially with all those women buzzing round him. "Let us wait here until the place is open."

"But there's the caretaker," objected Susannah; "it'll be such fun capturing her, and we shall miss it if we wait here."

I devoutly hoped that we should, for the "fun" might take an unexpected form. The caretaker was probably a retired soldier, and an Irish barrack-wife might give these ladies a little surprise,

accustomed, as they were, to the polite and long-suffering London
bobby. I wanted Susannah to be out of that little episode, and to
this end I detained her by expounding atrocious and impossible
misdeeds to be committed by us jointly as soon as we gained admission to the house, and thereby brought her to the verge of
hysterics.

"You *are* a wicked girl, Lydia!" she exclaimed rapturously, wiping her eyes; "I can't imagine how you think of such things. But
really we mustn't stay here any longer, or all the sport will be over."

As I thought that the caretaker-lady was probably disposed of
by this time, I assented, and we passed out along a narrow passage
to the back yard, where we found a short ladder reared against the
farther wall. I got to the ladder before Susannah and, ascending it
to the summit of the wall, became aware of a confused noise proceeding from McCarker's house. I paused to listen. Suddenly from
the din there separated itself a raucous voice—requesting somebody to "take that, ye divils!"—and then a piercing yelp. Evidently
there was no need for hurry.

"Look sharp, Lydia!" shouted Susannah from below, pinching
my ankles in her impatience.

"I can't get over," said I.

"Oh, tosh! Scramble over somehow."

"But I can't," I bleated, making ineffectual flourishes on the
top of the wall.

"Well, then, let me come and help you." With this benevolent
object she made a grab at my ankles, and the next moment we both
came slithering down the ladder to our starting-point.

"You *are* a clumsy guffin, Lydia," said Susannah, rubbing her
elbow; but, thank goodness, she didn't say "Oo-er!"

I began once more to crawl up the ladder, but she dragged me
back and scrambled up with surprising agility, halting at the top
to hold out her hand.

"Now, then, Lydia, up you come," she said peremptorily.

I clawed my way up as slowly and awkwardly as I could, and,
having at length been piloted over the wall, advanced with
Susannah towards the house.

As we entered I noted an unexpected silence—broken, however, by vigorous thumping on a door in the basement, accompanied by an expletive obligato. The ladies, gathered in the hall and dining-room, were mostly engaged in repairs and readjustment of garments; Miss Munker held an encrimsoned handkerchief to her nose and snuffled plaintively, while Miss Beedlestone surveyed the scene gloomily, with one eye—the other being temporarily occluded and presenting the phenomenon that Milkey would probably have described as a "dark 'un."

Clearly, Mrs. Caretaker was a person of a striking personality. Some of the ladies, however, who had remained outside her sphere of influence, proceeded cheerfully with their preparations, producing bundles of bills, a pot of paste, coloured chalks, and the apparatus for taking a flashlight photograph.

I seated myself on the sideboard and watched them sadly, as I trifled with a glass of sherry—I couldn't understand how that sherry came to be left there until I tasted it—watched them papering the walls with "Votes for Women," chalking propagandist labels on the family portraits, and setting up the ridiculous camera to photograph the wreckage. It was a silly spectacle, and, when one considered the elaborate and costly preparations it had entailed, it seemed a miserable anti-climax. It made me feel quite depressed.

But what had become of Milkey? As the question suddenly occurred to me, I looked round for him eagerly. But in vain. The "artificer" had vanished. Of course, he might have gone home. But then, on the other hand, he mightn't. Silently I dropped down from the sideboard, and, leaving Susannah chalking a pair of red whiskers on the portrait of Mr. McCarker's grandmother, stole unnoticed from the room.

Up the dark and softly carpeted stairs I crept, peering ahead for a tell-tale glimmer of light, and listening attentively. Nor had I far to go for confirmation of my fears. On the first-floor landing I detected a beam of light issuing from the crack of a door, and from within came the ominous sound of bursting woodwork. Oh, Milkey! Milkey!

The door had, with unpardonable carelessness, been left slightly ajar. Taking advantage of the noise, I pushed it farther open

and peeped in. Alas and alackaday! The artificer indeed! Two drawers had already been opened and their contents strewed on the
floor, and the jemmy was fast in the crack of a third. I was un-
speakably shocked.

But what filled me with utter amazement was the nature of the
raffle spread out on the floor. With one exception, indeed, the
things were of no negotiable value; but that one exception was a
staggerer. I could hardly believe my eyes. A magnificent diamond
pendant, worth a couple of thousand at least, left in a common
wooden drawer at the mercy of any casual burglar! I stared at it as
it lay in the open velvet-lined case, and marvelled at the insanity
of the owner. But only for a moment.

I am essentially a man of action. This immoral proceeding of
Milkey's was a distinct breach of contract, and could not be permitted. In a moment I had slipped off my shoes and, narrowly
watching the humped back of the "artificer" as he wrestled with
the obdurate lock, I softly tiptoed into the room, picked the pendant out of its case, backed out of the room, snatched up my shoes
and retreated silently down the stairs.

At the bottom of the flight I paused to slip the pendant into my
pocket and put on my shoes; and it was at this moment, I think,
that Milkey missed the sparkling bauble. I was glad Susannah was
not there. For Milkey soliloquised. Ostensibly he addressed his
remarks to a hypothetical person with a great many syllables to
his name; but actually he soliloquised. And his soliloquy was not
suitable for general distribution.

I was standing at the foot of the stairs listening to his inelegant
and ambiguous phrases, when suddenly the house resounded to
the pealing of a bell. A scuffling in the room above made me withdraw into an open doorway, and the next moment Milkey came
thundering down the stairs like a terrified elephant.

I was not long in following. If it was time for Milkey to go, it
was time for me to go also. But there was Susannah. I couldn't leave
her to be captured. Of course it was a ridiculous scruple. She really stood in no serious danger, whereas I, in my disguise and with
that pendant in my pocket, ran a risk that I shudder to think of.

I ought to have cleared off as Milkey had done, like a sensible man. However, I didn't. Instead, I hurried back to the dining-room, just in time to meet the raiders surging out in a body towards the back door.

Susannah greeted me with a cheerful smile, though she looked a little pale and nervous, and explained, "It's that caretaker woman. She's escaped from the coal-cellar and fetched the police. They're on the doorstep now. You'll have to get up the ladder a little quicker this time, Lydia."

"You won't get out at the back, my child," said I. "The police are sure to be there already." And, even as I spoke, there came a cry from the front that the police were climbing over the wall, and the mob of women forthwith surged back towards the dining-room.

"This way, Susannah!" said I. And seizing her by the arm, I hurried the now really terrified girl up the stairs, past the scene of Milkey's depredations, which I hastily described to her. As we reached the second floor, masculine voices from below announced the arrival of the guardians of the peace, and then as a confused scuffling mingled with shrieks of defiance, we ran softly up to the attic storey.

"Where are you going, Lydia?" my companion asked faintly.

"Out of the garret window and along the parapet," I replied.

"But we can't."

"We've got to. There has been a burglary committed, and we can't afford to get caught. Besides, it's quite easy."

As I made this mendacious statement, we entered a back garret. I softly opened the dormer window, and, having taken a precautionary peep out and ascertained that no one was watching from below, I set a chair against it and climbed out on to the narrow parapet.

I had some difficulty in persuading Susannah to follow, for she, as is apt to be the way of women, having started with wild foolhardiness, had suddenly collapsed into panic. However, she came out at last, whimpering with fright, and, when I had closed the window after her, we started to crawl away along the parapet.

It really was very unpleasant for the poor girl. The parapet was inconveniently narrow, and, to make it worse, the blockhead of a builder had set up a number of obstructions in the shape of low party-walls, the climbing over which in the darkness gave poor Susannah the most awful squirms.

"But where *are* we going to, Lydia?" she asked piteously, as I dragged her over the third.

"We are going to climb in at the first garret window that we find open," I replied; "then we shall go down stairs and out by the front door. It's quite simple."

And so it was—in theory. In practice, it turned out that every garret window was securely fastened. The domestics who inhabited those garrets knew no more of ventilation than a parcel of Eskimo. It was disgusting—in this enlightened age, too! As I tried one after another in vain, my heart sank. Of course I could have broken a pane of glass, but that would have instantly brought the police at our heels and complicated things generally.

At length we came to the last house of the row, and the end of the parapet. And still there was no unfastened window. But there was a glimmer of hope: a short ladder rested against the roof, and the parapet exhibited that state of dirt and litter that suggests the proximity of the British workman. Very cautiously I crept up the ladder to reconnoitre.

The roof was of the mansard type, and the upper slope was quite practicable to walk on; nevertheless I crawled over the low ridge on my hands and knees to avoid exhibiting myself against the sky. What I saw on the other side filled me with rapture. The front of the house was under repair; a complete scaffolding had been erected, and the ladder and hoisting tackle had been left *in situ* by the workmen.

I hurried back to Susannah with the glad tidings, and found her crouching on the parapet looking the picture of misery. I helped her on to the ladder and preceded her to the top—she didn't pinch my ankles this time—and then we crawled quadrupedally, side by side, across the ridge of the roof, and very absurd we must have looked.

On the farther side was another short ladder leading down to the top of the scaffolding, and when we had climbed down this, there remained the final descent to be considered. A pair of scaling ladders stood against the house, but they were closed with lashed planks. If I had been alone and in suitable clothes I could have got down easily; as it was, the ladders were useless.

But there was the hoisting tackle—an iron pulley-wheel with an ample length of stout rope. That would do, though, unfortunately, there was no windlass. I looked over the edge of the platform. Down in the street a crowd had collected, and as all faces were turned towards McCarker's residence, I concluded that our late colleagues were receiving constabulary attentions. But up to the present no one had observed us.

I rapidly made a large bowline on the end of the rope, and having jammed the knot securely, held the loop open.

"Now, Susannah," said I.

"What are you going to do, Lydia?" she inquired, peering over into the gulf below.

"You are going to sit in this loop and hold on tight to the rope above the knot, and I am going to lower you to the ground."

"Oh, I can't!" she exclaimed. "I shall fall out of it!"

"Nonsense!" said I. "You hold on, and you'll be perfectly safe."

"But how are you going to get down yourself?"

"Oh, I shall get down all right. Now."

I passed the loop over her and made her sit down in it and grasp the rope with both hands.

"You are a queer girl, Lydia," she remarked. "You were such an awful funker at first, and now you don't seem even a bit nervous."

As a matter of fact, I was perspiring with fright if she had only known it; but I made no reply— the circumstances not lending themselves to conversation—beyond entreating her to hold on for all she was worth. Then I hauled the rope taut, took a couple of turns with the fall round a scaffold pole, and gently eased her to the edge of the platform.

"I can't, Lydia; I can't really!" she gasped. But I only replied by bawling to her (in a voice like a coal-heaver's) to hold tight, and forthwith shoved her over the edge. As she swung clear she uttered a loud scream, which was unfortunate, for, of course, the people below looked up and spotted us. I paid out the rope as fast as I dared, with my head over the edge of the platform, watching Susannah as she descended, swinging slightly and turning round like a joint of roasting meat. After the first squeak she was perfectly quiet, which is more than the onlookers were, for they greeted her approach to *terra firma* with howls of flattering but misdirected applause, and a hansom cabby, who had pulled up to watch, stood up in his dickey and flourished his whip like a madman.

Down, down went Susannah, growing smaller and smaller to my anxious vision. The crowd closed round with frantic cheers; the fall of the rope suddenly slackened in my hands, and I saw her disengage herself from the loop. Now came my turn.

I had meant to haul up the bowline and go down in it myself. But there was no time with that yelling crowd below. Nor was it necessary, for an ample coil of rope remained above. Accordingly, holding the fall of the rope in my left hand, I grasped the hanging part with my right and boldly swung myself clear of the scaffold.

It was an awful moment when I felt myself dangling in mid air by one arm only, and assailed by the horrid doubt as to whether I could hang on long enough. I let the fall slip through my left hand as quickly as I could bear it, but still I seemed to descend with intolerable slowness. And my right arm felt as if it were dragging out of its socket whilst my left hand was being rapidly flayed by the chafing of the rope. As I came lower, indeed, the left hand took part of my weight, but the strain on the right shoulder grew agonising, and I felt that I could hold on only a few seconds more. But even in my agony I could see that I was rapidly drawing near the sea of upturned faces, and that each face had an open mouth emitting senseless noises. In fact, the crowd went stark mad to a man, and as for the cabby, he literally danced on the seat of his dickey.

I was within a dozen feet of the ground when I caught a warning yell from him.

"Look sharp, miss! The coppers is a-comin'."

That finished me. I simply let go with my left. The rope flew through the pulley; I came down like a thunderbolt on to the chest of a Grenadier Guardsman. Where the Guardsman went I never knew. He merely vanished. It was a winning hazard off the red.

"In yer come, miss!" screamed the cabman. I looked, and saw an ecstatic butcher bundling Susannah into the cab. I sprang on to the footboard; the whip swished, the horse bounded forward. I fell backwards and sat down heavily in Susannah's lap. We were saved.

The cab rattled along furiously for fully a mile; then, in the neighbourhood of Soho, it drew up, and a smiling face, or, at least, part of one, appeared in the trap.

"Where shall I put yer down, miss?" the proprietor of the face inquired.

"Cobden Statue, please," I answered promptly, and our progress was resumed.

That journey was really quite uncomfortable. Susannah's bearing was not merely obsequious and adulatory to an insufferable degree—it was rather embarrassingly affectionate. And the worst of it was that she was quite hurt at my matter-of-fact responses. I didn't know what to do. The removal of the incriminating ribbons from our hats and dresses occupied her partially, but it was a real relief to me when we pulled up at the statue in High Street, Camden Town, and I was able to jump out.

"Thank you so much, cabman!" I said effusively—but not more effusively than I felt. "It was *most* kind and chivalrous of you to help us as you did." I held up a half-sovereign, which I had in readiness, but, to my surprise, the cabman raised a deprecating hand.

"Not a farden!" he exclaimed. "What! Me take a fare from a young lady what can come down a rope like a bloomin' spider? Not me! Goodnight, ladies! I wishes yer every success!" With this he flicked his whip, flourished his hat, and finally vanished into the shadows of Hampstead Road.

I walked home with Susannah to a boardinghouse in a quiet side street. On the way she asked for my address, and I was reduced to the necessity of naming a certain stationer's shop, where letters could be received, and giving some humbugging excuse for not saying where I lived. But, bless you! Susannah didn't mind. In her eyes I was a superwoman—if there is such a thing or person—

a glorified creature who could do no wrong. In fact, she told me so as we stood on the boarding-house doorstep; and then, well, it wasn't my fault. I was afraid she would. And she did. And I couldn't possibly have prevented her without giving the whole show away. I hope that is clear?

Mind, in a general way, I have no objection to being kissed by a good-looking girl. Not at all! Far from it! But this was a different affair, and as I walked homeward I reviled myself angrily. For there is no denying that, as I said before, it was playing it rather low on poor, innocent Susannah.

I walked at a brisk pace towards my business premises, and was still wrapped in thought when I passed the front door in Poplar Grove and turned the corner. Ye gods, what a start I got then! For I nearly ran into the arms of two men who were lurking at my side door, and one of whom was actually listening at the letter-box!

Now, the expert eye has little difficulty in recognising the gentlemen connected with Scotland Yard—undisguised, at any rate. And these gentlemen were very undisguised. Fortunately I had the presence of mind to walk on without appearing to notice them, and thus I picked up a crumb of information. For, as I passed the door, I heard the listener remark, "I guess my nabs has smelt a rat." To which the other replied, "I reckon he has; and, if so, his lordship has let us in for an all-night sitting."

His lordship! Then it was that beastly candlestick! What a mercy I hadn't gone in at the front door! And what a mercy, too, that a slight distrust of the too-astute Judith had caused me to bring my keys and loose cash with me! I turned my back on Poplar Grove and walked rapidly—for it was getting late—in the direction of the studio. There was no human soul in the mews when I arrived, so that I plied my latchkey unembarrassed by suspicious observers. As I closed the friendly door behind me, I felt that I was secure, at least, for the moment.

As to the future—but sufficient for the day is the evil thereof!

8
THE GOOD SAMARITAN

CAN THERE BE anything more disconcerting than a moral anticlimax?
I think not. At any rate, I thought so when, on the morning after
the Suffragette raid on Mr. McCarker's house, I came to examine
the diamond pendant that I had snatched from the jaws of the
marauding Milkey. That pendant was the symbol of high and noble
resolve; of chivalrous, even Quixotic, action; of a splendid renun-
ciation. At the risk of a tap on the head with a jemmy had I captured it; of a seven, fourteen, or twenty-one years' lease of a prison
cell had I borne it away. And all that I might give it back freely to
its owner without fee or reward; surrender the equivalent of three
or four thousand pounds that the lady might not suffer loss nor
the Suffragettes incur undeserved discredit. It was a noble enterprise. The contemplation of it raised me several feet in my own
esteem. But—

I don't profess to be a judge of diamonds. In fact I am not. But
I know a piece of glass when I see it. And I saw it when I looked at
Mrs. McCarker's pendant. The very first glance by daylight brought
up before my mental optics the vision of three golden globes.

The baggage! She had popped the sparklers and had the setting filled in with what the jewellers euphemistically call "paste."
Now I understood why that pendant had been left in such an unprotected position. A burglary would suit her to a T. Incidentally,
I wondered if the Right Honourable Mac knew about "mine uncle."
But it was no affair of mine. Real or sham, diamond or glass, the
pendant was Mrs. McCarker's, and she should have it; and mighty

sick she would be, I suspected, when it came back, like bread cast upon the waters.

In a gloomily reflective frame of mind I made up the parcel. There was ample reason for gloominess over and above the vexation of the anticlimax. There were, for instance, those beastly detectives that I had seen on the previous night, lurking outside my business premises. Of course, they were after Tom Nagget if they only knew it. But they didn't. They thought they were after me. That is to say, they thought I was Tom Nagget; or, rather, they thought Tom Nagget was me; at least, they thought that Tom Nagget and I were one and the same person; or perhaps I should say—oh, hang! What an infernal muddle it all was!

The practical inference was that I dared not show my nose out of doors without some efficient disguise, and the only disguise available was Judith's silly costume and that ridiculous wig. In these borrowed plumes I accordingly invested myself, with ineffable distaste. For the joke was as extinct as yesterday's cigarette, and female dress was now but a mean and degrading masquerade.

I posted the pendant to Mrs. McCarker, registering it in the name of Boadicea Munker, the President of the Gadfly League. Then I drew an open cheque on my bank for fifty pounds, in favour of Miss Isabella Croker, and cashed it in person, receiving the amount in notes and gold, together with an inquisitive stare from the astonished cashier. Next, with infinite self-abasement and feeling myself the most miserable cad on earth, I visited one or two ladies' outfitters and furnished myself with a complete feminine costume—for Judith's things would have to be sent back to her, or there would certainly be trouble; and then, having laid in a stock of provisions in anticipation of a state of siege, I retired to the studio to consider my position behind a securely bolted door.

It was not a pleasing position. The police had got my business address; presumably they had got my name. At any moment they might obtain my private address, or Judith might give me away. I didn't trust Judith. Of course, if I were captured, I could play my trump card—my fingerprints. But I didn't want to play it. It mightn't take the trick after all. Your Scotland Yard bobby is a little like a. Christian Scientist: he sets a good deal more value on his own subjective states than on mere objective realities. I would eschew the society of bobbies if possible.

For three days I lived in a state of siege. Once only I stole forth at dusk to post off Judith's possessions and return laden with spoils from the grocer's. The rest of the time I spent (with my loins girded, literally, in the detestable feminine garments, ready for instant flight) making my abode snug in view of a possible raid. There was nothing actually incriminating, excepting a certain pearl necklace, which I was retaining in custody until I had decided whether it belonged to me, to the rascally pawnbroker from whom I had collected it, or to some other person. But I thought it discreet to obliterate the traces of my versatile activities and so forestall misleading interpretations.

And meanwhile I considered what move I should make before the bomb exploded. As a matter of fact, I made none; for the bomb exploded prematurely.

The catastrophe happened at about half-past ten on the third night. I was smoking a disconsolate pipe by the empty fireplace in the studio, with my heels on the mantelpiece and a contemptuous eye on my openwork stockings, when there came a gentle tapping at the door that opened on the mews.

I sprang to my high-heeled feet, clapped on my golden wig, and thrust my head out of the window. My elevated position enabled me to make out the ground plan of two men, and, as they both looked up on hearing the window open, I was able to recognise in one the well-remembered features of Detective-Sergeant Burbler.

"Who is that?" I demanded squeakily.

"Mr. Danby Croker at home?" was the irrelevant response.

"No. He hasn't come home yet," I answered.

"Can you tell us where he is?"

"I understood him to say that he was going to the Baptist Conference at Kentish Town," I answered.

Sounds of ribald mirth came up from below, and then the sergeant remarked:

"Little late for Baptist Conferences, isn't it?"

"Better late than never," I replied cheerfully; adding, "But who are you, and what do you want?"

"We want to see Mr. Croker very particularly," said the sergeant.

"But does *he* want to see *you* very particularly?" I asked. "Because, if not, you'd better call tomorrow at a more reasonable hour."

The two detectives consulted together, and decided to await Mr. Croker's return.

"Might we come in and wait?" the sergeant asked.

"No, you mightn't!" I squeaked acidly. "I'm not going to let you in here! I don't know you from Adam!"

This was not strictly correct. I have seen portraits of Adam, and they were not in the least like Detective-Sergeant Burbler. However, the sergeant took my meaning, and expressed his intention of waiting on the doorstep.

He was not a patient man, that Sergeant Burbler. The unrest of this neurotic age was upon him, impelling him to while away the time by trying skeleton keys in my lock, and making disparaging comments when he found the door bolted on the inside. But I paid little attention to his antics. I had occupation enough in getting into my outdoor jacket and reconnoitring the back window.

This window gave on the roof of a coach-house in an adjoining mews. The coach-house ended in a stable-loft, which was furnished with a practicable outside staircase. My observations showed that the back mews was entirely deserted, leaving a convenient route of escape. Noiselessly I threw up the window, and then returned to complete my preparations to evacuate the fortress.

Joe Dalby once informed me that I was a silly guffin. I resented it at the time, but I fear he was right; for I have to confess to an act of gratuitous folly that nearly spoiled everything. At this critical juncture I must needs indite a note to Sergeant Burbler. It was quite short, and moderately irrelevant; consisting, in fact, of nothing but the refrain of the delightful old English song, commencing:

"Adieu, adieu! Dear friends, adieu, adieu, adieu!
I may no longer stay with you—stay with you—hoo!"

And winding up with the promise to hang my harp on the weeping willow tree, a promise that I have had no opportunity to redeem, lacking both a suitable tree and the indispensable harp.

When I had placed this nonsensical effusion in an envelope, addressed it to the sergeant and laid it conspicuously on the table, I popped my head out of the window to see how things were progressing down below.

They were not progressing satisfactorily. One of the men was visible, doggedly prising at the door with a jemmy; but the sergeant had vanished. Could he have gone round to the back, and cut off my retreat while I was writing that fool of a note? It was a dreadful suspicion, unfounded, however, as it turned out, for as I stared up the mews he reappeared, carrying a ladder. I shut down the window, shot the catch, and, fetching a hammer and a three-quarter-inch clout nail, knocked the latter in behind the catch. That would keep them amused for a while.

My emergence on to the coach-house roof was far from dignified, and still farther from being ladylike. But there was no one to witness that unseemly exhibition. Unobserved, I ran along the leads, swung myself on to the loft staircase, and descended. Not a soul was stirring. The mews was silent as the grave until my ridiculous little wooden heels roused the echoes by tapping on the cobbles. As I went out I passed the entrance to my own proper mews, and halted for a moment to listen. The shattering of glass was borne to my ears, mingled with a sonorous thumping. Evidently friend Burbler was making hay with the landlord's fixtures.

Out in the Hampstead Road I hopped on to a passing yellow 'bus that was rumbling southward, and as I sat in the grateful darkness on the roof, I turned over my plans for the immediate future. At first I had thought of some quiet hotel in one of the streets off the Strand, but reflection convinced me that no respectable hotelkeeper would receive, at this time of night, a stray young woman without luggage or escort; and as for the non-respectable ones, they were probably unclean and unpleasant, and their staffs on undesirable terms with the police.

No; hotels were impossible. But what was I to do? I could not ramble about the street all night. Apart from the inevitable unpleasantness, and even danger, I should be certain to attract the notice of the police. It was quite an awkward dilemma.

Suddenly I caught the voice of the conductor, and with it a useful suggestion.

"'Ere yar, lady! Oxford Street, Charing Cross, Westminster!"

Exactly! That was the tip. Charing Cross Station. There were certain to be trains starting for somewhere. The exact destination was of no importance, but a train was an immediate refuge. My presence in it would present nothing unusual or suspicious, and the journey—on the South-Eastern—would certainly give me ample time to consider my plans.

I dropped off the 'bus at St. Martin's Church, and walked briskly down to the station. The wide space under the clock was occupied by a thin sprinkling of people, mostly in evening dress, evidently country folk who had just come from the theatres; and the cloaks of the ladies and their silken shawls, worn hoodwise, made me, in my plain morning costume and hat, look a little conspicuous. At least, that is what I thought as I walked across the station, past the ends of the platforms, and looked at the boards on which the destinations of the trains were written.

There were several trains leaving shortly, and I gave them all careful consideration, but finally decided on the one at the western end of the station, which was bound for Maidstone. It was due to leave, the collector informed me, at 11.42, and, as the clock now stood at 11.25, there was time and to spare. I procured a third-class ticket for Maidstone, and then proceeded slowly to perambulate the space under the clock. I should have liked to take a mild refresher at the buffet, but was not quite sure of the orthodox refection for a lady of my assumed station, and I was also a little nervous of the young ladies at the bar. These damsels must see a good deal of the seamy side of life, and they might spot me.

I had taken two turns along the space under the clock, reflecting profoundly on my position, but keeping a sharp lookout, when I became aware of an elderly person approaching me on the opposite tack. He had the look of an army officer; a copper-faced old reprobate, with a Roman nose ending in a purple knob, and baggy eyelids, with wicked little wrinkles in them that deepened as he drew nearer, and finally joined with other wrinkles to produce what he meant for an engaging smile. And then the old bounder raised his hat.

For a moment I was considerably startled, until I realised that he couldn't possibly know me, when I stalked past him with haughtily-averted face. But it was annoying. I didn't want notice of any kind, and, besides, I detest these elderly mohocks who go prowling about, making the common highways impossible for unprotected women. Moodily I perambulated the wide area, with an eye on the illuminated clock, and presently stopped to examine the barometer that it exhibited for the information of passengers. I don't quite know why it is there. South-Eastern trains have their peculiarities, but I never heard of one being held up in Charing Cross to wait for a favourable wind. Nor do I know why I stopped to look at it. I was not curious about the weather.

I had examined the top of the mercury column, and read off from the vernier the figures 30.6, when a man halted beside me so close that our shoulders touched. But he was not examining the barometer. Not at all. For when I glanced at him with quick suspicion, I caught the little pig-like grey eye of my military friend leering at me from its setting of wicked little wrinkles.

I must have turned crimson, for I felt the blood surge into my face and course up my neck with an audible hum. I suppose he took it for an indication of outraged modesty; but he was mistaken. A furious desire to batter that bulbous, Roman nose flat on his wicked old face was what was making my ears ring, and my fingers twitch within my tight suede gloves. But it would never have done. A skilful rat-tat with the knuckles of the left would have given the show away completely; and besides, it would hardly have been the ticket for a vigorous young man to hammer a broken-winded old knacker of near upon sixty.

As I stood trembling with rage and struggling to control my anger, I caught another eye, a fierce and critical eye that also looked out from a setting of wrinkles. But they were not wicked wrinkles. They spread out honestly, like the ribs of a fan, from the outer corner of the eye, and seemed to hint at a certain dry humour. And wrinkles and eye appertained to the brown, rather forbidding face of an elderly clergyman.

Instantly I decided to evade the army and seek sanctuary in the church. Pushing past the elderly buck, I walked slowly towards the parson, undismayed by the grimness of his visage. He touched his hat as I approached, and asked in a gruff voice:

"Do you know that person?"

"No, I do not," I replied emphatically.

"Is he annoying you?"

"Yes," I replied, "he's annoying me most—" I was going to say "damnably," but hastily substituted the adverb "abominably."

"I'll tell him not to," said the parson; and forthwith he strode off in the direction of my tormentor, who was in full and rapid retreat, and uncommonly red about the back of the neck. But the cleric soon overhauled him, and then there took place a little interview which I watched gloatingly out of the corner of my eye.

Elsewhere I have remarked upon the curious manner in which clothing appears to react upon personality; and it now seemed as if from the fal-lals and furbelows of my absurd costume something feminine had entered into my mental constitution. For, as I watched that hostile meeting whereof I was the bone of contention, my heart swelled with gratified vanity. Now I understood the feelings of the fair ladies of old, as they witnessed the splintering of lances and heard the clang of dinted armour; or of the barndoor hen as she watches the feathers flying in the scrimmage on the adjacent midden.

I didn't hear what passed. A gruff reference to someone who had "one foot in the grave, sir!" reached my ears, and I gathered that he was "old enough to be her grandfather." That was all. But it suggested that the parson was showing the rough side of his tongue.

The man of war did not take the rebuke meekly. He huffed and he puffed, he swaggered and he bounced; but it was no go. The parson was a head taller, and evidently had the gift of words. Finally the warrior went off spluttering like an elderly tomcat who had just had an unsatisfactory interview with a lump of coal, and the parson returned to me, as red as a turkey-cock and fairly gobbling with wrath.

"You've no business to be wandering about here alone," said he. "Where's your mother?"

I was so disconcerted by the sudden question that I was on the point of explaining that I had mislaid her. But I pulled myself together in time, though only enough to gibber inarticulately.

"Why are you here all by yourself?" he demanded.

"Well, you see," I explained, "I haven't got anyone with me."

The fan-like wrinkles spread out from the corners of his eyes, and his grim countenance softened. "That's a lady's reason," he growled.

And so it was. It must have been those confounded clothes.

I began to mumble some sort of explanation—I don't know what, for at that moment I got a violent shake up of another kind. A big, burly man entered the station with an appearance of hurry, and strode along, looking anxiously at the barriers. Now, as I have already mentioned, there is something about the gentlemen from Scotland Yard that the expert eye finds highly characteristic. And mine is an expert eye; and, as it followed the hurrying stranger from barrier to barrier, the diagnosis "plain-clothes bobby" came unsought. It was very disturbing. Of course, the fellow wasn't looking for me. Sergeant Burbler was doing that. But, all the same his presence here struck a discordant note.

"Whither are you bound?" my clerical friend asked,

I held out my ticket with a furtive eye on the detective.

He glanced at the ticket and remarked: "Maidstone. I am going that way myself—I get out at Aylesford—so I can put you into a carriage with some ladies, and look in on you from time to time to see that you are all right. There will be plenty of opportunities."

This was an excellent arrangement. It would see me safely past
the barrier, and that beastly detective. But it was susceptible of
improvement.

"Would you mind," I asked meekly, "if I traveled in your carriage? I should feel quite safe then."

I could see that he didn't "cotton to" the proposal, but what
could he say, poor old buffer? Nothing, obviously, but what he did
say, which was:

"Of course, I shouldn't mind, my dear young lady. I should be
delighted. Would you object to traveling in a smoking carriage?"

"Oh!" I replied gushingly, "I simply love smoke." Experience
had taught me that this was the orthodox thing for a girl to say.
And it happened to be true. I had a well-seasoned briar, and a
pouchful of navy-cut in my pocket at the very moment of speaking.

"Then, in that case," said the clergyman, with a glance at his
watch, "we had better take our seats. Have you any luggage?"

"Luggage!" I gasped, quite taken aback by the sudden question;
and then, like a fool, I added: "I'm afraid I've left it in the cab." It
must have been the sight of that detective prowling round our particular barrier that made me talk such blithering nonsense.

"Left it in the cab!" the parson repeated. "I'd better give notice
at once. What sort of luggage was it?"

"Oh, it doesn't matter," I stammered; "it was only a suitcase—
at least," I added hastily, as an expression of surprise appeared on
his grim countenance, "not a suitcase, you know, but a sort of
portmanteauy kind of a thing. But it really isn't of the least consequence."

"Isn't it, though," said he, with a quick glance at me. "Well, I
suppose you know best. Then we had better go to our train."

I followed him humbly, drawing down my veil as we went. A
little crowd of theatre-goers had collected at the barrier, and behind them stood the detective, looking them over eagerly. As we
approached him from behind, he drew a large blue envelope from
his pocket, and from the envelope a half-plate photograph. It
seemed to be an enlargement—I made it my business to get a good
look at it over the officer's shoulder—for it consisted merely of a

large face. And when I saw that face, I could have squeaked with fright. For it was—well, of course it was Tom Nagget's face, but, as Tom and I are as like as twins, it might just as well have been mine. So the detective was looking for me after all.

I glanced up at my chaperon to see if he had observed it; and I fancied he had, though his face was as a face of wood. I snuggled up close to him, and presented the back of my head to the detective as I passed him, and so sneaked through the bather on to the platform, shaking like an ill-made jelly on a rickety table.

We had taken our seats in an empty smoker, and were waiting for the train to start when another little incident occurred. It was "only a face at the window" as the song says, and a beastly ugly one at that; a face with a Roman nose ending in a purple blob, and with little pig-like eyes in a setting of baggy wrinkles. It broke into a slow, evil smile as it looked in on us, and then vanished; and the parson blew his nose wrathfully, and muttered something about an "ill-bred ruffian." And it really was very unpleasant for the poor old cock. I fancy he had foreseen the possibility of something of the kind.

At last the train rumbled out of the station. The parson produced his pipe, a death's-head clay bowl, marked "Gambier à Paris" and as black as a clerical hat. He filled it with dark brown flake, and puffed with the fierce enjoyment of a man who was starving for his weed; while I took deep sniffs and tried to get a smoke at second hand.

"I suppose there will be someone to meet you at Maidstone?" he said presently.

The sight of the detective at the barrier had suggested the same question though with a certain difference as to detail.

"No," I said, "I don't expect anyone to meet me."

"But you have friends there? Somewhere to go, I mean?"

"No. I don't know anyone there."

He blew out a cloud like the broadside of a two-decker and regarded me with a troubled expression.

"What are you going to do at Maidstone?" he asked presently.

That was precisely what I had been wondering myself, but I answered demurely:

"I thought I might get something to do there. It's not so crowded as London."

"What can you do?" he asked.

Now, if I had told the truth, I should have said that I was a good machine draughtsman, an expert fitter of oil and gas engines, could turn up a screw-bolt with anyone, and was a fair hand at lock-making. But I did not tell the truth. It was not politic.

"I write a fairly good hand," I said, "and I can do shorthand a little."

"H'm" (puff). "Can you work a typewriter?" Of course I could. Anyone can if he tries. I didn't say anything about speed.

The parson reflected cloudily. Presently he suggested: "I suppose you don't draw?"

I hesitated, but eventually admitted that I could.

"But only with a rule and T-square," I said. "I'm not much good at freehand."

My chaperon cogitated with a total disregard to the Smoke Abatement Act, and with a reflective and slightly disapproving eye on me. He didn't speak again for some time and station by station the interminable journey dragged out its weary length.

I awaited his next utterance with keen anxiety. Hunted, harassed, and desperate as I was, it seemed as if some haven of refuge were opening ahead. And still the parson sat silent and sphinx-like, puffing at his piratical pipe and scowling out through the open window on the invisible country. We were just entering the Greenhithe tunnel when he spoke again:

"Know anything about architecture?" he asked.

"A little, only quite a little, you know," I said modestly.

"Well, could you draw out the profile of a suite of mouldings, for instance?"

"Oh, lord, yes!" I replied eagerly. "That's just a matter of square, compass, and curves, all except the cherrybims." I stopped short, and he looked at me sharply.

"All except the what?" he asked.

"I mean to say," I answered, perspiring with embarrassment, and cursing my flippant colloquialisms, "that the mechanical part would be quite easy, but I mightn't be able to manage the figure ornaments—dripstone masks, and that sort of thing, you know."

He made no reply for a while, but continued to regard me inscrutably until the very marrow in my bones seemed to creep. What the deuce was he thinking about? Had he spotted me, and if so, what was he likely to do?

At length, to my unutterable relief, he resumed in quite a reassuring tone:

"I am asking these questions for a reason. I am preparing a series of papers for the *Archæologia Cantiana* on the churches of my district, and as my handwriting is—well, is the handwriting of an elderly clergyman, they will have to be typed. And I shall want someone to make drawings of the mouldings and capitals, and so forth. Now, if you are able to do the work, why shouldn't you? It will keep you out of mischief until you can get something better."

My heart leapt. Here was a harbour of refuge indeed! I could have fallen down and kissed the toes of his dear old boots.

"It would be quite a comfortable arrangement for you," he continued. "I am a bachelor, but my mother lives with me. She is a very old lady, of course, and not much in evidence, but still, she is there to act as your hostess. There is a nice little room that you could have, and I would pay you a pound a week as my private secretary. It wouldn't be hard work, you know. You would have plenty of leisure and liberty. Think it over and send me a line tomorrow."

"There is no need for that," I said huskily. "I accept thankfully; only I think a pound a week is a great deal too much for a girl secretary."

"I'd rather you thought it too much than too little," he said gruffly, and added, "Then we'll consider the matter settled."

"If you please," I murmured, and would have thanked him, but the fact is that, after all the excitement and agitation of my flight, I was rather overcome.

Once more we relapsed into silence. I pretended to doze, though, tired as I was, the mingled excitement and relief kept me wide awake. I watched my companion through the slits of my half-closed eyes, and caught him, now and again, looking at me with a troubled frown. Was he already repenting of the charitable impulse that had led him to gather this stray ewe lamb into the protecting fold? I hoped not. At any rate, he should have no cause in the future for repentance. But he was obviously very disturbed in his mind, and as the stations flitted by the contortions of his face became quite alarming, and he puffed at his pipe until the death's-head must have been nearly red-hot. At length, as we moved out of Snodland Station, he spoke, and his gruff, brusque tones really startled me.

"You say there's no one to meet you at Maidstone?"

"No, I'm afraid there isn't."

"But, you know," he said severely, "you can't go prowling about a strange town—or any other town, for that matter—at this time of night."

"Oh," I said, "I expect I shall be able to get a room for the night!"

"You won't," he growled; "and if you could, it wouldn't be proper at all. Now, I'll tell you what you'll have to do. You'll have to come home with me. My housekeeper will be sitting up—she will sit up for me, obstinate old fool—and she will get your room ready. That's what you'll have to do. So don't talk any more nonsense."

The last sentence he jerked out in a tone of absolute ferocity. I mumbled my thanks and heaved a deep sigh of contentment. At last the harbour lights were glimmering ahead.

At Aylesford we found a ridiculous little pony-cart waiting in charge of an aged rustic, who blinked at me in speechless amazement. I took my seat in the cart, my chaperon followed, and we started out of the station yard as the porter was putting out the lamps. For about twenty minutes we joggled along in silence through a labyrinth of dark lanes, and at length entered a drive that led up to the door of a large, square-looking house. The door opened as we rattled up to it, showing a brightly-lighted hall and the diminutive figure of a very prim-looking old lady.

"You are very late, Master Jeffrey," she said reprovingly, as my friend hopped out of the cart. "I'd almost given you up."

"She always says that," growled the parson, as he helped me out; and then he explained:

"It's the train, you know, Martha; would keep stopping at the public-houses. Oh, by the way, I've brought a young friend of mine to stay for a few days, Miss—er—Miss— What did you say your name was?" he demanded, in a fierce stage whisper.

"Tarkington," I whispered in return; "Lydia Tarkington."

"Yes, of course," he said hastily. "You remember the name, Martha? You've heard me speak of Miss Tar—Tar—"

"Tarkington," I whispered.

"Tarkington—Miss Tarkington, eh, Martha?"

"I expect I have," said Martha, devouring me with her eyes; "but my memory isn't what it used to be."

I thought I heard my protector murmur that "that was a mercy," but I may have been mistaken. At any rate, whatever Martha's views may have been, she provided us with an excellent hot supper, which "Master Jeffrey" supplemented with a glass or two of very reviving brown sherry; and, as the long-cased clock in the hall clanged out two o'clock, the little lady escorted me respectfully, but without comment, to a delightful room apparently overlooking an orchard.

I wished her good night, locked the door, took off my wig and plunged my head into a basinful of cold water. Then I threw open the window and slowly undressed. It was a delicious night, or rather morning. Down in the orchard a nightingale jug-jugged, as if he, too, had dropped into a soft billet. I reflected on dear innocent "Master Jeffrey," and hoped that my beastly masquerade wouldn't lead to embarrassing consequences for him. And then I thought of Susannah, also innocent and still more dear, and how she had kissed me on the strength of my deluding garments.

Once more I reviled myself for that unconscious kiss, and wondered if she would ever give me another. And all the time the nightingale sang "Jug-jug" down in the orchard. It seemed an ominous expression, with Maidstone Gaol so near at hand. But, of course, he wasn't referring to the "stone jug."

9
THE "PRISON JOSEPH"

OF ALL HUMAN ambitions, the most widespread in time and space is the desire to get something for nothing. It is universal. It has produced all the perpetual motion machines that have never worked. It has been behind all the projects for the abolition of poverty. In the past it sent the alchemist to his futile laboratory, just as at the present day it sends the widow and the clergyman to the bucket shop. The entire human race, in fact, seems to be bitten with it.

I don't pretend to be immune from the disease myself. Not at all. The idea of getting something without paying for it has an undoubted attraction. In fact, as the reader may have discovered, I am rather susceptible to one form of infection. I love a sale by auction. For there is always a chance that this dream may be realised. The faded portrait that you have bought for half a crown may turn out to be a Velasquez or a Van Dyck. Usually it doesn't, and then your half-crown is wasted. But it may. And the kitchen chairs may be unrecognised Heppelwhites, or they may not. And so on. At any rate, I have always been keen on the sporting chance of an auction.

Now, of all the sporting auctions, there is none to compare with a farmhouse sale. The things have been in the same place for generations. You may pick up anything from an antique four-poster to a set of missing crown jewels. It is a glorious gamble. I always keep a sharp look-out for farmhouse sales, and when I saw the notice of one pasted on a wall at Maidstone, I naturally stopped to read it through. At the first glance it was not so very alluring. Prime bullocks and short-horn cows were a little out of my line, and "useful farm carts" were not particularly useful to me. But when it came to "furniture and effects" casually thrown in at the end, I pricked up my eyes, so to speak, and made a careful mental note of the place and date.

It is necessary for me to explain, in view of what follows, that I was still under the painful necessity of disguising my personality by means of female costume and a golden wig. It was horrible, it was degrading, and it was most infernally uncomfortable. But it had to be. As the lady secretary of the Rev. Jeffrey Mostyn, I was comparatively secure from the attentions of the police; and security was a necessity, and necessity knows no law—if it can help it.

My natural advantages—my fair complexion, hairless face, and fluty, musical voice, had rendered the disguise a very efficient one; and I was becoming accustomed to it, though not reconciled. No, no, not reconciled; but accustomed. And hence, when a man halted some paces away and stood regarding me with rapt attention, I was not surprised. The thing had happened before; for, after all, good looks are good looks, and a comely young man is none the less comely for a halo of golden locks and a dainty straw hat trimmed with violets.

But, still, there are limits. A passing glance of admiration I say nothing to, but the fellow stood and stared at me as if I were a blooming waxwork. It was nothing short of beastly bad form; at least, so I thought, until, raising my eyes haughtily from the auction poster, I—

Great Zerubbabel! It was the "recognising officer" who had inspected me at Hunsgate Police-station! I knew the beggar at a glance. Here was a pretty kettle of fish! By the momentary peep at his face I knew he was trying to "place" me, and not succeeding. And no wonder. But I was afraid to move, for I remembered how attentively he had studied my gait as they walked me across the yard. And yet I couldn't stand there reading that poster all day.

I had come over to Maidstone in the rector's pony-cart, a circumstance that turned out to be my salvation. For at this critical moment it rattled up in charge of old Gammet, the gardener.

Gammet hopped out, touched his hat, and held the door open I turned slowly, minced delicately across the pavement, stepped into the cart, and arranged my skirts with ostentatious skill. Then Gammet jumped in and took the reins, and away we went; and, glancing back out of the tail of my eye at the recognising officer, I saw him take off his hat and scratch the back of his head.

On the way home I learned from Gammet what I ought to have learned before—that the Maidstone Assizes were on, and that the town was full of detectives and police who had come to give evidence. However, it was the last day but one, and my farmhouse sale was not due for nearly a week. The local railways would be safe by then.

The arrangements by which I was enabled to attend that sale really require more explanation than I have space to give, but some explanation is unavoidable.

My duties as the rector's secretary took me to various churches in the neighbourhood to make scale-drawings of architectural details, and among them to the little church of St. Cecily's. Of this quaint little building I shall have more to say on a future occasion, but I may now explain that the village appertaining to it was utterly depopulated during the Great Plague, and was never rebuilt. The church was consequently disused, but it was kept in repair; and, for reasons connected with the tenure of the benefice, a service was held in it four times a year.

Now, the very first time that I visited St. Cecily's, I saw that it was just the kind of *pied-à-terre* that I wanted. I had the keys, and could easily make myself a set of duplicates. The place was far from any village; it was never visited by anyone but myself, the rector, and old Gammet, who was the nominal sexton, and very seldom by either of them. Here I could secrete any property that I did not wish to be seen; and here, securely locked in, I could perform any little odd jobs (such as key-filing) that would excite remark if done *coram publico*. St. Cecily's was invaluable to me.

Among the property that I had thus secreted, magpie fashion, was a rather smart suit of tweeds, with the necessary appurtenances of brown boots, cap, etc. I had purchased them at Maidstone (explaining that they were for a sick brother, and handing the shopman a list of measurements), and, although I had, necessarily, no opportunity of trying them on, they were a perfectly satisfactory fit. That is the great advantage of having a really good figure. The slop-shop cutter is an idealist. He works with the perfect human form in his mind. Usually the result is disappointing, but in my case his optimism was justified.

I had no trouble in getting a day's leave. Father Jeffrey—as he allowed me to call him—was indulgent to a fault. Whatever suspicions of me he may have had at first, when once I had entered his house I was placed on a footing of absolute trust; in fact, for the guardian of an attractive young lady, the dear old buffer was a trifle casual. I came and went as I pleased, on foot or in the pony-cart, and when I announced that I wanted a day off he asked no question beyond inquiring if I had enough money.

Behold me, then, the original and only genuine Danby Croker, emerging cautiously from the vestry door of St. Cecily's, after a careful survey of the surrounding country from the summit of the little, squat Norman bell-tower. Ye, gods, what strides I took! How I kicked up my heels in glorious emancipation from entangling skirts! What unnecessary gates and fences I climbed over! How joyously I champed on the mouthpiece of my pipe and flourished my walking stick! On a footpath I met an elderly rustic, who touched his hat, and said, "Good-morning, sir." "Sir," mind you; not "miss"! The lord of creation had come into his own again. By gum! it was worth being alive to hear that "sir."

Mockett's Hill Farm, where the sale was to take place, was some ten miles down a branch line from Maidstone. It was close to the railway, though a mile and a half from the station, and, as I passed the house in the train, I recognised it by the signs of approaching dissolution and the little crowd of idlers The sight of the house brought my mind to a focus on the business of the day. What was I going to do?

It is very necessary to settle this question early, to avoid wild, impulsive bidding before the rostrum. I should have to keep myself in hand, for I had brought with me the entire residue of my little fortune, amounting now, after a few little purchases at Maidstone, to thirty pounds. That was a rash beginning. I must be careful. Furniture—my special weakness—must be taboo. St. Cecily's would hardly accommodate a Court cupboard, or a set of Chippendale chairs. Then china was impossible, and so were bulky clocks. In fact, when I came to consider it in cold blood the expedition looked rather like a wild-goose chase.

I got out at the little station and walked gaily to the farm, making extensive good resolutions as I went, and finally persuading myself that I was to be merely a spectator. The appearance of things when I arrived confirmed this view. A stout person in gaiters was sniffing round a red-wheeled cart labelled "Lot 49." I shouldn't compete with him. A party of horses moored in a corner of the yard gazed at the strangers in mild surprise. The prime bullocks looked over a low wall, and didn't care a single marigold. I didn't want *them*. And as to the reapers, horse-rakes, ploughs, harrows, and other engines of destruction I wouldn't have had them as a gift.

From the yard I entered the house, and looked round the rooms. The furniture stood about, abashed and disconsolate, and seemed quite ashamed of the little numbered tickets stuck on to mark its fallen estate; and I noted, almost with relief, that it all seemed to be modern and commonplace. Then I obtained a catalogue, and sat down in a sprawling Victorian armchair to read it. And very dull reading it was until, running my eye down the pages, I came to this entry

"Lot 108. Antique violin in carved oak case; said to be a genuine Prison Joseph."

"A Prison Joseph!" I exclaimed; and then added, "A prison grandmother!" For I don't believe in Prison Josephs. The instruments so described are as a rule simply bad old fiddles, or else unmitigated fakes. Let me explain.

There is a tradition that that incomparable master Giuseppe Guarneri (better known from the cipher I.H.S. on his labels as Giuseppe del Gesú) spent some years in prison, and that he occupied his too abundant leisure in making fiddles with crude materials supplied to him by the gaoler's daughter. Also that the fiddles produced by him in the prison years, and commonly known as "Prison Josephs," were quite rudely finished, and of generally inferior style.

I don't believe a word of it. Of course, it is possible that some fool may have clapped him into gaol. The very elect of humanity may chance to get popped into chokee. I have myself, for instance. But to suppose that, under any circumstances whatever, the divine Joseph would have made a bad fiddle! It is incredible. I reject the superstition with scorn.

But one thing was evident. The auctioneer didn't know much about fiddles. That was clear. So the matter was worth looking into.

Lot 108 was among the lumber in the loft, and I forthwith started up the wide staircase in search of it. On one of the landings I encountered a tall-case clock with a silver dial, the inscription whereon ("Thomae Tompion Londini fecit 1649") made me hurry away, as St. Anthony might have bustled past a bevy of painted hussies. I dared not stop to look at that clock.

The picturesque old loft was strewn with an indescribable collection of lumber, but I had no difficulty in finding Lot 108. And when I found it I saw at a glance that the auctioneer was a fool. It wasn't a Prison Joseph at all. The immortal Joey has turned out some of the noblest fiddles that have ever squeaked, not excepting the productions of Stradivari himself. But, so far as I am a judge—and I know a fiddle when I see one—he never laid varnish on a more perfect specimen than Lot 108. It was a beauty: a rather flat model of his second period, exquisite in its curves, and perfect in its proportions. The whole back was deliciously figured; the varnish was velvety and rich; the sound-holes would have brought tears to the eyes of the genuine connoisseur—I nearly had to wipe my own; the button was positively angelic; and as for the scroll, when you looked at it it made you smile and want to shake hands with it. Prison Joseph, indeed!

There was only one thing that I didn't quite like; it had ivory pegs. They seemed to be original; at any rate, they were old hippo ivory, probably Portuguese. But I don't care for ivory pegs. They detract from the dignity of a really fine scroll.

There was a rather fine old bow, apparently original; but, of course, the fiddle was unstrung, and there was no bridge or sound-post. So I couldn't try it; and I wouldn't have tried it if I could, for one didn't want to call attention to it. I managed to get a squint at the label through the sound-holes; not that there was any need; the instrument spoke for itself. Then I replaced it in its case, and shut down the carved lid.

I was about to turn away, when my eye lighted on another violin. This Farmer Mockett seemed to be an amateur of fiddles. But was he, though? On a second glance at number two I was inclined to doubt it. For number two was a rank duffer. Modern German in a flashy varnished case. I don't mean that it was one of those Teutonic masterpieces that are sent over here at eighteen marks the dozen. But it was a poor thing, with sham purfling and a machine-made scroll that set your teeth on edge. I shouldn't have given it a thought but for one rather odd circumstance; which was that, bad as it was, it had a certain hideous resemblance to the lovely creation in the oak case. At first I thought the likeness was merely accidental, and so, in part, it may have been. The general form followed the Guarneri model, but there was nothing in that. Machine-made fiddles, like slop-shop clothes, may be quite decently shaped. But, as I looked more closely, I seemed to see traces of "doctoring." The horrible, staring varnish had been carefully toned down with stain and pumice powder to a tint and surface crudely resembling those of the old *chef d'œuvre*, and fictitious signs of use and age had been artfully produced—I do verily believe with sandpaper.

I looked up the catalogue, without getting any fresh light on the subject. "Lot 201: (another property) violin, speculative, a.f." That seemed to be all plain sailing. The thing made no pretence to be other than it obviously was. And yet—

I am not a suspicious man—really straightforward people usually are not—but I could not get out of my mind the feeling that it was not for nothing that that German fiddle had been faked and put in with the Joseph; that, in short, there was a faint odour of what old Parmenter would call "chickery-pokery. "

I slowly descended the stairs, still cogitating on the mystery, hurried past the Tompion clock, and fell into the arms—so to speak—of a writing-table—a delicious little boudoir table fitted with what they called in 1750 a "tambour top," but which is now called an American roll-top, because it doesn't roll and isn't American. I was reminded of the well-worn story of old Dick Gillow and his noble patron. "Eighty guineas for a table, Mr. Gillow!" said his lordship. "It's a devil of a price!" "It's a devil of a table!" says Dicky.

And so was this. A sweet little piece, of fine Spanish mahogany, black with age and unspoiled by varnish, every inch of it spoke of the master craftsman. The drawers ran in and out like well-oiled slide-valves, the tambour top moved without a sound. It had been well cared for, too, for there was not a sign of injury or repair, and as I fingered it lovingly my heart turned to water. I really couldn't resist it. And what a delightful gift it would make for dear old Father Jeffrey!

I had just succeeded in humbugging myself to this extent, when I felt a hand laid on my arm I turned rather quickly, for I hadn't quite recovered from the recognising officer. But it was only an old woman—an anxious, troubled old woman, apparently belonging to the house. She looked eagerly into my face, and remarked:

"You seem to be rather taken with that table."

"I am," I replied, "and I am going to have it if I can."

"Well, then, you can't," said she. "It's Miss Lucy's table, and she's got to have it. The trustees would put it in the sale, but they'd no business to. It's Miss Lucy's, and she's going to buy it in; or, at least, I'm going to bid for her. It was her poor mother's table, and her mother had it from her mother before her, and she had it from her mother, and—" Here the good lady proceeded to genealogise after the bewildering fashion of the Book of Genesis, but she ended by an appeal: "You won't bid against us, will you? Because poor Miss Lucy has only got five pounds at present. So you won't, will you?"

"Certainly not!" I exclaimed. And it was no sacrifice to me. I would have fought a dealer for it tooth and nail, but I would far sooner think of it going back to the hands of those who had grown up with it and loved it as a fine old piece of cabinet work deserves to be loved.

She thanked me profusely, unnecessarily, and I then took the opportunity to ask:

"Do you happen to know anything about that old violin upstairs?"

"The old fiddle in the carved oak case? Well, it's supposed to be a real Prison Joseph, whatever that may be. It has been in the family for a hundred and fifty years, and they do say"—here she crept nearer and dropped her voice—"they do say that it wasn't honestly come by."

I need not say that I was shocked, but I refrained from censorious comment.

"You'd better not repeat it," she continued, "but that's what they have always said in the family. It's supposed that it belonged at one time to Sir Lawrence Bambury, the famous Jacobite, who lived close by here, and that Mr. Mockett's great-grandfather stole it from him. Nobody knows why, as he couldn't play the fiddle, and never tried. But they say he did steal it and hid it in a chest, where it was found after his death. Of course, it doesn't matter now. Sir Lawrence hasn't any need of fiddles now, poor soul!"

I agreed emphatically. As I hoped to be the purchaser, I wasn't going to admit a flaw in the vendor's title. Wishing the old lady "Good-afternoon," I retraced my steps up the stairs to take another look at my prospective property.

As I entered the loft I became aware of quick steps ascending the rough stairs behind me. Now, I didn't want to direct attention to the fiddle, so, instead of going to Lot 108, I interested myself for the moment in an invalid roasting-jack, and watched the newcomer furtively. He was a well-dressed, elderly man, obviously not a local person, and his face seemed to evoke some stirring of memory. He made no secret of the object of his visit, for he went direct to the place where the two fiddles were deposited. I avoided the appearance of watching him, and pretended to be absorbed in the roasting-jack, until he startled me by making a sort of clucking noise, as if he had laid an egg. Then I looked up, and saw him stooping over the fiddle-case and positively sniggering. It was very odd.

Presently he stood up, and slowly walked to the door, chuckling and rubbing his hands; and then he noticed me, and became, in an instant, as solemn as an owl.

That was very odd too.

As soon as he was gone, I stepped over to Lot 108 to see what had amused him so much. And it was at that moment that I remembered where I had seen him. It was at the shop in Wardour Street. That old gentleman was, in fact, the well-known violin-maker and dealer, Emanuel Slithers. That was rather unfortunate. I had only thirty pounds with me, and he wasn't likely to let a first-class Guarneri go for that. I was going to lose my treasure-trove after all.

But what was the old curmudgeon giggling about? That was the question.

It wasn't long before I got the answer. A single glance at my vanishing prize showed me that there had been a slight rearrangement of the exhibits. In a word, the two fiddles had changed cases. The noble Joseph reposed in the garish varnished case, while the blatant Vaterlander lay in the carved oak case like the impostor that he was. No wonder old Slithers had giggled.

It was not a mistake. The exchange had been made deliberately. There was no doubt about that, for not only had the fiddles got transposed, the ivory pegs had got transposed too. They now stuck out from the peg-box of the Teuton, while Joseph had come down to ebony. I understood now why the German had been so carefully faked. This little dodge had been planned in advance.

Now, if there is one thing that I cannot stand, it is deliberate dishonesty. I won't say that I am always absolutely straight myself, but I expect other people to be, and I see that they are, if possible.

Here was a case in point. For some reason the auction clerk had stuck the tickets on the cases instead of on the instruments; and some dishonest person had changed the fiddles for a manifestly fraudulent purpose. I wasn't going to have it. The good, honest, simple folk who came here to bid were not to be cheated in this disgraceful fashion. Certainly not.

I listened attentively to make sure that there was no one about; then, whisking the Joseph out of the miserable varnished box, I rapidly pulled out the wretched ebony pegs—they weren't even real ebony—and refitted him with the ancient ivory pegs proper to his station. The sham ebonies I replaced in the peg-box of the German, and finally laid each fiddle in its own proper case, carefully shutting the lids. Hardly had I finished my pious labours in restoring the *status quo ante bellum* when I heard a step on the stair. Hastily, I tip-toed across to the roasting-jack, and was deep in its disordered mechanism when a man in a green baize apron entered the loft.

"I'm afraid I shall have to turn you out, sir," said he. "They've finished selling the farm stock, and they've begun on the furniture."

I laid down the roasting-jack with a sigh of relief, and made my way downstairs to a large, low-ceiled room on the ground floor, where the rostrum had been set up and the sale was in full swing. The room was densely packed, and it was only by a vigorous and skilful use of my elbows that I eventually reached a position from which I could command the auctioneer's eye.

"Lot one hundred and three," the owner of the said eye chanted sonorously as I took my place; "bedroom pail, two fox-traps, a brass-bound church-service, a muzzle-loading pistol, and a mahogany child's arm-chair. A very useful little miscellaneous lot, this, gentlemen." He swept an inquiring eye over the sea of faces as if in search of someone who might possibly be the parent of a mahogany child. There was a solemn pause, and then a typical agricultural voice offered "a shullen."

During the competition for the "useful little lot" and the four that succeeded it, I examined the crowd with my habitual attention. Mr. Slithers occupied one of the seats of honour at the central table, and close to him sat the elderly servant who had been so severe with me on the subject of the table. Most of the other seated gentry appeared to be dealers, though there were one or two well-to-do outsiders.

At length Lot 107 was disposed of and the auctioneer turned his pince-nez once more on the catalogue. I edged a little more to the front, and girded up my loins for the fray.

"Lot one hundred and eight. Antique violin in carved oak case. Said to be a genuine Prison Joseph. Now, gentlemen, what shall we say for this fine old instrument?"

He glanced inquiringly at Mr. Slithers and so did the other dealers. They evidently knew the great London expert and were waiting for their cue.

"Ten shillings," said Mr. Slithers.

"Ten shillings!" gasped the auctioneer. "Ten shillings, Mr. Slithers, for a genuine Prison Joseph. Impossible! Would you like to see the lot, sir?"

"No, thank you," said Slithers, with a faint grin. "I've seen it."

The auctioneer was dismayed. Ten shillings!

"Would you like to see the lot, Mr. Fox?" he asked, addressing a dour-faced farmer who was seated at the table.

Mr. Fox shook his head emphatically, but gruffly offered fifteen shillings—"for the case," he explained after a pause.

Mr. Slithers looked at him in some surprise and with a slight frown, and reluctantly offered a pound, at which point I "weighed in" with a bid of "one-five." Thereafter the competition was between Slithers and me, and I firmly believe that he only went on bidding for the sake of appearances. Slowly the price crawled up to one-fifteen and when I capped this with "two pounds," there was no response. Slithers had reached his limit—for the case.

"Two pounds, gentlemen!" moaned the auctioneer. "This is incredible! Two pounds only for this unique instrument!" He looked round helplessly on the dealers; but they had their cue. If it wasn't good enough for Slithers it wasn't good enough for them. And as for Mr. Fox, he sat glowering at his catalogue—which trembled in his hand in a most singular manner—and cast an occasional glance of furtive suspicion at the London expert.

The pause, with an interlude of protests, lasted nearly half a minute, and all the time my heart was in my mouth. At length the hammer fell. The Prison Joseph was mine own. My efforts in the cause of Justice were not to go unrewarded.

"Cash!" I shouted, and held up two sovereigns. The clerk took them from me, and the precious oaken case was passed to me over the head of the crowd.

My instinct told me to make off with my treasure and save possible contention, though, of course, the purchase was quite regular and the identity of the instrument could be proved. But I wanted to see how Miss Lucy would fare with her table, and especially I wanted to be present when Lot 201 was put up.

Accordingly, I kept my place, resting the solid oak case on a chair and sitting on it for safety. The table was only a few numbers further down the catalogue. I would stay and see that sold, and then go out and get some fresh air before 201 was due.

Miss Lucy's table was Lot 115, and, as the auctioneer read out the entry, I saw that she had lost it. The way in which the dealers and Mr. Fox bucked up simultaneously showed me that five pounds would be of no use whatever.

And it wasn't. The bidding started at three pounds, and, before you could say "knife," had jumped up to fifteen. As her modest bid was extinguished by the "six" of a stolid dealer, the poor old dame banged the table with her poor old knobbly fist and then fell to wiping her eyes. I was quite distressed.

Seventeen, eighteen, nineteen, twenty; the bids mounted briskly, and then there was something of a pause. All the dealers but one retired and that one had but a single adversary—Mr. Fox. The old lady watched them narrowly, and so did I. Especially I watched Mr. Fox. As his face grew redder and more anxious, I thought I could see something of the working of his vulpine mind. He wanted the table, but he also wanted the fiddle. He knew about the transposition—the first one, I mean—and, for a very good reason, as I suspected.

But he had seen that Slithers had not been taken in, and feared that the expert had spotted the trick. Consequently, poor Mr. Fox didn't know how much he might have to pay for the fiddle; and how much, therefore, it was safe to spend on the table, his resources being limited. That was my reading of Mr. Fox's dilemma, and I think it was the right one. At any rate, having bid twenty pounds, he looked anxiously at the hostile dealer, and when that gentleman said "Twenty-one" he swore audibly. But after rather lengthy consideration he growled out "Twenty-two," and stared fiercely at the dealer. The latter, too, hesitated, but eventually went twenty-three, whereupon Mr. Fox flung down his catalogue, and shook his head fiercely. He had come to the end of his tether.

The dealer smiled faintly, and, as the auctioneer chanted the bid, he marked his catalogue with a pencil. This annoyed me. He was a little too previous.

"Twenty-four," said I. The dealer looked up at me with a decidedly startled expression. He hadn't supposed that there was another Richmond in the field. But he plucked up courage after a moment or two, and said, "Twenty-five," whereto I responded with "Twenty-six," as if I had the Bank of England behind me. This gave him pause, and I really hoped he had finished. But he hadn't. He reflected for quite a long time, but in the end he said, "Twenty-seven," and stooped over his catalogue.

"Twenty-eight," I chirped. It was my last stiver. For another pound the table was his, if he had only known it, But he didn't. He raised his eyebrows resignedly and, after a brief but excruciating interval, the hammer fell.

"Cash!" said I, and emptied my pocket to the last groat. Picking up my fiddle-case, I went out to the ante-room where the table was standing. There I met the old woman, who looked at me with dismal reproach.

"You said you weren't going to bid," said she.

"Well, I didn't bid against you."

"No, I know you didn't. You must forgive a crabbed old woman. But poor Miss Lucy! She'll be so dreadfully disappointed."

"She won't," said I. "The thing is hers. I bought it in for her."

The old woman's face turned a sort of dirty magenta. "Do you mean—" she began.

"I mean that it's Miss Lucy's table, that's all. Can't have a parcel of Shylocks hooking off with family property, you know. You just take it to her with my compliments."

"Won't you come and give it to her yourself?"

"No, I'm blowed if I will," said I, breaking out into a cold perspiration at the idea. "She doesn't know me from Adam, and I don't know her from Eve. It would be most embarrassing."

"Well, you must let me give you the five pounds that I bid. That would be only fair."

"Certainly not!" I exclaimed. "Why should she buy her own table? Oh, but I'll get you to give me one-and-ninepence, because I haven't got a return ticket."

She placed the exact amount in my hand, and as her nose began to work up and down at the end like a rabbit's when it smells a lettuce-leaf, I suspected that there were breakers ahead.

"What name shall I tell her?" she asked with an undeniable sniff.

"John Doe," I said hastily; "sometimes known as Richard Roe. And would you ask Miss Lucy to stand at the window as the four-fifty up train passes and wave her handkerchief, just to let me know that she has got the table safely?"

"She shall," the old lady assured me, with a most alarming sniff, "and I shall be there, too. We shall both"—here she became slightly incoherent, and, in my terror, I shook hands with her frantically. Then she mumbled something about "an old woman's blessing," but I didn't hear the end of it. I made a bee-line for the front door.

I spent some time prowling about unfrequented corners of the farm, horribly afraid that the old lady would run me to earth and exhibit me to Miss Lucy which would have been frightfully uncomfortable. However, she didn't, and when I had made a rough sketch for Father Jeffrey of a tablet on the gable of the house, I cautiously returned to the sale-room. And I was none too soon, for I had only just secured an inconspicuous point of vantage when I heard the auctioneer read out:

"Lot two hundred and one! Speculative violin; all faults."

He made no comment, and waited placidly for a bid. To his evident surprise, Mr. Slithers began with a pound. Mr. Fox followed with two. Slithers jumped to five. Mr. Fox retorted with ten, and scowled villainously at the dealer. The auctioneer stared at them open-mouthed, and so did the dealers. And I hugged the inestimable Joseph under my arm, and chuckled silently.

I was sorry 201 hadn't come earlier, because my train would be due quite soon; and it was really amusing. By the time the bidding had reached a hundred pounds, Fox was nearly purple and Slithers was distinctly snappy. But I had to go. I dared not lose the train, to say nothing of missing the fair Lucy's salute. The last bid that I heard as I left the room was two hundred and fifty-five pounds. I did not see who made it, but the voice was the voice of Mr. Fox, and the bid was accompanied by an unparliamentary expression.

I needn't have been in such a frantic hurry. I got to the station five minutes too soon, and the train was four minutes late. I walked up and down the platform, with Joseph under my arm, a little impatiently. I wanted to be clear of Mockett's Hill Farm as soon as possible. Not that I was in any way in the wrong, but I didn't want a fuss of any kind. Just now it would be exceedingly awkward.

At length the signal-bell ting-tinged, the semaphore fell, and almost at the very moment there appeared against the sky far away up the long white road, the figure of a man. He was tiny in the distance—a mere biped insect—but I could see that he was carrying something, and that something was of an elongated shape. Also, he seemed to be walking rapidly—very rapidly.

From the man on the road to the railway line my eye traveled, and then back to the man. He was getting sensibly nearer. And, along the line came a little white cloud, and under it a little black dot. And the man was drawing nearer, and walking faster than ever.

The train rushed forward with a triumphant whistle, and the man broke into a run. Very foolish of him; for now I could see that he was an elderly gentleman, and elderly gentlemen shouldn't run for trains. That is how they become deceased gentlemen. But he did run, and he swung, quite carelessly, what I could now see plainly was a fiddle-case.

The train rushed into the station. I rushed into the train. The guard looked at his watch, and stuck his whistle in his mouth. A faint halloo came down the wind from the elderly gent who would run when he didn't ought to. The guard looked at him, and then looked the other way. The stationmaster didn't look at all.

Then the stationmaster nodded, the guard blew his whistle, and waved his green flag. The elderly gentleman lifted up his voice, and addressed the guard in flowers of rhetoric—purple flowers; and the train moved slowly out of the station.

The road approached the up-side by a level crossing which we passed immediately after leaving the station. I looked out and I saw our elderly friend glaring over the gate, and shaking his fist at the train in general, but very especially at me. As I had suspected, the elderly one was Mr. Fox; and he was very much out of breath. But he had a little breath left, and a very indifferent use he made of it. Never before have I had such epithets applied to me.

Presently the train approached the neighbourhood of the farm. I looked out to see if there was anyone at the window. There was, or rather there were; two female figures of which I could recognise one by her white hair. And they waved frantically—not handkerchiefs surely! But, at any rate, they made the necessary signal, and only the providence that watches over indiscreet women saved them from falling out of window.

I leaned out, and waved my hat. I also smiled engagingly, but she couldn't see that, for her face was to me but a pinkish-white dot. But no doubt she smiled at me. I couldn't see the smile, but no doubt it was there. And doubtless it was an engaging smile. It might well have been.

You ought to be able to get a pretty decent smile for twenty-eight pounds.

10
PETER MOCKETT'S LEGACY

IN THE SATISFACTION of his desire for things of beauty the man of to-day is very largely a parasite on the past. Some few painters and sculptors, and even architects, still struggle worthily to maintain the old traditions; but, in general, he who desires the best that the mind of man has conceived and the skill of man executed, must seek it in "the touch of a vanished hand," on the impression whereof the dust of centuries has gathered.

Thus pessimistically did I cogitate as the sunbeams, streaming in through the windows of St. Cecily's, fell on scolloped capital and zigzag moulding, on the massive structures with their naive enrichments, that stood unmoved under the burden of eight hundred years; as the golden light called forth the mellow tones of the incomparable varnish, and threw into relief the swelling curves and subtle modeling of the old violin that lay on the credence table.

It was the morning after the sale at Mockett's Hill Farm, and I had come hot-foot to St. Cecily's to examine my treasure. Returning from the sale I had only had time to run into the church, change my clothes, and hide the violin before making my way back to the Rectory, and every moment since then I had been in a fever to have it once more in my hands.

Here let me make a brief but necessary digression. The little church of St. Cecily's had once served the villagers of Thorpe Dene. But Thorpe Dene was no more. One night, in the year 1665, the Pestilence stole into the valley and laid its skeleton hand on the smiling hamlet; and the villagers faded away, one by one, like the petals of a plucked dog-rose, until the last voice was hushed and the last grave was dug. Then the weeds grew up in the village street, the roofs fell in, and the walls crumbled, and wandering rustics from the neighbouring hamlets turned aside to avoid the sinister ruins with their unburied dead.

Thorpe Dene was as extinct as the Cities of the Plain.

But though the village had vanished, so that nothing remained but a few foundations, that notched the unwary ploughshare, and a long, grassy ridge in the churchyard, the church itself remained. The patron of the living still kept it in repair, and paid a small stipend, subject to the condition that service should be held in it four times a year. So that St. Cecily's was, at least technically, a going concern, and an invaluable retiring place I found it. But not only was the church kept in repair; some lunatic had actually presented it with an organ, a preposterously large instrument, with a swell-box constructed for five stops of pipes, but actually containing only a single stop.

Now, if the church was invaluable to me, the organ was simply a gift of the gods. The vacant space in the swell-box for the four rows of pipes furnished me with really sumptuous accommodation. When I had effected an entry by a little attention to the manhole door at the back, I found myself provided with a store-closet, a wardrobe, and a fairly commodious dressing-room; and all quite private and secure, not only from the outside world but even from persons who might inopportunely enter the church. It was a regular secret chamber.

To return now to the old Cremonese fiddle that I had just disinterred from its hiding-place. I gloated over its beauty with ecstasy, with a delight that was enhanced by anticipation. For my privileged ear, and mine alone, was about to hear that melodious voice burst forth once more after a century and a half of silence. It was a solemn thought.

I had bought the necessary appliances at Maidstone this very morning—a set of strings, a bridge, a sound-post, a cake of rosin, and a cheap bow—for the old one had lost most of its hairs—and forthwith I set to work to turn my treasure from a mere curio into an actual instrument. It took me some time, for bridge and sound-post required careful fitting to a valuable fiddle like this; but at length I had it strung, twanged the strings carefully into tune, rosined the bow with elaborate care, and tenderly grasped the neck of the fiddle. It was a tremendous moment. I had never before played upon a first-class violin, and I found myself, as my chin touched the rubbed spot on the belly, wondering whose chin had rested there last. Then I boldly swept the bow across the strings, striking out the opening bars of Rubenstein's "Melody in F."

The result was surprising. In fact, it was positively staggering. I can't say that Joseph had a bad tone. He simply had no tone at all. I could have got more resonance out of a soap-box.

I laid the fiddle down, and stared at it with my mouth agape. It was past belief, and quite past comprehension. True, I had heard that fiddles lose their tone if they lie long disused, and so they may. But a brand-new factory fiddle makes a noise. What it lacks is quality, not quantity, of sound. But this old Cremona was weak and muffled; it might almost as well have been a solid block of wood.

The more I thought about this phenomenon the more puzzled I became. Once or twice I was tempted to take off the belly and examine the interior, but the possibility of doing two or three hundred pounds' worth of damage was more than I dared face. And so, for the next few days, I went about my business, speculating profoundly and with deep discontent.

The ray of light that at length illumined the mystery came unexpectedly from a chance conversation with Father Jeffrey. We were sitting in the garden after dinner, and I remember that I was wearing a new blue-and-white striped frock that went rather well with my complexion.

"I suppose," said Father Jeffrey, as he filled the black and juicy death's-head clay pipe, "you have nearly finished with St. Cecily's?"

"Yes," I answered. "I am doing the west doorway now, but I've made an awful mucker of the old chappie with the nimbus."

"Ahem!" said Father Jeffrey. "You are referring, no doubt, to the figure of St. Paul?"

Of course I was, and I said so with suitable apologies, cursing inwardly my inveterate habit of using asinine colloquialisms. Then, by way of creating a diversion, I produced my sketch-book, and exhibited my 'prentice efforts at the rendering of architectural figures. Father Jeffrey examined them indulgently—I can't draw figures a bit—and turned over the leaves until he came to the drawing of the tablet on Mockett's Hill Farmhouse.

"P.J.M. 1724," he read aloud musingly. And, after a pause: "That will be old Peter Mockett and his wife Jane. Quite an historical character is old Peter; and an arrant old rascal, too, if there is any truth in local traditions—a notorious smuggler, a highwayman, and a murderer."

I was keenly interested. The worthy Peter would, no doubt, be the gentleman who acquired my violin, and was therefore a factor in its pedigree.

"Whom did he murder?" I asked.

"A neighbour of his, a certain Sir Lawrence Bambury—at least, that was the general belief. Sir Lawrence was found dead, with his drawn sword in his hand and a sword wound in his chest. Suspicion fell on Peter Mockett, though the crime was never actually brought home to him."

"Was there any quarrel, then?" said I.

"Yes. There was a chronic feud between the two men; but there was something else—something connected with one of the many queer stories of the '45. It seems that, shortly before the actual landing of the Pretender, an aged Italian lady sent to England an immensely valuable blue diamond, which was to form one of the new crown jewels if the rebellion was successful. It was a famous stone, and is mentioned by several contemporary writers by the name of the Ludovici Diamond—you will find it described in Moggridge's 'Historic Gems.' Well, the diamond was sent to this country in charge of a musician named Moroni, a well-known violinist, whose profession enabled him to travel with comparative safety. Moroni landed at Rye, and made his way across country to the house of Sir Lawrence Bambury, who was a zealous Jacobite.

And there he vanished, and the diamond with him. Neither the man nor the stone was ever seen or heard of again. Of course, there was a good deal of ugly rumour. People whispered that Sir Lawrence had made away with the musician, and stolen the diamond. But it never got beyond rumour.

"Then, not very long after, Sir Lawrence himself was found dead, and again rumour was busy; a good deal more busy this time, for Peter Mockett was known to be a desperate and unscrupulous man. But still nothing definite ever transpired. The mystery of Moroni's disappearance remains a mystery to this day, and the Ludovici Diamond has never been heard of since; which is rather more mysterious. It is probably lying in some forgotten hiding-place where it was secreted by the man who stole it, and who is now but a pinch of dust and a few crumbling bones. And long may it remain there!" Father Jeffrey concluded earnestly. "For, of all the devil's baubles, commend me to a great diamond. It goes down the ages generating hatred, avarice, treachery, and murder as the sun gives off light. You read Moggridge, and see if it isn't so." He puffed fiercely at the death's-head pipe, and, after a short pause, I asked:

"What became of Peter Mockett? Did he come to a peaceful end?"

"Not particularly," said Father Jeffrey. "He was found at the bottom of his own chalk pit, with his neck broken. He may have fallen in, but he was more probably pushed over the edge by some-one who had a grudge against him. At least, that is the opinion of a local antiquarian—an old fellow named Fox—who seems to know more about the affair than anybody. His property adjoins Mockett's Hill Farm, so he may have picked up some information on the spot. But however he got his knowledge, he is uncommonly close about it for some reason. Just run into the study and fetch Moggridge: he is on the top shelf by the door. We will see what he says about the Ludovici Diamond."

I fetched out the book, and we read the article through together. But beyond the very alluring description of this wonderful old jewel, we got no fresh light on the subject. It was clear that no one had set eyes on the Ludovici Diamond for more than a hundred and fifty years.

The reader who is gifted with a synthetic mind will have no difficulty in realising that Father Jeffrey's story put me in a considerable twitter. In fact, it started a train of thought which induced an elaborate census of chickens as yet unhatched.

Just consider the facts. The violin that I had bought had been stolen by Peter Mockett from Sir Lawrence Bambury. I had that from the old woman at the farm, as well as the fact that "he couldn't play the fiddle, and never tried." Now, there could hardly be a doubt that the violin was Moroni's instrument. But why had Peter Mockett stolen it if he couldn't play?

Then, there were the facts that Peter had died suddenly, and that the violin was found by accident in the chest where he had hidden it. And, finally, there was Mr. Fox.

Now, Fox obviously knew something about that violin, and was mighty eager to get possession of it. What did he know? And why did he want Miss Lucy's table? The answer to these questions seemed to be that Mr. Fox had come to the same conclusion as I had. What that conclusion was, I will not insult the reader's intelligence by stating.

That evening dragged out interminably. I was in a fever to get to work: to start hatching out my chickens—peacocks, every one of them. But nothing could be done until the morrow, and perhaps there might not be an opportunity even then. Yet the time was not wasted, for, as I strode up and down the paddock, while Father Jeffrey worked at his paper in the study, I shaped out a dear course of action, which saved delay in the end.

On the following morning I was dispatched in the pony-cart to Maidstone, to do the household shopping, and thereby save Martha's ancient legs; and among the battalion of parcels that assembled in the cart were two that did not appear in Martha's list. One was a bag of Portland cement, and the other a bag of plaster of Paris. They were the product of my evening's cogitations; and I secreted them, on my way home, in a disused barn near St. Cecily's.

The whole of the afternoon I was busy with the typewriter, re-
ducing Father Jeffrey's scrawl to intelligible script. But after tea I
escaped, and made a bee-line for St. Cecily's, only swerving aside
to collect my parcels from the barn. I let myself in at the vestry
door in a very ferment of excitement; for, apart from the momentous dip that I proposed to make blindfold into the lucky bag, I
was embarking on a very risky adventure. I was going to take the
belly off a violin worth, perhaps, from three to five hundred pounds.

It was a bold thing to attempt. A violin belly is but a thin plate
of pine, and pine is the very deuce for splitting. True, the purfling
binds the grain together at the edge, and strengthens it immensely,
but it was a risky job, and a crack in the belly would knock off half
the value of the instrument at a stroke.

However, I was not going to work blindly. I had once watched
a violin maker take off a belly, and I had noticed the procedure
attentively. I always do. To see an expert do a difficult thing is to
acquire valuable knowledge. So I knew what to do, and, especially,
what not to do. Moreover, I made certain preliminary investigations. Excise officers have a way of ascertaining the contents of a
cask by tapping on the outside, and doctors, by knocking little
double-knocks on your chest, can tell you to a nicety the density of
your lungs, or whether your heart is taking up an unfair amount of
room. In like manner, when I had got the fiddle out of its case, I
gently tapped with my knuckle on the back, going over it inch by
inch in the correct Brompton Hospital style. And, sure enough,
when I reached a spot a little below the centre of the lower bouts,
the hollow, boxy sound changed to a shorter, less resonant note.
There was what the doctors would call an area of dullness, and
with this confirmation of my diagnosis, I proceeded to operate.

But it was an anxious business. So anxious that I entirely forgot, for the moment, the ultimate object of the proceeding, and it
was only when, with a most alarming snap, the belly finally parted
from the ribs, that I remembered it. Then, indeed, I raised the loose
plate of wood, like the top shell of an oysters with a beating heart;
raised it, that is to say, as far as it would come, which was less

than an inch. Farther than that it refused to budge, and for a very good reason. Like the oyster-shell aforesaid, it had something sticking to it on the inside.

I peered in and saw a small leather bag, glued firmly to both back and belly, evidently to keep it from shifting. Cautiously I insinuated a sharp knife into the opening, and cut through the leather until the loose belly was free. I laid the belly on the table, and wiped my brow. My hand was trembling violently, and I was quite breathless with excitement.

The little leather bag, or case—for its opening had been sewn up—was stuck fast to the inside of the back. My knife had made a considerable opening in it, through which I could see what looked like a lace handkerchief. This I pulled out gently. Something jammed in the opening in the bag. I pulled a little harder. Suddenly it yielded, and with a sharp rattle, out into the cavity of the fiddle body tumbled a wonderful blue scintillating object about the size of a small greengage, that is to say, a little over an inch in diameter.

It was the Ludovici Diamond. There could be no doubt of it.

I laid it tenderly in the palm of my hand and looked at it, not without awe. It glinted and sparkled as if rejoicing at its new birth into the world of light, and was indeed a most beautiful object; and yet, in its uncanny blue lustre, in the strange gleams and prismatic flashes that darted forth from it as my hand moved, there was something weird and sinister. I thought of Moroni—murdered beyond a doubt—of Sir Lawrence and wicked old Peter Mockett, and wondered dimly what new mischief would befall now that this "devil's bauble" was at last let loose from its prison-house in the old violin. But there was no time to moralise. I had to be back at the Rectory for dinner, and a further item in my programme had to be performed before I went.

It is necessary now for me to explain the plan that I had laid out on the previous evening in anticipation of the discovery. Obviously a gem of the value of the Ludovici Diamond could not be left in so insecure a hiding-place as the swell-box of the organ. At any

moment my country might call me—through the agency of a policeman—and the call might involve a year or two of unavoidable absence. Some absolutely safe hiding-place for the diamond was a
necessity, and I believed that I had found one where it could be in
perfect security until the clouds should have rolled by, and I should
be free from the menace of the law.

High up on the south side of the little squat tower was a sundial that had attracted me from the first. It was surmounted by a
large figure of Time in high relief—in fact, nearly in the full round—
and, underneath, bore the inscription:

> "Grow olde along with mee:
> 1607: The Best is yet to be."

The pious intention of the words I am afraid I ignored, but I
read into them a message of Hope for better times, when my
troubles should be at an end. And so the amazing stroke of luck in
the discovery of the diamond had somehow connected itself with
the old sundial. Now, by some accident, the head of the figure of
Time had got knocked off—how, I cannot imagine. Father Jeffrey
had often lamented the injury and so had I; and hence, when, in
the course of raking over the rubbish in the old iron-bound church
chest, I had come across the broken-off head, I was greatly rejoiced,
and so was Father Jeffrey. The head was quite perfect, and the fracture clean, so that it could easily have been replaced; and when I
suggested to Father Jeffrey that I should stick it on with Portland
cement, he was delighted, and told me that I deserved to be the
wife of an archbishop.

It was to this separated head that my thoughts had turned on
the previous evening. Here was an ideal hiding-place for the diamond. And the sooner the jewel was put into it, the better.

I set to work with my customary energy, Fetching the head from
the old coffer, I took it into the vestry, scrubbed it clean and greased
it slightly with vaseline from a tube that I had brought in my pocket
for the purpose. Then I mixed a first installment of plaster in the

wash-hand basin—but I need not follow the process in tedious detail. Suffice it to say that I encased the stone head in a five-piece mould of plaster, and then I had to stow it, with my other effects, in the swell-box, and run home to dinner.

The next morning Father Jeffrey went to Rochester on church business, and old Gammet was busy in the kitchen garden, so that my time was my own, and St. Cecily's was safe from interruption. Thither I accordingly hurried after breakfast, and resumed my labours.

The mould came away from the stone head beautifully, thanks to the vaseline, and the pieces fitted together perfectly. All was ready for the final touches.

I mixed up a liberal quantity of Portland cement in two installments, making it rather liquid, and stirring a small proportion of the yellow, sandy loam from the churchyard to take off the raw, grey colour, and give it some texture. The first installment I poured into the well-soaped mould and shook it well, so that it should settle on the sides and form a hollow shell, and, while it was setting, I fetched the diamond and wrapped it in a covering of tissue paper. As soon as the shell of cement in the mould had set, I dropped the diamond into the cavity, and then mixed the rest of the cement and poured it in.

Although the cement that remained in the basin had set stone hard in half an hour, I did not disturb the mould for a full hour, but occupied myself in getting out the ladder that was kept in the tower, and mounting to the roof of the latter to survey the surrounding country and make sure that it was in its usual deserted state.

At length I thought it safe to examine my work, and began tentatively to pick off one of the pieces of the mould. The cement cast inside was perfectly hard and stony, as I ascertained by testing it with my fingernail, and when I thereupon picked off the rest of the mould, I had a replica of the head of Father Time identical with the original, save for a trifling difference of colour and texture.

Alter another look round from the tower, I proceeded to finish my work. Having trimmed up the cast with a knife, and mixed up a little fresh cement, I carried them up the ladder to the mutilated figure above the sundial. He is not to be mutilated any longer. A little dob of cement on the old fracture, another on the corresponding surface of the cast, a little adjustment and judicious pressure and the thing is done. Father Time is himself again, complete as of old; and not only is he complete, but

> "Even as the toad, ugly and venomous,
> Wears yet a precious jewel in his head."

I surveyed my masterpiece from below with profound complacency. The new head was not a perfect match to the old stonework, but the difference was inappreciable from the ground level, and time would improve it. I put the ladder back in its place, cleaned away the traces of plaster and cement, and then buried the original head beside an old tombstone, appropriately decorated with a scythe and hour-glass.

My work was done. Whatever might befall in the uncertain future, I should never be without resources. The idiotic laws of my country might claim me as their victim, but even so, Time—literally—would bring its compensations.

Of the restoration of the dismembered Joseph and of the wonderful improvement in his voice that resulted from the operation of opening his abdomen, I have no space to tell. For I now come to the catastrophe by which my peaceful sojourn at Dumbleton Rectory was brought to a sudden and untimely end.

I cannot say it was entirely unforeseen. Ever since my meeting with the recognising officer, I had felt that my security was gone. I had an uneasy feeling that the fellow would talk—how few persons appreciate the virtue of silence—and then some fool would show him photographs, and then—there would be the devil to pay.

And so it fell out. I had walked over to Maidstone one fine morning to buy a new sunshade. I had developed an interest in the absurd adjuvants of feminine vanity that often surprised me, and that I mention for the benefit of psychologists. The shop was one that I had often visited before, and I knew it well; which was fortunate. I was browsing round the outside, gaping in at the window and considering my prospective purchase, when my eye lighted on no less a person than Detective-Sergeant Burbler.

His eye lighted on me at the same moment. Fortunately, I did not lose my head. Without a moment's hesitation I walked into the shop, for I knew that it had what the Hunsgate policeman would call an "entrance out" into an adjoining street.

The sergeant did not know this, and hence he delayed; but not for long. As I slipped through a doorway hung with festooned lace curtains, I saw him enter and look round the shop. I bustled through to the other entrance. A large motor-car had just drawn up, and, as I emerged, a lady alighted and entered the shop, followed by her chauffeur carrying a large parcel. The engine had not been stopped. It was merely running free with the clutch out. In an instant I had hopped into the car and shoved over the lever.

It must have given the gear-wheel a nasty jar when the clutch went in, but I couldn't help that. The engine was a six or eight cylinder affair, and it picked up the car with a jerk that nearly sent me through the back of the seat.

Of course, the chauffeur came running out, bawling like a Bedlamite, and the sergeant followed, blowing a whistle. But what was the use of that? Before you could say Jack Robinson—supposing you wanted to, for any reason—the car was halfway down the street and gathering speed every moment. Still, I did not discourteously ignore them. I replied to their hubbub with a pretty little bugle flourish, and then swept round a corner; and so was lost to sight, though, no doubt, to memory dear.

I met with no obstruction from the traffic even in the High street. I just tootled the mechanical bugle, and, when the drivers saw a big car approaching in charge of a young lady, they pulled up on to the pavement. A few minutes of anxious steering in the heart of the town—for whatever the waggons might do, in the interests of safety, the lamp-posts declined to get out of the way—and then I whizzed over the bridge, and was off like a rocket along the Tonbridge road.

But I didn't go very far. To make for a seaport was impracticable, for I had only a few shillings in my pocket; and the road to London would hardly be safe. Nor should I be any better off there in my present costume and without money or even a cheque-book. But, apart from these considerations, I felt an unaccountable dislike to the idea of making off with another person's motor-car. Technically, of course, I had already stolen the car, but not actually. I had merely borrowed it in an emergency. Not that it is strictly legal to borrow property without the consent of the lender, but these subtleties I could not at the moment consider. The immediate question was what was to be my next move, and I turned it over at my leisure as I threaded the narrow Kentish lanes with a sharp eye for stray children and errant fowls.

I rather enjoyed the drive. It was long since I had driven a car, and this was a fine, capable machine. But I must not unduly prolong the jaunt, since other cars might by now be in pursuit. Circuitously, by many a winding lane, I approached the neighbourhood of St. Cecily's, and when at length the little church rose on the skyline above the wooded valley, I ran the car into a cart-track, switched off the accumulator, made all snug, and started off along a footpath through a coppice towards the church.

My first proceeding, after I had let myself in and locked the door, was to mount the summit of the little tower and survey the landscape. I could see quite a long way. Down in the valley was the abandoned car, invisible to me, though I could locate it exactly, and in several directions I could catch glimpses of a white, ribbon-like by-road.

But it was not long before I caught a glimpse of something else— a grey dot, sliding along one of those white ribbons with a smooth celerity unknown to horseflesh. I watched it closely. It glided swiftly round a curve and disappeared to reappear anon at another bend a full half-mile nearer. It was evidently following the road I had taken, and I pictured the chauffeur gripping the wheel, with his eyes on the tracks my tires had left in the dust.

So far, then, they had traced me, and it was well that I had cleared out in time. But when they found the deserted car, what would they do? Had anyone seen me? It was a momentous question, and as it occurred to me, I glanced once more over the country.

In the distance, a man was walking towards the coppice. Presently he would come to the abandoned car, where he would probably meet my pursuers. Well, he couldn't have seen me, anyhow. There was only one thing that made me uneasy. He was approaching along the footpath from the Rectory, and the question arose, Who was he?

Presently he disappeared behind the coppice, and then I turned my attention once more to the approaching car. It was buzzing down the lane now, and as it showed for an instant where the hedge was low, I could see that it contained two men besides the chauffeur. Then it vanished, and, for a long and anxious interval, I sat crouching below the parapet, peering out through the little embrasure.

Of a sudden my heart gave a bound. Three men had emerged from the coppice and were evidently coming towards the church, and one of them was Father Jeffrey!

I didn't stop to investigate further. Squeezing myself down the little winding stair, I made straightway for the organ and reconnoitred my citadel. It wasn't a bad retreat. The man-hole of the swell-box, to which I have referred, was a panel that was originally fixed in place by large screws. The screws were there still—at least they appeared to be. As a matter of fact, I had filed off their shanks so that only the heads remained. But they looked quite secure, and the bolts that I had fixed on inside, would assist the illusion.

I set the swell pedal in the top notch, which left the louvres that form the front of the swell-box slightly open. (I may explain that the "Venetian swell" is an arrangement of movable slats like a Venetian blind, the slats being opened or shut by a pedal to regulate the sound of the enclosed pipes.) Thus I could hear what was passing in the church, and even get a peep out, while, since it was totally dark in the swell-box, no one could possibly see in.

I had only just taken my place inside the box and shot the bolts, when I heard a key grate in the lock of the west door. There was a loud creaking of hinges, and then voices were audible.

"It's the most ridiculous thing I ever heard of," said the voice of Father Jeffrey. "You see the place is all locked up."

"Our friend is pretty handy with locks," was the reply; "and I don't suppose yours are Chubbs's. Besides, why did he stop the car there?"

"Can't say, I'm sure," snapped Father Jeffrey. "I thought you said it was a woman?"

"Man in woman's clothes, I said. Golden wig, hat trimmed with apple-blossom, blue-and-white striped dress, but a man all the same."

"Very well," growled Father Jeffrey "here's the church. You're at liberty to look round it if you want to."

The other person did want to. Dimly through the chink between two slats, I saw the two figures perambulate the church, looking into the benches one by one; I heard them open the old iron-bound chest, go into the vestry, ascend the tower stairs, and return; and all the time I hardly dared to breathe. Then they came round to the organ, and the stranger breathed in heavily between the front pipes; and from the front they proceeded to the rear.

Now was the critical moment.

"Does this thing open?" the stranger asked, banging on the back of the swell-box with his knuckles.

"It takes to pieces, I believe," said Father Jeffrey. "You can see it's screwed together. Your friend can hardly have screwed himself in, you know, sergeant, h'm?"

The sergeant received this shaft of irony with a disdainful grunt, and moved away.

"Are there any vaults?" he asked.

"Yes, there are," said Father Jeffrey, "closed up with masonry; but if you think I'm going to dig up the foundations of my church to look for a hypothetical variety artist, you're mistaken."

"I think, sir," said the sergeant, "that you might show a little more readiness to assist an officer of the law."

"An officer of the fiddlesticks!" was the gruff retort. "The fellow's off to the Continent while you are doddering about here."

Apparently a suspicion that this might really be the case entered the sergeant's mind, for he very shortly took his leave.

Father Jeffrey escorted him out, and, returning after a short interval, shut the door and, rather to my surprise, locked it. I supposed he was going out by the vestry door.

But he wasn't. I heard him go up the tower stair, where he remained for quite a considerable time, much to my discomfort. His presence disturbed me. I wanted him to go, that I might think over my plans in peace. The sound of a far-away motor-horn came faintly through an open window, and still he tarried aloft. At length he came down and I saw him, against the light of the west window, shutting up a silly little telescope that he habitually carried in his pocket. For some moments he stood, a motionless silhouette against the light. Then, to my utter consternation, he said aloud:

"Now then, Lydia, out you come! The coast's all clear!"

To say that I was flabbergasted would be to use a totally inadequate—as well as an intolerably vulgar—expression. It was what Milkey would call a "fair knock-out." It suddenly dawned upon me that I had considerably overestimated my chaperon's innocence.

I crawled out, feeling, and no doubt looking, a most miserable fool. He looked at me gravely, and said:

"You heard what the sergeant said, Lydia—that you are a man in woman's clothes. Is it true?"

"Yes, it is," I replied.

"Then you had better go and take off those things—that is, if you have got any others."

I crept back humbly to my lair, and rapidly made the desired change while Father Jeffrey did sentry-go up and down the nave. It was a miserable affair. Only now did I realise the deep affection that had grown up between this grim old parson and my unworthy self, and it cut me to the heart to think that he, who had trusted me so implicitly, should see me unmasked as the common, vulgar trickster that I was. For the first and only time in my life, I almost wished that I had been a woman, for then I had been entitled to indulge a strong inclination to blubber. Oh, blessed privilege! What the deuce do women want with the vote when they have the undisputed right to blubber?

When I came forth once more in the habiliments proper to my sex—and feeling a bigger fool than ever—Father Jeffrey surveyed me with a faint smile.

"Dear me, Lydia," said he, "how small you look!"

I expect I did. This is another of your confounded sex distinctions! An ordinary man in woman's clothes looks like a giantess; an ordinary woman in man's clothes looks like a shaved Persian cat.

"I don't look so small as I feel," said I.

The smile faded from his face. He looked really sorry for me, which made things worse. After a slightly embarrassing pause, he said:

"I don't know whether you would like to tell me anything. You are not bound to. It is not really any business of mine."

I understood the hint. He would rather I should say nothing than tell him a pack of lies.

"I should like to tell you the whole truth," I said, "but you'd never believe me. You'd only think me a barefaced and clumsy liar."

He laid his hand gently on my shoulder.

"You may take it, Lydia—my boy—that whatever you tell me on your honour I shall believe implicitly. I am sure you would not tell me a lie in cold blood."

I was profoundly touched, and thanked him rather huskily.

"It's a long story," I added.

"Then come up to the tower, where we can see about us, and tell it at your leisure. I am eager to hear it, for the sergeant gave me an account of you that I found quite incredible."

Accordingly we ascended the tower, and there, seated on the leads under the shelter of the parapet, I told him the story of that strange comedy of errors in which Tom Nagget and I played the leading parts; to which he listened with rapt attention as he swept the offing vigilantly with his telescope.

"It's a queer story," he said thoughtfully, when I had finished—"a very queer story. You have been the victim of circumstance with a vengeance; not that you haven't given circumstance every chance. You're rather a young scalliwag." He smiled at me indulgently, and then continued, "But I don't quite see why you shouldn't lay an information against this fellow Nagget. He is personating you deliberately."

"I couldn't do that," I said hastily. "I've taken his odds and played against him, you know."

Father Jeffrey chuckled.

"The inveterate sporting Briton," said he. But I could see that he agreed with me,

"Then there is only one other thing to do," he said, after a pause. "You must take a little trip to the Continent, and leave this gentleman to nibble at the toasted cheese until the trap nips him. Then you can come back and start fresh with a clean record. Have you got any money?"

"I've got a hundred pounds in the bank, if I could only get at it; and I have some capital invested."

"You can't touch that at present," said he; "but I can let you have enough to take you to Paris."

"I don't want to sponge on you," I said.

"You won't. You can send me a cheque from Paris or Jericho, or wherever you elect to stay for the present. And now we must settle how you are to get there. Dover or Folkestone will hardly do. The cross-Channel boats are pretty closely watched."

I fully agreed with this view, but could think of no better alternative. The continental packets from London were probably not entirely neglected by the police.

"I'll tell you what," said Father Jeffrey. "There is a pleasure boat that goes from the Old Swan Pier to Margate and Ramsgate, and then on to Boulogne. That ought to be pretty safe."

"Yes; but the train to London won't be, and I can't very well walk."

Father Jeffrey cogitated a while. Suddenly he looked up at me triumphantly, and smacked his knee.

"I have it!" he exclaimed. "The very thing! Old Jim Pollock—you don't know him, fortunately. His barge is lying just above Allington Lock, all ready to be off. The little Chatham tug will pick him up to-night about half-past nine. By to-morrow morning he will be down by Sheerness, or well up the Thames, according to the state of the wind. He will give you a passage to London if I ask him, and as he and his son Bill work the barge alone, you will be quite safe. Old Jim is as close as an oyster."

"But how shall I get on board the barge?" I asked.

"I will tell Jim that you will be on the bank below the castle ruins at nine o'clock; and mind you are there punctually. It will be nearly dark by then. You know the spot, and you'll probably find his boat waiting for you. And now, my dear boy, I must be off to make the necessary arrangements. I will hand the needful to Jim in a note addressed to you."

We descended the stairs and entered the dim nave, and, when I had displayed my late retreat—which he inspected with a grim smile—and commended the precious fiddle to his care, we passed into the tiny vestry. Here for a while we stood shaking hands silently, and both very much moved. Presently he opened the vestry door and looked out cautiously. Then he turned and gripped my hand once more.

"I shan't see you again, Lydia—my boy," he said, "but I wish you a safe passage and a good time in Paris. And don't forget what the old sundial says."

He was gone. The vestry door shut, the lock clicked, and I was alone.

I fell to pacing the silent nave, wrapped in profound thought. A new outlook on life was opening. But was it opening too late? It appeared as if the night of misfortune was closing in on me, and yet in this darkest hour I seemed to see on the far-away horizon the first, faint glimmer of the dawn.

II
AUNT JEMIMA

BEAUTIFUL SCENERY AND beautiful music have one property in common: the pleasurable emotions that they evoke are apt to be accompanied by a sort of induced current of melancholy. I do not pretend to explain the phenomenon. It is possible that just as the mingling of half-concealed dissonance is the essence of beautiful sound, so certain overtones of sadness are an integral part of the higher forms of pleasure. I cannot say. I only note the fact as it presented itself to me when, in the dusk of a summer's evening, I sat under a spreading beech to keep my tryst with old Jim Pollock.

My assignation was for nine o'clock, and it wanted ten minutes to the hour when I sat down. I had crept forth from my hiding-place betimes, and sneaked warily across the country, with the ruins of Allington Castle as my objective. And now I sat with the gentle river at my feet, looking across at the lovely wooded height over which the gauzy evening mist had gathered, and from whose depths poured forth an unceasing song from the countless choir of birds. Above it, rosy clouds floated in the violet eastern sky; below it, leaping fishes drew circles of silver on the surface of the quiet water.

It was all very peaceful. It breathed the quiet spirit of the English countryside, and was full of the beauty of our own fair land. And the contemplation of it filled me with profound melancholy; for I was bidding it all farewell. My pleasant life at the old Rectory was at an end. That haven of rest would shelter me no more. Once again must I go forth, a wandering Ishmaelite, into a hostile world.

Little wonder that I was melancholy.

The faint sound of a church clock coming from afar through the evening stillness made me cast an uneasy glance up the river. A barge was coming round the bend propelled by two men, one working a sweep and the other a setting-pole. I watched the deep-laden craft creeping down on the stream, and, as it approached my lurking place, I stood up and showed myself. Immediately the man who was working the sweep drew the long spar inboard, stepped down into the jolly-boat that was towing astern, cast off, and came sculling rapidly towards me.

"Are you Mr. Pollock?" I sang out, as the boat neared the bank.

"Yes," was the reply; "I'm Jim Pollock, I am." And the speaker, a walnut-faced shellback of about fifty-five, reached out an arm and clawed at the long grass, continuing, as I scrambled into the boat, "I suppose you be the parson's young gentleman?"

I replied that I was, whereupon Jim slewed the boat's head round and sculled back to the barge.

As I stepped on board, the other mariner, whom I correctly surmised to be Bill, saluted me with an admiring grin, which made me wonder what Father Jeffrey had said about me. But Bill made no remark, being apparently occupied with an endeavour to impale himself on the butt of the setting-pole; and Jim, having made the boat fast, beckoned to me mysteriously, and then shot, harlequin-wise, through the narrow opening of the cabin scuttle. I followed him, with less agility, and descended a ladder to a little cavern lighted by a smelly oil-lamp.

"Parson Mostyn," said Jim, "he told me as I was to give you this here letter, and these here clean dungaree trouseys, and this here jersey and cap. Says as how you'd best put on the trouseys and the jersey so's you won't be noticed aboard."

"Yes, I will," said I. "One doesn't want to make oneself conspicuous."

"Natoorally," said Jim. And he added, after a pause, "Seems as how you've been a-going it up at Maidstone."

"Oh, no," I said modestly. "Just a trifling misunderstanding with the authorities, that's all."

Jim received my explanation with a solemn wink, after which he retired up the ladder, and left me to make my toilet.

Father Jeffrey's letter (addressed to L. Tarkington, Esq.) contained five sovereigns and nine five-pound notes. The letter itself I need not transcribe, though its brief sentences remain engraved indelibly on my memory to this day: but I read it through several times, and then tore it into minute fragments, to be presently dropped into the Medway for safety. Then I put on the blue linen trousers, the jersey, and the blue cloth cap, and went up on deck. Jim surveyed me with an inscrutable blue eye, and remarked:

"Here's the noo apprentice, Bill. Looks a bit soft about the 'ands, don't he?"

Whereupon Bill rested from his labours, and let off a guffaw that woke the echoes and sent a water-vole hurrying into his burrow like a little grey streak of lightning.

"Now, what you wants to do," continued Jim, "is to learn the rudiments of navigation. And you begins by taking a hand at this here sweep."

I seized the handle of the unwieldly, overgrown oar and fell to work, while Jim stood by and instructed me, to the unmeasured joy of his offspring.

"When you flourishes the blade in the air," he explained, "you're a-wastin' your strength; and when you misses your stroke on the water you goes overboard. And there ain't no call for to dig up the bottom of the river; the conservancy dredger attends to the likes of that."

Here he had to suspend his instruction, as Bill had laughed himself into a state of temporary paralysis and the barge was approaching Allington Lock. Several other barges were preparing to pass through, and a considerable sprinkling of idlers had collected by the lock to look on; wherefore it was decided by Jim that it would be more discreet for me to go below, and stay there until we were through the lock and had been taken hold of by the tug.

Down below I accordingly remained, seated on a locker with my elbows on a little three-cornered table, thinking my thoughts, and speculating on the chances of a happy deliverance; while from above, the rattle of falling ropes, the clink of windlass pawls, and, later, the hoots of a steamer's whistle, told of the barge's progress. Then came an unmistakable jerk followed by the loud ripple of passing water, and Bill's head appeared at the scuttle to announce that it was "all clear now."

I came up on deck to discover that our barge, the *Little Nancy*, formed the end of a queue of similar craft that were being hustled down stream by a small screw tug. Memory supplies a confused vision of swiftly-passing woodland and meadow; of the fine old grey stone bridge at Aylesford with the clustering roofs of the village and the church tower brooding over all; then more woodland and meadow, and, as the light faded, grey expanses of marsh with shadowy hills beyond, shapeless factory buildings crowding to the water's edge, and lofty chimneys crowned with smoke-clouds. Within a couple of hours the lights of Strood and Rochester broke out of the gloom ahead; we plunged into the shadow of a great iron bridge and came out into a veritable constellation of anchor-lights, with the shapes of the cathedral and the castle-keep looming up faintly astern.

Here my role of spectator came temporarily to an end; for Bill obligingly placed an iron windlass crank in my hand and inducted me into the gentle art of hoisting. And though it was gratifying to see the heap of raffle on our deck gradually rise aloft and take on the shape of mast and sprit with intelligible rigging, the pleasure had its drawbacks in the form of blistered hands and aching shoulders. Further instruction in the "rudiments of navigation" concerned themselves with the fixing of sidelights and the loosing of sails; by which time we were in the very heart of the constellation and, as I gathered from Bill, had entered Chatham Reach.

Here the tug let go and abandoned us to our fate. We sheeted home the three sails—the *Little Nancy* was a "stumpy," that is to say, she carried no topsail—and started our voyage in earnest.

It was an astonishing experience. How old Jim found his way down the tortuous river I could not make out at all. And neither could he, to judge by his explanations. On all sides was a blank expanse of darkness, speckled with red and green lights that slid to and fro—the sidelights of other barges; and other lights, apparently on shore, glared and twinkled unmeaningly to me. And still old Jim stood calmly at the wheel and smoked his pipe. The barge tacked and twisted and turned; the sails shivered and filled, now on this side, now on that; and never once did we touch any of the countless shoals that stretch out from the marshy shores, or bump against one of the legion of barges that gyrated around us. I conceived a new respect for the bargee that night.

About three hours of this brought us abreast of Sheerness; the big red light on Garrison Point swept past, and presently Bill informed me that we were out in the "London River," and that presently we should "ketch the flood-tide." And no doubt we did; but it was all one to me. A void of darkness all around, sprinkled with endless lights; red, green, white, large, small, and all on the move in a bewildering procession. There were lights that snuffed out suddenly and then reappeared in a second or two brighter than ever; that bore down on us with a rush, swept close alongside, displaying the great, black shape of a gas-buoy with its little lantern on top, and slid away astern, still winking frantically. There were lights that turned red as we approached and then turned white again, and that popped in and out like the gas-buoys. And great steamers, aglow with lamps from stem to stern, roared past us bellowing like marine bulls of Bashan, slopping their wash over our deck, and bringing my heart into my mouth. And still old Jim sucked his pipe by the wheel while young Bill fetched an accordion out of the fore-peak and made the summer's night hideous.

Shortly after daybreak Jim sent me below to turn in, there being nothing for me to do, "unless," he added reassuringly, "someone runs over us." So I retired to a sort of cupboard and slept soundly until near upon noon; when I woke to find the *Little Nancy* anchored off Greenhithe while the ebb-tide ran out. Then Bill and I, after refreshing ourselves with a colossal can of tea and a massive breakfast of pickled pork, pulled the boat across to the beacon by St. Clement's Church and spent the afternoon playing a prehistoric form of cricket with a party of boys in a gravel pit. The bargee's life has its compensations.

At five o'clock we got up the anchor and resumed our voyage, but I retired early to the cupboard and knew no more until the following morning, when I was aroused by a vigorous shaking.

"Time to turn out, sir," said Jim. "Here's London Bridge close aboard and past eight o'clock. You'd best get on your shore togs and have your breakfast. We've got to get up to Battersea before high-water."

I rose and shed my nautical costume while Bill laid the table; and, having secretly tendered Jim a sovereign, which he rejected indignantly, informing me that he was going to settle up with the "paarson," I sat down to my last meal on board the *Little Nancy*.

It had been a pleasant interlude, and now that it was over I was once more face to face with my plan of escape. It all looked quite plain-sailing now. In another hour I should be on board the pleasure steamer, a harmless holiday-maker, taking a day trip to Boulogne. And once on French soil I should be safe.

We got up the anchor after breakfast—the mast had already been lowered—and worked the barge through the bridge with the sweeps. Here I took leave of Jim, and was ferried across in the boat to the Old Swan Pier by my shipmate Bill, who bundled me up on to the pontoon with scant ceremony, and with a hasty "So-long!" started off frantically after the retreating barge. My arrival was not unobserved. A pier official accosted me with inquiries as to what I wanted, and I replied that I wanted the Boulogne boat.

"Then," said he, "you've come to the wrong place. She don't start from here; she starts from Tilbury."

"The deuce she does!" said I. "What time does she start?"

"In about ten minutes," was the reply.

"But I can't get to Tilbury in ten minutes," I rejoined gloomily.

"No, you can't," said he, "and that's a fact. Better go to-morrow," and he turned away to attend to other matters. It was very disappointing. It might even be disastrous. And I had actually passed Tilbury yesterday morning in time to have caught the boat!

I looked wistfully at the receding form of the *Little Nancy*, and watched Bill climb on board and secure the boat. That refuge was gone. I should have to spend the night in London or else go down to Tilbury and wait there.

Suddenly my eye fell on a solitary figure standing apart from the crowd; the figure of a buxom girl dressed in black; and forthwith all thought of my present predicament and my future movements flew to the winds. I darted forward, seized her hand impulsively, and exclaimed, "Susannah!"

She turned quickly, and looked in my face with a curious mixture of amazement and recognition, and giving my hand a tepid shake, withdrew her own.

"Who *are* you?" she asked. "And how did you know I was Susannah?"

"Do you mean to say you don't remember me?" I exclaimed. And even as I asked the question I remembered myself, and saw what an idiotic mistake I had made. But I had to brazen it out.

"No, I don't," said she. "And I can't imagine how you knew I was Susannah."

"Oh, that's quite simple," I answered jauntily. "My sister Lydia told me about you."

"Really! Are you Lydia's brother?" She looked at me with a new and gratifying interest.

"Yes. Didn't you recognise me? We are considered to be very much alike."

"I thought you were like someone I knew," she replied. And added, "Yes, you are really extraordinarily like her. Is she here?"

Now, what was I to say? Was she here or wasn't she? It was a case for the casuists. I couldn't very well say that I was my own sister. That would have sounded absurd.

"No; she isn't," I answered.

"Then," said Susannah, "I don't quite see how you—you knew—"

I didn't quite see, either, so I broke in on the question:

"Oh, Lydia told me all about your little escapade, you know! What a joke it must have been! I should like to have seen you two on that roof."

"Yes, I know," said Susannah; "but, still, I don't quite see how you knew—"

The Lord knows how I should have got out of the mess but for a timely interruption. I suppose I should have had to confess to the beastly disguise, and admit that Lydia and I were one and the same person. But from this ignominy I was saved. At the height of my embarrassment I perceived an elderly woman approaching with a broad smile of recognition. I knew her in a moment. She was the old servant whom I had met at Mockett's Hill Farm.

"Well," she said as she came up, "you *are* a dreadful storyteller!"

Susannah looked at her in amazement. "Whatever do you mean?" she demanded. The old lady smiled blandly.

"He said he didn't know you," she explained.

"I really don't understand you, Priscilla," Susannah said stiffly. "Who said he didn't know whom?"

"Don't you remember, Miss Lucy?" said Priscilla. "This is the gentleman who bought in your writing-table for you at the farm sale."

Here was a pretty staggerer! Miss Lucy, hey! I felt myself turning the colour of a ripe tomato, and as for Susannah—or Miss Lucy—a blush-rose was anaemic compared with her cheeks.

"Did you?" she asked. And I guiltily admitted that I did.

She held out her hand warmly, and exclaimed: "How kind and generous it was of you! But how did you know I was Lucy Mockett?"

"I didn't," said I, telling the truth by way of a restful change. "What I said to Priscilla was the simple fact. I didn't know who Miss Lucy was."

"Then," said Susannah, as I prefer to call her, "it was perfectly sweet of you. It is just the sort of thing Lydia would do, I'm sure." (Evidently Lydia was still the super-woman of her worship.)

At this moment a beastly bell began to ring furiously on one of the boats. Priscilla looked round anxiously, and said:

"I think we must be getting on board, Miss Lucy. The boat is going to start."

I walked with them to the gangway, where we halted for a final word, undismayed by the glowering eye of the man on the bridge.

"Give Lydia my love," said Susannah, to the accompaniment of a protracted handshake, "and tell her that she's a perfectly horrid girl. I've written to her three times, and she has never replied once."

"Did you send your letters to the address I ga— she gave you?" I asked.

"Of course I did; and I expect they are there still." Which was, no doubt, the actual fact.

"Tell her," continued Susannah, "that we are going down to Lowestoft for a fortnight, and that you are both to meet me when I come back; and we'll go on the spree together."

"Now then, there," shouted the man on the bridge, "are you coming on or are you going to stay behind?"

Susannah answered by tripping across the gangway, and then stood by the bulwark waving her hand to me and smiling a last farewell.

"Mockett's Hill will always find me, you know," she called out, as a rope-bearing Caliban edged her away from the bulwark. I smiled in return and raised my hat. An amphibious ruffian cast off the last shore-rope; a steam windlass roared; the paddle-wheels began to revolve, and the steamer slowly drew away from the pier. The moment it was clear I fell to cursing my imbecility (but I continued to smile at Susannah); for I might have gone on board with her and traveled to Tilbury, which would have solved my difficulty effectually and pleasantly.

I was still gazing regretfully at the fast-receding steamer when a large and muscular hand took firm hold of my arm. I whisked to the rightabout like lightning to find myself confronted by a tall and massive man of peculiarly stolid aspect.

"What do you want?" I demanded breathlessly.

"I want you to step round to the police station with me," was the unmoved reply. "This lady has given you in custody on a charge of burglary, and I caution you that anything that you say may be used in evidence against you."

This lady! I looked round, and my horrified glance fell on a beetle-browed, forbidding old lady, who was regarding me with a smile that recalled Father Jeffrey's death's-head pipe. I seemed to remember her horrible old face. Where had I seen her before? Could it be?—yes, it was!

It was Aunt Jemima!

"There's some mistake here," I faltered, "I don't know this lady."

"No," said the officer; "but, you see, she says she knows you."

"It is a mistake—quite a mistake. I assure you it is," I said earnestly.

"Yes, I know," replied the officer. "But, you see, they always say that. You'd better come along quietly and not make a fuss."

I glanced despairingly at the shore-gangway. A uniformed constable was standing negligently in the entrance, with ill-feigned unconsciousness, and two pier officials were watching me with quite unfeigned interest. There was nothing for it but to go quietly.

I must admit that the plain-clothes man was very considerate. We walked ashore arm in arm, conversing amicably, with Aunt Jemima as a rearguard, and passed through the streets without attracting any notice. But it was a dismal end to my adventurous voyage, and I could only feel thankful that the catastrophe had been deferred until Susannah was off the scene.

The arrest was the merest fluke, which only made it the more exasperating. It appeared that Aunt Jemima had contemplated a trip to Margate and back. That was how she came to be on the pier. But she gladly gave up the trip, as she explained with fiendish satisfaction, for the pleasure of laying me by the heels. I suppose it was natural, but it struck me at the time as discreditably vindictive on her part.

I think the inspector was at first doubtful as to taking the charge. My appearance, no doubt, must have impressed him as absurdly incongruous with the alleged circumstances. But when I gave my name as John Smith, and was unable to furnish a satisfactory description of myself, his manner changed. "John Smith" was clearly a tactical mistake, but my reticence concerning myself and my place of abode was unavoidable. The end of it was that he entered the particulars, Aunt Jemima signed the charge-sheet, and I presently found myself, for the second time in my life, the inmate of a police cell.

Left to myself in the gloomy and none too clean apartment, my reflections, I need hardly say, were not of the most cheerful order. The crisis of my life had come, and with disconcerting suddenness. Viewed hitherto optimistically as a contingency perilous enough to give a certain piquancy to evasion, but remote enough to be looked at with a sort of impersonal amusement, the arrest had suddenly crystallised into grim reality. The pleasures of the chase were no more. Penal servitude stared me in the face unless I contrived in some way to secure, to use the old legal phrase, "a good deliverance."

I walked up and down the cell, turning the position over in my mind; and there fell upon me a strange feeling of aloofness, of isolation. Images of persons and things but lately seen came to me as to a dead man who should retain his consciousness when life had fled. The stony walls, the grated window, the massive door locked fast upon me, and the vault-like silence, seemed to cut me off from the land of the living. My thoughts were as the thoughts of some old Egyptian, lying in his sepulchral chamber, meditating on the world of light and life outside, where men still went to and fro, where the children were playing in the sunshine, where those who had loved him still spoke his name, still talked of him as of one who had been and was no more.

I thought of Susannah, gliding down the sunlit river that had borne me to my fate. Probably she was thinking of me at this very moment, and of the mythical Lydia and the "spree" that was now postponed *sine die*. I pictured my late shipmates drifting up by Westminster, and even now discussing "the paarson's young gentleman." And dear old Father Jeffrey, anxiously following in spirit the wanderings of his prodigal secretary, and wondering what time he should get the promised telegram from Boulogne.

From the present, my thoughts turned to the recent past; to the changed outlook on life that the atmosphere of the Rectory had engendered. It was only a week or two ago that I had discovered, from a chance newspaper report, the owner of the stolen pearl necklet that I had kept so long; and I had sent it back with a request—duly acceded to—that its receipt should be acknowledged in *The Times*. Thus had I wiped off, as I thought, the only definitely criminal act of my life, with the purpose of starting afresh with a clean record. But now it looked as if the fresh start might be considerably delayed.

There was, indeed, one way out. I could lay an information against Tom Nagget.

It would be quite fair. He was the real offender, and he had deliberately personated me. But I never entertained the idea for a moment. I had taken up his challenge, and I would abide by the consequences like a man.

I was not kept long without a hearing. The arrest had been made without a warrant, and it was accordingly necessary that I should be taken before a magistrate at once. An hour had barely elapsed since my capture when I was brought forth from my seclusion to be taken to the police court.

I was conveyed, at my request, in a cab, for which I paid, and was duly placed in the dock, an object of delighted interest to the mob of ragamuffins who were waiting as spectators. The magistrate gave me a casual glance as the charge was being stated, and then Aunt Jemima entered the witness-box with a grin of triumph.

I must admit that she described the circumstances of the burglary with admirable clearness, though, to my surprise, she made no reference to the finger-marked candle that I had left behind. This was a little awkward, for I couldn't very well mention it myself. I suppose she thought it unnecessary to go beyond her personal identification of me. Of that she had no doubt whatever, and she mistook, as ladies commonly do, her own complete conviction for conclusive proof.

Appearances were certainly against me. There was, for instance, the unfortunate name that I had chosen. It was the first name that came into my mind, but unluckily I was not the first who had made use of it.

"John Smith!" repeated the magistrate, as I answered to my wretched name. "What, another? Dear, dear! What a very wicked family these Smiths are, especially the Johns. Well, Smith, what is your occupation?"

"I am an engineer," I replied.

"Ah, that's better!" said the magistrate, who was evidently somewhat of a wag. "The Smiths—particularly the Johns—generally favour the calling of a clerk. And where are you engaged at present as an engineer?"

"I am not engaged anywhere at present."

"Where do you live?"

"I should prefer not to give my address," said I. The magistrate raised his eyebrows.

"Very well," he said; "then we will hear the evidence."

Then came Aunt Jemima, and, as I have said, she was exceedingly clear, highly circumstantial, excepting with regard to the candle, and absolutely cocksure.

"Are you quite certain that the prisoner is the man who entered your house?" the magistrate asked. And Aunt Jemima replied that she was quite certain.

At the conclusion of her evidence, the magistrate once more looked at me.

"You have heard what the prosecutrix says, Smith. She charges you with having broken into and entered her house on the date mentioned. Have you anything to say?"

"I say that she is mistaking me for someone else," I answered.

"That is quite possible," said the magistrate. "But can you bring forward any proof that it is so? Can you tell us, for instance, where you were on the night in question?"

"No, I can't," I replied. "It is too long ago."

"I must point out to you," the magistrate said, "that the concealment of your identity, in which you persist, is against you. Your best answer to the charge would be to prove that you are a person of known respectability. But if you continue to refuse any information as to who you are, where you live, how you live, and who is acquainted with you, that fact must weigh heavily against your claim of mistaken identity."

I fully perceived the truth of this, but I could give no account of myself that would be other than highly suspicious. Accordingly I maintained my attitude of complete reticence.

The magistrate was very fair, in spite of his ill-timed witticism. He gave me every assistance. But there was Aunt Jemima, with a clear and connected statement, to which I could give no answer but an unsupported denial.

I took it for granted that he would remand me for police inquiries. To my surprise, he did nothing of the kind. After hearing

all that I had to say—which was mighty little—he committed me
for trial at the Central Criminal Court; and I was forthwith whisked
out of the dock, and marched off to the cells attacked to the court.

The hours passed slowly, giving me ample opportunity for
meditation and pedestrian exercise up and down the cell. I was
furnished, at my own expense, with refreshment, which I consumed
with little relish in that unsavoury atmosphere, but made it last as
long as possible, nevertheless; for it formed, at least, a break in
the monotony. At last, late in the afternoon, the cell door again
opened, and I was "collected" by a constable, whom I followed
through the chilly passages until, through an open door, I caught
a glimpse of a squalid street, a waiting crowd of ragamuffins, and
the unlovely shape of the great, black, windowless omnibus. I hurried out with downcast face, stumbled up the steps, and plunged
into the dark and stuffy interior. A custodian ushered me into a
tiny compartment and bolted me in; and I sat down with shudder-
ing distaste and horrible speculations as to the previous tenant.

The outer door banged, and the police van rumbled off on its
melancholy errand. A faint glimmer of light came through the little
grating in my door—otherwise I was encompassed by a darkness
that might be smelt—and my circumscribed field of vision included
the grating in the opposite door; from whence presently issued a
faint cloud of cigarette smoke and a husky voice.

"What 'ave they got you for, Mr. 'Addon?"

"Eh?" said I, considerably startled. "I beg your pardon."

"Oh, it's all right," said the voice, "you needn't mind me. I'm
Milkey, I am."

I was horrified. This would never do. To be recognised by a
notorious rascal like Milkey would be absolutely fatal. It would
knock the bottom out of my "mistaken identity" defence at a blow.

"I don't quite understand," I said. "Did you say you were
Milkey?"

"Yus, I did," was the impatient answer.

"Really," said I. "How very unpleasant. I hope you won't catch
cold. You must ask them to rub you down when you get to
Holloway."

The rejoinder came in an angry growl.

"What are yer torkin' abaat, yer bloomin' silly—"

"Silence in there!" the brassy voice of the conductor commanded. "Stop that talking."

Milkey lowered his voice, but heightened the quality of his adjectives. As I persisted in misunderstanding him, he was good enough to furnish me with a perfectly frank estimate of my intellect and moral qualities, delivered in the very purest Anglo-Saxon. The late Professor Freeman would have been charmed. As to me, I was quite abashed. I knew I had my little defects of character, but I didn't think I was as bad as that.

As Milkey's conversational flourishes petered out, my interest in my surroundings revived. The late tenants of my compartment had bequeathed a certain reminiscent fragrance not particularly like that of old rose-leaves. But it was not with the past tenants that my attention was specially engaged; there were certain present inmates who began to introduce themselves modestly to my notice. I shuddered and wriggled uneasily. There was not even room to scratch oneself; a radical defect in the design of the van which ought not to have existed. The necessity of the proceeding should have been foreseen and provided for.

I speculated anxiously on the probable length of the journey, on the number of calls that the van would have to make, and the time it would take in getting to Holloway. Presently it stopped, and I assumed that we had brought up to take in more cargo. But I was mistaken. The constable entered the van, I heard a door unbolted, a passing figure excluded the light of my grating, and passed out. The process was repeated three times, and then my door opened.

"Out you come," said the constable; and out I came.

I stepped down on the pavement with a shock of surprise. This was not Holloway. Beyond the little group of spectators, I had a glimpse of a familiar thoroughfare, and before me was a small gateway, and an open gate, guarded by a couple of warders. The gate was massive and mediæval, crowned with rusty spikes; the gateway was set in a frowning façade of blackened stone. It was Newgate!

I ascended the steps, and plunged into the gloomy entrance in a state of profound surprise. I had supposed that Newgate was as extinct as the dodo, and should hardly have been more astonished if I had found myself entering the Tower of London by the Traitor's Gate. The outer gate clanged, its huge lock shot its colossal bolt, and our little procession of four started along the dark passage in charge of a couple of warders, who bore each a bunch of keys, any one of which might have been used to brain an ox.

I seemed to be in a dream. As I trudged along in the grim twilight and gate after gate was unlocked and then relocked after us, I found myself wondering into what sort of old-world dungeon I was to be thrust, and whether they would chain me to the wall.

Presently, however, we emerged from the old building into a wing constructed on more modern lines. My companions in misfortune were, one by one, deposited in cells on the ground floor, and I was conducted by one of the warders up a staircase to a gallery above.

"Here you are," said the warder, unlocking a door, and motioning me to enter. He looked me over doubtfully, and then asked, "Have you been in before?"

"No, I haven't," I said. "So, if you would kindly tell me anything I ought to know, I should be very greatly obliged."

The warder grinned. But he was a good-natured, genial man, and I dare say a polite prisoner who gives no trouble is somewhat of a relief. Besides, my appearance could hardly fail to impress him. He came into the cell, and, having fixed a numbered disc on my coat, explained to me the uses of the wretched appliances, and how I was expected to keep my apartment in order.

"I thought," said I, encouraged by his amiability, "that Newgate was closed long ago. I heard that it was to be pulled down."

"So it is," said he. "But after it was closed as an ordinary prison, it continued to be used during the Old Bailey Sessions to lodge the prisoners who were up for trial. It saved carrying them backwards and forwards to and from Holloway."

"But the Sessions aren't on now, are they?" I asked.

"No; they begin in four days' time. But we're all at sixes and sevens just now. Holloway is chockful on account of these strike riots, and Brixton isn't ready to open yet, so the overflow from Holloway has had to be stowed here. There are only three besides you, and I expect you are the last prisoners who will ever come to Newgate, because the place is going to be pulled down as soon as Brixton is opened. Quite an honour for you."

He shut up rather abruptly after this relaxation of discipline, and departed, banging the door on me.

Once more I was alone. The murmur of the streets filtered in faintly; impossible newsboys cried their wares in the softest pianissimo; an occasional engine whistle, muffled and far away, accentuated, by contrast, the sepulchral silence of the prison. The dim and ghostly sounds seemed to come in from another world; an infinitely distant world, a world of light and life, where people moved to and fro at their own wills, and no inexorable gaolers locked them, like precious documents, in an iron safe.

When should I re-enter that world? Ah, when?

> "Stone walls do not a prison make,
> Nor iron bars a cage!"

But, with the aid of a good, modern lock, a warder or two, and Black Maria waiting at the gate, they make an uncommonly good imitation.

12
THE HEAVENLY TWINS

I HAVE OFTEN thought that the position of a god must be far from a sinecure. To say nothing of the harassing responsibilities, the very miscellaneous nature of the duties appertaining to the post, and the absence of regular office hours, the appointment has many serious drawbacks. To take one only. Think of the annoyance that an omniscient individual must feel on having to view, as a mere inactive spectator, the imbecile proceedings of muddle-headed humanity! To be compelled to look on at a game of which he knows all the moves, to be able to see all the cards, and to see that everyone is playing wrong, and to be deprived, by Olympian etiquette, of the power to intervene and set the muddlers on the right track! It must really be supremely irritating.

I refer to the matter because it once fell to my lot to be placed in such a position myself; to hold, concealed in the recesses of my consciousness, the key that would have unlocked a great mystery, and to sit silent, gnashing my teeth, while that mystery was unraveled—all wrong—by an assembly of muddle-headed— But, as usual, I am beginning in the middle.

Let me go back to Newgate—in the spirit. Thank Heaven, I can never return there in the flesh. I spent three whole days in the grim old prison, and very anxious, miserable days they were. On the afternoon following my admission, I received a visit from an exceedingly spry young gentleman, with a most beautiful set of teeth and a fine open smile—it is interesting to note how frequently these two phenomena are associated. His hair was slightly thin on the

top, and he seemed to have a habit of wearing his hat indoors—
here is another of these strange correlations of function.

He seemed to be in a hurry. He danced into the cell and bumbled
about like a large blue-bottle, slapping a white-covered notebook and
a volume of *Tristram Shandy* down on the cell table, and requesting
me to "geg-geg-get my waistcoat unbuttoned." Then he lugged out
a stethoscope from some kind of stern-locker under his coat-tails,
and was in such a hurry that he brought out a toothbrush with it,
which fell on the floor, to his obvious dismay. And no wonder. You
don't want to sweep the floor of Newgate with your toothbrush.

When he had probed my internal mechanism with the stethoscope, and entered a few particulars in his notebook, he asked me
if I had any complaints to make. I ventured to remark that the
waiter had forgotten to come round with the cigars; whereupon he
snatched up his books and stethoscope, and danced out of the cell
without reply, banging the door after him. I was sorry to have
frightened him away. He was a pleasant-looking young gentleman,
and perfectly polite; and his teeth were really magnificent.

A little later a warder from Holloway called, bringing with him
a copper inking-slab, a roller, and a tube of fingerprint ink. I was a
little doubtful about allowing him to take my fingerprints, especially as the blue form on which he proposed to print them bore
the initials H.C.R. Why should an innocent man's fingerprints be
filed in the Habitual Criminals' Register? However, I thought it
politic to submit. My fingerprints were my sole defence, and if the
police had them I could insist on their being put in evidence.

Two more days dragged on their weary length. I took my allotted exercise in a dreary little yard in company with my three fel-
low-sufferers, watched by attendant warders and continually per-
secuted by Milkey. For my late purveyor strongly resented my refusal to recognise him, and, as he possessed in great perfection
the "old lag's" accomplishment of talking without moving his lips,
he was a constant source of trouble to the rest of us.

The very first time that we went out to exercise, he treated us
to a display of his powers as a ventriloquist that nearly got us into
hot water.

"Don't know me, don't yer?" said Milkey, staring straight before him, and not moving a muscle of his face. "Bloomin' sneak of a fence, tryin' to pass 'isself off as a toff—"

"Stop that talking, Smith!" said the warder, in a stern voice. "You know you're not allowed to speak here."

"Oo's a-torkin'?" growled Milkey, with the immovable face of a hideous figurehead. "It's the birds a-singin' in the trees. That's what you heard."

"That was you, Atkins!" the warder exclaimed fiercely. "I saw your lips move. I've spoken to you before. Now, don't let me have to speak again."

"Oo arst yer to speak?" demanded Milkey, as rigid as a graven image. "Got too much lip, you 'ave. Why don't yer keep quiet?"

"I warn you, Smith," said the warder, "if you don't keep silence, I shall report you for punishment."

And so on, during the whole of the exercise hours. Milkey was a regular thorn in our flesh, and it was only a lurking suspicion in the mind of the warder as to the true state of the case that saved us from being put on the report.

The fourth morning of my incarceration brought a change. The warder who brought my breakfast informed me that the sessions opened to-day, and that I was one of the first batch to be tried. This was good hearing, but it put me in no end of a twitter. I should probably know my fate before the evening; but what was that fate to be?

An hour or two later the cell door opened and the warder beckoned me out. I followed him down the stairs and found the other three prisoners toeing a line in the corridor. I took my place at the end of the line, and at the command "Right turn!" we slewed round and marched off to meet our doom. Through various passages we walked in silence, save for Milkey's obscure mutterings, and presently came out into a narrow, paved yard, roofed in with iron bars like a huge aviary.

This was the famous "Birdcage Walk"—the murderers' burial-ground—and, as we tramped slowly through it, my eye traveled over the sinister initials carved on the left-hand wall. "Ship *Flowery*

Land," I read, near the middle of the wall, and dimly recalled the old story of the *Flowery Land* pirates; and meanwhile Milkey obligingly supplied details in a ventriloquial mumble.

"Now, Smith," said the warder severely; "talking again!" He fixed a reproving eye on me as the other warder unlocked the massive iron-bound gate at the end. We passed out of the ill-omened cage, through which many a poor devil has walked to meet the black cap and the chaplain's "Amen!" and I think we all breathed more freely when the gate banged behind us.

Presently we descended some steps and entered a subterranean passage, ill-savoured and dark, and lined by old-fashioned cell-doors. Here we halted while some of the doors were unlocked, and the inmates of the cells, prisoners who had that morning been brought from Holloway, were haled forth to join our procession. It was too dark to see what they were like, but I observed that they were four or five in number.

With this new accession to our strength, we again, moved forward until we came to a winding flight of worn and dirty stairs, up which we stumbled into the daylight. The change was quite theatrical. The stairs led straight up into the dock, and, as I came out of the well like a stage demon, to take my place at the end of the line of prisoners, the scene burst upon me with a suddenness that was quite startling. After the solitude and silence of the prison, the confined space of my cell and the dimness of the underground passage, the light and spaciousness of the court and the throng of strangers who filled it had a quite bewildering effect.

Immediately opposite was the bench, pervaded by a general sense of redness. The cushions were red, the judge's canopy was lined with red, and the judge himself, who looked like a rather showy sort of waxwork, wore a scarlet robe. The colour effect was unpleasantly suggestive.

I ran my eye over the assembly; the oddly-dressed functionaries on the bench, the prosaic-looking occupants of the jury box, the knot of counsel—reproductions in black and white of the judge—the attorneys and reporters, the long-robed ushers, the grey-wigged clerk, the City Lands Commissioners, the jurors in waiting, and the sprinkling of police officers; and I found it far more impressive than agreeable.

The proceedings were well under way before I had recovered from my bewilderment. I had a confused consciousness of the Clerk of Arraigns reading from a paper and addressing us severally by name, and I noticed with surprise that he addressed me twice (the second time in connection with a candlestick "of the goods and chattels of Edward, Lord Barmington"—that gave me a nasty jar), and that when I said "Not guilty" someone else said "Not guilty" too. What business was it of his? And how could he know? Then came the swearing-in of the jury, a tedious affair, involving everlastingly repeated references to "our Sovereign Lord the King and the prisoners at the bar," a sort of diabolical litany that seemed to want an organ accompaniment and a choir to sing "Amen!"

About halfway through this ceremony I happened to look at the judge, and was a little disconcerted to find him regarding me intently and with a very odd expression of surprise. It was, indeed, not unnatural. I don't suppose he had often seen a person of my appearance in the dock, though queer things must happen in a criminal court. He looked at me through his spectacles and over them, and finally took them off to see how I looked to the unaided or unobstructed vision. And the curious expression of half-amused perplexity gathered on his face as he looked from me to the other prisoners, and then back again to me. No doubt the contrast was very absurd.

The judge was not the only person who noticed it. Chancing to look towards the counsel's benches, I observed that one of the banisters was staring at me open-mouthed, and, as I caught his eye, he broke into an undeniable grin, and nudged an adjacent colleague. The second counsel looked, swept his eye along the line of prisoners, looked at me again, grinned, and nudged another neighbour. The sensation spread until all the counsel were, with one accord, gazing at me and comparing me with my companions in misfortune. There was evidently something ludicrous in the comparison, for they discussed it with broad smiles, and one or two laughed outright, which struck me as slightly indecorous, considering the place and the solemn occasion. But the ordinary barrister is a somewhat irresponsible creature.

The sensation, however, was not limited to the counsel. The jurors, who had been sworn, had clearly noticed me, and were talking together eagerly with their eyes fixed on me, and the same odd mixture of surprise and amusement on their faces. The functionaries on the bench looked at me and whispered together; the jurors in waiting, observing the general attention, craned round from their corner to get a look at the dock; and the reporters, in their box, positively fermented with excitement. I was quite interested.

When the jury was sworn, the usher addressed a few eloquent remarks to nobody in particular on the subject of "treason, murder, felony, or misdemeanour, committed or done by them or any of them," and wound up by pointing out that "the prisoners at the bar stood on their deliverance." As a matter of fact, one of them stood on my toe, and I had to mention the matter to him, and got a prod in the back from the warder and a whispered request for "silence."

The usher's address or proclamation was followed by a solemn pause. The entire court, even including the sphinx-like Clerk of Arraigns, seemed to be gazing at me. The circumstance was so noticeable that the police superintendent standing below the dock looked up to ascertain the cause, and then backed away stealthily down the court to get a better view, until, catching his heel in some obstruction, he staggered wildly backwards and fell into the arms of an usher; which relieved the general tension and caused universal gratification.

Then the judge spoke, with his eyes still glued on me. "What is the name of that prisoner on the left?" indicating me.

The warder communicated with the usher, who then replied: "John Smith, my lord."

The judge ran his eye down a paper on his desk and looked up.

"And the name of the second prisoner on the right?" he asked.

Again there was a whispered consultation, and the usher answered, "His name is also John Smith, my lord," at which everybody laughed; and it really was rather absurd. One of us might have had more imagination.

The judge was highly amused; and as for the counsel, they might have been viewing the antics of Charley's Aunt.

"How long have these men been in custody?" the judge asked.

"They were both arrested on the ninth, my lord," was the reply; at which everybody laughed again. And it *was* a quaint coincidence.

"Have they both been detained at Holloway since their committal?" pursued the judge.

"No, my lord," was the answer. "The man on the left has been kept at Newgate; the other man has been at Holloway."

"Ha!" said the judge, "that probably accounts for it." (Accounts for what? I asked myself). "Now, I see that one John Smith is charged with having stolen a candlestick. Which one is that?"

"That is the man from Holloway, my lord," was the answer; and a very proper answer too.

"The other John Smith," continued the judge, "is charged with breaking into and entering the dwelling house of Jemima Dalby."

"That is the man from Newgate, my lord."

"Very well," said the judge; then, turning to the counsel for the Crown, he asked, "What is the general character of the evidence against these two men?"

"They both appear to have been seen and identified, my lord," replied the counsel.

"Does the charge in both cases rest upon identification alone?"

"No, m'lord. There are fingerprints as well."

"What!" exclaimed the judge, "have they both got the same fingerprints?" Whereupon there was a general laugh, and I laughed myself. It was getting quite amusing.

"No, my lord," said the counsel. "The fingerprints are those of Holloway Smith. The other man's fingerprints have been taken and examined at Scotland Yard, but they are not known there."

"Then," said the judge, "I must ask a question which ought not to be asked at this stage, but which is unavoidable under the circumstances. Are there any previous convictions against the John Smith from Holloway?"

"It is believed, m'lord," said the counsel, "that he is a convict named Barrett, who escaped from Ashbury Gaol about a year ago, but the identification is not quite certain, as that prisoner escaped before his fingerprints were taken, and he then had black hair."

"But," said the judge, "if he escaped before his fingerprints were taken, how comes it that his fingerprints are known to the police?"

The counsel glanced at his notes and answered:

"It appears, m'lord, that the prisoner left some very distinct impressions of his fingers on a candle which came into the possession of the police."

"Was that at Lord Barmington's house?" his lordship asked.

"No, m'lord. At Lord Barmington's house he left prints of his fingers on a silver salver, but they were already known then; in fact, that was how the police identified him with that particular burglary. The candle was found—er"—here the counsel put on his pince-nez and examined his brief—"was found in the house of a Miss Dalby, which he had entered."

"Miss Dalby!" exclaimed the judge. "But it is the other man—Newgate Smith—who is charged with entering Miss Dalby's house."

The counsel hastily bent over his brief with his hand to his pince-nez. "Your lordship is perfectly correct," said he, "but—er—it seems—er—in fact, it appears that both men are charged with entering Miss Dalby's house. It would seem as if there had been some mistake or confusion of two different persons."

"It would indeed," said the judge, "and it is very necessary that the mistake should be rectified at once. Let the other prisoners be removed. We must settle this question of identity before anything else is done."

The other prisoners were marched down into the underground passage, and the two John Smiths stood alone in the dock, save for the warder seated at his desk. During the last few minutes a light had been gradually breaking on me. Now, as I looked at my namesake and our eyes met in mutual recognition, it blazed up into dazzling effulgence. For "Holloway Smith" was Tom Nagget!

The rascal had been impersonating me again, and the Lord only knows what a record of crime he had been establishing for me while I had been away. I must do him the justice to say that his impersonation was as nearly perfect as it could be. He had bleached his

hideous black hair and eyebrows with peroxide until they were almost identical in appearance with the spun gold that Nature had
adorned me withal. It was no wonder that, as we stood side by side
at the warder's command, a murmur of astonishment arose from
the court. Tweedledum and Tweedledee in the dock must have been
something of a novelty.

The judge looked from one of us to the other with positive fascination, and chuckled delightedly.

"Really," said he, "it is most astonishing! The two men are absolutely indistinguishable. They are perfect duplicates. It is the
most amazing *lusus naturæ* that I have ever seen—that is," he
added, "if it is really a *lusus naturæ*—if it owes, I mean, nothing to
art. But you mentioned, Mr. Grayling, that the prisoner who escaped from Ashbury Gaol had black hair. May I ask if the hair of
these two men has been examined?"

"I have no instructions to that effect, m'lord," replied the counsel.

"Then," said the judge, "I think it should be done now. Perhaps
the Medical Officer of Holloway, who, I see, is present, would make
the necessary examination and report."

Here the spry young medico who had visited me in Newgate
made his appearance from some corner of the court, and was admitted to the dock. He was still sprightly and debonair, though
unavoidably shorn of his hat. But he was less bumbly and more
sedate; there wasn't so much of the blue-bottle about him. He displayed his teeth in great perfection when he was confronted by the
Heavenly Twins, and requested us, very politely, to turn up our
sleeves.

I complied readily. I am, in fact, rather proud of my arms. They
are muscular without being knobbly, and the fair, silken skin is
entirely undisfigured with hair save for a delicate golden down.
Some people call that condition effeminate, but I don't agree; man
is not supposed to be a furry animal. So I rolled up my sleeves
above the elbow and held out my arms with modest pride.

Not so Tom Nagget. That unfortunate malefactor knew his
weakness, and just turned back his coat cuffs enough to show a pair
of dirty wristbands. But the doctor wasn't to be put off in that way.

"Right up above the elbows, please," said he, and Tom had no choice but to obey. Unwillingly he rolled back his shirtsleeves—and gave the whole show away at once. For poor Tom's arms were like those of a monkey, covered with hideous black hair. It was a disgusting spectacle. I felt quite sorry for Tom.

But, conclusive as it was, the doctor was not satisfied. He was a very thorough young man. First he passed his hand over my head and picked up a lock of hair which he twiddled between his finger and thumb, passing on to Tom and repeating the proceeding, much to Tom's discomfort. Then he rummaged in a posterior pocket somewhere under his coat-tails (he seemed to keep all his portable property there, being apparently provided with a sort of dorsal pouch like that of a wrong-sided kangaroo), and I hoped he would bring out another toothbrush.

But he didn't. What he eventually produced from the lucky-bag was a pocket lens, and with this he minutely examined the roots of my hair and eyebrows, and having, with my permission, pulled out a hair from my head, he viewed its roots against the light. Then he went on to Tom Nagget and repeated the proceeding, excepting that Tom wouldn't let him pull out a hair—said "he wasn't going to be made bald for anybody." However, it didn't seem to matter. The doctor put away his lens and bustled off to the witness-box with the air of a man who knew all about it.

"You have examined the two prisoners?" said the judge when the doctor had been sworn; and the witness having replied that he had, the judge asked: "What is the result of your examination?"

"I find," said the doctor, "that the prisoner on the left"—indicating me—"is a naturally blonde man. His hair and eyebrows appear to be in their natural state and not to have been treated by any dye, or bleach, or anything that might alter their colour or appearance. The other prisoner"—here he pointed to Tom Nagget—"is a dark-haired man. His eyebrows and the hair on his scalp have been bleached by some chemical—apparently peroxide of hydrogen—but the natural dark colour is visible at the roots."

"That is a very important fact," said the judge; and when he had asked the doctor one or two questions in verification of his statement, he continued: "The next question that we have to settle before we proceed to try either of these prisoners is, which of them is the one to whom the statements of the respective prosecutors actually apply? In view of the astonishing resemblance between the two men, and of what looks like an attempt at personation, it is necessary that the persons who have identified them respectively should see them together. The witnesses to identity had better, therefore, be called now."

The first witness who was called was Aunt Jemima. She paddled briskly down the court with a confident and resolute air, but when she got into the witness-box and turned her eyes on the dock, her jaw dropped considerably. In fact, I could see that she was absolutely stumped. But she wasn't going to admit it. Not she! There are some people who can't say "I don't know," and Aunt Jemima was one of them.

"On the ninth of this month, Miss Dalby," said the counsel for the crown, "you gave a man into custody on a charge of burglary. Do you see that man in court?"

Aunt Jemima looked anxiously from me to Tom Nagget, and from Tom Nagget to me, and said: "Yes, I do."

"Kindly point him out," said the counsel.

For one agonising moment Aunt Jemima's eyes oscillated to and fro like those of a mechanical figure on a Dutch clock; then she shot out an accusing forefinger at Tom Nagget.

"That's the man!" said she.

The counsel showed no surprise, but merely asked: "Are you sure that is the man?"

"Quite sure. I should know him among a thousand."

Evidently Aunt Jemima was like the late Captain Bunsby. What she said she stuck to.

"Where, and at what hour, did you give him into custody?" the counsel asked.

"On the Old Swan Pier, at ten minutes past nine in the morning."

Here Tom Nagget began to protest, but the judge silenced him.

"You will be heard presently," said he.

Following Aunt Jemima were the constable, the sergeant, and the inspector whom I had admitted to her house on that eventful evening. Of course, they had no doubts. They had identified Tom at Holloway; they knew about the fingerprints, and they had heard what had passed in court. So they all plumped for "Holloway Smith."

Then came Lord Barmington, and a rare twitter he was in when he saw Tweedledum and Tweedledee in the dock. I believe he thought at first that there was something wrong with his eyesight, for I saw him rub his eyes and blink. Then he was sworn, and the examination commenced.

"You identified a man at Marlborough Street Police-court on the ninth," said the counsel. "Can you tell us which of those two men is the one?"

Lord Barmington blinked at us dubiously.

"They are very much alike," said he, "but I am inclined to think that the man on the left is the one; or perhaps it may have been the one on the right. And yet—"

"Oh, come, Lord Barmington," said the counsel, "this will not do! Can you, or can you not, say which is the man you identified?"

"Well, d'you know, I'm afraid I really can't. They are so *very* alike."

This closed the preliminary inquiry, and I had some hopes that I should be released without further trouble. But the judge was of opinion that my case must go to the jury, and he directed the counsel for the prosecution to proceed with the case against me in the regular manner. Tom Nagget was removed to the cells, and the counsel made his opening statement.

"The prisoner, John Smith, is charged with breaking into and entering the dwelling-house of Jemima Dalby on the sixth of October last, at about half-past eleven o'clock at night. There are some singular features in the case, but as they will appear in the evidence I shall not recapitulate them now, but proceed to call the witnesses."

He glanced at the usher, who called out "Jemima Dalby!" and Aunt Jemima came forth from some corner behind the dock and re-entered the witness-box. The counsel requested her to tell the jury what she remembered of the burglary, and she plunged, without pre-amble, into the story, to which I listened with the keenest interest.

"On the sixth of October, at half-past eleven at night, I was awakened by a noise."

"What sort of noise?" the counsel asked.

"Oh, an ordinary sort of noise! You see, I was asleep before I woke, and when you are asleep you don't notice noises particu-larly. Well, when I woke I listened, and then I heard my cockatoo calling for a hansom."

"Dear me!" exclaimed the judge. "Did you, really?"

"Yes. And after that he called loudly for a pot of beer. And then I knew there was something wrong. He only calls for a hansom when he is very excited, and for beer only under the most excep-tional circumstances."

"In the ordinary way," said the judge, "I suppose he is content with lemonade and a four-wheeler?"

But Aunt Jemima only sniffed, and went on with her narrative:

"So I got out of bed and put on my flan—"

"Never mind what you put on, Miss Dalby," said the counsel, "though I'm sure you looked very charming in it. It isn't of any consequence."

"It isn't now," snapped Aunt Jemima, "but it was then! How-ever, I lit my candle and came downstairs. The gas was alight in the dining-room, and when I pushed the door open and looked in I saw him."

"Saw whom, Miss Dalby?"

"Him!" she replied tartly, pointing at me.

"Indeed!" said the counsel, clearly as much surprised as I was. "Well, you looked in and saw the prisoner. Are you quite sure the prisoner is the person you saw?"

"Of course I am. Quite certain. I should know him among ten thousand."

"Yes. And did you speak to him? Did you ask him what he was doing there?"

"No. I could see what he was doing. He was drinking my beer. But he spoke to me. He asked me what I was doing in his dining-room, if you ever heard such impudence. And then he snatched up the poker, and I ran down to the coal-cellar and bolted myself in. Then three idiots of policemen came and pretended I was a bur-glar—in my own house, mind you—and when I came out I found they had let the man go."

"Did he steal anything?"

"No; but he left a candle with his fingerprints on it."

"How do you know they were his?"

"Well, they weren't mine, so they must have been his."

This was the sum of Aunt Jemima's evidence. She was suc-ceeded by the constable whom I had been compelled to admit to the house, and who gave his evidence with some embarrassment.

"On the sixth of October, at eleven-thirty p.m., I was called to the house of Miss Dalby."

"Who called you?" the counsel asked.

The constable turned a lively pink.

"I was called by a man who turned out to be a burglar," said he.

"Is the prisoner the man who called you in?"

"No, he is not."

"Are you sure he is not?"

"I am quite sure he is not," the constable replied. And to his great relief, and mine, he was hustled out of the box.

The next witness was the inspector whom I had invited into Aunt Jemima's house. Like the constable, he spoke with diffidence and did not seem to enjoy himself, though he received some moral support from a glass case which he handed to the usher. This case interested me considerably. It contained a candle in a flat candle-stick, a tumbler and a beer-bottle, the two latter being dusted over with white powder. I had seen those articles before, and now hailed them affectionately as friends in need.

"On the sixth of October at eleven-forty-five p.m.," the inspec-tor began, "I entered the house of Miss Dalby in company with Sergeant Guffet."

"How did you gain entrance to the house?" asked the counsel.

"I was let in by a man who represented himself as the owner of the house, but who was in reality a burglar." (Here a universal snigger arose from the court and the inspector turned the colour of a beetroot.)

"Is the prisoner the man who let you in?"

"No, he is not."

"Have you, since that night, seen the man who let you in?"

"Yes, I saw him on the tenth instant at Marlborough Police Court."

"When you were in Miss Dalby's house, did you discover any clue to the identity of the burglar?"

"Yes; I found on the dining-room mantelpiece a candle which bore the very distinct impressions of the fingers and thumb of a left hand. On the table I found a tumbler and a beer-bottle, on both of which were very clear prints of the fingers and thumb of a right hand. I took possession of these articles and conveyed them, my-self, to Scotland Yard and handed them to an officer of the Finger-print Department. Those are the articles in that glass case."

The case was passed up to the judge, who inspected the en-closed specimens curiously while the inspector stepped down from the box and gave place to a gentleman whom I had not seen be-fore, and who answered to the name of Singleton. The prosecuting counsel opened fire on him as soon as he had been sworn, and the judge passed the glazed case down and settled himself to listen.

"You are one of the officers of the Fingerprint Department, I believe, Mr. Singleton?"

"I am."

"Do you know anything about the articles in this glass case?"

"Yes. They were brought to me on the seventh of October last by Inspector Barber. I examined them and found that they bore a complete set of fingerprints, ten different impressions, correspond-ing to the ten digits of a pair of hands. All the impressions were remarkably clear and perfect. I compared them with our register and found that they belonged to some person unknown to us. I then photographed the fingerprints and attached the photographs to a blank form which I filed in the register."

"Are those impressions which you found on the candle and other articles the fingerprints of the prisoner?"

"No. I have here, on this form, the prisoner's fingerprints. They were taken at Newgate on the tenth instant. They do not bear the slightest resemblance to the fingerprints on the candle, the tumbler, or the bottle."

At this point the foreman of the jury rose and indicated that his colleagues had heard enough evidence and had come to a decision on the case. The witness then stepped down from the box, the judge asked me if I wished to say anything—to which I replied that I did not—and the grey-wigged Clerk of Arraigns stood up in his pew and faced the jury.

"Are you all agreed upon your verdict, gentlemen?" he asked.

"We are," replied the foreman.

"What do you say, gentlemen? Is the prisoner guilty or not guilty?"

"Not guilty," the foreman answered.

I suppose it was a foregone conclusion, but, all the same, when the words were spoken, I felt my knees tremble in the most alarming manner and the court seemed to shimmer as if seen through rippling water. But I leaned heavily on the edge of the dock and pulled myself together in time to catch the judge's address.

"A very proper verdict," said he. "It was clearly a case of mistaken identity and a very instructive one. It furnishes a warning to all who may be called upon to swear to the identity of suspected persons, and it offers an admirable illustration of the great value of fingerprint evidence. I congratulate you, Smith—if that is really your name—on a very fortunate escape; and I trust, for your sake, that there are no more members of the great Smith family who bear such an inconvenient resemblance to you."

A murmur of laughter arose from the court, and I smiled a sickly smile. Then the door of the dock was opened, and I came down the steps, feeling uncommonly shaky and hardly able to realise the sudden turn in the wheel of fortune. I was free! The Law had no terrors for me now. The sword of Damocles hung over me no longer. The Fingerprint Department had obligingly hooked it up securely to the ceiling, to let it down again presently for some other poor devil's benefit.

My first impulse was to rush forth into the open air, but curiosity held me back. I wanted to see what was going to happen to the perfidious Thomas. So I got permission from the clerk to stay and hear the case, and took my seat as a spectator. But it was a maddening experience. There I sat, knowing all the facts of the case and listening to their balderdash until I could have stood on the table and screeched. I had to hear that donkey of an expert expound the infallibility of his silly system while all those guffins sat round like a lot of half-witted owls and solemnly took it in for absolute gospel.

Of course, they brought out my prepared candle again and showed Tom his fingerprints on it; and when the poor devil swore, with tears in his eyes, that he had never seen the candle and never heard of Aunt Jemima, the judge waxed quite facetious, and told him what a pity it was that he hadn't called some witness whose fingers gave the same print as his own. It was perfectly incredible. In all that court there was not a single person who was not totally obsessed by the great Fingerprint Superstition. The simple and obvious plan of duplicating fingerprints never seemed to occur to any of them. Why, the judge actually suggested—as a wild joke—what had really happened; and even then he didn't see it.

"You seem to imply," he said, "that you may have put these prints on your own candle at home and that some burglar may have taken the candle and left it at Miss Dalby's house. And I suppose we are to understand that the other man wore gloves so that his own fingerprints shouldn't get on the candle." Whereupon all the bobbies in the court laughed aloud. But it was no laughing matter for Tom.

At last, unable to stand it any longer, I got up and went out. I was sorry for Tom, but he had played and he had lost, and now he had got to pay. But he didn't do so badly. Later in the day I bought an evening paper, and read that he had got off with three years, which was really less than he deserved.

Once outside the court, I pranced along with the gait of an antelope, reveling in my new-found freedom and safety. Insensibly I drifted northward, stopping once only to send off an explanatory letter-card to Father Jeffrey; and as I went I shaped a course for the conduct of my future. I had had a lesson, and that lesson should not be wasted. Life, like a lady's frock, looks best on the side that is not seamy. I would have done with my shady curio-dealer's business. My predecessor there was an unmitigated fence, the place was known to the police, and the circumstances of the business offered a premium to dishonesty. I would hand the stock bodily to some auctioneer and wash my hands of the whole affair.

Thus I reflected somewhat disjointedly as I looked down from the omnibus roof on to the crowded pavements. My spirits rose higher as I more fully realised my freedom. Like a sparrow that has found an unexpected hole in the bird-catcher's cage, I felt it, at first, too good to be true. But now I spread my wings and tasted of the joy of living; and I meant henceforth to look at the cage from the outside.

The house at Poplar Grove was a seedy-looking affair, I thought, as I stood at the side door sorting out my keys. The bunch had grown a trifle since I started on my travels, for it still held the keys of St. Cecily's, but I found the latch-key, and inserted it. As the door swung inwards, it seemed to creak with unwonted loudness, and my step in the passage called forth cavernous echoes. I walked through into the parlour that had been called the "back shop." Eureka! The place was as empty as a museum egg. There was not a stick left. My business premises had been gutted to the very cobwebs.

Of course, it was Judith Lyon. True daughter of the guileful Jacob, she had heard of my arrest—or, more probably, Tom's—and had concluded that I was in for a "stretch."

And this was her return for all my kindness and good-fellowship!

Oh! Woman! woman! (Or, as my friend McAlarney will pronounce it—Wumman! Wumman!)

EPILOGUE
SUSANNAH'S DOWRY

THE JOY THAT obtains among the angels over the one sinner that repenteth (with a certain apparent indifference to the chronically righteous) is not fully shared by the mere man of the world. Mr. Worldly Wiseman, in this, as in other matters, is not in accord with angelic views; and I suspect that even the most piously inclined banker or solicitor would not elect to fill the places of trust in his office with repentant sinners.

Nevertheless, to a person like myself, with a slightly piebald moral record, it is a great satisfaction to reflect on the superlative merit of tardy repentance as compared with mere monotonously good conduct. For Danby Croker is a reformed character. He has repented; not in sackcloth and ashes (which is a dirty and disagreeable method), but in becoming costume and amidst such delicate surroundings as are congruous with his refined personality. As I write the closing lines of these records of an ill-spent life, seated— in a delightful little elbow-chair by old Dick Heppelwhite—at my writing-table (a charming piece by Shearer, quite in his happiest manner) by the open window, through which I look out on the score or two of acres that form my modest demesne, I reflect sorrowfully— But here I am, falling into my old mistake of beginning at the wrong end. Let me take up the thread of my narrative.

It was about three months after that little episode at the Old Bailey. A soft breeze twiddled the weathercock of St. Cecily's gently to and fro, and the mellow autumn sunlight fell on the old dial, thereby enabling it to inform the world at large that it was half-past ten. I had a special and immediate interest in the dial at that moment, and read once more, with renewed pleasure, the words of its quaint inscription

> "Grow olde along with mee:
> 1607: The Best is yet to be."

The chappie who carved that inscription knew what he was about. I was going to prove it anon.

There were three persons in the churchyard; perhaps I should say three and a half, for Priscilla was just vanishing through the wicket, sniveling into her pocket-handkerchief—I didn't see what she had to snivel about, and don't now; but Lord! as old Pepys would say, to think how these elderly females will blubber about nothing! The three persons were Father Jeffrey, Susannah, and myself. Susannah was not in tears. Not a bit of it. She knew which side her bread was buttered.

"Well," said Father Jeffrey, peeling off his surplice, and hanging it on a tombstone, "now you're married I wish you joy." Here he pulled up rather abruptly—but none too soon—and punctuated the remark with a slightly embarrassed "Hem!" Quite right, too! There is enough of that sort of thing in the Marriage Service, without importing it into general conversation.

"But," he added, after a pause, "I don't quite see what you two young idiots are going to live upon."

"Oh, that's all right," Susannah replied jauntily. "Lyd—Danby's awfully clever, you know, and I can do chip-carving and paper flowers, and—and all that sort of thing."

Father Jeffrey waved her away with an indulgent smile.

"Seriously, though, Lydia—my boy," said he, "what do you propose to do?"

"I don't know that I propose to do anything," I answered, "but live very comfortably on the interest of my wife's property."

There was a moment of speechless amazement which I enjoyed exceedingly, and then Susannah remarked:

"You must be a very economical young man if you're going to live comfortably on the interest of four hundred and thirty pounds."

"But I'm not," said I. "My proposal is to realise the family jewels and live on the proceeds."

"Oh, don't talk such nonsense, Danby," said Susannah; "and it's no use trying to pull our legs, because we know you."

But if Susannah did know me, Father Jeffrey knew me better; and he now looked at me doubtfully out of the corner of his eye, and scratched his chin (he had a habit of scratching his chin when perplexed, and opening his mouth to facilitate the process. The effect was very quaint).

"I wonder what new bedevilment you are up to now, my son?" he said thoughtfully; and, turning to Susannah, he asked: "Are there any family jewels?"

"I've got a garnet brooch," said she. "There's nothing else that I know of."

But Father Jeffrey was suspicious. He knew my little ways of old.

"Come now, Lydia—my boy," said he, "just explain yourself. Where is the property that you are talking about?"

"At the present moment," I said, "it's up there in the sundial, but I'm going to get it down now."

That "knocked" them both, as the vernacular of the Old Kent Road has it. They seated themselves on a flat tombstone and waited humbly and without comment for further developments.

We all like a little theatrical display now and again, and I confess that I am not immune from this very human weakness. I had made all necessary preparations for what poor Tom Nagget would have called the "denoomong." A geological hammer and chisel were in my pockets; a small tin of cement was hidden in the vestry; I had seen that the ladder was handy, and had stowed a gardener's trowel in the porch.

The latter came into requisition first. Stepping over to the well-remembered tombstone, I lifted the turf and disinterred the stone head of Father Time, which I placed in the hand of my quondam guardian; who stared at it speechlessly, and from it to the counterfeit head above the dial. Next, I placed the ladder against the tower, and, climbing up to the level of the dial, seized the cement head of the figure of Time and drew the hammer from my pocket. A careful tap with the handle cracked the head off neatly at the neck, and down I came with my prize in my hand. Father Jeffrey and Susannah craned forward eagerly as I held the head in my hand and balanced the hammer ready to strike. With careful precision, I gave a smart blow with the sharp edge of the hammer; the head splintered into three large fragments, disclosing a cavity in which lay a little tissue-paper packet. I tore open the packet, and, daintily picking out the great blue stone, held it up, all flashing and scintillating in the sunlight.

"Gobblessmysoul!" exclaimed Father Jeffrey.

I laid it in the palm of his hand, and he gazed at it awhile in silent wonder, while, as for Susannah, she pored over it with—I regret to say—her mouth open as if it were an oyster, and she was about to consume it at a single gulp.

"But, my son," Father Jeffrey at length asked, "what is this, and where did it come from?"

"This," I replied melodramatically, "is the Ludovici Diamond."

I gave them a little time to recover—which they didn't—and, meanwhile, I reconstituted Father Time with a little cement and his original head. Then I related the moving history of the discovery of the diamond in the old fiddle. They listened enthralled, and, even for some time after I had finished, neither spoke, but both sat gazing at the "devil's bauble" sparkling in Father Jeffrey's hand. At last Susannah looked up at me with an admiring glance that somehow recalled the night of the Great Raid.

"I don't see, Danby dear," said she, "how you make out that it's mine."

"We needn't go into that," said Father Jeffrey. "'With all my worldly goods I thee endow,' you know. But the question is, was it Peter Mockett's?"

"I don't think we need go into that either," said I, hastily picking the stone out of his hand and slipping it into my pocket. And I didn't. Neither did Mr. Theophilus B. Guffey, who eventually bought it of me for a prince's ransom, as a wedding gift to his aristocratic but impecunious bride. It now diffuses envy and discord through the United States of America, but its equivalent, invested in gilt-edged securities, lubricates very pleasantly the wheels of a deserving man's life.

My modest *pied-à-terre* overlooks the Medway, and is within a quarter of a mile of the Rectory; a pleasant circumstance for us all, since Father Jeffrey and Susannah are devoted to one another; and I may mention that they both foolishly persist in calling me Lydia even unto this day.

A PRINCE OF SWINDLERS

GUY BOOTHBY

PREFACE

By the Right Honourable the Earl of Amberley,
*for many years Governor of the Colony of New South Wales,
and sometime Viceroy of India*

AFTER NO SMALL amount of deliberation, I have come to the conclusion that it is only fit and proper I should set myself right with the world in the matter of the now famous 18— swindles. For, though I have never been openly accused of complicity in those miserable affairs, yet I cannot rid myself of the remembrance that it was I who introduced the man who perpetrated them to London society, and that in more than one instance I acted, innocently enough, Heaven knows, as his *Deus ex machinâ*, in bringing about the very results he was so anxious to achieve. I will first allude, in a few words, to the year in which the crimes took place, and then proceed to describe the events that led to my receiving the confession which has so strangely and unexpectedly come into my hands.

Whatever else may be said on the subject, one thing at least is certain—it will be many years before London forgets that season of festivity. The joyous occasion which made half the sovereigns of Europe our guests for weeks on end, kept foreign princes among us until their faces became as familiar to us as those of our own aristocracy, rendered the houses in our fashionable quarters unobtainable for love or money, filled our hotels to repletion, and produced daily pageants the like of which few of us have ever seen or imagined, can hardly fail to go down to posterity as one of the

223

most notable in English history. Small wonder, therefore, that the
wealth, then located in our great metropolis, should have attracted
swindlers from all parts of the globe.

That it should have fallen to the lot of one who has always
prided himself on steering clear of undesirable acquaintances, to
introduce to his friends one of the most notorious adventurers our
capital has ever seen, seems like the irony of fate. Perhaps, however, if I begin by showing how cleverly our meeting was contrived,
those, who would otherwise feel inclined to censure me, will pause
before passing judgment, and will ask themselves whether they
would not have walked into the snare as unsuspectingly as I did.

It was during the last year of my term of office as Viceroy, and
while I was paying a visit to the Governor of Bombay, that I decided upon making a tour of the northern Provinces, beginning with
Peshawur, and winding up with the Maharajah of Malar-Kadir. As
the latter potentate is so well known, I need not describe him. His
forcible personality, his enlightened rule, and the progress his state
has made within the last ten years, are well known to every student of the history of our magnificent Indian Empire.

My stay with him was a pleasant finish to an otherwise monotonous business, for his hospitality has a world-wide reputation.
When I arrived he placed his palace, his servants, and his stables
at my disposal to use just as I pleased. My time was practically my
own. I could be as solitary as a hermit if I so desired; on the other
hand, I had but to give the order, and five hundred men would
cater for my amusement. It seems therefore the more unfortunate
that to this pleasant arrangement I should have to attribute the
calamities which it is the purpose of this series of stories to narrate.

On the third morning of my stay I woke early. When I had examined my watch I discovered that it wanted an hour of daylight,
and, not feeling inclined to go to sleep again, I wondered how I
should employ my time until my servant should bring me my *chota
hazri*, or early breakfast. On proceeding to my window I found a
perfect morning, the stars still shining, though in the east they were
paling before the approach of dawn. It was difficult to realize that
in a few hours the earth which now looked so cool and wholesome

would be lying, burnt up and quivering, beneath the blazing Indian sun.

I stood and watched the picture presented to me for some minutes, until an overwhelming desire came over me to order a horse and go for a long ride before the sun should make his appearance above the jungle trees. The temptation was more than I could resist, so I crossed the room and, opening the door, woke my servant, who was sleeping in the antechamber. Having bidden him find a groom and have a horse saddled for me, without rousing the household, I returned and commenced my toilet. Then, descending by a private staircase to the great courtyard, I mounted the animal I found awaiting me there, and set off.

Leaving the city behind me I made my way over the new bridge with which His Highness has spanned the river, and, crossing the plain, headed towards the jungle, that rises like a green wall upon the other side. My horse was a *waler* of exceptional excellence, as every one who knows the Maharajah's stable will readily understand, and I was just in the humour for a ride. But the coolness was not destined to last long, for, by the time I had left the second village behind me, the stars had given place to the faint grey light of dawn. A soft breeze stirred the palms and rustled the long grass, but its freshness was deceptive; the sun would be up almost before I could look round, and then nothing could save us from a scorching day.

After I had been riding for nearly an hour it struck me that, if I wished to be back in time for breakfast, I had better think of returning. At the time I was standing in the centre of a small plain, surrounded by jungle. Behind me was the path I had followed to reach the place; in front, and to right and left, others leading whither I could not tell. Having no desire to return by the road I had come, I touched up my horse and cantered off in an easterly direction, feeling certain that, even if I had to make a divergence, I should reach the city without very much trouble.

By the time I had put three miles or so behind me the heat had become stifling, the path being completely shut in on either side by the densest jungle I have ever known. For all I could see to the contrary, I might have been a hundred miles from any habitation.

Imagine my astonishment, therefore, when, on turning a corner of the track, I suddenly left the jungle behind me, and found myself standing on the top of a stupendous cliff, looking down upon a lake of blue water. In the centre of this lake was an island, and on the island a house. At the distance I was from it the latter appeared to be built of white marble, as indeed I afterwards found to be the case. Anything, however, more lovely than the effect produced by the blue water, the white building, and the jungle-clad hills upon the other side, can scarcely be imagined. I stood and gazed at it in delighted amazement. Of all the beautiful places I had hitherto seen in India this, I could honestly say, was entitled to rank first. But how it was to benefit me in my present situation I could not for the life of me understand.

Ten minutes later I had discovered a guide, and also a path down the cliff to the shore, where, I was assured, a boat and a man could be obtained to transport me to the palace. I therefore bade my informant precede me, and after some minutes' anxious scrambling my horse and I reached the water's edge.

Once there, the boatman was soon brought to light, and, when I had resigned my horse to the care of my guide, I was rowed across to the mysterious residence in question.

On reaching it we drew up at some steps leading to a broad stone esplanade, which, I could see, encircled the entire place. Out of a grove of trees rose the building itself, a confused jumble of Eastern architecture crowned with many towers. With the exception of the vegetation and the blue sky, everything was of a dazzling white, against which the dark green of the palms contrasted with admirable effect.

Springing from the boat I made my way up the steps, imbued with much the same feeling of curiosity as the happy Prince, so familiar to us in our nursery days, must have experienced when he found the enchanted castle in the forest. As I reached the top, to my unqualified astonishment, an English man-servant appeared through a gateway and bowed before me.

"Breakfast is served," he said, "and my master bids me say that he waits to receive your lordship."

Though I thought he must be making a mistake, I said nothing, but followed him along the terrace, through a magnificent gateway, on the top of which a peacock was preening himself in the sunlight, through court after court, all built of the same white marble, through a garden in which a fountain was playing to the rustling accompaniment of pipal and pomegranate leaves, to finally enter the verandah of the main building itself.

Drawing aside the curtain which covered a finely-carved doorway, the servant invited me to enter, and as I did so announced "His Excellency the Viceroy."

The change from the vivid whiteness of the marble outside to the cool semi-European room in which I now found myself was almost disconcerting in its abruptness. Indeed, I had scarcely time to recover my presence of mind before I became aware that my host was standing before me. Another surprise was in store for me. I had expected to find a native, instead of which he proved to be an Englishman.

"I am more indebted than I can say to your Excellency for the honour of this visit," he began, as he extended his hand. "I can only wish I were better prepared for it."

"You must not say that," I answered. "It is I who should apologise. I fear I am an intruder. But to tell you the truth I had lost my way, and it is only by chance that I am here at all. I was foolish to venture out without a guide, and have no one to blame for what has occurred but myself."

"In that case I must thank the Fates for their kindness to me," returned my host. "But don't let me keep you standing. You must be both tired and hungry after your long ride, and breakfast, as you see, is upon the table. Shall we show ourselves sufficiently blind to the conventionalities to sit down to it without further preliminaries?"

Upon my assenting he struck a small gong at his side, and servants, acting under the instructions of the white man who had conducted me to his master's presence, instantly appeared in answer to it. We took our places at the table, and the meal immediately commenced.

While it was in progress I was permitted an excellent opportunity of studying my host, who sat opposite me, with such light as penetrated the *jhilmills* falling directly upon his face. I doubt, however, vividly as my memory recalls the scene, whether I can give you an adequate description of the man who has since come to be a sort of nightmare to me.

In height he could not have been more than five feet two. His shoulders were broad, and would have been evidence of considerable strength but for one malformation, which completely spoilt his whole appearance. The poor fellow suffered from curvature of the spine of the worst sort, and the large hump between his shoulders produced a most extraordinary effect. But it is when I endeavour to describe his face that I find myself confronted with the most serious difficulty.

How to make you realize it I hardly know.

To begin with, I do not think I should be overstepping the mark were I to say that it was one of the most beautiful countenances I have ever seen in my fellow men. Its contour was as perfect as that of the bust of the Greek god, Hermes, to whom, all things considered, it is only fit and proper he should bear some resemblance. The forehead was broad, and surmounted with a wealth of dark hair, in colour almost black. His eyes were large and dreamy, the brows almost penciled in their delicacy; the nose, the most prominent feature of his face, reminded me more of that of the great Napoleon than any other I can recall.

His mouth was small but firm, his ears as tiny as those of an English beauty, and set in closer to his head than is usual with those organs. But it was his chin that fascinated me most. It was plainly that of a man accustomed to command; that of a man of iron will whom no amount of opposition would deter from his purpose. His hands were small and delicate, and his fingers taper, plainly those of the artist, either a painter or a musician. Altogether he presented a unique appearance, and one that once seen would not be easily forgotten.

During the meal I congratulated him upon the possession of such a beautiful residence, the like of which I had never seen before.

"Unfortunately," he answered, "the place does not belong to me, but is the property of our mutual host, the Maharajah. His Highness, knowing that I am a scholar and a recluse, is kind enough to permit me the use of this portion of the palace; and the value of such a privilege I must leave you to imagine."

"You are a student, then?" I said, as I began to understand matters a little more clearly.

"In a perfunctory sort of way," he replied. "That is to say, I have acquired sufficient knowledge to be aware of my own ignorance."

I ventured to inquire the subject in which he took most interest. It proved to be china and the native art of India, and on these two topics we conversed for upwards of half an hour. It was evident that he was a consummate master of his subject. This I could the more readily understand when, our meal being finished, he led me into an adjoining room, in which stood the cabinets containing his treasures. Such a collection I had never seen before. Its size and completeness amazed me.

"But surely you have not brought all these specimens together yourself?" I asked in astonishment.

"With a few exceptions," he answered. "You see it has been the hobby of my life. And it is to the fact that I am now engaged upon a book upon the subject, which I hope to have published in England next year, that you may attribute my playing the hermit here."

"You intend, then, to visit England?"

"If my book is finished in time," he answered, "I shall be in London at the end of April or the commencement of May. Who would not wish to be in the chief city of Her Majesty's dominions upon such a joyous and auspicious occasion?"

As he said this he took down a small vase from a shelf, and, as if to change the subject, described its history and its beauties to me. A stranger picture than he presented at that moment it would be difficult to imagine. His long fingers held his treasure as carefully as if it were an invaluable jewel, his eyes glistened with the fire of the true collector, who is born but never made, and when he came to that part of his narrative which described the long hunt for, and the eventual purchase of, the ornament in question, his voice fairly shook with excitement. I was more interested than at any other time I should have thought possible, and it was then that I committed the most foolish action of my life. Quite carried away by his charm I said:

"I hope when you *do* come to London, you will permit me to be of any service I can to you."

"I thank you," he answered gravely. "Your lordship is very kind, and if the occasion arises, as I hope it will, I shall most certainly avail myself of your offer."

"We shall be very pleased to see you," I replied; "and now, if you will not consider me inquisitive, may I ask if you live in this great place alone?"

"With the exception of my servants I have no companions."

"Really! You must surely find it very lonely?"

"I do, and it is that very solitude which endears it to me. When His Highness so kindly offered me the place for a residence, I inquired if I should have much company. He replied that I might remain here twenty years and never see a soul unless I chose to do so. On hearing that I accepted his offer with alacrity."

"Then you prefer the life of a hermit to mixing with your fellow men?"

"I do. But next year I shall put off my monastic habits for a few months, and mix with my fellow men, as you call them, in London."

"You will find hearty welcome, I am sure."

"It is very kind of you to say so; I hope I shall. But I am forgetting the rules of hospitality. You are a great smoker, I have heard. Let me offer you a cigar."

As he spoke, he took a small silver whistle from his pocket, and blew a peculiar note upon it. A moment later the same English servant who had conducted me to his presence, entered, carrying a number of cigar boxes upon a tray. I chose one, and as I did so glanced at the man. In outward appearance he was exactly what a body servant should be, of medium height, scrupulously neat, clean shaven, and with a face as devoid of expression as a blank wall. When he had left the room again my host immediately turned to me.

"Now," he said, "as you have seen my collection, will you like to explore the Palace?"

To this proposition I gladly assented, and we set off together. An hour later, satiated with the beauty of what I had seen, and feeling as if I had known the man beside me all my life, I bade him good-bye upon the steps, and prepared to return to the spot where my horse was waiting for me.

"One of my servants will accompany you," he said, "and will conduct you to the city."

"I am greatly indebted to you," I answered. "Should I not see you before, I hope you will not forget your promise to call upon me either in Calcutta, before we leave, or in London next year."

He smiled in a peculiar way.

"You must not think me so blind to my own interests as to forget your kind offer," he replied. "It is just possible, however, that I may be in Calcutta before you leave."

"I shall hope to see you then," I said, and having shaken him by the hand, stepped into the boat which was waiting to convey me across.

Within an hour I was back once more at the Palace, much to the satisfaction of the Maharajah and my staff, to whom my absence had been the cause of considerable anxiety.

It was not until the evening that I found a convenient opportunity, and was able to question His Highness about his strange *protégé*. He quickly told me all there was to know about him. His name, it appeared, was Simon Carne. He was an Englishman, and had been a great traveler. On a certain memorable occasion he had saved His Highness' life at the risk of his own, and ever since that time a close intimacy had existed between them. For upwards of three years the man in question had occupied a wing of the island palace, going away for months at a time, presumably in search of specimens for his collection, and returning when he became tired of the world. To the best of His Highness' belief he was exceedingly wealthy, but on this subject little was known. Such was all I could learn about the mysterious individual I had met earlier in the day.

Much as I wanted to do so, I was unable to pay another visit to the palace on the lake. Owing to pressing business, I was compelled to return to Calcutta as quickly as possible. For this reason it was nearly eight months before I saw or heard anything of Simon Carne again. When I *did* meet him we were in the midst of our preparations for returning to England. I had been for a ride, I remember, and was in the act of dismounting from my horse, when an individual came down the steps and strolled towards me. I recognised him instantly as the man in whom I had been so much interested in Malar-Kadir. He was now dressed in fashionable European attire, but there was no mistaking his face. I held out my hand.

"How do you do, Mr. Carne?" I cried. "This is an unexpected pleasure. Pray how long have you been in Calcutta?"

"I arrived last night," he answered, "and I leave to-morrow morning for Burma. You see, I have taken Your Excellency at your word."

"I am very pleased to see you," I replied. "I have the liveliest recollection of your kindness to me the day that I lost my way in the jungle. As you are leaving so soon, I fear we shall not have the pleasure of seeing much of you, but possibly you can dine with us this evening?"

"I shall be very glad to do so," he answered simply, watching me with his wonderful eyes, which somehow always reminded me of those of a collie.

"Her ladyship is devoted to Indian pottery and brass work," I said, "and she would never forgive me if I did not give her an opportunity of consulting you upon her collection."

"I shall be very proud to assist in any way I can," he answered.

"Very well, then, we shall meet at eight. Good-bye."

That evening we had the pleasure of his society at dinner, and I am prepared to state that a more interesting guest has never sat at a vice-regal table. My wife and daughters fell under his spell as quickly as I had done. Indeed, the former told me afterwards that she considered him the most uncommon man she had met during her residence in the East, an admission scarcely complimentary to the numerous important members of my council who all prided themselves upon their originality. When he said good-bye we had extorted his promise to call upon us in London, and I gathered later that my wife was prepared to make a lion of him when he should put in an appearance.

How he *did* arrive in London during the first week of the following May; how it became known that he had taken Porchester House, which, as every one knows, stands at the corner of Belverton Street and Park Lane, for the season, at an enormous rental; how he furnished it superbly, brought an army of Indian servants to wait upon him, and was prepared to astonish the town with his entertainments, are matters of history. I welcomed him to England, and he dined with us on the night following his arrival, and thus it was that we became, in a manner of speaking, his sponsors in Society. When one looks back on that time, and remembers how vigorously, even in the midst of all that season's gaiety, our social world took him up, the fuss that was made of him, the manner in which his doings were chronicled by the Press, it is indeed hard to realize how egregiously we were all being deceived.

During the months of June and July he was to be met at every house of distinction. Even royalty permitted itself to become on friendly terms with him, while it was rumoured that no fewer than three of the proudest beauties in England were prepared at any moment to accept his offer of marriage. To have been a social lion during such a brilliant season, to have been able to afford one of the most perfect residences in our great city, and to have written a book which the foremost authorities upon the subject declare to be a masterpiece, are things of which any man might be proud. And yet this was exactly what Simon Carne was and did.

And now, having described his advent among us, I must refer to the greatest excitement of all that year. Unique as was the occasion which prompted the gaiety of London, constant as were the arrivals and departures of illustrious folk, marvelous as were the social functions, and enormous the amount of money expended, it is strange that the things which attracted the most attention should be neither royal, social, nor political.

As may be imagined, I am referring to the enormous robberies and swindles which will forever be associated with that memorable year. Day after day, for weeks at a time, the Press chronicled a series of crimes, the like of which the oldest Englishman could not remember. It soon became evident that they were the work of one person, and that that person was a master hand was as certain as his success.

At first the police were positive that the depredations were conducted by a foreign gang, located somewhere in North London, and that they would soon be able to put their fingers on the culprits. But they were speedily undeceived. In spite of their efforts the burglaries continued with painful regularity. Hardly a prominent person escaped. My friend Lord Orpington was despoiled of his priceless gold and silver plate; my cousin, the Duchess of Wiltshire, lost her world famous diamonds; the Earl of Calingforth his race-horse "Vulcanite"; and others of my friends were despoiled of their choicest possessions. How it was that I escaped I can understand now, but I must confess that it passed my comprehension at the time.

Throughout the season Simon Carne and I scarcely spent a day apart. His society was like chloral; the more I took of it the more I wanted. And I am now told that others were affected in the same way. I used to flatter myself that it was to my endeavours he owed his social success, and I can only, in justice, say that he tried to prove himself grateful. I have his portrait hanging in my library now, painted by a famous Academician, with this inscription upon the lozenge at the base of the frame:

"To my kind friend, the Earl of Amberley, in remembrance of a happy and prosperous visit to London, from Simon Carne"

The portrait represents him standing before a bookcase in a half-dark room. His extraordinary face, with its dark penetrating eyes, is instinct with life, while his lips seem as if opening to speak. To my thinking it would have been a better picture had he not been standing in such a way that the light accentuated his deformity; but it appears that this was the sitter's own desire, thus confirming what, on many occasions, I had felt compelled to believe, namely, that he was, for some peculiar reason, proud of his misfortune.

It was at the end of the Cowes week that we parted company. He had been racing his yacht, the *Unknown Quantity*, and, as if not satisfied with having won the Derby, must needs appropriate the Queen's Cup. It was on the day following that now famous race that half the leaders of London Society bade him farewell on the deck of the steam yacht that was to carry him back to India.

A month later, and quite by chance, the dreadful truth came out. Then it was discovered that the man of whom we had all been making so much fuss, the man whom royalty had condescended to treat almost as a friend, was neither more nor less than a Prince of Swindlers, who had been utilising his splendid opportunities to the very best advantage.

Every one will remember the excitement which followed the first disclosure of this dreadful secret, and the others which followed it. As fresh discoveries came to light, the popular interest became more and more intense, while the public's wonderment at the man's almost superhuman cleverness waxed every day greater than before. My position, as you may suppose, was not an enviable one. I saw how cleverly I had been duped, and when my friends, who had most of them suffered from his talents, congratulated me on my immunity, I could only console myself with the reflection that I was responsible for more than half the acquaintances the wretch had made. But, deeply as I was drinking of the cup of sorrow, I had not come to the bottom of it yet.

One Saturday evening—the 7th of November, if I recollect aright—I was sitting in my library, writing letters after dinner, when I heard the postman come round the square and finally ascend the steps of my house. A few moments later a footman entered bearing some letters, and a large packet, upon a salver. Having read the former, I cut the string which bound the parcel, and opened it.

To my surprise, it contained a bundle of manuscript and a letter. The former I put aside, while I broke open the envelope and extracted its contents. To my horror, it was from Simon Carne, and ran as follows:

"On The High Seas.

"My Dear Lord Amberley,—

"It is only reasonable to suppose that by this time you have become acquainted with the nature of the peculiar services you have rendered me. I am your debtor for as pleasant, and, at the same time, as profitable a visit to London as any man could desire. In order that you may not think me ungrateful, I will ask you to accept the accompanying narrative of my adventures in your great metropolis. Since I have placed myself beyond the reach of capture, I will permit you to make any use of it you please. Doubtless you will blame me, but you must at least do me the justice to remember that, in spite of the splendid opportunities you permitted me, I invariably spared yourself and family. You will think me mad thus to betray myself, but, believe me, I have taken the greatest precautions against discovery, and as I am proud of my London exploits, I have not the least desire to hide my light beneath a bushel.

"With kind regards to Lady Amberley and yourself,

"I am, yours very sincerely,

"Simon Carne."

Needless to say I did not retire to rest before I had read the manuscript through from beginning to end, with the result that the morning following I communicated with the police. They were hopeful that they might be able to discover the place where the packet had been posted, but after considerable search it was found that it had been handed by a captain of a yacht, name unknown, to the commander of a homeward bound brig, off Finisterre, for postage in Plymouth. The narrative, as you will observe, is written in the third person, and, as far as I can gather, the handwriting is not that of Simon Carne. As, however, the details of each individual swindle coincide exactly with the facts as ascertained by the police, there can be no doubt of their authenticity.

A year has now elapsed since my receipt of the packet. During that time the police of almost every civilized country have been on the alert to effect the capture of my whilom friend, but without success. Whether his yacht sank and conveyed him to the bottom of the ocean, or whether, as I suspect, she only carried him to a certain part of the seas where he changed into another vessel and so eluded justice, I cannot say. Even the Maharajah of Malar-Kadir has heard nothing of him since. The fact, however, remains, I have, innocently enough, compounded a series of felonies, and, as I said at the commencement of this preface, the publication of the narrative I have so strangely received is intended to be, as far as possible, my excuse.

INTRODUCTION

THE NIGHT WAS close and muggy, such a night, indeed, as only Calcutta, of all the great cities of the East, can produce. The reek of the native quarter, that sickly, penetrating odour which, once smelt, is never forgotten, filled the streets and even invaded the sacred precincts of Government House, where a man of gentlemanly appearance, but sadly deformed, was engaged in bidding Her Majesty the Queen of England's representative in India an almost affectionate farewell.

"You will not forget your promise to acquaint us with your arrival in London," said His Excellency as he shook his guest by the hand. "We shall be delighted to see you, and if we can make your stay pleasurable as well as profitable to you, you may be sure we shall endeavour to do so."

"Your lordship is most hospitable, and I think I may safely promise that I will avail myself of your kindness," replied the other. "In the meantime 'good-bye,' and a pleasant voyage to you."

A few minutes later he had passed the sentry, and was making his way along the Maidan to the point where the Chitpore Road crosses it. Here he stopped and appeared to deliberate. He smiled a little sardonically as the recollection of the evening's entertainment crossed his mind, and, as if he feared he might forget something connected with it, when he reached a lamp-post, took a notebook from his pocket and made an entry in it.

"Providence has really been most kind," he said as he shut the book with a snap, and returned it to his pocket. "And what is more,

I am prepared to be properly grateful. It was a good morning's work for me when His Excellency decided to take a ride through the Maharajah's suburbs. Now I have only to play my cards carefully and success should be assured."

He took a cigar from his pocket, nipped off the end, and then lit it. He was still smiling when the smoke had cleared away.

"It is fortunate that Her Excellency is, like myself, an enthusiastic admirer of Indian art," he said. "It is a trump card, and I shall play it for all it's worth when I get to the other side. But to-night I have something of more importance to consider. I have to find the sinews of war. Let us hope that the luck which has followed me hitherto will still hold good, and that Liz will prove as tractable as usual."

Almost as he concluded his soliloquy a *ticca-gharri* made its appearance, and, without being hailed, pulled up beside him. It was evident that their meeting was intentional, for the driver asked no question of his fare, who simply took his seat, laid himself back upon the cushions, and smoked his cigar with the air of a man playing a part in some performance that had been long arranged.

Ten minutes later the coachman had turned out of the Chitpore Road into a narrow bye street. From this he broke off into another, and at the end of a few minutes into still another. These offshoots of the main thoroughfare were wrapped in inky darkness, and, in order that there should be as much danger as possible, they were crowded to excess. To those who know Calcutta this information will be significant.

There are slums in all the great cities of the world, and every one boasts its own peculiar characteristics. The Ratcliffe Highway in London, and the streets that lead off it, can show a fair assortment of vice; the Chinese quarters of New York, Chicago, and San Francisco can more than equal them; Little Bourke Street, Melbourne, a portion of Singapore, and the shipping quarter of Bombay, have their own individual qualities, but surely for the lowest of all the world's low places one must go to Calcutta, the capital of our great Indian Empire.

Surrounding the Lal, Machua, Burra, and Joira Bazaars are to be found the most infamous dens the mind of man can conceive.

But that is not all. If an exhibition of scented, high-toned, gold-lacquered vice is required, one has only to make one's way into the streets that lie within a stone's throw of the Chitpore Road to be accommodated.

Reaching a certain corner, the *gharri* came to a standstill and the fare alighted. He said something in an undertone to the driver as he paid him, and then stood upon the footway placidly smoking until the vehicle had disappeared from view. When it was no longer in sight he looked up at the houses towering above his head; in one a marriage feast was being celebrated; across the way the sound of a woman's voice in angry expostulation could be heard. The passers-by, all of whom were natives, scanned him curiously, but made no remark. Englishmen, it is true, were *sometimes* seen in that quarter and at that hour, but this one seemed of a different class, and it is possible that nine out of every ten took him for the most detested of all Englishmen, a police officer.

For upwards of ten minutes he waited, but after that he seemed to become impatient. The person he had expected to find at the rendezvous had, so far, failed to put in an appearance, and he was beginning to wonder what he had better do in the event of his not coming.

But, badly as he had started, he was not destined to fail in his enterprise; for, just as his patience was exhausted, he saw, hastening towards him, a man whom he recognised as the person for whom he waited.

"You are late," he said in English, which he was aware the other spoke fluently, though he was averse to owning it. "I have been here more than a quarter of an hour."

"It was impossible that I could get away before," the other answered cringingly; "but if your Excellency will be pleased to follow me now, I will conduct you to the person you seek, without further delay."

"Lead on," said the Englishman; "we have wasted enough time already."

Without more ado the Babu turned himself about and proceeded in the direction he had come, never pausing save to glance over his shoulder to make sure that his companion was following. Seemingly countless were the lanes, streets, and alleys through which they passed. The place was nothing more or less than a rabbit warren of small passages, and so dark that, at times, it was as much as the Englishman could do to see his guide ahead of him. Well acquainted as he was with the quarter, he had never been able to make himself master of all its intricacies, and as the person whom he was going to meet was compelled to change her residence at frequent intervals, he had long given up the idea of endeavouring to find her himself.

Turning out of a narrow lane, which differed from its fellows only in the fact that it contained more dirt and a greater number of unsavoury odours, they found themselves at the top of a short flight of steps, which in their turn conducted them to a small square, round which rose houses taller than any they had yet discovered. Every window contained a balcony, some larger than others, but all in the last stage of decay. The effect was peculiar, but not so strange as the quiet of the place; indeed, the wind and the far off hum of the city were the only sounds to be heard.

Now and again figures issued from the different doorways, stood for a moment looking anxiously about them, and then disappeared as silently as they had come. All the time not a light was to be seen, or the sound of a human voice. It was a strange place for a white man to be in, and so Simon Carne evidently thought as he obeyed his guide's invitation and entered the last house on the right hand side.

Whether the buildings had been originally intended for residences or for offices it would be difficult to say. They were almost as old as John Company himself, and would not appear to have been cleaned or repaired since they had been first inhabited.

From the centre of the hall, in which he found himself, a massive staircase led to the other floors, and up this Carne marched behind his conductor. On gaining the first landing he paused while the Babu went forward and knocked at a door. A moment later the shutter of a small *grille* was pulled back, and the face of a native woman looked out. A muttered conversation ensued, and after it was finished the door was opened and Carne was invited to enter. This summons he obeyed with alacrity, only to find that once he was inside, the door was immediately shut and barred behind him.

After the darkness of the street and the semi-obscurity of the stairs, the dazzling light of the apartment in which he now stood was almost too much for his eyes. It was not long, however, before he had recovered sufficiently to look about him. The room was a fine one, in shape almost square, with a large window at the further end covered with a thick curtain of native cloth. It was furnished with considerable taste, in a mixture of styles, half European and half native. A large lamp of worked brass, burning some sweet-smelling oil, was suspended from the ceiling. A quantity of tapestry, much of it extremely rare, covered the walls, relieved here and there with some superb specimens of native weapons; comfortable divans were scattered about, as if inviting repose, and as if further to carry out this idea, beside one of the lounges, a silver-mounted narghyle was placed, its tube curled up beside it in a fashion somewhat suggestive of a snake.

But, luxurious as it all was, it was evidently not quite what Carne had expected to find, and the change seemed to mystify as much as it surprised him. Just as he was coming to a decision, however, his ear caught the sound of chinking bracelets, and next moment the curtain which covered a doorway in the left wall was drawn aside by a hand glistening with rings and as tiny as that of a little child. A second later Trincomalee Liz entered the room.

Standing in the doorway, the heavily embroidered curtain falling in thick folds behind her and forming a most effective background, she made a picture such as few men could look upon without a thrill of admiration. At that time she, the famous Trincomalee Liz, whose doings had made her notorious from the Saghalian coast to the shores of the Persian Gulf, was at the prime of her life and beauty—a beauty such as no man who has ever seen it will ever forget.

It was a notorious fact that those tiny hands had ruined more men than any other half-dozen pairs in the whole of India, or the East for that matter. Not much was known of her history, but what had come to light was certainly interesting. As far as could be ascertained she was born in Tonquin; her father, it had been said, was a handsome but disreputable Frenchman, who had called himself a count, and over his absinthe was wont to talk of his possessions in Normandy; her mother hailed from Northern India, and she herself was lovelier than the pale hibiscus blossom. To tell in what manner Liz and Carne had become acquainted would be too long a story to be included here. But that there *was* some bond between the pair is a fact that may be stated without fear of contradiction.

On seeing her, the visitor rose from his seat and went to meet her.

"So you have come at last," she said, holding out both hands to him. "I have been expecting you these three weeks past. Remember, you told me you were coming."

"I was prevented," said Carne. "And the business upon which I desired to see you was not fully matured."

"So there is business then?" she answered with a pretty petulance. "I thought as much. I might know by this time that you do not come to see me for anything else. But there, do not let us talk in this fashion when I have not had you with me for nearly a year. Tell me of yourself, and what you have been doing since last we met."

As she spoke she was occupied preparing a *huqa* for him. When it was ready she fitted a tiny amber mouthpiece to the tube, and presented it to him with a compliment as delicate as her own rose-leaf hands. Then, seating herself on a pile of cushions beside him, she bade him proceed with his narrative.

"And now," she said, when he had finished, "what is this business that brings you to me?"

A few moments elapsed before he began his explanation, and during that time he studied her face closely.

"I have a scheme in my head," he said, laying the *huqa* stick carefully upon the floor, "that, properly carried out, should make us both rich beyond all telling, but to carry it out properly I must have your co-operation."

She laughed softly, and nodded her head.

"You mean that you want money," she answered. "Ah, Simon, you always want money."

"I *do* want money," he replied without hesitation. "I want it badly. Listen to what I have to say, and then tell me if you can give it to me. You know what year this is in England?"

She nodded her head. There were few things with which she had not some sort of acquaintance.

"It will be a time of great rejoicing," he continued. "Half the princes of the earth will be assembled in London. There will be wealth untold there, to be had for the mere gathering in; and who is so well able to gather it as I? I tell you, Liz, I have made up my mind to make the journey and try my luck, and, if you will help me with the money, you shall have it back with such jewels, for interest, as no woman ever wore yet. To begin with, there is the Duchess of Wiltshire's necklace. Ah, your eyes light up; you have heard of it?"

"I have," she answered, her voice trembling with excitement. "Who has not?"

"It is the finest thing of its kind in Europe, if not in the world," he went on slowly, as if to allow time for his words to sink in. "It consists of three hundred stones, and is worth, apart from its historic value, at least fifty thousand pounds."

He saw her hands tighten on the cushions upon which she sat.

"Fifty thousand pounds! That is five lacs of rupees?"

"Exactly! Five lacs of rupees, a king's ransom," he answered. "But that is not all. There will be twice as much to be had for the taking when once I get there. Find me the money I want, and those stones shall be your property.

"How much *do* you want?"

"The value of the necklace," he answered. "Fifty thousand pounds."

"It is a large sum," she said, "and it will be difficult to find."

He smiled, as if her words were a joke and should be treated as such.

"The interest will be good," he answered.

"But are you certain of obtaining it?" she asked.

"Have I ever failed yet?" he replied.

"You have done wonderful things, certainly. But this time you are attempting so much."

"The greater the glory!" he answered. "I have prepared my plans, and I shall not fail. This is going to be the greatest undertaking of my life. If it comes off successfully, I shall retire upon my laurels. Come, for the sake of—well, you know for the sake of what—will you let me have the money? It is not the first time you have done it, and on each occasion you have not only been repaid, but well rewarded into the bargain."

"When do you want it?"

"By mid-day to-morrow. It must be paid in to my account at the Bank before twelve o'clock. You will have no difficulty in obtaining it I know. Your respectable merchant friends will do it for you if you but hold up your little finger. If they don't feel inclined, then put on the screw and make them."

She laughed as he paid this tribute to her power. A moment later, however, she was all gravity.

"And the security?"

He leant towards her and whispered in her ear.

"It is well," she replied. "The money shall be found for you to-morrow. Now tell me your plans; I must know all that you intend doing."

"In the first place," he answered, drawing a little closer to her, and speaking in a lower voice, so that no eavesdropper should hear, "I shall take with me Abdul Khan, Ram Gafur, Jowur Singh, and Nur Ali, with others of less note as servants. I shall engage the best house in London, and under the wing of our gracious Viceroy, who has promised me the light of his countenance, will work my way into the highest society. That done I shall commence operations. No one will ever suspect!"

"And when it is finished, and you have accomplished your desires, how will you escape?"

"That I have not yet arranged. But of this you may be sure, I shall run no risks."

"And afterwards?"

He leant a little towards her again, and patted her affectionately upon the hand.

"Then we shall see what we shall see," he said. "I don't think you will find me ungrateful."

She shook her pretty head.

"It is good talk," she cried, "but it means nothing. You always say the same. How am I to know that you will not learn to love one of the white mem-sahibs when you are so much among them?"

"Because there is but one Trincomalee Liz," he answered; "and for that reason you need have no fear."

Her face expressed the doubt with which she received this assertion. As she had said, it was not the first time she had been cajoled into advancing him large sums with the same assurance. He knew this, and, lest she should alter her mind, prepared to change the subject.

"Besides the others, I must take Hiram Singh and Wajib Baksh. They are in Calcutta, I am told, and I must communicate with them before noon to-morrow. They are the most expert craftsmen in India, and I shall have need of them."

"I will have them found, and word shall be sent to you."

"Could I not meet them here?"

"Nay, it is impossible. I shall not be here myself. I leave for Madras within six hours."

"Is there, then, trouble toward?"

She smiled, and spread her hands apart with a gesture that said: "Who knows?"

He did not question her further, but after a little conversation on the subject of the money, rose to bid her farewell.

"I do not like this idea," she said, standing before him and looking him in the face. "It is too dangerous. Why should you run such risk? Let us go together to Burma. You shall be my vizier."

"I would wish for nothing better," he said, "were it not that I am resolved to go to England. My mind is set upon it, and when I have done, London shall have something to talk about for years to come."

"If you are determined, I will say no more," she answered; "but when it is over, and you are free, we will talk again."

"You will not forget about the money?" he asked anxiously.

She stamped her foot.

"Money, money, money," she cried. "It is always the money of which you think. But you shall have it, never fear. And now when shall I see you again?"

"In six months' time at a place of which I will tell you before-hand."

"It is a long time to wait."

"There is a necklace worth five lacs to pay you for the waiting."

"Then I will be patient. Good-bye."

"Good-bye, little friend," he said. And then, as if he thought he had not said enough, he added: "Think sometimes of Simon Carne."

She promised, with many pretty speeches, to do so, after which he left the room and went downstairs. As he reached the bottom step he heard a cough in the dark above him and looked up. He could just distinguish Liz leaning over the rail. Then something dropped and rattled upon the wooden steps behind him. He picked it up to find that it was an antique ring set with rubies.

"Wear it that it may bring thee luck," she cried, and then dis-appeared again.

He put the present on his finger and went out into the dark square.

"The money is found," he said, as he looked up at the starlit heavens. "Hiram Singh and Wajib Baksh are to be discovered be-fore noon to-morrow. His Excellency the Viceroy and his amiable lady have promised to stand sponsors for me in London society. If with these advantages I don't succeed, well, all I can say is, I don't deserve to. Now where is my Babuji?"

Almost at the same instant a figure appeared from the shadow of the building and approached him.

"If the Sahib will permit me, I will guide him by a short road to his hotel."

"Lead on then. I am tired, and it is time I was in bed." Then to himself he added: "I must sleep to-night, for to-morrow there are great things toward."

THE DUCHESS OF WILTSHIRE'S DIAMONDS

TO THE REFLECTIVE mind the rapidity with which the inhabitants of the world's greatest city seize upon a new name or idea, and familiarise themselves with it, can scarcely prove otherwise than astonishing. As an illustration of my meaning let me take the case of Klimo—the now famous private detective, who has won for himself the right to be considered as great as Lecocq, or even the late lamented Sherlock Holmes.

Up to a certain morning London had never even heard his name, nor had it the remotest notion as to who or what he might be. It was as sublimely ignorant and careless on the subject as the inhabitants of Kamtchatka or Peru. Within twenty-four hours, however, the whole aspect of the case was changed. The man, woman, or child who had not seen his posters, or heard his name, was counted an ignoramus unworthy of intercourse with human beings.

Princes became familiar with it as their trains bore them to Windsor to luncheon with the Queen; the nobility noticed and commented upon it as they drove about the town; merchants, and business men generally, read it as they made their ways by omnibus or underground, to their various shops and counting-houses; street boys called each other by it as a nickname; music hall artistes introduced it into their patter, while it was even rumoured that the Stock Exchange itself had paused in the full flood tide of business to manufacture a riddle on the subject.

That Klimo made his profession pay him well was certain, first from the fact that his advertisements must have cost a good round sum, and, second, because he had taken a mansion in Belverton Street, Park Lane, next door to Porchester House, where, to the dismay of that aristocratic neighbourhood, he advertised that he was prepared to receive and be consulted by his clients. The invitation was responded to with alacrity, and from that day forward, between the hours of twelve and two, the pavement upon the north side of the street was lined with carriages, every one containing some person desirous of testing the great man's skill.

I must here explain that I have narrated all this in order to show the state of affairs existing in Belverton Street and Park Lane when Simon Carne arrived, or was supposed to arrive, in England. If my memory serves me correctly, it was on Wednesday, the 3rd of May, that the Earl of Amberley drove to Victoria to meet and welcome the man whose acquaintance he had made in India under such peculiar circumstances, and under the spell of whose fascination he and his family had fallen so completely.

Reaching the station, his lordship descended from his carriage, and made his way to the platform set apart for the reception of the Continental express. He walked with a jaunty air, and seemed to be on the best of terms with himself and the world in general. How little he suspected the existence of the noose into which he was so innocently running his head!

As if out of compliment to his arrival, the train put in an appearance within a few moments of his reaching the platform. He immediately placed himself in such a position that he could make sure of seeing the man he wanted, and waited patiently until he should come in sight. Carne, however, was not among the first batch; indeed, the majority of passengers had passed before his lordship caught sight of him.

One thing was very certain, however great the crush might have been, it would have been difficult to mistake Carne's figure. The man's infirmity and the peculiar beauty of his face rendered him easily recognisable. Possibly, after his long sojourn in India, he found the morning cold, for he wore a long fur coat, the collar of which he had turned up round his ears, thus making a fitting frame for his delicate face. On seeing Lord Amberley he hastened forward to greet him.

"This is most kind and friendly of you," he said, as he shook the other by the hand. "A fine day and Lord Amberley to meet me. One could scarcely imagine a better welcome."

As he spoke, one of his Indian servants approached and salaamed before him. He gave him an order, and received an answer in Hindustani, whereupon he turned again to Lord Amberley.

"You may imagine how anxious I am to see my new dwelling," he said. "My servant tells me that my carriage is here, so may I hope that you will drive back with me and see for yourself how I am likely to be lodged?"

"I shall be delighted," said Lord Amberley, who was longing for the opportunity, and they accordingly went out into the station yard together to discover a brougham, drawn by two magnificent horses, and with Nur Ali, in all the glory of white raiment and crested turban, on the box, waiting to receive them. His lordship dismissed his Victoria, and when Jowur Singh had taken his place beside his fellow servant upon the box, the carriage rolled out of the station yard in the direction of Hyde Park.

"I trust her ladyship is quite well," said Simon Carne politely, as they turned into Gloucester Place.

"Excellently well, thank you," replied his lordship. "She bade me welcome you to England in her name as well as my own, and I was to say that she is looking forward to seeing you."

"She is most kind, and I shall do myself the honour of calling upon her as soon as circumstances will permit," answered Carne. "I beg you will convey my best thanks to her for her thought of me."

While these polite speeches were passing between them they were rapidly approaching a large hoarding, on which was displayed a poster setting forth the name of the now famous detective, Klimo.

Simon Carne, leaning forward, studied it, and when they had passed, turned to his friend again.

"At Victoria and on all the hoardings we meet I see an enormous placard, bearing the word 'Klimo.' Pray, what does it mean?"

His lordship laughed.

"You are asking a question which, a month ago, was on the lips of nine out of every ten Londoners. It is only within the last fortnight that we have learned who and what 'Klimo' is."

"And pray what is he?"

"Well, the explanation is very simple. He is neither more nor less than a remarkably astute private detective, who has succeeded in attracting notice in such a way that half London has been induced to patronize him. I have had no dealings with the man myself. But a friend of mine, Lord Orpington, has been the victim of a most audacious burglary, and, the police having failed to solve the mystery, he has called Klimo in. We shall therefore see what he can do before many days are past. But, there, I expect you will soon know more about him than any of us."

"Indeed! And why?"

"For the simple reason that he has taken No. 1, Belverton Terrace, the house adjoining your own, and sees his clients there."

Simon Carne pursed up his lips, and appeared to be considering something.

"I trust he will not prove a nuisance," he said at last. "The agents who found me the house should have acquainted me with the fact. Private detectives, on however large a scale, scarcely strike one as the most desirable of neighbours—particularly for a man who is so fond of quiet as myself."

At this moment they were approaching their destination. As the carriage passed Belverton Street and pulled up, Lord Amberley pointed to a long line of vehicles standing before the detective's door.

"You can see for yourself something of the business he does," he said. "Those are the carriages of his clients, and it is probable that twice as many have arrived on foot."

"I shall certainly speak to the agent on the subject," said Carne, with a shadow of annoyance upon his face. "I consider the fact of this man's being so close to me a serious drawback to the house."

Jowur Singh here descended from the box and opened the door in order that his master and his guest might alight, while portly

Ram Gafur, the butler, came down the steps and salaamed before them with Oriental obsequious ness. Carne greeted his domestics with kindly condescension, and then, accompanied by the ex-Viceroy, entered his new abode.

"I think you may congratulate yourself upon having secured one of the most desirable residences in London," said his lordship ten minutes or so later, when they had explored the principal rooms.

"I am very glad to hear you say so," said Carne. "I trust your lordship will remember that you will always be welcome in the house as long as I am its owner."

"It is very kind of you to say so," returned Lord Amberley warmly. "I shall look forward to some months of pleasant intercourse. And now I must be going. To-morrow, perhaps, if you have nothing better to do, you will give us the pleasure of your company at dinner. Your fame has already gone abroad, and we shall ask one or two nice people to meet you, including my brother and sister-in-law, Lord and Lady Gelpington, Lord and Lady Orpington, and my cousin, the Duchess of Wiltshire, whose interest in china and Indian art, as perhaps you know, is only second to your own."

"I shall be most glad to come."

"We may count on seeing you in Eaton Square, then, at eight o'clock?"

"If I am alive you may be sure I shall be there. Must you really go? Then good-bye, and many thanks for meeting me."

His lordship having left the house, Simon Carne went upstairs to his dressing-room, which it was to be noticed he found without inquiry, and rang the electric bell, beside the fireplace, three times. While he was waiting for it to be answered he stood looking out of the window at the long line of carriages in the street below.

"Everything is progressing admirably," he said to himself. "Amberley does not suspect any more than the world in general. As a proof he asks me to dinner to-morrow evening to meet his brother and sister-in-law, two of his particular friends, and above all Her Grace of Wiltshire. Of course I shall go, and when I bid Her Grace good-bye it will be strange if I am not one step nearer the interest on Liz's money."

At this moment the door opened, and his valet, the grave and respectable Belton, entered the room. Carne turned to greet him impatiently.

"Come, come, Belton," he said, "we must be quick. It is twenty minutes to twelve, and if we don't hurry, the folk next door will become impatient. Have you succeeded in doing what I spoke to you about last night?"

"I have done everything, sir."

"I am glad to hear it. Now lock that door and let us get to work. You can let me have your news while I am dressing."

Opening one side of a massive wardrobe, that completely filled one end of the room, Belton took from it a number of garments. They included a well-worn velvet coat, a baggy pair of trousers— so old that only a notorious pauper or a millionaire could have afforded to wear them—a flannel waistcoat, a Gladstone collar, a soft silk tie, and a pair of embroidered carpet slippers upon which no old clothes man in the most reckless way of business in Petticoat Lane would have advanced a single halfpenny. Into these he assisted his master to change.

"Now give me the wig, and unfasten the straps of this hump," said Carne, as the other placed the garments just referred to upon a neighbouring chair.

Belton did as he was ordered, and then there happened a thing the like of which no one would have believed. Having unbuckled a strap on either shoulder, and slipped his hand beneath the waistcoat, he withdrew a large *papier-maché* hump, which he carried away and carefully placed in a drawer of the bureau. Relieved of his burden, Simon Carne stood up as straight and well-made a man as any in Her Majesty's dominions. The malformation, for which so many, including the Earl and Countess of Amberley, had often pitied him, was nothing but a hoax intended to produce an effect which would permit him additional facilities of disguise.

The hump discarded, and the grey wig fitted carefully to his head in such a manner that not even a pinch of his own curly locks could be seen beneath it, he adorned his cheeks with a pair of *crépu*-hair whiskers, donned the flannel vest and the velvet coat previously mentioned, slipped his feet into the carpet slippers, placed a pair of smoked glasses upon his nose, and declared himself ready to proceed about his business. The man who would have known him for Simon Carne would have been as astute as, well, shall we say, as the private detective—Klimo himself.

"It's on the stroke of twelve," he said, as he gave a final glance at himself in the pier-glass above the dressing-table, and arranged his tie to his satisfaction. "Should any one call, instruct Ram Gafur to tell them that I have gone out on business, and shall not be back until three o'clock."

"Very good, sir."

"Now undo the door and let me go in."

Thus commanded, Belton went across to the large wardrobe which, as I have already said, covered the whole of one side of the room, and opened the middle door. Two or three garments were seen inside suspended on pegs, and these he removed, at the same time pushing towards the right the panel at the rear. When this was done a large aperture in the wall between the two houses was disclosed. Through this door Carne passed, drawing it behind him.

In No. 1, Belverton Terrace, the house occupied by the detective, whose presence in the street Carne seemed to find so objectionable, the entrance thus constructed was covered by the peculiar kind of confessional box in which Klimo invariably sat to receive his clients, the rearmost panels of which opened in the same fashion as those in the wardrobe in the dressing-room. These being pulled aside, he had but to draw them to again after him, take his seat, ring the electric bell to inform his housekeeper that he was ready, and then welcome his clients as quickly as they cared to come.

Punctually at two o'clock the interviews ceased, and Klimo, having reaped an excellent harvest of fees, returned to Porchester House to become Simon Carne once more.

Possibly it was due to the fact that the Earl and Countess of Amberley were brimming over with his praise, or it may have been the rumour that he was worth as many millions as you have fingers upon your hand that did it; one thing, however, was self evident, within twenty-four hours of the noble earl's meeting him at Victoria Station, Simon Carne was the talk, not only of fashionable, but also of unfashionable London.

That his household were, with one exception, natives of India, that he had paid a rental for Porchester House which ran into five figures, that he was the greatest living authority upon china and Indian art generally, and that he had come over to England in search of a wife, were among the smallest of the *canards* set afloat concerning him.

During dinner next evening Carne put forth every effort to please. He was placed on the right hand of his hostess and next to the Duchess of Wiltshire. To the latter he paid particular attention, and to such good purpose that when the ladies returned to the drawing-room afterwards, Her Grace was full of his praises. They had discussed china of all sorts, Carne had promised her a specimen which she had longed for all her life, but had never been able to obtain, and in return she had promised to show him the quaintly carved Indian casket in which the famous necklace, of which he had, of course, heard, spent most of its time. She would be wearing the jewels in question at her own ball in a week's time, she informed him, and if he would care to see the case when it came from her bankers on that day, she would be only too pleased to show it to him.

As Simon Carne drove home in his luxurious brougham afterwards, he smiled to himself as he thought of the success which was attending his first endeavour. Two of the guests, who were stewards of the Jockey Club, had heard with delight his idea of purchasing a horse, in order to have an interest in the Derby. While another, on hearing that he desired to become the possessor of a yacht, had offered to propose him for the R.C.Y.C. To crown it all, however, and much better than all, the Duchess of Wiltshire had promised to show him her famous diamonds.

"By this time next week," he said to himself, "Liz's interest should be considerably closer. But satisfactory as my progress has been hitherto, it is difficult to see how I am to get possession of the stones. From what I have been able to discover, they are only brought from the bank on the day the Duchess intends to wear them, and they are taken back by His Grace the morning following.

"While she has got them on her person it would be manifestly impossible to get them from her. And as, when she takes them off, they are returned to their box and placed in a safe, constructed in the wall of the bedroom adjoining, and which for the occasion is occupied by the butler and one of the under footmen, the only key being in the possession of the Duke himself, it would be equally foolish to hope to appropriate them. In what manner, therefore, I am to become their possessor passes my comprehension. However, one thing is certain, obtained they must be, and the attempt must be made on the night of the ball if possible. In the meantime I'll set my wits to work upon a plan."

Next day Simon Carne was the recipient of an invitation to the ball in question, and two days later he called upon the Duchess of Wiltshire, at her residence in Belgrave Square, with a plan prepared. He also took with him the small vase he had promised her four nights before. She received him most graciously, and their talk fell at once into the usual channel. Having examined her collection, and charmed her by means of one or two judicious criticisms, he asked permission to include photographs of certain of her treasures in his forthcoming book, then little by little he skillfully guided the conversation on to the subject of jewels.

"Since we are discussing gems, Mr. Carne," she said, "perhaps it would interest you to see my famous necklace. By good fortune I have it in the house now, for the reason that an alteration is being made to one of the clasps by my jewelers."

"I should like to see it immensely," answered Carne. "At one time and another I have had the good fortune to examine the jewels of the leading Indian princes, and I should like to be able to say that I had seen the famous Wiltshire necklace."

"Then you shall certainly have that honour," she answered with a smile. "If you will ring that bell I will send for it."

Carne rang the bell as requested, and when the butler entered he was given the key of the safe and ordered to bring the case to the drawing-room.

"We must not keep it very long," she observed while the man was absent. "It is to be returned to the bank in an hour's time."

"I am indeed fortunate," Carne replied, and turned to the description of some curious Indian wood carving, of which he was making a special feature in his book. As he explained, he had collected his illustrations from the doors of Indian temples, from the gateways of palaces, from old brass work, and even from carved chairs and boxes he had picked up in all sorts of odd corners. Her Grace was most interested.

"How strange that you should have mentioned it," she said. "If carved boxes have any interest for you, it is possible my jewel case itself may be of use to you. As I think I told you during Lady Amberley's dinner, it came from Benares, and has carved upon it the portraits of nearly every god in the Hindu Pantheon."

"You raise my curiosity to fever heat," said Carne.

A few moments later the servant returned, bringing with him a wooden box, about sixteen inches long, by twelve wide, and eight deep, which he placed upon a table beside his mistress, after which he retired.

"This is the case to which I have just been referring," said the Duchess, placing her hand on the article in question. "If you glance at it you will see how exquisitely it is carved."

Concealing his eagerness with an effort, Simon Carne drew his chair up to the table, and examined the box.

It was with justice she had described it as a work of art. What the wood was of which it was constructed Carne was unable to tell. It was dark and heavy, and, though it was not teak, closely resembled it. It was literally covered with quaint carving, and of its kind was an unique work of art.

"It is most curious and beautiful," said Carne when he had finished his examination. "In all my experience I can safely say I have never seen its equal. If you will permit me I should very much like to include a description and an illustration of it in my book."

"Of course you may do so; I shall be only too delighted," answered Her Grace. "If it will help you in your work I shall be glad to lend it to you for a few hours, in order that you may have the illustration made."

This was exactly what Carne had been waiting for, and he accepted the offer with alacrity.

"Very well, then," she said. "On the day of my ball, when it will be brought from the bank again, I will take the necklace out and send the case to you. I must make one proviso, however, and that is that you let me have it back the same day."

"I will certainly promise to do that," replied Carne.

"And now let us look inside," said his hostess.

Choosing a key from a bunch she carried in her pocket, she unlocked the casket, and lifted the lid. Accustomed as Carne had all his life been to the sight of gems, what he then saw before him almost took his breath away. The inside of the box, both sides and bottom, was quilted with the softest Russia leather, and on this luxurious couch reposed the famous necklace. The fire of the stones when the light caught them was sufficient to dazzle the eyes, so fierce was it.

As Carne could see, every gem was perfect of its kind, and there were no fewer than three hundred of them. The setting was a fine example of the jeweler's art, and last, but not least, the value of the whole affair was fifty thousand pounds, a mere fleabite to the man who had given it to his wife, but a fortune to any humbler person.

"And now that you have seen my property, what do you think of it?" asked the Duchess as she watched her visitor's face.

"It is very beautiful," he answered, "and I do not wonder that you are proud of it. Yes, the diamonds are very fine, but I think it is their abiding place that fascinates me more. Have you any objection to my measuring it?"

"Pray do so, if it is likely to be of any assistance to you," replied Her Grace.

Carne thereupon produced a small ivory rule, ran it over the box, and the figures he thus obtained he jotted down in his pocket-book.

Ten minutes later, when the case had been returned to the safe, he thanked the Duchess for her kindness and took his departure, promising to call in person for the empty case on the morning of the ball.

Reaching home he passed into his study, and, seating himself at his writing table, pulled a sheet of note paper towards him and began to sketch, as well as he could remember it, the box he had seen. Then he leant back in his chair and closed his eyes.

"I have cracked a good many hard nuts in my time," he said reflectively, "but never one that seemed so difficult at first sight as this. As far as I see at present, the case stands as follows: the box will be brought from the bank where it usually reposes to Wiltshire House on the morning of the dance. I shall be allowed to have possession of it, without the stones of course, for a period possibly extending from eleven o'clock in the morning to four or five, at any rate not later than seven, in the evening. After the ball the necklace will be returned to it, when it will be locked up in the safe, over which the butler and a footman will mount guard.

"To get into the room during the night is not only too risky, but physically out of the question; while to rob Her Grace of her treasure during the progress of the dance would be equally impossible. The Duke fetches the casket and takes it back to the bank himself, so that to all intents and purposes I am almost as far off the solution as ever."

Half an hour went by and found him still seated at his desk, staring at the drawing on the paper, then an hour. The traffic of the streets rolled past the house unheeded. Finally Jowur Singh announced his carriage, and, feeling that an idea might come to him with a change of scene, he set off for a drive in the park.

By this time his elegant mail phaeton, with its magnificent horses and Indian servant on the seat behind, was as well-known as Her Majesty's state equipage, and attracted almost as much attention. To-day, however, the fashionable world noticed that Simon Carne looked preoccupied. He was still working out his problem, but so far without much success. Suddenly something, no one will ever be able to say what, put an idea into his head. The notion was no sooner born in his brain than he left the park and drove quickly home. Ten minutes had scarcely elapsed before he was back in his study again, and had ordered that Wajib Baksh should be sent to him.

When the man he wanted put in an appearance, Carne handed him the paper upon which he had made the drawing of the jewel case.

"Look at that," he said, "and tell me what thou seest there."

"I see a box," answered the man, who by this time was well accustomed to his master's ways.

"As thou say'st, it is a box," said Carne. "The wood is heavy and thick, though what wood it is I do not know. The measurements are upon the paper below. Within, both the sides and bottom are quilted with soft leather, as I have also shown. Think now, Wajib Baksh, for in this case thou wilt need to have all thy wits about thee. Tell me is it in thy power, oh most cunning of all craftsmen, to insert such extra sides within this box that they, being held by a spring, shall lie so snug as not to be noticeable to the ordinary eye? Can it be so arranged that, when the box is locked, they shall fall flat upon the bottom, thus covering and holding fast what lies beneath them, and yet making the box appear to the eye as if it were empty. Is it possible for thee to do such a thing?"

Wajib Baksh did not reply for a few moments. His instinct told him what his master wanted, and he was not disposed to answer hastily, for he also saw that his reputation as the most cunning craftsman in India was at stake.

"If the Heaven-born will permit me the night for thought," he said at last, "I will come to him when he rises from his bed and tell him what I can do, and he can then give his orders as it pleases him."

"Very good," said Carne. "Then to-morrow morning I shall expect thy report. Let the work be good, and there will be many rupees for thee to touch in return. As to the lock and the way it shall act, let that be the concern of Hiram Singh."

Wajib Baksh salaamed and withdrew, and Simon Carne for the time being dismissed the matter from his mind.

Next morning, while he was dressing, Belton reported that the two artificers desired an interview with him. He ordered them to be admitted, and forthwith they entered the room. It was noticeable that Wajib Baksh carried in his hand a heavy box, which, upon Carne's motioning him to do so, he placed upon the table.

"Have ye thought over the matter?" he asked, seeing that the men waited for him to speak.

"We have thought of it," replied Hiram Singh, who always acted as spokesman for the pair. "If the Presence will deign to look, he will see that we have made a box of the size and shape such as he drew upon the paper."

"Yes, it is certainly a good copy, "said Carne condescendingly, after he had examined it.

Wajib Baksh showed his white teeth in appreciation of the compliment, and Hiram Singh drew closer to the table.

"And now, if the Sahib will open it, he will in his wisdom be able to tell if it resembles the other that he has in his mind."

Carne opened the box as requested, and discovered that the interior was an exact counterfeit of the Duchess of Wiltshire's jewel case, even to the extent of the quilted leather lining which had been the other's principal feature. He admitted that the likeness was all that could be desired.

"As he is satisfied," said Hiram Singh, "it may be that the Protector of the Poor will deign to try an experiment with it. See, here is a comb. Let it be placed in the box, so—now he will see what he will see."

The broad, silver-backed comb, lying upon his dressing-table, was placed on the bottom of the box, the lid was closed, and the key turned in the lock. The case being securely fastened, Hiram Singh laid it before his master.

"I am to open it, I suppose?" said Carne, taking the key and replacing it in the lock.

"If my master pleases," replied the other.

Carne accordingly turned it in the lock, and, having done so, raised the lid and looked inside. His astonishment was complete. To all intents and purposes the box was empty. The comb was not to be seen, and yet the quilted sides and bottom were, to all appearances, just the same as when he had first looked inside.

"This is most wonderful," he said. And indeed it was as clever a conjuring trick as any he had ever seen.

"Nay, it is very simple," Wajib Baksh replied. "The Heaven-born told me that there must be no risk of detection."

He took the box in his own hands and, running his nails down the centre of the quilting, dividing the false bottom into two pieces; these he lifted out, revealing the comb lying upon the real bottom beneath.

"The sides, as my lord will see," said Hiram Singh, taking a step forward, "are held in their appointed places by these two springs. Thus, when the key is turned the springs relax, and the sides are driven by others into their places on the bottom, where the seams in the quilting mask the join. There is but one disadvantage. It is as follows: When the pieces which form the bottom are lifted out in order that my lord may get at whatever lies concealed beneath, the springs must of necessity stand revealed. However, to any one who knows sufficient of the working of the box to lift out the false bottom, it will be an easy matter to withdraw the springs and conceal them about his person."

"As you say that is an easy matter," said Carne, "and I shall not be likely to forget. Now one other question. Presuming I am in a position to put the real box into your hands for say eight hours, do you think that in that time you can fit it up so that detection will be impossible?"

"Assuredly, my lord," replied Hiram Singh with conviction. "There is but the lock and the fitting of the springs to be done. Three hours at most would suffice for that."

"I am pleased with you," said Carne. "As a proof of my satisfaction, when the work is finished you will each receive five hundred rupees. Now you can go."

According to his promise, ten o'clock on the Friday following found him in his hansom driving towards Belgrave Square. He was a little anxious, though the casual observer would scarcely have been able to tell it. The magnitude of the stake for which he was playing was enough to try the nerve of even such a past master in his profession as Simon Carne.

Arriving at the house he discovered some workmen erecting an awning across the footway in preparation for the ball that was to take place at night. It was not long, however, before he found himself in the boudoir, reminding Her Grace of her promise to permit him an opportunity of making a drawing of the famous jewel case. The Duchess was naturally busy, and within a quarter of an hour he was on his way home with the box placed on the seat of the carriage beside him.

"Now," he said, as he patted it good-humouredly, "if only the notion worked out by Hiram Singh and Wajib Baksh holds good, the famous Wiltshire diamonds will become my property before very many hours are passed. By this time to-morrow, I suppose, London will be all agog concerning the burglary."

On reaching his house he left his carriage, and himself carried the box into his study. Once there he rang his bell and ordered Hiram Singh and Wajib Baksh to be sent to him. When they arrived he showed them the box upon which they were to exercise their ingenuity.

"Bring your tools in here," he said, "and do the work under my own eyes. You have but nine hours before you, so you must make the most of them."

The men went for their implements, and as soon as they were ready set to work. All through the day they were kept hard at it, with the result that by five o'clock the alterations had been effected and the case stood ready. By the time Carne returned from his afternoon drive in the Park it was quite prepared for the part it was to play in his scheme. Having praised the men, he turned them out and locked the door, then went across the room and unlocked a drawer in his writing table. From it he took a flat leather jewel case, which he opened. It contained a necklace of counterfeit diamonds, if anything a little larger than the one he intended to try to obtain. He had purchased it that morning in the Burlington Arcade for the purpose of testing the apparatus his servants had made, and this he now proceeded to do.

Laying it carefully upon the bottom he closed the lid and turned the key. When he opened it again the necklace was gone, and even though he knew the secret he could not for the life of him see where the false bottom began and ended. After that he reset the trap and tossed the necklace carelessly in. To his delight it acted as well as on the previous occasion. He could scarcely contain his satisfaction.

His conscience was sufficiently elastic to give him no trouble. To him it was scarcely a robbery he was planning, but an artistic trial of skill, in which he pitted his wits and cunning against the forces of society in general.

At half-past seven he dined, and afterwards smoked a meditative cigar over the evening paper in the billiard room. The invitations to the ball were for ten o'clock, and at nine-thirty he went to his dressing-room.

"Make me tidy as quickly as you can," he said to Belton when the latter appeared, "and while you are doing so listen to my final instructions.

"To-night, as you know, I am endeavouring to secure the Duchess of Wiltshire's necklace. To-morrow morning all London will resound with the hubbub, and I have been making my plans in such a way as to arrange that Klimo shall be the first person consulted. When the messenger calls, if call he does, see that the old woman next door bids him tell the Duke to come personally at twelve o'clock. Do you understand?"

"Perfectly, sir."

"Very good. Now give me the jewel case, and let me be off. You need not sit up for me."

Precisely as the clocks in the neighbourhood were striking ten Simon Carne reached Belgrave Square, and, as he hoped, found himself the first guest.

His hostess and her husband received him in the ante-room of the drawing-room.

"I come laden with a thousand apologies," he said as he took Her Grace's hand, and bent over it with that ceremonious politeness which was one of the man's chief characteristics. "I am most unconscionably early, I know, but I hastened here in order that I might personally return the jewel case you so kindly lent me. I must trust to your generosity to forgive me. The drawings took longer than I expected."

"Please do not apologise," answered Her Grace. "It is very kind of you to have brought the case yourself. I hope the illustrations have proved successful. I shall look forward to seeing them as soon as they are ready. But I am keeping you holding the box. One of my servants will take it to my room."

She called a footman to her, and bade him take the box and place it upon her dressing-table.

"Before it goes I must let you see that I have not damaged it either externally or internally," said Carne with a laugh. "It is such a valuable case that I should never forgive myself if it had even received a scratch during the time it has been in my possession."

So saying he lifted the lid and allowed her to look inside. To all appearance it was exactly the same as when she had lent it to him earlier in the day.

"You have been most careful," she said. And then, with an air of banter, she continued: "If you desire it, I shall be pleased to give you a certificate to that effect."

They jested in this fashion for a few moments after the servant's departure, during which time Carne promised to call upon her the following morning at 11 o'clock, and to bring with him the illustrations he had made and a queer little piece of china he had had the good fortune to pick up in a dealer's shop the previous afternoon. By this time fashionable London was making its way up the grand staircase, and with its appearance further conversation became impossible.

Shortly after midnight Carne bade his hostess good-night and slipped away. He was perfectly satisfied with his evening's entertainment, and if the key of the jewel case were not turned before the jewels were placed in it, he was convinced they would become his property. It speaks well for his strength of nerve when I record the fact that on going to bed his slumbers were as peaceful and untroubled as those of a little child.

Breakfast was scarcely over next morning before a hansom drew up at his front door and Lord Amberley alighted. He was ushered into Carne's presence forthwith, and on seeing that the latter was surprised at his early visit, hastened to explain.

"My dear fellow," he said, as he took possession of the chair the other offered him, "I have come round to see you on most important business. As I told you last night at the dance, when you

so kindly asked me to come and see the steam yacht you have purchased, I had an appointment with Wiltshire at half-past nine this
morning. On reaching Belgrave Square, I found the whole house
in confusion. Servants were running hither and thither with scared
faces, the butler was on the borders of lunacy, the Duchess was
well-nigh hysterical in her boudoir, while her husband was in his
study vowing vengeance against all the world."

"You alarm me," said Carne, lighting a cigarette with a hand
that was as steady as a rock. "What on earth has happened?"

"I think I might safely allow you fifty guesses and then wager a
hundred pounds you'd not hit the mark; and yet in a certain measure it concerns you."

"Concerns me? Good gracious! What have I done to bring all
this about?"

"Pray do not look so alarmed," said Amberley. "Personally you
have done nothing. Indeed, on second thoughts, I don't know that
I am right in saying that it concerns you at all. The fact of the matter is, Carne, a burglary took place last night at Wiltshire House,
and the famous necklace has disappeared."

"Good heavens! You don't say so?"

"But I *do*. The circumstances of the case are as follows: When
my cousin retired to her room last night after the ball, she
unclasped the necklace, and, in her husband's presence, placed it
carefully in her jewel case, which she locked. That having been
done, Wiltshire took the box to the room which contained the safe,
and himself placed it there, locking the iron door with his own key.
The room was occupied that night, according to custom, by the
butler and one of the footmen, both of whom have been in the family since they were boys.

"Next morning, after breakfast, the Duke unlocked the safe and
took out the box, intending to convey it to the Bank as usual. Before leaving, however, he placed it on his study-table and went
upstairs to speak to his wife. He cannot remember exactly how long
he was absent, but he feels convinced that he was not gone more
than a quarter of an hour at the very utmost.

"Their conversation finished, she accompanied him downstairs, where she saw him take up the case to carry it to his carriage. Before he left the house, however, she said: 'I suppose you have looked to see that the necklace is all right?' 'How could I do so?' was his reply. 'You know you possess the only key that will fit it?'

"She felt in her pockets, but to her surprise the key was not there."

"If I were a detective I should say that that is a point to be remembered," said Carne with a smile. "Pray, where did she find her keys?"

"Upon her dressing-table," said Amberley. "Though she has not the slightest recollection of leaving them there."

"Well, when she had procured the keys, what happened?"

"Why, they opened the box, and, to their astonishment and dismay, *found it empty. The jewels were gone!*"

"Good gracious! What a terrible loss! It seems almost impossible that it can be true. And pray, what did they do?"

"At first they stood staring into the empty box, hardly believing the evidence of their own eyes. Stare how they would, however, they could not bring them back. The jewels had, without doubt, disappeared, but when and where the robbery had taken place it was impossible to say. After that they had up all the servants and questioned them, but the result was what they might have foreseen, no one from the butler to the kitchen-maid could throw any light upon the subject. To this minute it remains as great a mystery as when they first discovered it."

"I am more concerned than I can tell you," said Carne. "How thankful I ought to be that I returned the case to Her Grace last night. But in thinking of myself I am forgetting to ask what has brought you to me. If I can be of any assistance I hope you will command me."

"Well, I'll tell you why I have come," replied Lord Amberley. "Naturally, they are most anxious to have the mystery solved and the jewels recovered as soon as possible. Wiltshire wanted to send to Scotland Yard there and then, but his wife and I eventually persuaded him to consult Klimo. As you know, if the police authorities are called in first, he refuses the business altogether. Now, we thought, as you are his next door neighbour, you might possibly be able to assist us."

"You may be very sure, my lord, I will do everything that lies in my power. Let us go in and see him at once."

As he spoke he rose and threw what remained of his cigarette into the fireplace. His visitor having imitated his example, they procured their hats and walked round from Park Lane into Belverton Street to bring up at No. 1. After they had rung the bell the door was opened to them by the old woman who invariably received the detective's clients.

"Is Mr. Klimo at home?" asked Carne. "And if so, can we see him?"

The old lady was a little deaf, and the question had to be repeated before she could be made to understand what was wanted. As soon, however, as she realized their desire, she informed them that her master was absent from town, but would be back as usual at twelve o'clock to meet his clients.

"What on earth's to be done?" said the Earl, looking at his companion in dismay. "I am afraid I can't come back again, as I have a most important appointment at that hour."

"Do you think you could entrust the business to me?" asked Carne. "If so, I will make a point of seeing him at twelve o'clock, and could call at Wiltshire House afterwards and tell the Duke what I have done."

"That's very good of you," replied Amberley. "If you are sure it would not put you to too much trouble, that would be quite the best thing to be done."

"I will do it with pleasure," Carne replied. "I feel it my duty to help in whatever way I can."

"You are very kind," said the other. "Then, as I understand it, you are to call upon Klimo at twelve o'clock, and afterwards to let my cousins know what you have succeeded in doing. I only hope he will help us to secure the thief. We are having too many of these burglaries just now. I must catch this hansom and be off. Good-bye, and many thanks."

"Good-bye," said Carne, and shook him by the hand.

The hansom having rolled away, Carne retraced his steps to his own abode.

"It is really very strange," he muttered as he walked along, "how often chance condescends to lend her assistance to my little schemes. The mere fact that His Grace left the box unwatched in his study for a quarter of an hour may serve to throw the police off on quite another scent. I am also glad that they decided to open the case in the house, for if it had gone to the bankers' and had been placed in the strong room unexamined, I should never have been able to get possession of the jewels at all."

Three hours later he drove to Wiltshire House and saw the Duke. The Duchess was far too much upset by the catastrophe to see any one.

"This is really most kind of you, Mr. Carne," said His Grace when the other had supplied an elaborate account of his interview with Klimo. "We are extremely indebted to you. I am sorry he cannot come before ten o'clock to-night, and that he makes this stipulation of my seeing him alone, for I must confess I should like to have had some one else present to ask any questions that might escape me. But if that's his usual hour and custom, well, we must abide by it, that's all. I hope he will do some good, for this is the greatest calamity that has ever befallen me. As I told you just now, it has made my wife quite ill. She is confined to her bedroom and quite hysterical."

"You do not suspect any one, I suppose?" inquired Carne.

"Not a soul," the other answered. "The thing is such a mystery that we do not know what to think. I feel convinced, however, that my servants are as innocent as I am. Nothing will ever make me think them otherwise. I wish I could catch the fellow, that's all. I'd make him suffer for the trick he's played me."

Carne offered an appropriate reply, and after a little further conversation upon the subject, bade the irate nobleman good-bye and left the house. From Belgrave Square he drove to one of the clubs of which he had been elected a member, in search of Lord Orpington, with whom he had promised to lunch, and afterwards

took him to a ship-builder's yard near Greenwich, in order to show
him the steam yacht he had lately purchased.

It was close upon dinner time before he returned to his own
residence. He brought Lord Orpington with him, and they dined
in state together. At nine the latter bade him good-bye, and at ten
Carne retired to his dressing-room and rang for Belton.

"What have you to report," he asked, "with regard to what I
bade you do in Belgrave Square?"

"I followed your instructions to the letter," Belton replied. "Yesterday morning I wrote to Messrs. Horniblow and Jimson, the
house agents in Piccadilly, in the name of Colonel Braithwaite, and
asked for an order to view the residence to the right of Wiltshire
House. I asked that the order might be sent direct to the house,
where the Colonel would get it upon his arrival. This letter I posted
myself in Basingstoke, as you desired me to do.

"At nine o'clock yesterday morning I dressed myself as much
like an elderly army officer as possible, and took a cab to Belgrave
Square. The caretaker, an old fellow of close upon seventy years of
age, admitted me immediately upon hearing my name, and proposed that he should show me over the house. This, however, I
told him was quite unnecessary, backing my speech with a present
of half a crown, whereupon he returned to his breakfast perfectly
satisfied, while I wandered about the house at my own leisure.

"Reaching the same floor as that upon which is situated the
room in which the Duke's safe is kept, I discovered that your supposition was quite correct, and that it would be possible for a man,
by opening the window, to make his way along the coping from
one house to the other, without being seen. I made certain that
there was no one in the bedroom in which the butler slept, and
then arranged the long telescope walking-stick you gave me, and
fixed one of my boots to it by means of the screw in the end. With
this I was able to make a regular succession of footsteps in the
dust along the ledge, between one window and the other.

"That done, I went downstairs again, bade the caretaker good-
morning, and got into my cab. From Belgrave Square I drove to
the shop of the pawnbroker whom you told me you had discovered
was out of town. His assistant inquired my business, and was anx-

ious to do what he could for me. I told him, however, that I must see his master personally, as it was about the sale of some diamonds I had had left me. I pretended to be annoyed that he was not at home, and muttered to myself, so that the man could hear, something about its meaning a journey to Amsterdam.

"Then I limped out of the shop, paid off my cab, and, walking down a by-street, removed my moustache, and altered my appearance by taking off my great coat and muffler. A few streets further on I purchased a bowler hat in place of the old-fashioned topper I had hitherto been wearing, and then took a cab from Piccadilly and came home."

"You have fulfilled my instructions admirably," said Carne. "And if the business comes off, as I expect it will, you shall receive your usual percentage. Now I must be turned into Klimo and be off to Belgrave Square to put His Grace of Wiltshire upon the track of this burglar."

Before he retired to rest that night Simon Carne took something, wrapped in a red silk handkerchief, from the capacious pocket of the coat Klimo had been wearing a few moments before. Having unrolled the covering, he held up to the light the magnificent necklace which for so many years had been the joy and pride of the ducal house of Wiltshire. The electric light played upon it, and touched it with a thousand different hues.

"Where so many have failed," he said to himself, as he wrapped it in the handkerchief again and locked it in his safe, "it is pleasant to be able to congratulate oneself on having succeeded. It is without its equal, and I don't think I shall be over-stepping the mark if I say that I think when she receives it Liz will be glad she lent me the money."

Next morning all London was astonished by the news that the famous Wiltshire diamonds had been stolen, and a few hours later Carne learnt from an evening paper that the detectives who had taken up the case, upon the supposed retirement from it of Klimo, were still completely at fault.

That evening he was to entertain several friends to dinner. They included Lord Amberley, Lord Orpington, and a prominent member of the Privy Council. Lord Amberley arrived late, but filled to overflowing with importance. His friends noticed his state, and questioned him.

"Well, gentlemen," he answered, as he took up a commanding position upon the drawing-room hearthrug, "I am in a position to inform you that Klimo has reported upon the case, and the upshot of it is that the Wiltshire Diamond Mystery is a mystery no longer."

"What do you mean?" asked the others in a chorus.

"I mean that he sent in his report to Wiltshire this afternoon, as arranged. From what he said the other night, after being alone in the room with the empty jewel case and a magnifying glass for two minutes or so, he was in a position to describe the *modus operandi*, and, what is more, to put the police on the scent of the burglar."

"And how *was* it worked?" asked Carne.

"From the empty house next door," replied the other. "On the morning of the burglary a man, purporting to be a retired army officer, called with an order to view, got the caretaker out of the way, clambered along to Wiltshire House by means of the parapet outside, reached the room during the time the servants were at breakfast, opened the safe, and abstracted the jewels."

"But how did Klimo find all this out?" asked Lord Orpington.

"By his own inimitable cleverness," replied Lord Amberley. "At any rate it has been proved that he was correct. The man *did* make his way from next door, and the police have since discovered that an individual, answering to the description given, visited a pawnbroker's shop in the city about an hour later, and stated that he had diamonds to sell."

"If that is so it turns out to be a very simple mystery after all," said Lord Orpington as they began their meal.

"Thanks to the ingenuity of the cleverest detective in the world," remarked Amberley.

"In that case here's a good health to Klimo," said the Privy Councilor, raising his glass.

"I will join you in that," said Simon Carne. "Here's a very good health to Klimo and his connection with the Duchess of Wiltshire's diamonds. May he always be equally successful!"

"Hear, hear to that," replied his guests.

HOW SIMON CARNE WON THE DERBY

IT WAS SEVEN o'clock on one of the brightest mornings of all that year. The scene was Waterloo Station, where the Earl of Amberley, Lord Orpington, and the Marquis of Laverstock were pacing up and down the main line departure platform, gazing anxiously about them. It was evident, from the way they scrutinised every person who approached them, that they were on the lookout for someone. This someone ultimately proved to be Simon Carne, who, when he appeared, greeted them with considerable cordiality, at the same time apologising for his lateness in joining them.

"I think this must be our train," he said, pointing to the carriages drawn up beside the platform on which they stood. "At any rate, here is my man. By dint of study he has turned himself into a sort of walking Bradshaw, and he will certainly be able to inform us."

The inimitable Belton deferentially insinuated that his master was right in his conjecture, and then led the way towards a Pullman car, which had been attached to the train for the convenience of Carne and his guests. They took their seats, and a few moments later the train moved slowly out of the station. Carne was in the best of spirits, and the fact that he was taking his friends down to the stables of his trainer, William Bent, in order that they might witness a trial of his candidate for the Derby, seemed to give him the greatest possible pleasure.

On reaching Merford, the little wayside station nearest the village in which the training stables were situated, they discovered a

273

comfortable four-wheeled conveyance drawn up to receive them. The driver touched his hat, and stated that his master was awaiting them on the Downs; this proved to be the case, for when they left the high road and turned on to the soft turf they saw before them a string of thoroughbreds, and the trainer himself mounted upon his well-known white pony, Columbine.

"Good-morning, Bent," said Carne, as the latter rode up and lifted his hat to himself and friends. "You see we have kept our promise, and are here to witness the trial you said you had arranged for us."

"I am glad to see you, sir," Bent replied. "And I only hope that what I am about to show you will prove of service to you. The horse is as fit as mortal hands can make him, and if he don't do his best for you next week there will be one person surprised in England, and that one will be myself. As you know, sir, the only horse I dread is Vulcanite, and the fact cannot be denied that he's a real clinker."

"Well," said Carne, "when we have seen our animal gallop we shall know better how much trust we are to place in him. For my own part I'm not afraid. Vulcanite, as you say, is a good horse, but, if I'm not mistaken, Knight of Malta is a better. Surely this is he coming towards us."

"That's him," said the trainer, with a fine disregard for grammar. "There's no mistaking him, is there? And now, if you'd care to stroll across we'll see them saddle."

The party accordingly descended from the carriage, and walked across the turf to the spot where the four thoroughbreds were being divested of their sheets. They made a pretty group; but even the most inexperienced critic could scarcely have failed to pick out Knight of Malta as the best among them. He was a tall, shapely bay, with black points, a trifle light of flesh perhaps, but with clean, flat legs, and low, greyhound-like thighs, sure evidence of the enormous propelling power he was known to possess. His head was perfection itself, though a wee bit too lop-eared if anything. Taken altogether, he looked, what he was, thoroughbred every inch of him. The others of the party were Gasometer, Hydrogen, and Young Romeo, the last named being the particular trial horse of the party.

It was a favourite boast of the trainer that the last named was so reliable in his habits, his condition, and his pace, that you would not be far wrong if you were to set your watch by him.

"By the way, Bent," said Carne, as the boys were lifted into their saddles, "what weights are the horses carrying?"

"Well, sir, Young Romeo carries 8st. 9lb.; Gasometer, 7st. 8lb.; Hydrogen, 7st. 1lb.; and the Knight, 9st. 11lb. The distance will be the Epsom course, one mile and a half, and the best horse to win. Now, sir, if you're ready we'll get to work."

He turned to the lad who was to ride Hydrogen.

"Once you are off you will make the running, and bring them along at your best pace to the dip, where Gasometer will, if possible, take it up. After that I leave it to you other boys to make the best race of it you can. You, Blunt," calling up his head lad, "go down with them to the post, and get them off to as good a start as possible."

The horses departed, and Simon Carne and his friends accompanied the trainer to a spot where they would see the finish to the best advantage. Five minutes later an ejaculation from Lord Orpington told them that the horses had started. Each man accordingly clapped his glasses to his eyes, and watched the race before them. Faithful to his instructions, the lad on Hydrogen came straight to the front, and led them a cracker until they descended into the slight dip which marked the end of the first half-mile.

Then he retired to the rear, hopelessly done for, and Gasometer took up the running, with Knight of Malta close alongside him, and Young Romeo only half a length away. As they passed the mile post Young Romeo shot to the front, but it soon became evident he had not come to stay. Good horse as he was, there was a better catching him hand over fist. The pace was all that could be desired, and when Knight of Malta swept past the group, winner of the trial by more than his own length, the congratulations Simon Carne received were as cordial as he could possibly desire.

"What did I tell you, sir?" said Bent, with a smile of satisfaction upon his face. "You see what a good horse he is. There's no mistake about that."

"Well, let us hope he will do as well a week hence," Carne replied simply, as he replaced his glasses in their case.

"Amen to that," remarked Lord Orpington.

"And now, gentlemen," said the trainer, "if you will allow me, I will drive you over to my place to breakfast."

They took their places in the carriage once more, and, Bent having taken the reins, in a few moments they were bowling along the high road towards a neat modern residence standing on a slight eminence on the edge of the Downs. This was the trainer's own place of abode, the stables containing his many precious charges lying a hundred yards or so to the rear.

They were received on the threshold by the trainer's wife, who welcomed them most heartily to Merford. The keen air of the Downs had sharpened their appetites, and when they sat down to table they found they were able to do full justice to the excellent fare provided for them. The meal at an end, they inspected the stables, once more carefully examining the Derby candidate, who seemed none the worse for his morning's exertion, and then Carne left his guests in the big yard to the enjoyment of their cigars, while he accompanied his trainer into the house for a few moments' chat.

"And now sit down, sir," said Bent, when they reached his own sanctum, a cosy apartment, half sitting-room and half office, bearing upon its walls innumerable mementoes of circumstances connected with the owner's lengthy turf experiences. "I hope you are satisfied with what you saw this morning?"

"Perfectly satisfied," said Carne, "but I should like to hear exactly what you think about the race itself."

"Well, sir, as you may imagine, I have been thinking a good deal about it lately, and this is the conclusion I have come to. If this were an ordinary year, I should say that we possess out and away the best horse in the race; but we must remember that this is not by any means an ordinary year—there's Vulcanite, who they tell me is in the very pink of condition, and who has beaten our horse each time they have met; there's the Mandarin, who won the Two Thousand this week, and who will be certain to come into greater favour as the time shortens, and The Filibuster, who won the Biennial Stakes at the Craven Meeting, a nice enough horse, though I must say I don't fancy him over much myself."

"I take it, then, that the only horse you really fear is Vulcanite?"

"That's so, sir. If he were not in the list, I should feel as certain of seeing you leading your horse back a winner as any man could well be."

On looking at his watch Carne discovered that it was time for him to rejoin his friends and be off to the railway station if they desired to catch the train which they had arranged should convey them back to town. So bidding the trainer and his wife good-bye, they took their places in the carriage once more, and were driven away.

Arriving at Waterloo, they drove to Lord Orpington's club to lunch.

"Do you know you're a very lucky fellow, Carne?" said the Earl of Amberley as they stood on the steps of that institution afterwards, before separating in pursuit of the pleasures of the afternoon. "You have health, wealth, fame, good looks, one of the finest houses in London, and now one of the prospective winners of the Derby. In fact, you only want one thing to make your existence perfect."

"And what is that?" asked Carne.

"A wife," replied Lord Amberley. "I wonder the girls have let you escape so long."

"I am not a marrying man," said Carne; "how could a fellow like myself, who is here to-day and gone to-morrow, expect any woman to link her lot with his? Do you remember our first meeting?"

"Perfectly, "replied Lord Amberley. "When I close my eyes I can see that beautiful marble palace, set in its frame of blue water, as plainly as if it were but yesterday I breakfasted with you there."

"That was a very fortunate morning for me," said the other. "And now here is my cab. I must be off. Good-bye."

"Good-bye," cried his friends, as he went down the steps and entered the vehicle. "Don't forget to let us know if anything further turns up."

"I will be sure to do so," said Simon Carne, and then, as he laid himself back on the soft cushions and was driven by way of Waterloo Place to Piccadilly, he added to himself, "Yes, if I can bring off the little scheme I have in my mind, and one or two others which I am preparing, and can manage to get out of England without any one suspecting that I am the burglar who has outwitted all London, I shall have good cause to say that was a very fortunate day for me when I first met his lordship."

That evening he dined alone. He seemed pre-occupied, and it was evident that he was disappointed about something. Several times on hearing noises in the street outside he questioned his servants as to the cause. At last, however, when Ram Gafur entered the room carrying a telegram upon a salver, his feelings found vent in a sigh of satisfaction. With eager fingers he broke open the envelope, withdrew the contents, and read the message it contained:

"Seven Stars Music Hall—Whitechapel Road. Ten o'clock."

There was no signature, but that fact did not seem to trouble him very much. He placed it in his pocket-book, and afterwards continued his meal in better spirits. When the servants had left the room he poured himself out a glass of port, and taking a pencil proceeded to make certain calculations upon the back of an envelope. For nearly ten minutes he occupied himself in this way, then he tore the paper into tiny pieces, replaced his pencil in his pocket, and sipped his wine with a satisfaction that was the outcome of perfected arrangements.

"The public excitement," he said to himself, not without a small touch of pride, "has as yet scarcely cooled down from the robbery of the famous Wiltshire jewels. Lord Orpington has not as yet discovered the whereabouts of the gold and silver plate which disappeared from his house so mysteriously a week or two ago, while several other people have done their best to catch a gang of burglars who would seem to have set all London at defiance. But if I bring off this new *coup*, they'll forget all their grievances in consideration of the latest and greatest scandal. There'll be scarcely a man in England who won't have something to say upon the subject. By the way, let me see how he stands in the betting to-night."

He took a paper from the table in the window, and glanced down the sporting column. Vulcanite was evidently the public's choice, Knight of Malta being only second favourite, with The Mandarin a strong third.

"What a hubbub there will be when it becomes known," said Carne, as he placed the paper on the table again. "I shall have to take especial care, or some of the storm may blow back on me. I fancy I can hear the newsboys shouting: 'Latest news of the turf scandal. The Derby favourite stolen. Vulcanite missing. An attempt made to get at Knight of Malta.' Why! It will be twenty years before old England will forget the sensation I am about to give her."

With a grim chuckle at the idea, he went upstairs to his dressing-room and locked the door. It must have been well after nine o'clock when he emerged again, and, clad in a long ulster, left the house in his private hansom. Passing down Park Lane he drove along Piccadilly, then by way of the Haymarket, Strand, Ludgate Hill, and Fenchurch Street to the Whitechapel Road. Reaching the corner of Leman Street, he signaled to his man to stop, and jumped out.

His appearance was now entirely changed. Instead of the deformed, scholar-like figure he usually presented, he now resembled a common-place, farmerish individual, with iron grey hair, a somewhat crafty face, ornamented with bushy eyebrows and a quantity of fluffy whiskers. How he had managed it as he drove along goodness only knows, but that he had effected the change was certain.

Having watched his cab drive away, he strolled along the street until he arrived at a building, the flaring lights of which proclaimed it the Seven Stars Music Hall. He paid his money at the box office, and then walked inside to find a fair-sized building, upon the floor of which were placed possibly a hundred small tables. On the stage at the further end a young lady, boasting a minimum of clothing and a maximum of self-assurance, was explaining, to the dashing accompaniment of the orchestra, the adventures she had experienced "When Billy and me was courting."

Acting up to his appearance, Carne called for a "two of Scotch cold," and, having lit a meerschaum pipe which he took from his waistcoat pocket, prepared to make himself at home. As ten o'clock struck he turned his chair a little, in order that he might have a better view of the door, and waited.

Five minutes must have elapsed before his patience was rewarded. Then two men came in together, and immediately he saw them he turned his face in an opposite direction, and seemed to be taking an absorbing interest in what was happening upon the stage.

One of the men who had entered, and whom he had seemed to recognise—a cadaverous-looking individual in a suit of clothes a size too small for him, a velvet waistcoat at least three sizes too large, a check tie, in which was stuck an enormous horseshoe pin composed of palpably imitation diamonds, boasting no shirt as far as could be seen, and wearing upon his head a top hat of a shape that had been fashionable in the early sixties—stopped, and placed his hand upon his shoulder.

"Mr. Blenkins, or I'm a d'isy," he said. "Well, who'd ha' thought of seeing you here of all places? Why, it was only this afternoon as me and my friend, Mr. Brown here, was a-speaking of you. To think as how you should ha' come up to London just this very time, and be at the Seven Stars Music Hall, of all other places! It's like what the noospapers call a go-insidence, drat me if it ain't. 'Ow are yer, old pal?"

He extended his hand, which Mr. Blenkins took, and shook with considerable cordiality. After that, Mr. Brown, who from outward appearances was by far the most respectable of the trio, was introduced in the capacity of a gentleman from America, a citizenship that became more apparent when he opened his mouth to speak.

"And what was 'ee speaking of I about?" asked Mr. Blenkins, when the trio were comfortably seated at table.

This the diffident Mr. Jones, for by that commonplace appellative the seedy gentleman with the magnificent diamonds chose to be called, declined to state. It would appear that he was willing to discuss the news of the day, the price of forage, the prospects of war, the programme proceeding upon the stage, in fact, anything rather than declare the subject of his conversation with Mr. Brown that afternoon.

It was not until Mr. Brown happened to ask Mr. Blenkins what horse he fancied for the Derby that Mr. Jones in any degree recovered his self-possession. Then an animated discussion on the forthcoming race was entered upon. How long it would have lasted had not Mr. Jones presently declared that the music of the orchestra was too much for him, I cannot say.

Thereupon Mr. Brown suggested that they should leave the Hall and proceed to a place of which he knew in a neighbouring street. This they accordingly did, and when they were safely installed in a small room off the bar, Mr. Jones, having made certain that there was no one near enough to overhear, unlocked his powers of conversation with whisky and water, and proceeded to speak his mind.

For upwards of an hour they remained closeted in the room together, conversing in an undertone. Then the meeting broke up, Mr. Blenkins bidding his friends "good-night" before they left the house.

From the outward appearances of the party, if in these days of seedy millionaires and overdressed bankrupts one may venture to judge by them, he would have been a speculative individual who would have given a five pound note for the worldly wealth of the trio. Yet, had you taken so much trouble, you might have followed Mr. Blenkins and have seen him picked up by a smart private hansom at the corner of Leman Street. You might then have gone back to the "Hen and Feathers," and have followed Mr. Brown as far as Osborn Street, and have seen him enter a neat brougham, which was evidently his own private property. Another hansom, also a private one, met Mr. Jones in the same thoroughfare, and an hour later two of the number were in Park Lane, while the third was discussing a bottle of Heidseck in a gorgeous private sitting-room on the second floor of the Langham Hotel.

As he entered his dressing-room on his return to Porchester House, Simon Carne glanced at his watch. It was exactly twelve o'clock.

"I hope Belton will not be long," he said to himself. "Give him a quarter of an hour to rid himself of the other fellow, and say half an hour to get home. In that case he should be here within the next few minutes."

The thought had scarcely passed through his brain before there was a deferential knock at the door, and next moment Belton, clad in a long great coat, entered the room.

"You're back sooner than I expected," said Carne. "You could not have stayed very long with our friend?"

"I left him soon after you did, sir," said Belton. "He was in a hurry to get home, and as there was nothing more to settle I did not attempt to prevent him. I trust you are satisfied, sir, with the result of our adventure."

"Perfectly satisfied," said Carne. "Tomorrow I'll make sure that he's good for the money, and then we'll get to work. In the meantime you had better see about a van and the furniture of which I spoke to you, and also engage a man upon whom you can rely."

"But what about Merford, sir, and the attempt upon Knight of Malta?"

"I'll see about that on Monday. I have promised Bent to spend the night there."

"You'll excuse my saying so, sir, I hope," said Belton, as he poured out his master's hot water and laid his dressing-gown upon the back of a chair, ready for him to put on, "but it's a terrible risky business. If we don't bring it off, there'll be such a noise in England as has never been heard before. You might murder the Prime Minister, I believe, and it wouldn't count for so much with the people generally as an attempt to steal the Derby favourite."

"But we shall not fail," said Carne confidently. "By this time you ought to know me better than to suppose that. No, no, never fear, Belton; I've got all my plans cut and dried, and even if we fail to get possession of Vulcanite, the odds are a thousand to one against our being suspected of any complicity in the matter. Now you can go to bed. Goodnight."

"Good-night, sir," said Belton respectfully, and left the room.

It was one of Simon Carne's peculiarities always to fulfill his engagements in spite of any inconvenience they might cause himself. Accordingly the four o'clock train from Waterloo, on the Monday following the meeting at the Music Hall just narrated, carried him to Merford in pursuance of the promise he had given his trainer.

Reaching the little wayside station on the edge of the Downs, he alighted, to find himself welcomed by his trainer, who lifted his hat respectfully, and wished him good afternoon.

During the drive, Carne spoke of the impending race, and among other things of a letter he had that morning received, warning

him of an attempt that would probably be made to obtain possession of his horse. The trainer laughed good humouredly.

"Bless you, sir," he said, "that's nothing. You should just see
some of the letters I've got pasted into my scrap book. Most of 'em
comes a week or fortnight before a big race. Some of 'em warns me
that if I don't prevent the horse from starting, I'm as good as a
dead man; others ask me what price I will take to let him finish
outside the first three; while more still tell me that if I don't put
'im out of the way altogether, I'll find my house and my wife
and family flying up to the clouds under a full charge of dynamite within three days of the race being run. Don't you pay any
attention to the letters you receive. I'll look after the horse, and
you may be very sure I'll take good care that nothing happens to
him."

"I know that, of course," said Carne, "but I thought I'd tell you.
You see, I'm only a novice at racing, and perhaps I place more importance just now upon a threat of that kind than I shall do a couple
of years hence."

"Of course," replied the trainer. "I understand exactly how you
feel, sir. It's quite natural. And now here we are, with the missis
standing on the steps to help me give you a hearty welcome."

They drove up to the door, and when Carne had alighted he
was received by the trainer's wife as her lord and master had predicted. His bedroom he discovered, on being conducted to it to
prepare for dinner, was at the back of the house, overlooking the
stableyard, and possessed a lovely view, extending across the gar-
dens and village towards where the Downs ended and the woods
of Herberford began.

"A pretty room," he said to Belton, as the latter laid out his
things upon the bed, "and very convenient for our purpose. Have
you discovered where you are located?"

"Next door, sir."

"I am glad of that; and what room is beneath us?"

"The kitchen and pantry, sir. With the exception of one at the
top of the house, there are no other bedrooms on this side."

"That is excellent news. Now get me ready as soon as you can."

During dinner that evening Simon Carne made himself as pleasant as possible to his host and hostess. So affable, indeed, was he that when they retired to rest they confessed to each other that they had never entertained a more charming guest. It was arranged that he should be called at five o'clock on the morning following, in order that he might accompany the trainer to the Downs to see his horse at his exercise.

It was close upon eleven o'clock when he dismissed his valet and threw himself upon his bed with a novel. For upwards of two hours he amused himself with his book; then he rose and dressed himself in the rough suit which his man had put out for him. Having done so, he took a strong rope ladder from his bag, blew out his light, and opened his window. To attach the hooks at the end of the ropes to the inside of the window sill, and to throw the rest outside was the work of a moment. Then, having ascertained that his door was securely locked, he crawled out and descended to the ground. Once there, he waited until he saw Belton's light disappear, and heard his window softly open. Next moment a small black bag was lowered, and following it, by means of another ladder, came the servant himself.

"There is no time to be lost," said Carne, as soon as they were together. "You must set to work on the big gates, while I do the other business. The men are all asleep; nevertheless, be careful that you make no noise."

Having given his instructions, he left his servant and made his way across the yard towards the box where Knight of Malta was confined. When he reached it he unfastened the bag he had brought with him, and took from it a brace and a peculiar shaped bit, resembling a pair of compasses. Uniting these, he oiled the points and applied them to the door, a little above the lock. What he desired to do did not occupy him for more than a minute.

Then he went quietly along the yard to the further boundary, where he had that afternoon noticed a short ladder. By means of this he mounted to the top of the wall, then lifted it up after him and lowered it on the other side, still without making any noise. Instead of dismounting by it, however, he seated himself for a moment astride of it, while he drew on a pair of clumsy boots he had brought with him, suspended round his neck. Then, having chosen his place, he jumped. His weight caused him to leave a good mark on the soft ground on the other side.

He then walked heavily for perhaps fifty yards, until he reached the high road. Here he divested himself of the boots, put on his list slippers once more, and returned as speedily as possible to the ladder, which he mounted and drew up after him. Having descended on the other side, he left it standing against the wall, and hastened across the yard towards the gates, where he found Belton just finishing the work he had set him to do.

With the aid of a brace and bit similar to that used by Carne upon the stable door, the lock had been entirely removed and the gate stood open. Belton was evidently satisfied with his work; Carne, however, was not so pleased. He picked up the circle of wood and showed it to his servant. Then, taking the bit, he inserted the screw on the reverse side and gave it two or three turns.

"You might have ruined everything," he whispered, "by omitting that. The first carpenter who looked at it would be able to tell that the work was done from the inside. But, thank goodness, I know a trick that will set that right. Now then, give me the pads, and I'll drop them by the door. Then we can return to our rooms."

Four large blanket pads were handed to him, and he went quietly across and dropped them by the stable door. After that he rejoined Belton, and they made their way, with the assistance of the ladders, back to their own rooms once more.

Half an hour later Carne was wrapped in a sweet slumber from which he did not wake until he was aroused by a tapping at his chamber door. It was the trainer.

"Mr. Carne," cried Bent, in what were plainly agitated tones, "if you could make it convenient I should be glad to speak to you as soon as possible."

In something under twenty minutes he was dressed and downstairs. He found the trainer awaiting him in the hall, wearing a very serious face.

"If you will stroll with me as far as the yard, I should like to show you something," he said.

Carne accordingly took up his hat and followed him out of the house.

"You look unusually serious," said the latter, as they crossed the garden.

"An attempt has been made to get possession of your horse."

Carne stopped short in his walk and faced the other.

"What did I tell you yesterday?" he remarked. "I was certain that that letter was more than an idle warning. But how do you know that an attempt *has* been made?"

"Come, sir, and see for yourself," said Bent. "I am sorry to say there is no gainsaying the fact."

A moment later they had reached the entrance to the stableyard.

"See, sir," said Bent, pointing to a circular hole which now existed where previously the lock had been. "The rascals cut out the lock, and thus gained an entry to the yard."

He picked up the round piece of wood with the lock still attached to it, and showed it to his employer.

"One thing is very certain, the man who cut this hole is a master of his trade, and is also the possessor of fine implements."

"So it would appear," said Carne grimly. "Now what else is there for me to hear? Is the horse much hurt?"

"Not a bit the worse, sir," answered Bent. "They didn't get in at him, you see. Something must have frightened them before they could complete their task. Step this way, sir, if you please, and examine the door of the box for yourself. I have given strict orders that nothing shall be touched until you have seen it."

They crossed the yard together, and approached the box in question. On the woodwork the commencement of a circle similar to that which had been completed on the yard gates could be plainly distinguished, while on the ground below lay four curious shaped pads, one of which Carne picked up.

"What on earth are these things," he asked innocently enough.

"Their use is easily explained, sir," answered the trainer. "They are intended for tying over the horse's feet, so that when he is led out of his box his plates may make no noise upon the stones. I'd like to have been behind 'em with a whip when they got him out, that's all. The double-dyed rascals to try such a trick upon a horse in my charge!"

"I can understand your indignation," said Carne. "It seems to me we have had a narrow escape."

"Narrow escape, or no narrow escape, I'd have had 'em safely locked up in Merford Police Station by this time," replied Bent vindictively. "And now, sir, let me show you how they got out. As far as I can see they must have imagined they heard somebody coming from the house, otherwise they would have left by the gates instead of by this ladder."

He pointed to the ladder, which was still standing where Carne had placed it, and then led him by a side door round to the other side of the wall. Here he pointed to some heavy footmarks upon the turf. Carne examined them closely.

"If the size of his foot is any criterion of his build," he said, "he must have been a precious big fellow. Let me see how mine compares with it."

He placed his neat shoe in one of the imprints before him, and smiled as he noticed how the other overlapped it.

They then made their way to the box, where they found the animal at his breakfast. He lifted his head and glanced round at them, bit at the iron of the manger, and then gave a little playful kick with one of his hind legs.

"He doesn't seem any the worse for his adventure," said Carne, as the trainer went up to him and ran his hand over his legs.

"Not a bit," answered the other. "He's a wonderfully even-tempered horse, and it takes a lot to put him out. If his nerves had been at all upset he wouldn't have licked up his food as clean as he has done."

Having given another look at him, they left him in charge of his lad, and returned to the house.

The gallop after breakfast confirmed their conclusion that there was nothing the matter, and Simon Carne returned to town ostensibly comforted by Bent's solemn assurance to that effect. That afternoon Lord Calingforth, the owner of Vulcanite, called upon him. They had met repeatedly, and consequently were on the most intimate terms.

"Good afternoon, Carne," he said as he entered the room. "I have come to condole with you upon your misfortune, and to offer you my warmest sympathy."

"Why, what on earth has happened?" asked Carne, as he offered his visitor a cigar.

"God bless my soul, my dear fellow! Haven't you seen the afternoon's paper? Why, it reports the startling news that your stables were broken into last night, and that my rival, Knight of Malta, was missing this morning."

Carne laughed.

"I wonder what they'll say next," he said quietly. "But don't let me appear to deceive you. It is perfectly true that the stables were broken into last night, but the thieves were disturbed, and decamped just as they were forcing the lock of The Knight's box."

"In that case I congratulate you. What rascally inventions some of these sporting papers do get hold of to be sure. I'm indeed glad to hear that it is not true. The race would have lost half its interest if your horse were out of it. By the way, I suppose you are still as confident as ever?"

"Would you like to test it?"

"Very much, if you feel inclined for a bet."

"Then I'll have a level thousand pounds with you that my horse beats yours. Both to start or the wager is off. Do you agree?"

"With pleasure. I'll make a note of it."

The noble Earl jotted the bet down in his book, and then changed the subject by inquiring whether Carne had ever had any transactions with his next door neighbour, Klimo.

"Only on one occasion," the other replied. "I consulted him on behalf of the Duke of Wiltshire at the time his wife's diamonds were stolen. To tell the truth, I was half thinking of calling him in to see if he could find the fellow who broke into the stables last night, but on second thoughts I determined not to do so. I did not want to make any more fuss about it than I could help. But what makes you ask about Klimo?"

"Well, to put the matter in a nutshell, there has been a good deal of small pilfering down at my trainer's place lately, and I want to get it stopped."

"If I were you I should wait till after the race, and then have him down. If one excites public curiosity just now, one never knows what will happen."

"I think you are right. Anyhow, I'll act on your advice. Now what do you say to coming along to the Rooms with me to see how our horses stand in the market? Your presence there would do more than any number of paper denials towards showing the fallacy of this stupid report. Will you come?"

"With pleasure," said Carne, and in less than five minutes he was sitting beside the noble Earl in his mail phaeton, driving towards the rooms in question.

When he got there, he found Lord Calingforth had stated the case very correctly. The report that Knight of Malta had been stolen had been widely circulated, and Carne discovered that the animal was, for the moment, almost a dead letter in the market. The presence of his owner, however, was sufficient to stay the panic, and when he had snapped up two or three long bets, which a few moments before had been going begging, the horse began steadily to rise towards his old position.

That night, when Belton waited upon his master at bedtime, he found him, if possible, more silent than usual. It was not until his work was well-nigh completed that the other spoke.

"It's a strange thing, Belton," he said, "and you may hardly believe it, but if there were not certain reasons to prevent me from being so magnanimous, I would give this matter up, and let the race be run on its merits. I don't know that I ever took a scheme in hand with a worse grace. However, as it can't be helped, I suppose I must go through with it. Is the van prepared?"

"It is quite ready, sir."

"All the furniture arranged as I directed?"

"It is exactly as you wished, sir. I have attended to it myself."

"And what about the man?"

"I have engaged the young fellow, sir, who assisted me before. I know he's quick, and I can stake my life that he's trustworthy."

"I am glad to hear it. He will have need to be. Now for my arrangements. I shall make the attempt on Friday morning next, that is to say, two days from now. You and the man you have just mentioned will take the van and horses to Market Stopford, traveling by the goods train which, I have discovered, reaches the town between four and five in the morning. As soon as you are out of the station, you will start straight away along the high road towards Exbridge, reaching the village between five and six. I shall meet you in the road alongside the third milestone on the other side, made up for the part I am to play. Do you understand?"

"Perfectly, sir."

"That will do then. I shall go down to the village to-morrow evening, and you will not hear from me again until you meet me at the place I have named. Good-night."

"Good-night, sir."

Now, it is a well-known fact that if you wish to excite the anger of the inhabitants of Exbridge village, and more particularly of any member of the Pitman Training Establishment, you have but to ask for information concerning a certain blind beggar who put in an appearance there towards sunset on the Thursday preceding the Derby of 18—, and you will do so. When that mysterious individual first came in sight he was creeping along the dusty high road that winds across the Downs from Market Stopford to Beaton Junction, dolorously quavering a ballad that was intended to be, though few would have recognised it, "The Wearing of the Green."

On reaching the stables he tapped along the wall with his stick, until he came to the gate. Then, when he was asked his business by the head lad, who had been called up by one of the stable boys, he stated that he was starving, and, with peculiar arts of his own, induced them to provide him with a meal. For upwards of an hour he remained talking with the lads, and then wended his way down the hill towards the village, where he further managed to induce the rector to permit him to occupy one of his outhouses for the night.

After tea he went out and sat on the green, but towards eight o'clock he crossed the stream at the ford, and made his way up to a little copse, which ornamented a slight eminence, on the opposite side of the village to that upon which the training stables were situated.

How he found his way, considering his infirmity, it is difficult to say, but that he did find it was proved by his presence there. It

might also have been noticed that when he was once under cover
of the bushes, he gave up tapping the earth with his stick, and
walked straight enough, and without apparent hesitation, to the
stump of a tree, upon which he seated himself.

For some time he enjoyed the beauty of the evening undisturbed
by the presence of any other human being. Then he heard a step
behind him, and next moment a smart-looking stable lad parted
the bushes and came into view.

"Hullo," said the newcomer. "So you managed to get here first?"

"So I have," said the old rascal, "and it's wonderful when you
come to think of it, considering my age, and what a poor old blind
chap I be. But I'm glad to find ye've managed to get away, my lad.
Now what have ye got to say for yourself?"

"I don't know that I've got anything to say," replied the boy.
"But this much is certain, what you want can't be done."

"And a fine young cockerel you are to be sure, to crow so loud
that it can't be done," said the old fellow, with an evil chuckle. "How
do you know it can't?"

"Because I don't see my way," replied the other. "It's too dangerous by a long sight. Why, if the Guv'nor was to get wind of what
you want me to do, England itself wouldn't be big enough to hold
us both. You don't know 'im as well as I do."

"I know him well enough for all practical purposes," replied
the beggar. "Now, if you've got any more objections to raise, be
quick about it. If you haven't, then I'll talk to you. You haven't?
Very good then. Now, just hold your jaw, open your ears, and listen to what I've got to say. What time do you go to exercise to-
morrow morning?"

"Nine o'clock."

"Very good then. You go down on to the Downs, and the Boss
sends you off with Vulcanite for a canter. What do you do? Why,
you go steadily enough as long as he can see you, but directly you're
round on the other side of the hill you stick in your heels, and nip
into the wood that runs along on your right hand, just as if your
horse was bolting with you. Once in there, you go through for half
a mile until you come to the stream, ford that, and then cut into

the next wood, riding as if the devil himself were after you, until you reach the path above Hangman's Hollow. Do you know the place?"

"I reckon I ought to."

"Well, then, you just make tracks for it. When you get there you'll find me waiting for you. After that I'll take over command, and get both you and the horse out of England in such a way that nobody will ever suspect. Then there'll be five hundred pounds for your trouble, a safe passage with the horse to South America, and another five hundred the day the nag is set ashore. There's not as much risk as you could take between your finger and thumb, and a lad with a spirit like yours could make a fortune with a thousand pounds on the other side. What have you to say now?"

"It's all very well," replied the lad, "but how am I to know that you'll play straight with me?"

"What do you take me for?" said the beggar indignantly, at the same time putting his hand in his coat pocket and producing what looked like a crumpled piece of paper. "If you doubt me, there's something that may help to convince you. But don't go showing it around to-night, or you'll be giving yourself away, and that'll mean the Stone Jug for you, and 'Amen' to all your hopes of a fortune. You'll do as I wish now, I suppose?"

"I'll do it," said the lad sullenly, as he crumpled the bank-note up and put it in his pocket. "But now I must be off. Since there's been this fuss about Knight of Malta, the Guv'nor has us all in before eight o'clock, and keeps the horse under lock and key, with the head lad sleeping in the box with him."

"Well, good-night to you, and don't you forget about to-morrow morning; niggle the horse about a bit just to make him impatient like, and drop a hint that he's a bit fresh. That will make his bolting look more feasible. Don't leave the track while there's any one near you, but, as soon as you do, ride like thunder to the place I told you of. I'll see that they're put off the scent as to the way you've gone."

"All right," said the lad. "I don't like it, but I suppose I'm in too deep now to draw back. Good-night."

"Good-night, and good luck to you."

Once he had got rid of the youth, Carne (for it was he) returned by another route to the rector's out-building, where he laid himself down on the straw, and was soon fast asleep. His slumbers lasted till nearly daybreak, when he rose and made his way across country to the small copse above Hangman's Hollow, on the road from Exbridge to Beaton Junction. Here he discovered a large van drawn up, apparently laden with furniture both inside and out. The horses were feeding beneath a tree, and a couple of men were eating their breakfast beside them. On seeing Carne, the taller of the pair—a respectable-looking workman, with a big brown beard—rose and touched his hat. The other looked with astonishment at the disreputable beggar standing before them.

"So you arrived here safely," said Carne. "If anything you're a little before your time. Boil me a cup of tea, and give me something to eat as quickly as possible, for I am nearly famished. When you have done that, get out the clothes I told you to bring with you, and let me change into them. It wouldn't do for any of the people from the village back yonder to be able to say afterwards that they saw me talking with you in this rig out."

As soon as his hunger was appeased he disappeared into the wood, and dressed himself in his new attire. Another suit of clothes, and an apron such as might be worn by a furniture remover's foreman, a grey wig, a short grey beard and moustache, and a bowler hat, changed his identity completely; indeed, when his rags had been hidden in the hollow of a tree, it would have been a difficult matter to have traced any resemblance between the respectable-looking workman eating his breakfast and the disreputable beggar of half an hour before.

It was close upon nine o'clock by this time, and as soon as he realized this Carne gave the order to put the horses to. This done, they turned their attention to the back of the van, and then a strange thing became apparent. Though to all appearances, viewed from the open doors at the end, the inside of this giant receptacle was filled to its utmost holding capacity with chests of drawers, chairs, bedsteads, carpets, and other articles of household furniture, yet by pulling a pair of handles it was possible for two men easily to withdraw what looked like half the contents of the van.

The poorest observer would then have noticed that in almost every particular these articles were dummies, affixed to a screen, capable of being removed at a moment's notice. The remainder of the van was fitted after the fashion of a stable, with a manger at the end and a pair of slings dependent from the roof.

The nervous tension produced by the waiting soon became almost more than the men could bear. Minute after minute went slowly by, and still the eagerly expected horse did not put in an appearance. Then Belton, whom Carne had placed on the look-out, came flying towards them with the report that he could hear a sound of galloping hoofs in the wood. A few seconds later the noise could be plainly heard at the van, and almost before they had time to comment upon it, a magnificent thoroughbred, ridden by the stable boy who had talked to the blind beggar on the previous evening, dashed into view, and pulled up beside the van.

"Jump off," cried Carne, catching at the horse's head, "and remove the saddle. Now be quick with those cloths; we must rub him down or he'll catch cold."

When the horse was comparatively dry he was led into the van, which was to be his stable for the next few hours, and, in spite of his protests, slung in such a fashion that his feet did not touch the floor. This business completed, Carne bade the frightened boy get in with him, and take care that he did not, on any account, neigh.

After that the mask of furniture was replaced, and the doors closed and locked. The men mounted to their places on the box and roof, and the van continued its journey along the high road towards the Junction. But satisfactory as their attempt had so far proved, the danger was by no means over. Scarcely had they proceeded three miles on their way before Carne distinguished the sound of hoofs upon the road behind him. A moment later a young man, mounted on a well-bred horse, came into view, rode up alongside, and signaled to the driver to stop.

"What's the matter?" inquired the latter, as he brought his horses to a standstill. "Have we dropped anything?"

"Have you seen anything of a boy on a horse?" asked the man, who was so much out of breath that he could scarcely get his words out.

"What sort of a boy, and what sort of a horse?" asked the man on the van.

"A youngish boy," was the reply, "seven stone weight, with sandy hair, on a thoroughbred."

"No: we ain't seen no boy with sandy 'air, ridin' of a thoroughbred 'orse seven stone weight," said Carne. "What's 'e been an' done?"

"The horse has bolted with him off the Downs, back yonder," answered the man. "The Guv'nor has sent us out in all directions to look for him."

"Sorry we can't oblige you," said the driver as he prepared to start his team again. "Good day to you."

"Much obliged," said the horseman, and, when he had turned off into a side road, the van continued its journey till it reached the railway station. A quarter of an hour later it caught the eleven o'clock goods train and set off for the small seaside town of Barworth, on the south coast, where it was shipped on board a steamer which had arrived that morning from London.

Once it was safely transferred from the railway truck to the deck, Carne was accosted by a tall, swarthy individual, who, from his importance, seemed to be both the owner and the skipper of the vessel. They went down into the saloon together, and a few moments later an observer, had one been there, might have seen a cheque for a considerable sum of money change hands.

An hour later the *Jessie Branker* was steaming out to sea, and a military-looking individual, not at all to be compared with the industrious mechanic, who had shipped the furniture van on board the vessel bound for Spain, stood on the platform of the station waiting for the express train to London. On reaching the metropolis he discovered it surging beneath the weight of a great excitement. The streets re-echoed with the raucous cries of the news-vendors:

"The Derby favourite stolen—Vulcanite missing from his stable!"

Next morning an advertisement appeared in every paper of consequence, offering "A reward of Five Hundred Pounds for any information which might lead to the conviction of the person or persons who on the morning of May 28th had stolen, or caused to be stolen, from the Pitman Training Stables, the Derby favourite, Vulcanite, the property of the Right Honourable the Earl of Calingforth."

The week following, Knight of Malta, owned by Simon Carne, Esq., of Porchester House, Park Lane, won the Derby by a neck, in a scene of intense excitement. The Mandarin being second, and The Filibuster third. It is a strange fact that to this day not a member of the racing world has been able to solve the mystery surrounding the disappearance of one of the greatest horses that ever set foot on an English racecourse.

To-day, if Simon Carne thinks of that momentous occasion, when, amid the shouting crowd of Epsom he led his horse back a winner, he smiles softly to himself, and murmurs beneath his breath:

"Valued at twenty thousand pounds, and beaten in the Derby by a furniture van."

A SERVICE TO THE STATE

IT WAS THE day following that upon which Simon Carne, presented by the Earl of Amberley, had made his bow before the Heir Apparent at the second *levée* of the season, that Klimo entered upon one of the most interesting cases which had so far come into his experience. The clock in his consulting room had just struck one when his elderly housekeeper entered, and handed him a card, bearing the name of Mrs. George Jeffreys, 14, Bellamer Street, Bloomsbury. The detective immediately bade his servant admit the visitor, and, almost before he had given the order, the lady in question stood before him.

She was young, not more than twenty-four at most, a frail wisp of a girl, with light brown hair and eyes that spoke for her nationality as plain as any words. She was neatly, but by no means expensively dressed, and showed evident signs of being oppressed by a weight of trouble. Klimo looked at her, and in that glance took in everything. In spite of the fact, that he was reputed to possess a heart as hard as any flint, it was noticeable that his voice, when he spoke to her, was not as gruff as that in which he usually addressed his visitors.

"Pray sit down," he said, "and tell me in as few words as possible what it is you desire that I should do for you. Speak as clearly as you can, and, if you want my help, don't hesitate to tell me everything."

The girl sat down as ordered, and immediately commenced her tale.

"My name is Eileen Jeffreys," she said. "I am the wife of an English Bank Inspector, and the daughter of Septimus O'Grady, of Chicago, U.S.A."

"I shall remember," replied Klimo. "And how long have you been married?"

"Two years," answered the girl. "Two years next September. My husband and I met in America, and then came to England to settle."

"In saying good-bye to your old home, you left your father behind, I presume?"

"Yes, he preferred to remain in America."

"May I ask his profession?"

"That, I'm afraid, foolish as it may seem to say so, I cannot tell you," answered the girl, with a slightly heightened colour. "His means of earning a living were always kept a secret from me."

"That was rather strange, was it not?" said Klimo. "Had he private resources?"

"None that I ever heard of," replied the girl.

"Did no business men ever come to see him?"

"But very few people came to us at all. We had scarcely any friends."

"Of what nationality were the friends who *did* come?"

"Mostly Irish, like ourselves," answered Mrs. Jeffreys.

"Was there ever any quarrel between your father and your husband, prior to your leaving America?"

"Never any downright quarrel," said the girl. "But I am sorry to say they were not always the best of friends. In those days my father was a very difficult man to get on with."

"Indeed?" said Klimo. "Now, perhaps you had better proceed with your story."

"To do that, I must explain that at the end of January of this present year, my father, who was then in Chicago, sent us a cablegram to say he was leaving for England that very day, and, that upon his arrival in England, if we had no objection, he would like to take up his residence with us. He was to sail from New York on the Saturday following, and, as you know, the passage takes six days or thereabouts. Arriving in England he came to London and put up at our house in Bellamer Street, Bloomsbury. That was during the first week in February last, and off and on he has been living with us ever since."

"Have you any idea what brought him to England?"

"Not the least," she answered deliberately, after a few seconds' pause, which Klimo did not fail to notice.

"Did he do business with any one that you are aware of?"

"I cannot say. On several occasions he went away for a week at a time into the Midlands, but what took him there I have no possible idea. On the last occasion he left us on the fifteenth of last month, and returned on the ninth of this, the same day that my husband was called away to Marseilles on important banking business. It was easy to see that he was not well. He was feverish, and within a short time of my getting him to bed began to wander in his mind, declaring over and over again that he bitterly repented some action he had taken, and that if he could once consider himself safe again would be quit of the whole thing for ever.

"For close upon a fortnight I continued to nurse him, until he was so far recovered as to recognise me once more. The day that he did so I took in at the door this cablegram, from which I may perhaps date the business that has brought me to you."

She took a paper from her pocket and handed it to Klimo, who glanced at it, examined the post-mark and the date, and then placed it upon the desk before him. It was from Chicago, and ran as follows:—

O'Grady,
    13, Bellamer Street, London, England.
Why no answer? Reply chances of doing business.
                                Nero.

"Of course, it was impossible for me to tell what this meant. I was not in my father's confidence, and I had no notion who his mysterious correspondent might be. But as the doctor had distinctly stated that to allow him to consider any business at all would bring on a relapse and probably kill him, I placed the message in a drawer, and determined to let it remain there until he should be well enough to attend to it without danger to himself. The week following he was not quite so well, and fortunately there was complete silence on the part of his correspondents. Then this second message arrived. As you will see it is also from Chicago and from the same person.

> Reply immediately, or remember consequences.
> Time presses, if do not realise at present price, market will be lost.
>
> > > Nero.

"Following my previous line of action, I placed this communication also in the drawer, and determined to let Nero wait for a reply. By doing so, however, I was incurring greater trouble than I dreamt of. Within forty-eight hours I received the following message, and upon that I made up my mind and came off at once to you. What it means I do not know, but that it bodes some ill to my father I feel certain. I had heard of your fame, and as my husband is away from home, my father unable to protect himself, and I am without friends at all in England, I thought the wisest course I could pursue would be to consult you."

"Let me look at the last cablegram," said Klimo, putting his hand from the box, and taking the slip of paper.

The first and second messages were simplicity itself; this, however, was a complete enigma. It was worded as follows:—

> Uneasy—Alpha—Omega—Nineteen—Twelve—to-day—five—lacs—arrange—seventy—eight—Brazils—one—twenty—nine.
>
> > > Nero.

Klimo read it through, and the girl noticed that he shook his head over it.

"My dear young lady," he said, "I am afraid that it would be safer for you not to tell me any further, for I fear it is not in my power to help you."

"You will not help me now that I have told you my miserable position? Then there is nothing before me but despair. Oh, sir, is your decision quite irrevocable? You cannot think how I have counted on your assistance."

"I regret exceedingly that I am compelled to disappoint you," he answered. "But my time is more than occupied as it is, and I could not give your case my attention, even if I would."

His decision had been too much for her fortitude, and before he could prevent it, her head was down upon her hands and she had begun to weep bitterly. He attempted to comfort her, but in vain; and when she left him, tears were still coursing down her cheeks. It was not until she had been gone about ten minutes, and he had informed his housekeeper that he would see no more clients that day, that he discovered that she had left her precious cablegrams behind her.

Actuated by a feeling of curiosity, he sat down again and spread the three cablegrams out upon his writing-table. The first two, as I have said, required no consideration, they spoke for themselves, but the third baffled him completely. Who was this Septimus O'Grady who lived in Chicago, and whose associates spent their time discussing the wrongs of Ireland? How was it that, being a man innocent of private means, he engaged in no business?

Then another question called for consideration. If he had no business, what brought him to London and took him so repeatedly into the Midlands? These riddles he set aside for the present, and began to pick the last cablegram to pieces. That its author was not easy in his mind when he wrote it was quite certain.

Then who and what were the Alpha and Omega mentioned? What connection had they with Nero; also what did nineteen and twelve mean when coupled with To-day? Further, why should five lacs arrange seventy-eight Brazils? And what possible sense could be made out of the numbers one—twenty—and nine? He read the message from beginning to end again, after that from the end to the beginning, and, like a good many other men in a similar position, because he could not understand it, found himself taking a greater interest in it. This feeling had not left him when he had put off disguise as Klimo and was Simon Carne once more.

While he was eating his lunch the thought of the lonely Irishman lying ill in a house, where he was without doubt an unwelcome guest, fascinated him strangely, and when he rose from the table he found he was not able to shake off the impression it had given him. That the girl had some notion of her father's business he felt as certain as of his own name, even though she had so strenuously denied the fact. Otherwise why should she have been so frightened by what might have been simply innocent business messages in cypher? That she was frightened was as plain as the sun then shining into his room. Despite the fact that he had resolved not to take up the case, he went into his study, and took the cablegrams from the drawer in which he had placed them. Then drawing a sheet of paper towards him, he set to work upon the puzzle.

"The first word requires no explanation," he said as he wrote it down. "For the two next, Alpha and Omega, we will, for the sake of argument, write The Beginning and The End, and as that tells us nothing, we will substitute for them The First and The Last. Now, who or what are The First and The Last? Are they the first and last words of a code, or of a word, or do they refer to two individuals who are the principal folk in some company or conspiracy? If the latter, it is just possible they are the people who are so desperately uneasy. The next two words, however, are too much for me altogether."

Uninteresting as the case had appeared at first sight, he soon discovered that he could think of nothing else. He found himself puzzling over it during an afternoon concert at the Queen's Hall, and he even thought of it while calling upon the wife of the Prime Minister afterwards. As he drove in the Park before dinner, the wheels of his carriage seemed to be saying "Alpha and Omega, nineteen, twelve" over and over again with pitiless reiteration, and by the time he reached home once more he would gladly have paid a ten-pound note for a feasible solution of the enigma, if only to get its weight off his mind.

While waiting for dinner he took pen and paper and wrote the message out again, this time in half a dozen different ways. But the effect was the same, none of them afforded him any clue. He

then took the second letter of each word, after that the third, then
the fourth, and so on until he had exhausted them. The result in
each case was absolute gibberish, and he felt that he was no nearer
understanding it than when Mrs. Jeffreys had handed it to him
nearly eight hours before.

During the night he dreamt about it, and when he woke in the
morning its weight was still upon his mind. "Nineteen—twelve," it
is true had left him, but he was no better off for the reason that
"Seventy-eight Brazils" had taken its place. When he got out of bed
he tried it again. But at the end of half an hour his patience was
exhausted.

"Confound the thing," he said, as he threw the paper from him,
and seated himself in a chair before his looking-glass in order that
his confidential valet, Belton, might shave him. "I'll think no more
of it. Mrs. Jeffreys must solve the mystery for herself. It has wor-
ried me too much already."

He laid his head back upon the rest and allowed his valet to
run the soap brush over his chin. But, however much he might desire it his Old Man of the Sea was not to be discarded so easily; the
word "Brazils" seemed to be printed in letters of fire upon the ceiling. As the razor glided over his cheek he thought of the various
constructions to be placed upon the word—The Country—Stocks—
and even nuts—Brazil nuts, Spanish nuts, Barcelona nuts, walnuts,
cob nuts—and then, as if to make the nightmare more complete,
no less a thing than Nuttall's Dictionary. The smile the last suggestion caused him came within an ace of leaving its mark upon
his cheek. He signed to the man to stay his hand.

"Egad!" he cried, "who knows but this may be the solution of
the mystery? Go down to the study, Belton, and bring me Nuttall's
Dictionary."

He waited with one side of his face still soaped until his valet
returned, bringing with him the desired volume. Having received
it he placed it upon the table and took up the telegram.

"Seventy—eight Brazils," it said, "one—twenty—nine."

Accordingly he chose the seventieth page, and ran his fingers
down the first column. The letter was B, but the eighth word proved

useless. He thereupon turned to the seventy-eighth page, and in the first column discovered the word *Bomb*. In a second the whole aspect of the case changed, and he became all eagerness and excitement. The last words on the telegram were "one-twenty-nine," yet it was plain that there were barely a hundred upon the page. The only explanation, therefore, was that the word "One" distinguished the column, and the "twenty-nine" referred to the number of the word in it.

Almost trembling with eagerness he began to count. Surely enough the twenty-ninth word *was* Bomb. The coincidence was, to say the least of it, extraordinary. But presuming that it was correct, the rest of the message was simplicity itself. He turned the telegram over, and upon the back transcribed the communication as he imagined it should be read. When he had finished, it ran as follows:

> Owing to O'Grady's silence, the Society in Chicago is growing uneasy. Two men, who are the first and last, or, in other words, the principal members, are going to do something (Nineteen-twelve) to-day with fifty thousand somethings, so arrange about the bombs.

Having got so far, all that remained to be done was to find out to what "nineteen-twelve" referred. He turned to the dictionary again, and looked for the twelfth word upon the nineteenth page. This proved to be "Alkahest," which told him nothing. So he reversed the proceedings and looked for the nineteenth word upon the twelfth page; but this proved even less satisfactory than before. However much the dictionary might have helped him hitherto, it was plainly useless now. He thought and thought, but without success. He turned up the almanac, but the dates did not fit in.

He then wrote the letters of the alphabet upon a sheet of paper, and against each placed its equivalent number. The nineteenth letter was S, the twelfth L. Did they represent two words, or were they the first and the last letters of a word? In that case, what could it be. The only three he could think of were *soil*, *sell*, and *sail*. The two first were hopeless, but the last seemed better. But how would that fit in? He took up his pen and tried it.

> Owing to O'Grady's silence, the Society in Chicago is growing uneasy. Two men, who are the first and last, or, in other words, the principal members, sail to-day with fifty thousand somethings, probably pounds or dollars, so prepare bombs.
>
> Nero.

He felt convinced that he had hit it at last. Either it was a very extraordinary coincidence, or he had discovered the answer to the riddle. If his solution were correct, one thing was certain, he had got in his hands, quite by chance, a clue to one of the biggest Fenian conspiracies ever yet brought to light. He remembered that at that moment London contained half the crowned heads, or their representatives, of Europe. What better occasion could the enemies of law and order desire for striking a blow at the Government and society in general? What was he to do?

To communicate with the police and thus allow himself to be drawn into the affair, would be an act of the maddest folly; should he therefore drop the whole thing, as he had at first proposed, or should he take the matter into his own hands, help Mrs. Jeffreys in her trouble by shipping her father out of harm's way, outwit the Fenians, and appropriate the fifty thousand pounds mentioned in the cablegram himself?

The last idea was distinctly a good one. But, before it could be done, he felt he must be certain of his facts. Was the fifty thousand referred to money, or was it something else? If the former, was it pounds or was it dollars? There was a vast difference, but in either case, if only he could hit on a safe scheme, he would be well repaid for whatever risk he might run. He decided to see Mrs. Jeffreys without loss of time. Accordingly, after breakfast, he sent her a note asking her to call upon him, without fail, at twelve o'clock.

Punctuality is not generally considered a virtue possessed by the sex of which Mrs. Jeffreys was so unfortunate a member, but the clock upon Klimo's mantelpiece had scarcely struck the hour before she put in an appearance. He immediately bade her be seated.

"Mrs. Jeffreys," he began with a severely judicial air, "it is with much regret I find that while seeking my advice yesterday you were all the time deceiving me. How was it that you failed to tell me that your father was connected with a Fenian Society, whose one aim and object is to destroy law and order in this country?"

The question evidently took the girl by surprise. She became deathly pale, and for a moment Klimo thought she was going to faint. With a marvelous exhibition of will, however, she pulled herself together and faced her accuser.

"You have no right to say such a thing," she began. "My father is—"

"Pardon me," he answered quietly, "but I am in the possession of information which enables me to understand exactly what he is. If you answer me correctly it is probable that after all I will take your case up, and will help you to save your father's life, but if you decline to do so, ill as he is, he will be arrested within twenty-four hours, and then nothing on earth can save him from condign punishment. Which do you prefer?"

"I will tell you everything," she said quickly. "I ought to have done so at first, but you can understand why I shrank from it. My father has for a long time past been ashamed of the part he has been playing, but he could not help himself. He was too valuable to them, and they would not let him slip. They drove him on and on, and it was his remorse and anxiety that broke him down at last."

"I think you have chosen the better course in telling me this. I will ask my questions, and you can answer them. To begin with, where are the headquarters of the Society?"

"In Chicago."

"I thought as much. And is it possible for you to tell me the names of the two principal members?"

"There are many members, and I don't know that one *is* greater than another."

"But there must be some who are more important than others. For instance, the pair referred to in this telegram as Alpha and Omega?"

"I can only think," she answered, after a moment's thought, "that they must be the two men who came oftenest to our house, Messrs. Maguire and Rooney."

"Can you describe them, or, better still, have you their photographs?"

"I have a photograph of Mr. Rooney. It was taken last year."

"You must send it to me as soon as you get home," he said; "and now give me as close a description as possible of the other person to whom you refer, Mr. Maguire."

Mrs. Jeffreys considered for a few moments before she answered.

"He is tall, standing fully six feet, I should think," she said at last, "with red hair and watery blue eyes, in the left of which there is a slight cast. He is broad shouldered and, in spite of his long residence in America, speaks with a decided brogue. I know them for desperate men, and if they come over to England may God help us all. Mr. Klimo, you don't think the police will take my father?"

"Not if you implicitly obey my instructions," he answered.

Klimo thought for a few seconds, and then continued: "If you wish me to undertake this business, which I need hardly tell you is out of my usual line, you will now go home and send me the photograph you spoke of a few moments since. After that you will take no sort of action until you hear from me again. For certain reasons of my own I shall take this matter up, and will do my utmost to save your father. One word of advice first, say nothing to anybody, but pack your father's boxes and be prepared to get him out of England, if necessary, at a moment's notice."

The girl rose and made as if she would leave the room, but instead of doing so she stood irresolute. For a few moments she said nothing, but fumbled with the handle of her parasol and breathed heavily. Then the pluck which had so far sustained her gave way entirely, and she fell back on her chair crying as if her heart would break. Klimo instantly left his box and went round to her. He made a figure queer enough to please any one, in his old-fashioned clothes, his skull cap, his long grey hair reaching almost to his shoulders, and with his smoked glass spectacles perched upon his nose.

"Why cry, my dear young lady?" said Klimo. "Have I not promised to do my best for you? Let us, however, understand each other thoroughly. If there is anything you are keeping back you must tell me. By not speaking out you are imperiling your own and your father's safety."

"I know that you must think that I am endeavouring to deceive you," she said; "but I am so terribly afraid of committing myself that I hardly know what to tell and what not to tell. I have come to you, having no friends in the whole world save my husband, who is in Marseilles, and my father, who, as I have said, is lying dangerously ill in our house.

"Of course I know what my father has been. Surely you cannot suppose that a grown up girl like myself could be so dense as not to guess why few save Irishmen visited our house, and why at times there were men staying with us for weeks at a time, who lived in the back rooms and never went outside our front door, and who, when they did take their departure, sneaked out in the dead of night.

"I remember a time in the fall of the last year that I was at home, when there were more meetings than ever, and when these men, Maguire and Rooney, almost lived with us. They and my father were occupied day and night in a room at the top of the house, and then, in the January following, Maguire came to England. Three weeks later the papers were full of a terrible dynamite explosion in London, in which forty innocent people lost their lives. Mr. Klimo, you must imagine for yourself the terror and shame that seized me, particularly when I remembered that my father was a companion of the men who had been concerned in it.

"Now my father repents, and they are edging him on to some fresh outrage. I cannot tell you what it is, but I know this, that if Maguire and Rooney are coming to England, something awful is about to happen, and if they distrust him, and there is any chance of any one getting into trouble, my father will be made the scapegoat.

"To run away from them would be to court certain death. They have agents in almost every European city, and, unless we could get right away to the other side of the world, they would be certain to catch us. Besides, my father is too ill to travel. The doctors say he must not be disturbed under any pretence whatever."

"Well, well!" said Klimo, "leave the matter to me, and I will see what can be done. Send me the photograph you spoke of, and let me know instantly if there are any further developments."

"Do you mean that after all I can rely upon you helping me?"

"If you are brave," he answered, "not without. Now, one last question, and then you must be off. I see in the last telegram, mention made of fifty lacs; I presume that means money?"

"A lac is their term for a thousand pounds," she answered without hesitation.

"That will do," said Klimo. "Now go home and don't worry yourself more than you can help. Above all, don't let any one suspect that I have any interest in the case. Upon your doing that will in a great measure depend your safety."

She promised to obey him in this particular as in the others, and then took her departure.

When Klimo had passed into the adjoining house, he bade his valet accompany him to his study.

"Belton," he said, as he seated himself in a comfortable chair before his writing table, "I have this morning agreed to undertake what promises to be one of the most dangerous, and at the same time most interesting, cases that has yet come under my notice. A young lady, the wife of a respectable Bank Inspector, has been twice to see me lately with a very sad story. Her father, it would appear, is an Irish American, with the usual prejudice against this country. He has been for some time a member of a Fenian Society, possibly one of their most active workers. In January last the executive sent him to this country to arrange for an exhibition of their powers.

"Since arriving here the father has been seized with remorse, and the mental strain and fear thus entailed have made him seriously ill. For weeks he has been lying at death's door in his

daughter's house. Hearing nothing from him the Society has tele-
graphed again and again, but without result. In consequence, two
of the chief and most dangerous members are coming over here
with fifty thousand pounds at their disposal, to look after their
erring brother, to take over the management of affairs, and to commence the slaughter as per arrangement.

"Now as a peaceable citizen of the City of London, and a humble
servant of Her Majesty the Queen, it is manifestly my duty to de-
liver these rascals into the hands of the police. But to do that would
be to implicate the girl's father, and to kill her husband's faith in
her family; for it must be remembered he knows nothing of the
father's Fenian tendencies. It would also mix me up in a most undesirable matter at a time when I have the best of reasons for desiring to keep quiet.

"Well, the long and the short of the matter is that I have been
thinking the question out, and I have arrived at the following conclusion. If I can hit upon a workable scheme I shall play policeman and public benefactor, checkmate the dynamiters, save the
girl and her father, and reimburse myself to the extent of fifty thousand pounds. Fifty thousand pounds, Belton, think of that. If it
hadn't been for the money I should have had nothing at all to do
with it."

"But how will you do it, sir?" asked Belton, who had learnt by
experience never to be surprised at anything his master might say
or do.

"Well, so far," he answered, "it seems a comparatively easy
matter. I see that the last telegram was dispatched on Saturday,
May 26th, and says, or purports to say, 'sail to-day' In that case,
all being well, they should be in Liverpool some time to-morrow,
Thursday. So we have a clear day at our disposal in which to prepare a reception for them. Tonight I am to have a photograph of
one of the men in my possession, and to-morrow I shall send you
to Liverpool to meet them. Once you have set eyes on them you
must not lose sight of them until you have discovered where they
are domiciled in London. After that I will take the matter in hand
myself."

"At what hour do you wish me to start for Liverpool, sir?" asked Belton.

"First thing to-morrow morning," his master replied. "In the meantime you must, by hook or crook, obtain a police inspector's, a sergeant's, and two constable's, uniforms with belts and helmets complete. Also I shall require three men in whom I can place absolute and implicit confidence. They must be big fellows with plenty of pluck and intelligence, and the clothes you get must fit them so that they shall not look awkward in them. They must also bring plain clothes with them, for I shall want two of them to undertake a journey to Ireland. They will each be paid a hundred pounds for the job, and to ensure their silence afterwards. Do you think you can find me the men without disclosing my connection with the matter?"

"I know exactly where to put my hand upon them, sir," remarked Belton, "and for the sum you mention it's my belief they'd hold their tongues for ever, no matter what pressure was brought to bear upon them."

"Very good. You had better communicate with them at once, and tell them to hold themselves in readiness, for I may want them at any moment. On Friday night I shall probably attempt the job, and they can get back to town when and how they like."

"Very good, sir. I'll see about them this afternoon without fail."

Next morning, Belton left London for Liverpool, with the photograph of the mysterious Rooney in his pocket-book. Carne had spent the afternoon with a fashionable party at Hurlingham, and it was not until he returned to his house that he received the telegram he had instructed his valet to send him. It was short, and to the point.

Friends arrived. Reach Euston nine o'clock.

The station clocks wanted ten minutes of the hour when the hansom containing a certain ascetic looking curate drove into the yard. The clergyman paid his fare, and, having inquired the platform upon which the Liverpool express would arrive, strolled leisurely in that direction. He would have been a clever man who would have recognised in this unsophisticated individual either deformed Simon Carne, of Park Lane, or the famous detective of Belverton Street.

Punctual almost to the moment the train put in an appearance, and drew up beside the platform. A moment later the curate was engulfed in a sea of passengers. A bystander, had he been sufficiently observant to notice such a thing, would have been struck by the eager way in which he looked about him, and also by the way in which his manner changed directly he went forward to greet the person he was expecting.

To all appearances they were both curates, but their social positions must have been widely different if their behaviour to each other could have been taken as any criterion. The new arrival, having greeted his friend, turned to two gentlemen standing beside him, and after thanking them for their company during the journey, wished them a pleasant holiday in England, and bade them good-bye. Then, turning to his friend again, he led him along the platform towards the cab rank.

During the time Belton had been speaking to the two men just referred to, Carne had been studying their faces attentively. One, the taller of the pair, if his red hair and watery blue eyes went for anything, was evidently Maguire, the other was Rooney, the man of the photograph. Both were big, burly fellows, and Carne felt that if it ever came to a fight, they would be just the sort of men to offer a determined resistance.

Arm in arm the curates followed the Americans towards the cab rank. Reaching it, the latter called up a vehicle, placed the bags they carried upon the roof, and took their places inside. The driver had evidently received his instructions, for he drove off without delay. Carne at once called up another cab, into which Belton sprang without ceremony. Carne pointed to the cab just disappearing through the gates ahead.

"Keep that hansom in sight, cabby," he said; "but whatever you do don't pass it."

"All right, sir," said the man, and immediately applied the whip to his horse.

When they turned into Seymour Street, scarcely twenty yards separated the two vehicles, and in this order they proceeded across the Euston Road, by way of Upper Woburn Place and Tavistock Square.

The cab passed through Bloomsbury Square, and turned down one of the thoroughfares leading therefrom, and made its way into a street flanked on either side by tall, gloomy-looking houses. Leaning over the apron, Carne gazed up at the corner house, on which he could just see the plate setting forth the name of the street. What he saw there told him all he wanted to know.

They were in Bellamer Street, and it was plain to him that the men had determined to thrust themselves upon the hapless Mrs. Jeffreys. He immediately poked his umbrella through the shutter, and bade the cabman drive on to the next corner, and then pull up. As soon as the horse came to a standstill, Carne jumped out, and, bidding his companion drive home, crossed the street, and made his way back until he arrived at a spot exactly opposite the house entered by the two men.

His supposition that they intended to domicile themselves there was borne out by the fact that they had taken their luggage inside, and had dismissed their cab. There had been lights in two of the windows when the cab had passed, now a third was added, and this he set down as emanating from the room allotted to the new arrivals.

For upwards of an hour and a half Carne remained standing in the shadow of the opposite houses, watching the Jeffreys' residence. The lights in the lower room had by this time disappeared, and within ten minutes that on the first floor followed suit. Being convinced, in his own mind, that the inmates were safely settled for the night, he left the scene of his vigil, and, walking to the corner of the street, hailed a hansom and was driven home. On reaching No. 1, Belverton Street, he found a letter lying on the hall table addressed to Klimo. It was in a woman's handwriting, and it did not take him long to guess that it was from Mrs. Jeffreys. He opened it and read as follows:

"Bellamer Street,
"Thursday Evening.

"Dear Mr. Klimo,—

"I am sending this to you to tell you that my worst
suspicions have been realised. The two men whose
coming I so dreaded, have arrived, and have taken
up their abode with us. For my father's sake I dare
not turn them out, and to-night I have heard from
my husband to say that he will be home on Saturday
next. What is to be done? If something does not happen soon, they will commence their dastardly business in England, and then God help us all. My only
hope is in Him and you.

"Yours ever gratefully,
"Eileen Jeffreys."

Carne folded up the letter with a grave face, and then let himself into Porchester House and went to bed to think out his plan of
action. Next morning he was up betimes, and by the breakfast hour
had made up his mind as to what he was going to do. He had also
written and dispatched a note to the girl who was depending so
much upon him. In it he told her to come and see him without fail
that morning. His meal finished, he went to his dressing-room and
attired himself in Klimo's clothes, and shortly after ten o'clock
entered the detective's house. Half an hour later Mrs. Jeffreys was
ushered into his presence. As he greeted her he noticed that she
looked pale and wan. It was evident she had spent a sleepless night.

"Sit down," he said, "and tell me what has happened since last
I saw you."

"The most terrible thing of all has happened," she answered,
"As I told you in my note, the men have reached England, and are
now living in our house. You can imagine what a shock their arrival was to me. I did not know what to do. For my father's sake I
could not refuse them admittance, and yet I knew that I had no
right to take them in during my husband's absence. Be that as it
may, they are there now, and to-morrow night George returns. If

he discovers their identity, and suspects their errand, he will hand
them over to the police without a second thought, and then we shall
be disgraced for ever. Oh, Mr. Klimo, you promised to help me,
can you not do so? Heaven knows how badly I need your aid."

"You shall have it. Now listen to my instructions. You will go
home and watch these men. During the afternoon they will probably go out, and the instant they do so, you must admit three of my
servants and place them in some room where their presence will
not be suspected by our enemies. A friend, who will hand you my
card, will call later on, and as he will take command, you must do
your best to help him in every possible way."

"You need have no fear of my not doing that," she said. "And I
will be grateful to you till my dying day."

"Well, we'll see. Now good-bye."

After she had left him, Klimo returned to Porchester House and
sent for Belton. He was out, it appeared, but within half an hour
he returned and entered his master's presence.

"Have you discovered the bank?" asked Carne.

"Yes, sir, I have," said Belton. "But not till I was walked off my
legs. The men are as suspicious as wild rabbits, and they dodged
and played about so, that I began to think they'd get away from me
altogether. The bank is the 'United Kingdom,' Oxford Street
branch."

"That's right. Now what about the uniforms?"

"They're quite ready, sir, helmets, tunics, belts and trousers
complete."

"Well then have them packed as I told you yesterday, and ready
to proceed to Bellamer Street with the men, the instant we get the
information that the folk we are after have stepped outside the
house door."

"Very good, sir. And as to yourself?"

"I shall join you at the house at ten o'clock, or thereabouts. We
must, if possible, catch them at their supper."

London was half through its pleasures that night, when a tall,
military-looking man, muffled in a large cloak, stepped into a hansom outside Porchester House, Park Lane, and drove off in the

direction of Oxford Street. Though the business which was taking
him out would have presented sufficient dangers to have deterred
many men who consider themselves not wanting in pluck, it did
not in the least oppress Simon Carne; on the contrary, it seemed
to afford him no small amount of satisfaction. He whistled a tune
to himself as he drove along the lamplit thoroughfares, and smiled
as sweetly as a lover thinking of his mistress when he reviewed the
plot he had so cunningly contrived.

He felt a glow of virtue as he remembered that he was undertaking the business in order to promote another's happiness, but
at the same time reflected that, if fate were willing to pay him fifty
thousand pounds for his generosity, well, it was so much the better for him. Reaching Mudie's Library, his coachman drove by way
of Hart Street into Bloomsbury Square, and later on turned into
Bellamer Street.

At the corner he stopped his driver and gave him some instructions in a low voice. Having done so, he walked along the pavement as far as No. 14, where he came to a standstill. As on the last
occasion that he had surveyed the house, there were lights in three
of the windows, and from this illumination he argued that his men
were at home. Without hesitation he went up the steps and rang
the bell. Before he could have counted fifty it was opened by Mrs.
Jeffreys herself, who looked suspiciously at the person she saw
before her. It was evident that in the tall, well-made man with iron-
grey moustache and dark hair, she did not recognise her elderly
acquaintance, Klimo, the detective.

"Are you Mrs. Jeffreys?" asked the newcomer, in a low voice.

"I am," she answered. "Pray, what can I do for you?"

"I was told by a friend to give you this card."

He thereupon handed to her a card on which was written the
one word "Klimo." She glanced at it, and, as if that magic name
were sufficient to settle every doubt, beckoned to him to follow
her. Having softly closed the door she led him down the passage
until she arrived at a door on her right hand. This she opened
and signed to him to enter. It was a room that was half office half
library.

"I am to understand that you come from Mr. Klimo?" she said, trembling under the intensity of her emotion. "What am I to do?"

"First be as calm as you can. Then tell me where the men are with whom I have to deal."

"They are having their supper in the dining-room. They went out soon after luncheon, and only returned an hour ago."

"Very good. Now, if you will conduct me upstairs, I shall be glad to see if your father is well enough to sign a document I have brought with me. Nothing can be done until I have arranged that."

"If you will come with me I will take you to him. But we must go quietly, for the men are so suspicious that they send for me to know the meaning of every sound. I was dreadfully afraid your ring would bring them out into the hall."

Leading the way up the stairs she conducted him to a room on the first floor, the door of which she opened carefully. On entering, Carne found himself in a well-furnished bedroom. A bed stood in the centre of the room, and on this lay a man. In the dim light, for the gas was turned down till it showed scarcely a glimmer, he looked more like a skeleton than a human being. A long white beard lay upon the coverlet, his hair was of the same colour, and the pallor of his skin more than matched both. That he was conscious was shown by the question he addressed to his daughter as they entered.

"What is it, Eileen?" he asked faintly. "Who is this gentleman, and why does he come to see me?"

"He is a friend, father," she answered. "One who has come to save us from these wicked men."

"God bless you, sir," said the invalid, and as he spoke he made as if he would shake him by the hand.

Carne, however, checked him.

"Do not move or speak," he said, "but try and pull yourself together sufficiently to sign this paper."

"What is the document?"

"It is something without which I can take no sort of action. My instructions are to do nothing until you have signed it. You need not be afraid; it will not hurt you. Come, sir, there is no time to be wasted. If these rascals are to be got out of England our scheme must be carried out to-night."

"To do that I will sign anything. I trust your honour for its contents. Give me a pen and ink."

His daughter supported him in her arms, while Carne dipped a pen in the bottle of ink he had brought with him and placed it in the tremulous fingers. Then, the paper being supported on a book, the old man laboriously traced his signature at the place indicated. When he had done so he fell back upon the pillow completely exhausted.

Carne blotted it carefully, then folded the paper up, placed it in his pocket and announced himself ready for work. The clock upon the mantelpiece showed him that it was a quarter to eleven, so that if he intended to act that night he knew he must do so quickly. Bidding the invalid rest happy in the knowledge that his safety was assured, he beckoned the daughter to him.

"Go downstairs," he said in a whisper, "and make sure that the men are still in the dining-room."

She did as he ordered her, and in a few moments returned with the information that they had finished their supper and had announced their intention of going to bed.

"In that case we must hurry," said Carne. "Where are my men concealed?"

"In the room at the end of that passage," was the girl's reply.

"I will go to them. In the meantime you must return to the study downstairs, where we will join you in five minutes' time. Just before we enter the room in which they are sitting, one of my men will ring the front door bell. You must endeavour to make the fellows inside believe that you are trying to prevent us from gaining admittance. We shall arrest you, and then deal with them. Do you understand?"

"Perfectly."

She slipped away, and Carne hastened to the room at the end of the passage. He scratched with his fingernail upon the door, and a second later it was opened by a sergeant of police. On stepping inside he found two constables and an inspector awaiting him.

"Is all prepared, Belton?" he inquired of the latter.

"Quite prepared, sir."

"Then come along, and step as softly as you can."

As he spoke he took from his pocket a couple of papers, and led the way along the corridor and down the stairs. With infinite care they made their way along the hall until they reached the dining-room door, where Mrs. Jeffreys joined them. Then the street bell rang loudly, and the man who had opened the front door a couple of inches shut it with a bang. Without further hesitation Carne called upon the woman to stand aside, while Belton threw open the dining-room door.

"I tell you, sir, you are mistaken," cried the terrified woman.

"I am the best judge of that," said Carne roughly, and then, turning to Belton, he added: "Let one of your men take charge of this woman."

On hearing them enter, the two men they were in search of had risen from the chairs they had been occupying on either side of the fire, and stood side by side upon the hearth rug, staring at the intruders as if they did not know what to do.

"James Maguire and Patrick Wake Rooney," said Carne, approaching the two men, and presenting the papers he held in his hand, "I have here warrants, and arrest you both on a charge of being concerned in a Fenian plot against the well being of Her Majesty's Government. I should advise you to submit quietly. The house is surrounded, constables are posted at all the doors, and there is not the slightest chance of escape."

The men seemed too thunderstruck to do anything, and submitted quietly to the process of handcuffing. When they had been secured, Carne turned to the inspector and said:

"With regard to the other man who is ill upstairs, Septimus O'Grady, you had better post a man at his door."

"Very good, sir."

Then turning to Messrs. Maguire and Rooney, he said: "I am authorised by Her Majesty's Government to offer you your choice between arrest and appearance at Bow Street, or immediate return to America. Which do you choose? I need not tell you that we have proof enough in our hands to hang the pair of you if necessary.

You had better make up your minds as quickly as possible, for I have no time to waste."

The men stared at him in supreme astonishment.

"You will not prosecute us?"

"My instructions are, in the event of your choosing the latter alternative, to see that you leave the country at once. In fact, I shall conduct you to Kingstown myself to-night, and place you aboard the mail-boat there."

"Well, so far as I can see, it's Hobson's choice," said Maguire. "I'll pay you the compliment of saying that you're smarter than I thought you'd be. How did you come to know we were in England?"

"Because your departure from America was cabled to us more than a week ago. You have been shadowed ever since you set foot ashore. Now passages have been booked for you on board the out-going boat, and you will sail in her. First, however, it will be necessary for you to sign this paper, pledging yourselves never to set foot in England again."

"And supposing we do not sign it?"

"In that case I shall take you both to Bow Street forthwith, and you will come before the magistrates in the morning. You know what that will mean. You had better make up your minds quickly, for there is no time to lose."

For some moments they remained silent. Then Maguire said sullenly: "Bedad, sir, since there's nothing else for it, I consent."

"And so do I," said Rooney. "Where's the paper?"

Carne handed them a formidable-looking document, and they read it in turn with ostentatious care. As soon as they had professed themselves willing to append their signatures to it, the sham detective took it to a writing-table at the other end of the room, and then ordered them to be unmanacled, so that they could come up in turn and sign. Had they been less agitated it is just possible they would have noticed that two sheets of blotting paper covered the context, and that only a small space on the paper, which was of a bluish grey tint, was left uncovered.

Then placing them in charge of the police officials, Carne left the room and went upstairs to examine their baggage. Evidently he discovered there what he wanted to know, for when he returned to the room his face was radiant.

Half an hour later they had left the house in separate cabs. Rooney was accompanied by Belton and one of his subordinates, now in plain clothes, while Carne and another took charge of Maguire. At Euston they found special carriages awaiting them, and the same procedure was adopted in Ireland. The journey to Queenstown proved entirely uneventful; not for one moment did the two men suspect the trick that was being played upon them; nevertheless, it was with ill-concealed feelings of satisfaction that Carne and Belton bade them farewell upon the deck of the out-ward-bound steamer.

"Good-bye," said Maguire, as their captors prepared to pass over the side again. "An' good luck to ye. I'll wish ye that, for ye've treated us well, though it's a scurvy trick ye've played us in turning us out of England like this. First, however, one question. What about O'Grady?"

"The same course will be pursued with him, as soon as he is able to move," answered the other. "I can't say more."

"A word in your ear first," said Rooney. He leant towards Carne. "The girl's a good one," he said. "An' ye may do what ye can for her, for she knows nought of our business."

"I'll remember that if ever the chance arises," said Carne. "Now, good-bye."

"Good-bye."

On the Wednesday morning following, an elderly gentleman, dressed in rather an antiquated fashion, but boasting an appearance of great respectability, drove up in a brougham to the branch of the United Kingdom Bank in Oxford Street, and presented a cheque for no less a sum than forty-five thousand pounds, signed with the names of Septimus O'Grady, James Maguire, and Patrick Rooney, and bearing the date of the preceding Friday.

The cheque was in perfect order, and, in spite of the largeness of the amount, it was cashed without hesitation.

That afternoon Klimo received a visit from Mrs. Jeffreys. She came to express her gratitude for his help, and to ask the extent of her debt.

"You owe me nothing but your gratitude. I will not take a halfpenny. I am quite well enough rewarded now," said Klimo with a smile.

When she had gone he took out his pocketbook and consulted it.

"Forty-five thousand pounds," he said with a chuckle. "Yes, that is good. I did not take her money, but I *have* been rewarded in another way."

Then he went into Porchester House and dressed for the Garden Party at Marlborough House, to which he had been invited.

THE WEDDING GUEST

ONE BRIGHT SUMMER morning Simon Carne sat in his study, and reflected on the slackness of things in general. Since he had rendered such a signal service to the State, as narrated in the previous chapter, he had done comparatively nothing to raise himself in his own estimation. He was thinking in this strain when his butler entered, and announced "Kelmare Sahib." The interruption was a welcome one, and Carne rose to greet his guest with every sign of pleasure on his face.

"Good-morning, Kelmare," he said, as he took the other's outstretched hand; "I'm delighted to see you. How are you this morning?"

"As well as a man can hope to be under the circumstances," replied the new arrival, a somewhat *blasé* youth, dressed in the height of fashion. "You are going to the Greenthorpe wedding, of course. I hear you have been invited."

"You are quite right; I have," said Carne, and presently produced a card from the basket, and tossed it across the table.

The other took it up with a groan.

"Yes," he said, "that's it, by Jove! And a nice-looking document it is. Carne, did you ever hate anybody so badly that it seemed as if it would be scarcely possible to discover anything you would not do to hurt them?"

"No," answered Carne, "I cannot say that I have. Fate has always found me some way or another in which I might get even with my enemies. But you seem very vindictive in this matter. What's the reason of it?"

"Vindictive?" said Kelmare, "of course I am; think how they have treated me. A year ago, this week, Sophie Greenthorpe and I were engaged. Old Greenthorpe had not then turned his business into a limited liability company, and my people were jolly angry with me for making such a foolish match; but I did not care. I was in love, and Sophie Greenthorpe is as pretty a girl as can be found in the length and breadth of London. But there, you've seen her, so you know for yourself. Well, three months later, old Greenthorpe sold his business for upwards of three million sterling. On the strength of it he went into the House, gave thirty thousand to the funds of his party, and would have received a baronetcy for his generosity, had his party not been shunted out of power.

"Inside another month all the swells had taken them up; dukes and earls were as common at the old lady's receptions as they had been scarce before, and I began to understand that, instead of being everybody to them as I had once been, the old fellow was beginning to think his daughter might have done much better than become engaged to the third son of an impecunious earl.

"Then Kilbenham came upon the scene. He's a fine-looking fellow, and a marquis, but, as you know as well as I do, a real bad hat. He hasn't a red cent in the world to bless himself with, and he wanted money—well—just about as badly as a man *could* want it. What's the result? Within six weeks I am thrown over, and she has accepted Kilbenham's offer of marriage. Society says—'What a good match!' and, as if to endorse it, you received an invitation to the ceremony."

"Forgive me, but *you* are growing cynical now," said Carne, as he lit a fresh cigar.

"Haven't I good cause to be?" asked Kelmare. "Wait till you've been treated as I have, and then we'll see how you'll feel. When I think how every man you meet speaks of Kilbenham, and of the stories that are afloat concerning him, and hear the way old Greenthorpe and his pretensions are laughed at in the clubs, and sneered at in the papers, and am told that they are receiving presents of enormous value from all sorts and conditions of people, from Royalty to the poor devils of workmen he still underpays, just because Kilbenham is a marquis and she is the daughter of a millionaire, why, I can tell you it is enough to make any one cynical."

"In the main, I agree with you," said Carne. "But, as life is made up of just such contradictions, it seems to me absurd to butt your head against a stone wall, and then grumble because it hurts and you don't make any impression on it. Do you think the presents are as wonderful as they say? I want to know, because I've not given mine yet. In these days one gives as others give. If they have not received anything very good, then a pair of electroplated entrée dishes will meet the case. If the reverse—well—diamonds, perhaps, or an old Master that the Americans are wild to buy, and can't."

"Who is cynical now, I should like to know?" said Kelmare. "I was told this morning that up to the present, with the superb diamonds given by the bride's father, they have totaled a value of something like twenty thousand pounds."

"You surprise me," answered Carne.

"I am surprised myself," said Kelmare, as he rose to go. "Now, I must be off. I came in to see if you felt inclined for a week's cruise in the Channel. Burgrave has lent me his yacht, and somehow I think a change of air will do me good."

"I am very sorry," said Carne, "but it would be quite impossible for me to get away just now. I have several important functions on hand that will keep me in town."

"I suppose this wedding is one of them?"

"To tell the honest truth, I had scarcely thought of it," replied Carne. "Must you be off? Well, then, good-bye, and a pleasant holiday to you."

When Kelmare had disappeared, Carne went back to his study, and seated himself at his writing-table. "Kelmare is a little oversensitive," he said, "and his pique is spoiling his judgment. He does not seem to realize that he has come very well out of a jolly bad business. I am not certain which I pity most—Miss Greenthorpe, who is a heartless little hussy, or the Marquis of Kilbenham, who is a thorough-paced scoundrel. The wedding, however, promises to be a fashionable one, and—"

He stopped midway, rose, and stood leaning against the mantelpiece, staring into the empty fireplace. Presently he flipped the ash off his cigar, and turned round. "It never struck me in that light before," he said, as he pressed the button of the electric bell in the wall beside him. When it was answered, he ordered his carriage, and a quarter of an hour later was rolling down Regent Street.

Reaching a well-known jeweler's shop, he pulled the check string, and, the door having been opened, descended, and went inside. It was not the first time he had had dealings with the firm, and as soon as he was recognised the proprietor hastened forward himself to wait upon him.

"I want a nice wedding present for a young lady," he said, when the other had asked what he could have the pleasure of showing him. "Diamonds, I think, for preference."

A tray containing hairpins, brooches, rings, and aigrettes set with stones was put before him, but Carne was not satisfied. He wanted something better, he said—something a little more imposing. When he left the shop a quarter of an hour later he had chosen a diamond bracelet, for which he had paid the sum of one thousand pounds. In consequence, the jeweler bowed him to his carriage with almost Oriental obsequiousness.

As Carne rolled down the street, he took the bracelet from its case and glanced at it. He had long since made up his mind as to his line of action, and having done so, was now prepared to start business without delay. On leaving the shop, he had ordered his coachman to drive home; but on second thoughts he changed his mind, and, once more pulling the check string, substituted Berkeley Square for Park Lane.

"I must be thoroughly convinced in my own mind," he said, "before I do anything, and the only way to do that will be to see old Greenthorpe himself without delay. I think I have a good and sufficient excuse in my pocket. At any rate, I'll try it."

On reaching the residence in question, he instructed his footman to inquire whether Mr. Greenthorpe was at home, and if so, if he would see him. An answer in the affirmative was soon forthcoming,

and a moment later Carne and Greenthorpe were greeting each
other in the library.

"Delighted to see you, my dear sir," the latter said as he shook
his guest warmly by the hand, at the same time hoping that old Sir
Mowbray Mowbray next door, who was a gentleman of the old
school, and looked down on the plutocracy, could see and recognise
the magnificent equipage standing before his house. "This is most
kind of you, and indeed I take it as most friendly too."

Carne's face was as smiling and fascinating as it was wont to
be, but an acute observer might have read in the curves of his lips
a little of the contempt he felt for the man before him. Matthew
Greenthorpe's face and figure betrayed his origin as plainly as any
words could have done. If this had not been sufficient, his dress and
the profusion of jewelry—principally diamonds—that decked his person would have told the tale. In appearance he was short, stout,
very red about the face, and made up what he lacked in breeding by
an effusive familiarity that sometimes bordered on the offensive.

"I am afraid," said Carne, when his host had finished speaking,
"that I ought to be ashamed of myself for intruding on you at such
an early hour. I wanted, however, to thank you personally for the
kind invitation you have sent me to be present at your daughter's
wedding."

"I trust you will be able to come," replied Mr. Greenthorpe a
little anxiously, for he was eager that the world should know that
he and the now famous Simon Carne were on familiar terms.

"That is exactly what has brought me to see you," said Carne.
"I regret to say I hardly know yet whether I shall be able to give
myself that pleasure or not. An important complication has arisen
in connection with some property in which I am interested, and it
is just possible that I shall be called to the Continent within the
next few days. My object in calling upon you this morning was to
ask you to permit me to withhold my answer until I am at liberty
to speak more definitely as to my arrangements."

"By all means, by all means," answered his host, placing himself with legs wide apart upon the hearthrug, and rattling the money

in his trouser pockets. "Take just as long as you like so long as you don't say you can't come. Me and the missus—hem! I mean Mrs. Greenthorpe and I—are looking forward to the pleasure of your society, and I can tell you we shan't think our company complete if we don't have you with us."

"I am extremely flattered," said Carne sweetly, "and you may be sure it will not be my fault if I am *not* among your guests."

"Hear, hear, to that, sir," replied the old gentleman. "We shall be a merry party, and, I trust, a distinguished one. We *did* hope to have had Royalty present among us, but, unfortunately, there were special reasons, that I am hardly privileged to mention, which prevented it. However, the Duke of Rugby and his duchess, the father and mother of my future son-in-law, you know, are coming; the Earl of Boxmoor and his countess have accepted; Lord Southam and his lady, half a dozen baronets or so, and as many Members of Parliament and their wives as you can count on one hand. There'll be a ball the night before, given by the Mayor at the Assembly Rooms, a dinner to the tenants at the conclusion of the ceremony, and a ball in my own house after the young couple have gone away. You may take it from me, my dear sir, that nothing on a similar scale has ever been seen at Market Stopford before."

"I can quite believe it," said Carne. "It will mark an epoch in the history of the county."

"It will do more than that, sir. The festivities alone will cost me a cool five thousand pounds. At first *I* was all for having it in town, but I was persuaded out of it. After all, a country house is better suited to such jinks. And we mean to do it well."

He took Carne familiarly by the button of his coat, and, sinking his voice to an impressive whisper, asked him to hazard a guess how much he thought the whole affair, presents and all, would cost.

Carne shook his head. "I have not the very remotest notion," he said. "But if you wish me to guess, I will put it at fifty thousand pounds."

"Not enough by half, sir—not enough by half. Why, I'll let you into a little secret that even my wife knows nothing about."

As he spoke, he crossed the room to a large safe in the wall. This he unlocked, and having done so took from it an oblong box, wrapped in tissue paper. This he placed on the table in the centre of the room, and then, having looked out into the hall to make sure that no one was about, shut and locked the door. Then, turning to Carne, he said:

"I don't know what you may think, sir, but there are some people I know as try to insinuate that if you have money you can't have taste. Now, I've got the money"—here he threw back his shoulders, and tapped himself proudly on the chest—"and I'm going to convince you, sir, that I've got as pretty an idea of taste as any man could wish to have. This box will prove it."

So saying, he unwrapped the tissue paper, and displayed to Carne's astonished gaze a large gilded casket, richly chased, standing upon four massive feet.

"There, sir, you see," he said, "an artistic bit of workmanship, and I'll ask you to guess what it's for."

Carne, however, shook his head. "I'm afraid I'm but a poor hand at guessing, but, if I must venture an opinion, I should say a jewel case."

Thereupon Mr. Greenthorpe lifted the lid.

"And you would be wrong, sir. I will tell you what it is for. That box has been constructed to contain exactly fifty thousand sovereigns, and on her wedding day it will be filled, and presented to the bride, as a token of her father's affection. Now, if that isn't in good taste, I shall have to ask you to tell me what is."

"I am astonished at your munificence," said Carne. "To be perfectly candid with you, I don't know that I have ever heard of such a present before."

"I thought you'd say so. I said to myself when I ordered that box, 'Mr. Carne is the best judge of what is artistic in England, and I'll take his opinion about it.'"

"I suppose your daughter has received some valuable presents?"

"Valuable, sir? Why, that's no name for it. I should put down what has come in up to the present at not a penny under twenty thousand pounds. Why, you may not believe it, sir, but Mrs. Green-thorpe has presented the young couple with a complete toilet-set of solid gold. I doubt if such another has been seen in this country before."

"I should say it would be worth a burglar's while to pay a visit to your house on the wedding day," said Carne with a smile.

"He wouldn't get much for his pains," said the old gentleman warmly. "I have already provided for that contingency. The bil-liard-room will be used as a treasure-chamber for the time being, as there is a big safe like that over yonder in the wall. This week bars are being placed on all the windows, and on the night preced-ing, and also on the wedding day, one of my gardeners will keep watch in the room itself, while one of the village policemen will mount guard at the door in the passage. Between them they ought to be sufficient to keep out any burglars who may wish to try their hands upon the presents. What do you think?"

At that moment the handle of the door turned, and an instant later the bride-elect entered the room. On seeing Simon Carne she paused upon the threshold with a gesture of embarrassment, and made as if she would retreat. Carne, however, was too quick for her. He advanced and held out his hand.

"How do you do, Miss Greenthorpe?" he said, looking her steadily in the face. "Your father has just been telling me of the many beautiful presents you have received. I am sure I congratu-late you most heartily. With your permission I will add my mite to the list. Such as it is, I would beg your acceptance of it."

So saying, he took from his pocket the case containing the bracelet he had that morning purchased. Unfastening it, he with-drew the circlet and clasped it upon her wrist. So great was her surprise and delight that for some moments she was at a loss how to express her thanks. When she recovered her presence of mind and her speech, she attempted to do so, but Carne stopped her.

"You must not thank me too much," he said, "or I shall begin to think I have done a meritorious action. I trust Lord Kilbenham is well?"

"He was very well when I last saw him," answered the girl after a momentary pause, which Carne noticed, "but he is so busy just now that we see very little of each other. Good-bye."

All the way home Simon Carne sat wrapped in a brown study. On reaching his residence he went straight to his study, and to his writing-desk, where he engaged himself for some minutes jotting down certain memoranda on a sheet of note-paper. When he had finished he rang the bell and ordered that Belton, his valet, should be sent to him.

"Belton," he said, when the person he wanted had arrived in answer to the summons, "on Thursday next I shall go down to Market Stopford to attend the wedding of the Marquis of Kilben-ham with Miss Greenthorpe. You will, of course, accompany me. In the meantime" (here he handed him the sheet of paper upon which he had been writing) "I want you to attend to these few details. Some of the articles, I'm afraid, you will find rather difficult to obtain, but at any cost I must have them to take down to the country with me."

Belton took the paper and left the room with it, and for the time being Carne dismissed the matter from his mind.

The sun was in the act of setting on the day immediately preceding the wedding when Simon Carne and his faithful valet reached the wayside station of Market Stopford. As the train came to a standstill, a footman wearing the Greenthorpe livery opened the door of the reserved carriage and informed his master's guest that a brougham was waiting outside the station to convey him to his destination. Belton was to follow with the luggage in the servants' omnibus.

On arrival at Greenthorpe Park, Simon Carne was received by his host and hostess in the hall, the rearmost portion of which was furnished as a smoking-room. Judging from the number of guests passing, re-passing, and lolling about in the easy chairs, most of the company invited had already arrived. When he had greeted those with whom he was familiar, and had taken a cup of tea from the hands of the bride-elect, who was dispensing it at a small table near the great oak fireplace, he set himself to be agreeable to those about him for the space of a quarter of an hour, after which he was escorted to his bedroom, a pretty room situated in the main portion of the building at the head of the grand staircase. He found Belton awaiting him there. His luggage had been unpacked, and a glance at his watch told him that in a few minutes' time it would be necessary for him to prepare for dinner.

"Well, Belton," he said, as he threw himself into a chair beside the window that looked out over the rose garden, "here we are, and the next question is, how are we going to succeed?"

"I have never known you fail yet, sir," replied the deferential valet, "and I don't suppose you'll do so on this occasion."

"You flatter me, Belton, but I will not be so falsely modest as to say that your praise is altogether undeserved. This, however, is a case of more than usual delicacy and danger, and it will be necessary for us to play our cards with considerable care. When I have examined this house I shall elaborate my plans more fully. We have none too much time, for the attempt must be made tomorrow night. You have brought down with you the things I mentioned on that list, I suppose?"

"They are in these chests, sir," said Belton. "They make a precious heavy load, and once or twice I was fearful lest they might arouse suspicion."

"You need have no fear, my good Belton," said Carne. "I have a very plausible excuse to account for their presence here. Every one by this time knows that I am a great student, and also that I never travel without at least two cases of books. It is looked upon as a harmless fad. Here is my key. Open the box standing nearest to you."

Belton did as he was commanded, when it was seen that it was filled to its utmost holding capacity with books.

"No one would think," said Carne, with a smile at the astonishment depicted on the other's face, "that there are only two layers of volumes there, would they? If you lift out the tray upon which they rest, you will discover that the balance of the box is now occupied by the things you placed in it. Unknown to you, I had the trays fitted after you had packed the others. There is nothing like being prepared for all emergencies. Now, pay attention to what I am about to say to you. I have learned that the wedding presents, including the fifty thousand sovereigns presented by Mr. Greenthorpe to his daughter in that absurd casket, of which I spoke to you, will be on view to-morrow afternoon in the billiard-room; to-night, and to-morrow before the ball commences, they will be placed in the safe. One of Mr. Greenthorpe's most trusted servants will keep watch over them in the room, while a constable will be on duty in the lobby outside. Bars have been placed on all the windows, and, as I understand, the village police will patrol the building at intervals during the night. The problem of how we are to get hold of them would seem rather a hard nut to crack, would it not?"

"I must confess I don't see how you are going to do it at all, sir," said Belton.

"Well, we'll see. I have a plan in my head now, but before I can adopt it I must make a few inquiries. I believe there is a staircase leading from the end of this corridor down to the lobby outside the billiard and smoking-rooms. If this is so, we shall have to make use of it. It must be your business to discover at what time the custodians of the treasure have their last meal. When you have found that out let me know. Now you had better get me ready for dinner as soon as possible."

When Carne retired to rest that evening, his inimitable valet was in a position to report that the sentries were already installed, and that their supper had been taken to them, by Mr. Greenthorpe's orders, at ten o'clock precisely, by one of the under-footmen, who had been instructed to look after them.

"Very good," said Carne; "I think I see my way now. I'll sleep on my scheme and let you know what decision I have come to in the morning. If we pull this little business off successfully, there will be ten thousand pounds for you to pay into your credit, my friend."

Belton bowed and thanked his master without a sign of emotion upon his face. After which Simon Carne went to bed.

When he was called next morning, he discovered a perfect summer day. Brilliant sunshine streamed in at the windows, and the songs of birds came from the trees outside.

"An excellent augury," he said to himself as he jumped out of bed and donned the heavy dressing-gown his valet held open for him. "Miss Greenthorpe, my compliments to you. My lord marquis is not the only man upon whom you are conferring happiness today."

His good humour did not leave him, for when he descended to the breakfast-room an hour later his face was radiant with smiles, and every one admitted that it would be impossible to meet a more charming companion.

During the morning he was occupied in the library, writing letters.

At one he lunched with his fellow-guests, none of the family being present, and at half-past went off to dress for the wedding ceremony. This important business completed, a move was made for the church; and in something less than a quarter of an hour the nuptial knot was tied, and Miss Sophie Greenthorpe, only daughter of Matthew Greenthorpe, erstwhile grocer and provision merchant, of Little Bexter Street, Tottenham Court Road, left the building, on her husband's arm, Marchioness of Kilbenham and future Duchess of Rugby.

Simon Carne and his fellow-guests followed in her wake down the aisle, and, having entered their carriages, returned to the Park.

The ball that evening was an acknowledged success, but, though he was an excellent dancer, and had his choice of the prettiest women in the room, Carne was evidently ill at ease. The number of times he stealthily examined his watch said this as plainly as any words. As a matter of fact, the last guest had scarcely arrived before he left the ball-room, and passed down the lobby towards the back staircase, stopping *en route* to glance at the billiard-room door.

As he expected, it was closed, and a stalwart provincial policeman stood on guard before it.

He made a jocular reference about the treasure the constable was guarding, and, with a laugh at himself for forgetting the way to his bedroom, retraced his steps to the stairs, up which he passed to his own apartment Belton was awaiting him there.

"It is ten minutes to ten, Belton," he said abruptly. "It must be now or never. Go down to the kitchen, and hang about there until the tray upon which the suppers of the guard are placed is prepared. When the footman starts with it for the billiard-room, accompany him, and, as he opens the green baize door leading from the servants' quarters into the house, manage, by hook or crook, to hold him in conversation. Say something, and interrupt yourself by a severe fit of coughing. That will give me my cue. If anything should happen to me as I come downstairs, be sure that the man puts his tray down on the slab at the foot of the stairs and renders me assistance. I will manage the rest. Now be off."

Belton bowed respectfully, and left the room. As he did so, Carne crossed to the dressing-table, and unlocked a small case standing upon it. From this he took a tiny silver-stoppered scent bottle, containing, perhaps, half an ounce of white powder. This he slipped into his waistcoat pocket, and then made for the door.

On the top of the back staircase he paused for a few moments to listen. He heard the spring of the green baize door in the passage below creak as it was pushed open. Next moment he distinguished Belton's voice. "It's as true as that I'm standing here," he was saying. "As I went up the stairs with the governor's hot water there she was coming along the passage. I stood back to let her pass, and as I did she—" (Here the narrative was interrupted by a violent fit of coughing.) On hearing this Carne descended the stairs, and, when he had got halfway down, saw the footman and his valet coming along the passage below. At the same instant he must have caught his foot in the stair carpet, for he tripped and fell headlong to the bottom.

"Heaven's alive!" cried Belton. "I do believe that's my governor, and he's killed." At the same time he ran forward to the injured man's assistance.

Carne lay at the foot of the stairs just as he had fallen, his head thrown back, his eyes shut, and his body curled up and motionless.

Belton turned to the footman, who still stood holding the tray where he had stopped on seeing the accident, and said: "Put down those things and go and find Mr. Greenthorpe as quickly as you can. Tell him Mr. Carne has fallen downstairs, and I'm afraid is seriously injured."

The footman immediately disappeared. His back was scarcely turned, however, before Carne was on his feet.

"Excellent, my dear Belton," he whispered; and, as he spoke, he slipped his fingers into his waistcoat pocket. "Hand me up that tray, but be quiet, or the policeman round the corner will hear you."

Belton did as he was ordered, and Carne thereupon sprinkled upon the suppers provided for the two men some of the white powder from the bottle he had taken from his dressing-case. This done, he resumed his place at the foot of the stairs, while Belton, kneeling over him and supporting his head, waited for assistance. Very few minutes elapsed before Mr. Greenthorpe, with his scared face, appeared upon the scene. At his direction Belton and the footman carried the unconscious gentleman to his bedroom, and placed him upon his bed. Restoratives were administered, and in something under ten minutes the injured man once more opened his eyes.

"What is the matter?" he asked feebly. "What has happened?"

"You have met with a slight accident, my dear sir," said the old gentleman, "but you are better now. You fell downstairs."

As if he scarcely comprehended what was said, Carne feebly repeated the last sentence after his host, and then closed his eyes again. When he opened them once more, it was to beg Mr. Greenthorpe to leave him and return to his guests downstairs. After a small amount of pressing, the latter consented to do so, and retired, taking the footman with him. The first use Carne made of their departure was to turn to Belton.

"The powder will take effect in five hours," he said. "See that you have all the things prepared."

"They are quite ready," replied Belton. "I arranged them this evening."

"Very good," said Carne. "Now, I am going to sleep in real earnest."

So saying, he closed his eyes, and resigned himself to slumber as composedly as if nothing out of the common had occurred. The clock on the stables had struck three when he woke again. Belton was still sleeping peacefully, and it was not until he had been repeatedly shaken that he became conscious that it was time to get up.

"Wake up," said Carne; "it is three o'clock, and time for us to be about our business. Unlock that box, and get out the things."

Belton did as he was ordered, placing the packets as he took them from the cases in small Gladstone bags. Having done this, he went to one of his master's trunks, and took from it two suits of clothes, a pair of wigs, two excellently contrived false beards, and a couple of soft felt hats. These he placed upon the bed. Ten minutes later he had assisted his master to change into one of the suits, and when this was done waited for further instructions.

"Before you dress, take a tumbler from that table, and go downstairs. If you should meet any one, say that you are going to the butler's pantry in search of filtered water, as you have used all the drinking water in this room. The ball should be over by this time, and the guests in bed half an hour ago. Ascertain if this is the case, and as you return glance at the policeman on duty outside the billiard-room door. Let me know his condition."

"Very good, sir," said Belton; and, taking a tumbler from the table in question, he left the room. In less than five minutes he had returned to report that, with the exception of the corridor outside the billiard-room, the house was in darkness.

"And how is the guardian of the door?" Carne inquired.

"Fast asleep," said Belton, "and snoring like a pig, sir."

"That is right," said Carne. "The man inside should be the same, or that powder has failed me for the first time in my experience. We'll give them half an hour longer, however, and then get to work. You had better dress yourself."

While Belton was making himself up to resemble his master, Carne sat in an easy chair by his dressing-table, reading Ruskin's *Stones of Venice*. It was one of the most important of his many peculiarities that he could withdraw his thoughts from any subject, however much it might hitherto have engrossed him, and fasten them upon another, without once allowing them to wander back to their original channel. As the stable clock chimed the half-hour, he put the book aside, and sprang to his feet.

"If you're ready, Belton," he said, "switch off the electric light and open that door."

When this had been done he bade his valet wait in the bed-room while he crept down the stairs on tip-toe. On turning into the billiard-room lobby, he discovered the rural policeman propped up in the corner fast asleep. His heavy breathing echoed down the corridors, and one moment's inspection showed Carne that from him he had nothing to fear. Unlocking the door with a key which he took from his pocket, he entered the room, to find the gardener, like the policeman, fast asleep in an armchair by the window. He crossed to him, and, after a careful examination of his breathing, lifted one of his eyelids.

"Excellent," he said. "Nothing could be better. Now, when Belton comes, we shall be ready for business."

So saying, he left the room again, and went softly up the stairs to find his valet. The latter was awaiting him, and, before a wit-ness, had there been one, could have counted twenty, they were standing in the billiard-room together. It was a large apartment, luxuriously furnished, with a bow window at one end and an al-cove, surrounded with seats, at the other. In this alcove, cleverly hidden by the wainscotting, as Mr. Greenthorpe had once been at some pains to point out to Simon Carne, there existed a large iron safe of the latest burglar-proof pattern and design.

The secret was an ingenious one, and would have baffled any ordinary craftsman. Carne, however, as has already been explained, was far from being a commonplace member of his profession. Turn-ing to Belton, he said, "Give me the tools." These being forthcom-ing, in something less than ten minutes he had picked the lock and was master of the safe's contents.

When these, including the fifty thousand sovereigns, had been safely carried upstairs and stowed away in the portmanteaux and chests, and the safe had been filled with the spurious jewelry he had brought with him for that purpose, he signed to Belton to bring him a long pair of steps which stood in a corner of the room, and which had been used for securing the sky-light above the billiard table. These he placed in such a position as would enable him to reach the window.

With a diamond-pointed instrument, and a hand as true as the eye that guided it, he quickly extracted a square of coloured glass, filed through the catch, and was soon standing on the leads outside. A few moments later, the ladder, which had already rendered him such signal service, had enabled him to descend into the garden on the other side.

There he arranged a succession of footsteps in the soft mould, and having done so, returned to the roof, carefully wiped the end of the ladder, so that it should not betray him, and climbed down into the room below, pulling it after him.

"I think we have finished now," he said to Belton, as he took a last look at the recumbent guardians of the room. "These gentlemen sleep soundly, so we will not disturb them further. Come, let us retire to bed."

In less than half an hour he was in bed and fast asleep. Next morning he was still confined to his room by his accident, though he expressed himself as suffering but slight pain. Everyone was quick to sympathise with him, and numerous messages were conveyed to him expressive of sorrow that he should have met with his accident at such a time of general rejoicing. At ten o'clock the first batch of guests took their departure. It was arranged that the Duke and Duchess of Rugby, the Earl and Countess of Raxter, and Simon Carne, who was to be carried downstairs, should travel up to town together by the special train leaving immediately after lunch.

When they bade their host good-bye, the latter was nearly overcome.

"I'm sure it has been a real downright pleasure to me to entertain you, Mr. Carne," he said, as he stood by the carriage door and shook his guest warmly by the hand. "There is only one thing bad about it, and that is your accident."

"You must not speak of that," said Carne, with a little wave of his hand. "The pleasure I have derived from my visit to you amply compensates me for such a minor inconvenience."

So saying he shook hands and drove away to catch his train.

Next morning it was announced in all the Society papers that, owing to an unfortunate accident he had sustained while visiting Mr. Matthew Greenthorpe, at Greenthorpe Park, on the occasion of his daughter's marriage, Mr. Simon Carne would be unable to fulfill any of the engagements he might have entered into.

Any intelligent reader of the aforesaid papers might have been excused had he pictured the gentleman in question confined to his bed, tended by skilled nurses, and watched over by the most fashionable West End physicians obtainable for love or money. They would doubtless, therefore, have been surprised could they have seen him at a late hour on the following evening hard at work in the laboratory he had constructed at the top of his house, as hale and hearty a man as any to be found in the great Metropolis.

"Now those Apostle spoons," he was saying, as he turned from the crucible at which he was engaged to Belton, who was busy at a side table. "The diamonds are safely disposed of, their settings are melted down, and, when these spoons have been added to the list, he will be a wise man who can find in my possession any trace of the famous Kilbenham-Greenthorpe wedding presents."

He was sitting before the fire in his study next morning, with his left foot lying bound up upon a neighbouring chair, when Ram Gafur announced "Kelmare Sahib."

"So sorry to hear that you are under the weather, Carne," said the newcomer as he shook hands. "I only heard of your accident from Raxter last night, or I should have been round before. Beastly hard luck, but you shouldn't have gone to the wedding, you know!"

"And, pray, why not?"

"You see for yourself you haven't profited by your visit, have you?"

"That all depends upon what you consider profit," replied Carne. "I was an actor in an interesting Society spectacle. I was permitted an opportunity of observing my fellow-creatures in many new lights. Personally, I think I did very well. Besides that, to be laid up just now is not altogether a thing to be despised, as you seem to imagine."

"What do you mean?"

"It isn't everybody who can boast such a valid excuse for declining invitations as I now possess," said Carne. "When I tell you that I had a dinner, a lecture at the Imperial Institute, two 'at homes,' and three dances on my list for to-night, you will understand what I mean. Now I am able to decline every one of them without risk of giving offence or fear of hurting the susceptibilities of any one. If you don't call that luck, I do. And now tell me what has brought you here, for I suppose you have some reason, other than friendship, for this early call. When you came in I observed that you were bursting with importance. You are not going to tell me that you have abandoned your yachting trip and are going to be married?"

"You need have no fear on that score. All the same, I have the greatest and most glorious news for you. It isn't every day a man finds Providence taking up his case and entering into judgment against his enemies for him. That is my position. Haven't you heard the news?"

"What news?" asked Carne innocently.

"The greatest of all possible news," answered Kelmare, "and one which concerns you, my dear fellow. You may not believe it, but it was discovered last evening that the Kilbenham-Greenthorpe wedding presents have all been stolen, including the fifty thousand sovereigns presented to the bride in the now famous jeweled casket. What do you think of that?"

"Surely you must be joking," said Carne incredulously. "I cannot believe it."

"Nevertheless it's a fact," replied Kelmare.

"But when did it happen? and how did they discover it?" asked Carne.

"When it took place nobody can tell, but they discovered it when they came to put the presents together after the guests had departed. On the morning after the wedding old Greenthorpe had visited the safe himself, and glanced casually at its contents, just to see that they were all right, you know; but it was not until the afternoon, when they began to do them up, that they discovered that every single article of value the place contained had been abstracted, and dummies substituted. Their investigation proved that the sky-light had been tampered with, and one could see unmistakable footmarks on the flower beds outside.

"Good gracious!" said Carne. "This is news indeed. What a haul the thieves must have had, to be sure! I can scarcely believe it even now. But I thought they had a gardener in the room, a policeman at the door, and a patrol outside, and that old Greenthorpe went to sleep with the keys of the room and safe under his pillow?"

"Quite right," said Kelmare, "so he did; that's the mysterious part of it. The two chaps swear positively that they were wide-awake all night, and that nothing was tampered with while they were there. Who the thieves were, and how they became so familiar with the place, are riddles that it would puzzle the Sphinx, or your friend Klimo next door, to unravel."

"What an unfortunate thing," said Carne. "It's to be hoped the police will catch them before they have time to dispose of their booty."

"You are thinking of your bracelet, I suppose?"

"It may seem egotistical, but I must confess I was; and now I suppose you'll stay to lunch?"

"I'm afraid that's impossible. There are at least five families who have not heard the news, and I feel that it is my bounden duty to enlighten them."

"You're quite right, it is not often a man has such glorious vengeance to chronicle. It behoves you to make the most of it."

The other looked at Carne as if to discover whether or not he was laughing at him. Carne's face, however, was quite expressionless.

"Good-bye; I suppose you won't be at the Wilbringham's tonight?"

"I'm afraid not. You evidently forget that, as I said just now, I have a very good and sufficient excuse."

When the front door had closed behind his guest, Carne lit a third cigar.

"I'm overstepping my allowance," he said reflectively, as he watched the smoke circle upward, "but it isn't every day a man gives a thousand pounds for a wedding present and gets upwards of seventy thousand back. I think I may congratulate myself on having brought off a very successful little speculation."

A CASE OF PHILANTHROPY

IF ONE CONSULTS a dictionary one finds that the word dipsomaniac means a man who spends his life continually desiring alcoholic liquor; a name that properly classifies it has not yet been invented for the individual who exhibits a perpetual craving for notoriety, and yet one is, perhaps, as much a nuisance to society as the other. After his run of success there came a time when Simon Carne, like Alexander the Great, could have sat down and wept, for the reason that he had no more worlds to conquer. For the moment it seemed as if he had exhausted, to put it plainly, every species of artistic villainy.

He had won the Derby, under peculiar circumstances, as narrated elsewhere; he had rendered a signal, though an unostentatious, service to the State; he had stolen, under enormous difficulty, the most famous family jewels in Europe; and he had relieved the most fashionable bride and bridegroom of the season of the valuable presents that their friends and relations had lavished on them.

Having accomplished so much, it would seem as if he had done all that mortal man could do to create a record for himself, but, like the dipsomaniac above mentioned, he was by no means satisfied, he craved for more. It delighted him beyond all measure to hear the comments of his friends upon each daring crime as it became known to the world. What he wanted now was something before which all the rest would sink into insignificance. Day after day he had puzzled his brains, but without success. All he wanted was a hint. When he got it he could be trusted to follow it up for himself. At present, however, even that was wanting.

On a morning following a banquet at the Mansion House, at which he had been a welcome, as well as a conspicuous guest, he was sitting alone in his study smoking a meditative cigar. Though the world would scarcely have thought it, a fashionable life did not suit him, and he was beginning to wonder whether he was not, after all, a little tired of England. He was hungering for the warmth and colour of the East, and, perhaps, if the truth must be told, for something of the rest he had known in the Maharajah of Kadir's lake palace, where he had been domiciled when he had first made the acquaintance of the man who had been his sponsor in English society, the Earl of Amberley.

It was a strange coincidence that, while he was thinking of that nobleman, and of the events which had followed the introduction just referred to, his quick ears should have caught the sound of a bell that was destined eventually to lead him up to one of the most sensational adventures of all his sensational career. A moment later his butler entered to inform him that Lady Caroline Weltershall and the Earl of Amberley had called, and would like to see him. Tossing his cigar into the grate, he passed through the door Ram Gafur held open for him, and, having crossed the hall, entered the drawing-room.

As he went he wondered what it was that had brought them to see him at such an early hour. Both were among his more intimate acquaintances, and both occupied distinguished positions in the social life of the world's great metropolis. While her friends and relations spent their time in search of amusement, and a seemingly eternal round of gaieties, which involved a waste of both health and money, Lady Caroline, who was the ugly duckling of an otherwise singularly handsome family, put her life to a different use.

Philanthropy was her hobby, and scarcely a day passed in which she did not speak at some meeting, preside over some committee, or endeavour in some way, as she somewhat grandiloquently put it: "To better the lives and ameliorate the conditions of our less fortunate fellow creatures." In appearance she was a short, fair woman, of about forty-five years of age, with a not unhandsome face, the effect of which, however, was completely spoilt by two large and protruding teeth.

"My dear Lady Caroline, this is indeed kind of you," said Carne, as he shook hands with her, "and also of you, Lord Amberley. To what happy circumstance may I attribute the pleasure of this visit?"

"I fear it is dreadfully early for us to come to see you," replied her ladyship, "but Lord Amberley assured me that as our business is so pressing you would forgive us."

"Pray do not apologise," returned Carne. "It gives me the greatest possible pleasure to see you. As for the hour I am ashamed to confess that, while the morning is no longer young, I have only just finished breakfast. But won't you sit down?"

They seated themselves once more, and when they had done so, Lady Caroline unfolded her tale.

"As you are perhaps aware, my friends say that I never come to see them unless it is to attempt to extort money from them for some charitable purpose," she said. "No, you need not prepare to button up your pockets, Mr. Carne. I am not going to ask you for anything to-day. What I *do* want, however, is to endeavour to persuade you to help us in a movement we are inaugurating to raise money with which to relieve the great distress in the Canary Islands, brought about by the late disastrous earthquake. My cousin, the Marquis of Laverstock, has kindly promised to act as president, and, although we started it but yesterday, ten thousand pounds have already been subscribed. As you are aware, however, if we are to attract public attention and support, the funds raised must be representative of all classes. Our intention, therefore, is to hold a drawing-room meeting at my house to-morrow afternoon, when a number of the most prominent people of the day will be invited to give us their views upon the subject.

"I feel sure, if you will only consent to throw in your lot with us, and to assist in carrying out what we have in view, we shall be able to raise a sum of at least one hundred thousand pounds for the benefit of the sufferers. Our kind friend here, Lord Amberley, has promised to act as secretary, and his efforts will be invaluable to us. Royalty has signified its gracious approval, and it is expected will head the list with a handsome donation. Every class will be appealed to. Ministers of religion, of all known denominations, will be invited to co-operate, and if you will only consent to allow your name to appear upon the *personnel* of the committee, and will allow us to advertise your name as a speaker at to-morrow's meeting, I feel sure there is nothing we shall not be able to achieve."

"I shall be delighted to help you in any way I can," Carne replied. "If my name is likely to be of any assistance to you, I beg you will make use of it. In the meantime, if you will permit me, I will forward you a cheque for one thousand pounds, being my contribution to the fund you have so charitably started."

Her ladyship beamed with delight, and even Lord Amberley smiled gracious approval.

"You are generous, indeed," said Lady Caroline. "I only wish others would imitate your example."

She did not say that, wealthy though she herself was, she had only contributed ten pounds to the fund. It is well known that while she inaugurated large works of charity, she seldom contributed very largely to them. As a wit once remarked: "Philanthropy was her virtue, and meanness was her vice."

"Egad," said Amberley, "if you're going to open your purse strings like that, Carne, I shall feel called upon to do the same."

"Then let me have the pleasure of booking both amounts at once," cried her ladyship, at the same time whipping out her notebook and pencil with flattering alacrity.

"I shall be delighted," said Carne, with a smile of eagerness.

"I also," replied Amberley, and in a trice both amounts were written down. Having gained her point, her ladyship rose to say goodbye. Lord Amberley immediately imitated her example.

"You will not forget, will you, Mr. Carne?" she said. "I am to have the pleasure of seeing you at my house to-morrow afternoon at three o'clock. We shall look forward to hearing your speech, and I need not remind you that every word you utter will be listened to with the closest attention."

"At three to-morrow afternoon," said Carne, "I shall be at your house. You need have no fear that I shall forget. And now, since you think you must be going, good-bye, and many thanks to you for asking me."

He escorted them to the carriage which was waiting outside, and when he had watched it drive away, returned to his study to write the cheque he had promised her. Having done so, he did not rise from his chair, but continued to sit at his writing-table, biting the feather of his quill pen and staring at the blotting pad before him. A great and glorious notion had suddenly come into his head, and the majesty of it was for the moment holding him spellbound.

"If only it could be worked," he said to himself, "what a glorious *coup* it would be. The question for my consideration is, can it be done? To invite the people of England to subscribe its pounds, shillings, and pence, for my benefit, would be a glorious notion, and just the sort of thing I should enjoy. Besides which I have to remember that I am a thousand pounds to the bad already, and that must come back from somewhere. For the present, however, I'll put the matter aside. After the meeting to-morrow I shall have something tangible to go upon, and then, if I still feel in the same mind, it will be strange if I can't find some way of doing what I want. In the meantime I shall have to think out my speech; upon that will depend a good deal of my success. It is a strange world in which it is ordained that so much should depend upon so little!"

At five minutes to three o'clock on the following afternoon Simon Carne might have been observed—that, I believe, is the correct expression—strolling across from Apsley House to Gloucester Place. Reaching Lord Weltershall's residence, he discovered a long row of carriages lining the pavement, and setting down their occupants at his lordship's door. Carne followed the stream into the house, and was carried by it up the stairs towards the large drawing-room where the meeting was to be held. Already about a hundred persons were present, and it was evident that, if they continued to arrive at the same rate, it would not be long before the room would be filled to overflowing. Seeing Lady Caroline bidding her friends welcome near the door, Carne hastened to shake hands with her.

"It is so very good of you to come," she said, as she took his hand. "Remember, we are looking to you for a rousing speech this afternoon. We want one that will inflame all England, and touch the heart-strings of every man and woman in the land."

"To touch their purse-strings would, perhaps, be more to the point," said Carne, with one of his quiet smiles.

"Let us hope we shall touch them, too," she replied. "Now would you mind going to the dais at the other end of the room? You will find Lord Laverstock there, talking to my husband, I think."

Carne bowed, and went forward as he had been directed.

So soon as it was known that the celebrities had arrived, the meeting was declared open and the speechmaking commenced. Clever as some of them were it could not be doubted that Carne's address was the event of the afternoon. He was a born speaker, and what was more, despite the short notice he had received, had made himself thoroughly conversant with his subject. His handsome face was on fire with excitement, and his sonorous voice rang through the large room like a trumpet call. When he sat down it was amidst a burst of applause. Lord Laverstock leant forward and shook hands with him.

"Your speech will be read all over England to-morrow morning," he said. "It should make a difference of thousands of pounds to the fund. I congratulate you most heartily upon it."

Simon Carne felt that if it was really going to make that difference he might, in the light of future events, heartily congratulate himself. He, however, accepted the praise showered upon him with becoming modesty, and, during the next speaker's exhibition of halting elocution, amused himself watching the faces before him, and speculating as to what they would say when the surprise he was going to spring upon them became known. Half an hour later, when the committee had been elected and the meeting had broken up, he bade his friends goodbye and set off on his return home. That evening he was dining at home, intending to call at his club afterwards, and to drop in at a reception and two dances between ten and midnight. After dinner, however, he changed his mind, and having instructed Ram Gafur to deny him to all callers, and countermanding his order for his carriage, went to his study, where he locked himself in and sat down to smoke and think.

He had set himself a puzzle which would have taxed the brain of that arch schemer Machiavelli himself. He was not, however, going to be beaten by it. There *must* be some way, he told himself, in which the fraud could be worked, and if there was he was going to find it. Numberless were the plans he formed, only to discover a few moments later that some little difficulty rendered each impracticable.

Suddenly, throwing down the pencil with which he had been writing, he sprang to his feet and began eagerly to pace the room. It was evident, from the expression upon his face, that he had touched upon a train of thought that was at last likely to prove productive. Reaching the fireplace for about the thirtieth time, he paused and gazed into the fireless grate. After standing there for a few moments he turned, and, with his hands in his pockets, said solemnly to himself: "Yes! I think it can be done!"

Whatever the train of thought may have been that led him to make this declaration, it was plain that it afforded him no small amount of satisfaction. He did not, however, commit himself at once to a decision, but continued to think over the scheme he had hit upon until he had completely mastered it. It was nearly midnight before he was thoroughly satisfied. Then he followed his invariable practice on such occasions, and rang for the inimitable Belton. When he had admitted him to the room, he bade him close and lock the door behind him.

By the time this had been done he had lit a fresh cigar, and had once more taken up his position on the hearthrug.

"I sent for you to say that I have just made up my mind to try a little scheme, compared with which all I have done so far will sink into insignificance."

"What is it, sir?" asked Belton.

"I will tell you, but you must not look so terrified. Put in a few words, it is neither more nor less than to attempt to divert the enormous sum of money which the prodigal English public is taking out of its pocket in order to assist the people of the Canary Islands, who have lost so severely by the recent terrible earthquake, into my own."

Belton's face expressed his astonishment.

"But, my dear sir," he said, "that's a fund of which the Marquis of Laverstock is president, and of whose committee you are one of the principal members."

"Exactly," answered Carne. "It is to those two happy circumstances I shall later on attribute the success I now mean to attain. Lord Laverstock is merely a pompous old nobleman, whose hobby is philanthropy. This lesson will do him good. It will be strange if, before I am a week older, I cannot twist him round my finger. Now for my instructions. In the first place, you must find me a moderate-sized house, fit for an elderly lady, and situated in a fairly fashionable quarter, say South Kensington. Furnish it on the hire system from one of the big firms, and engage three servants who can be relied upon to do their work, and, what is more important, who can hold their tongues.

"Next find me an old lady to impersonate the mistress of the house. She must be very frail and delicate-looking, and you will arrange with some livery stable people in the neighbourhood to supply her with a carriage, in which she will go for an airing every afternoon in order that the neighbourhood may become familiar with her personality. Both she and the servants must be made to thoroughly understand that their only chance of obtaining anything from me depends upon their carrying out my instructions to the letter. Also, while they are in the house, they must keep themselves to themselves. My identity, of course, must not transpire.

"As soon as I give the signal, the old lady must keep to the house, and the neighbourhood must be allowed to understand that she is seriously ill. The day following she will be worse, and the next she will be dead. You will then make arrangements for the funeral, order a coffin, and arrange for the conveyance of the body to Southampton, *en route* for the Channel Islands, where she is to be buried. At Southampton a yacht, which I will arrange for myself, will be in readiness to carry us out to sea. Do you think you understand?"

"Perfectly, sir," Belton replied, "but I wish I could persuade you to give up the attempt. You will excuse my saying so, sir, I hope, but it does seem to me a pity, when you have done so much, to risk losing it all over such a dangerous bit of business as this. It surely can't succeed, sir?"

"Belton," said Carne very seriously, "you strike me as being in a strange humour tonight, and I cannot say that I like it, Were it not that I have the most implicit confidence in you, I should begin to think you were turning honest. In that case our connection would be likely to be a very short one."

"I hope, sir," Belton answered in alarm, "that you still believe I am as devoted as ever to your interests."

"I do believe it," Carne replied. "Let the manner in which you carry out the various instructions I have just given you, confirm me in that belief. This is Wednesday. I shall expect you to come to me on Saturday with a report that the house has been taken and furnished, and that the servants are installed and the delicate old lady in residence."

"You may rely upon my doing my best, sir."

"I feel sure of that," said Carne, "and now that all is arranged I think that I will go to bed."

A week later a committee of the Canary Islands Relief Fund was able to announce to the world, through the columns of the Daily Press, that the generous public of England had subscribed no less a sum than one hundred thousand pounds for the relief of the sufferers by the late earthquake. The same day Carne attended a committee meeting in Gloucester Place. A proposition advanced by Lady Weltershall and seconded by Simon Carne was carried unanimously. It was to the effect that in a week's time such members of the Relief Committee as could get away should start for the scene of the calamity in the chairman's yacht, which had been placed at their disposal, taking with them, for distribution among the impoverished inhabitants of the Islands, the sum already subscribed, namely, one hundred thousand pounds in English gold. They would then be able, with the assistance of the English Consul, to personally superintend the distribution of their money, and also be in a position to report to the subscribers, when they returned to England, the manner in which the money had been utilised.

"In that case," said Carne, who had not only seconded the motion, but had put the notion into Lady Weltershall's head, "it might be as well if our chairman would interview the authorities of the bank, and arrange that the amount in question shall be packed, ready for delivery to the messengers he may select to call for it before the date in question."

"I will make it my business to call at the bank to-morrow morning," replied the chairman, "and perhaps you, Mr. Carne, would have no objection to accompany me."

"If it will facilitate the business of this committee I shall be only too pleased to do so," said Carne, and so it was settled.

On a Tuesday afternoon, six days later, and two days before the date upon which it had been arranged that the committee should sail, the Marquis of Laverstock received a letter. Lady Caroline Weltershall, the Earl of Amberley, and Simon Carne were with him when he opened it. He read it through, and then read it again, after which he turned to his guests.

"This is really a very extraordinary communication," he said, "and as it affects the matter we have most at heart, perhaps I had better read it to you:

> 154, Great Chesterton Street,
> Tuesday Evening.
> To the Most Noble the Marquis of Laverstock,
> K.G., Berkeley Square.
> My Lord—As one who has been permitted to enjoy a long and peaceful life in a country where such visitations are happily unknown, I take the liberty of writing to your Lordship to say how very much I should like to subscribe to the fund so nobly started by you and your friends to assist the poor people who have lost so much by the earthquake in the Canary Islands. Being a lonely old woman, blessed by Providence with some small share of worldly wealth, I feel

it my duty to make some small sacrifice to help others who have not been so blessed.

Unfortunately, I do not enjoy very good health, but if your Lordship could spare a moment to call upon me, I would like to thank you in the name of Womanhood for all you have done, and, in proof of my gratitude, would willingly give you my cheque for the sum of ten thousand pounds to add to the amount already subscribed. I am permitted by my doctors to see visitors between the hours of eleven and twelve in the morning, and five and six in the after-noon. I should then be both honoured and pleased to see your Lordship.

Trusting you will concede me this small favour, I have the honour to be,

Yours very sincerely,

Janet O'Halloran.

There was a momentary pause after his lordship had finished reading the letter.

"What will you do?" inquired Lady Caroline.

"It is a noble offering," put in Simon Carne.

"I think there cannot be two opinions as to what is my duty," replied the chairman. "I shall accede to her request, though why she wants to see me is more than I can tell."

"As she hints in the letter, she wishes to congratulate you per-sonally on what you have done," continued the Earl of Amberley; "and as it will be the handsomest donation we have yet received, it will, perhaps, be as well to humour her."

"In that case I will do as I say, and make it my business to call there this afternoon between five and six. And now it is my duty to report to you that Mr. Simon Carne and I waited upon the authori-ties at the Bank this morning, and have arranged that the sum of one hundred thousand pounds in gold shall be ready for our mes-sengers when they call for it, either to-morrow morning or to-mor-row afternoon at latest."

"It is a large sum to take with us," said Lady Caroline. "I trust it will not prove a temptation to thieves!"

"You need have no fear on that score," replied his lordship. "As I have explained to the manager, my own trusted servants will effect the removal of the money, accompanied by two private detectives, who will remain on board my yacht until we weigh anchor. We have left nothing to chance. To make the matter doubly sure, I have also arranged that the money shall not be handed over except to a person who shall present my cheque, and at the same time show this signet ring which I now wear upon my finger."

The other members of the committee expressed themselves as perfectly satisfied with this arrangement, and when certain other business had been transacted the meeting broke up.

As soon as he left Berkeley Square Carne returned with all haste to Porchester House. Reaching his study he ordered that Belton should be at once sent to him.

"Now, Belton," he said, when the latter stood before him, "there is not a moment to lose. Lord Laverstook will be at Great Chesterton Street in about two hours. Send a messenger to Waterloo to inquire if they can let us have a special train at seven o'clock to take a funeral party to Southampton. Use the name of Merryburn, and you may say that the amount of the charge, whatever it may be, will be paid before the train starts. As soon as you obtain a reply, bring it to 154, Great Chesterton Street. In the meantime I shall disguise myself and go on to await you there. On the way I shall wire to the captain of the yacht at Southampton to be prepared for us. Do you understand what you have to do?"

"Perfectly, sir," Belton replied. "But I must confess that I am very nervous."

"There is no need to be. Mark my words, everything will go like clockwork. Now I am going to change my things and prepare for the excursion."

He would have been a sharp man who would have recognised in the dignified-looking clergyman who drove up in a hansom to 154, Great Chesterton Street, half an hour later, Simon Carne, who had attended the committee meeting of the Canary Island Relief

Fund that afternoon. As he alighted he looked up, and saw that all the blinds were drawn down, and that there were evident signs that Death had laid his finger on the house. Having dismissed his cab he rang the bell, and when the door was opened entered the house. The butler who admitted him had been prepared for his coming. He bowed respectfully, and conducted him to the drawing-room. There he found an intensely respectable old lady, attired in black silk, seated beside the window.

"Go upstairs," he said peremptorily, "and remain in the room above this until you are told to come down. Be careful not to let yourself be seen. As soon as it gets dark to-night you can leave the house, but not till then. Before you go the money promised you will be paid. Now be off upstairs, and make sure that none of the neighbours catch sight of you."

Ten minutes later a man, who might have been a retired military officer, and who was dressed in deepest black, drove up, and was admitted to the house. Though no one would have recognised him, Carne addressed him at once as "Belton."

"What have you arranged about the train?" he asked, as soon as they were in the drawing-room together.

"I have settled that it shall be ready to start for Southampton punctually at seven o'clock," the other answered.

"And what about the hearse?"

"It will be here at a quarter to seven, without fail."

"Very good; we will have the corpse ready meanwhile. Now, before you do anything else, have the two lower blinds in the front drawn up. If he thinks there is trouble in the house he may take fright, and we must not scare our bird away after all the bother we have had to lure him here."

For the next hour they were busily engaged perfecting their arrangements. These were scarcely completed before a gorgeous landau drove up to the house, and Belton reported that the footman had alighted and was ascending the steps.

"Let his lordship be shown into the drawing-room," said Simon Carne, "and as soon as he is there do you, Belton, wait at the door. I'll call you when I want you."

Carne went into the drawing-room and set the door ajar. As he did so he heard the footman inquire whether Mrs. O'Halloran was at home, and whether she would see his master. The butler answered in the affirmative, and a few moments later the Marquis ascended the steps.

"Will you be pleased to step this way, my lord," said the servant. "My mistress is expecting you, and will see you at once."

When he entered the drawing-room he discovered the same portly, dignified clergyman whom the neighbours had seen enter the house an hour or so before, standing before the fireplace.

"Good-afternoon, my lord," said this individual, as the door closed behind the butler. "If you will be good enough to take a seat, Mrs. O'Halloran will be down in a few moments."

His lordship did as he was requested, and while doing so commented on the weather, and allowed his eyes to wander round the room. He took in the grand piano, the easy chairs on either side of the book-case, and the flower-stand in the window. He could see that there was plain evidence of wealth in these things. What his next thought would have been can only be conjectured, for he was suddenly roused from his reverie by hearing the man say in a gruff voice: "It's all up, my lord. If you move or attempt to cry out, you're a dead man!"

Swinging round he discovered a revolver barrel pointed at his head. He uttered an involuntary cry of alarm, and made as if he would rise.

"Sit down, sir," said the clergyman authoritatively. "Are you mad that you disobey me? You do not know with whom you are trifling."

"What do you mean?" cried the astonished peer, his eyes almost starting from his head. "I demand to be told what this behaviour means. Are you aware who I am?"

"Perfectly," the other replied. "As to your other question, you will know nothing more than I choose to tell you. What's more, I should advise you to hold your tongue, unless you desire to be gagged. That would be unpleasant for all parties."

Then, turning to the door, he cried: "Come in, Dick!"

A moment later the military individual, who had been to Water-loo to arrange about the train, entered the room to find the Most Noble the Marquis of Laverstock seated in an easy chair, almost beside himself with terror, with the venerable clergyman standing over him revolver in hand.

"Dick, my lad," said the latter quietly, "his lordship has been wise enough to hear reason. No, sir, thank you, your hands behind your back, as arranged, if you please. If you don't obey me I shall blow your brains out, and it would be a thousand pities to spoil this nice Turkey carpet. That's right. Now Dick, my lad, I want his lordship's pocket-book from his coat and those sheets of note-paper and envelopes we brought with us. I carry a stylographic pen myself, so there is no need of ink."

These articles having been obtained, they were placed on a table beside him, and Carne took possession of the pocket-book. He leisurely opened it, and from it took the cheque for one hundred thousand pounds, signed by the chairman and committee of the Canary Island Relief Fund, which had been drawn that afternoon.

"Now take the pen," he said, "and begin to write. Endeavour to remember that I am in a hurry, and have no time to waste. Let the first letter be to the bank authorities. Request them, in your capacity of Chairman of the Relief Fund, to hand to the bearers the amount of the cheque in gold."

"I will do no such thing," cried the old fellow sturdily. "Nothing shall induce me to assist you in perpetrating such a fraud."

"I am sorry to hear that," said Carne sweetly, "for I am afraid in that case we shall be compelled to make you submit to a rather unpleasant alternative. Come, sir, I will give you three minutes in which to write that letter. If at the end of that time you have not done so, I shall proceed to drastic measures."

So saying, he thrust the poker into the fire in a highly suggestive manner. Needless to say, within the time specified the letter had been written, placed in its envelope, and directed.

"Now I shall have to trouble you to fill in this telegraph form to your wife, to tell her that you have been called out of town, and do not expect to be able to return until tomorrow."

The other wrote as directed, and when he had done so Carne placed this paper also in his pocket.

"Now I want that signet ring upon your finger, if you please."

The old gentleman handed it over to his persecutor with a heavy sigh. He had realized that it was useless to refuse.

"Now that wine-glass on the sideboard, Dick," said the clergyman, "also that carafe of water. When you have given them to me, go and see that the other things I spoke to you about are ready."

Having placed the articles in question upon the table Belton left the room. Carne immediately filled the glass, into which he poured about a tablespoonful of some dark liquid from a bottle which he took from his pocket, and which he had brought with him for that purpose.

"I'll have to trouble you to drink this, my lord," he said, as he stirred the contents of the glass with an ivory paper knife taken from the table. "You need have no fear. It is perfectly harmless, and will not hurt you."

"I will not touch it," replied the other. "Nothing you can do or say will induce me to drink a drop of it."

Carne examined his watch ostentatiously.

"Time flies, I regret to say," he answered impressively, "and I cannot stay to argue the question with you. I will give you three minutes to do as I have ordered you. If you have not drunk it by that time we shall be compelled to repeat the little persuasion we tried with such success a few moments since."

"You wish to kill me," cried the other. "I will not drink it. I will not be murdered. You are a fiend to attempt such a thing."

"I regret to say you are wasting time," replied his companion. "I assure you if you drink it you will not be hurt. It is merely an opiate intended to put you to sleep until we have time to get away in safety. Come, that delightful poker is getting hot again, and if you do not do what I tell you, trouble will ensue. Think well before you refuse."

There was another pause, during which the unfortunate nobleman gazed first at the poker, which had been thrust between the bars of the grate, and then at the relentless being who stood before him, revolver in hand. Never had a member of the House of Lords been placed in a more awkward and unenviable position.

"One minute," said Carne quietly.

There was another pause, during which the Marquis groaned in a heartrending manner. Carne remembered with a smile that the family title had been bestowed upon one of the Marquis' ancestors for bravery on the field of battle.

"Two minutes!"

As he spoke he stooped and gave the poker a little twist.

"Three minutes!"

The words were scarcely out of his mouth before Lord Laverstock threw up his hands.

"You are a heartless being to make me, but I will drink," he cried, and with an ashened face he immediately swallowed the contents of the glass.

"Thank you," said Carne politely.

The effect produced by the drug was almost instantaneous. A man could scarcely have counted a hundred before the old gentleman, who had evidently resigned himself to his fate, laid himself back in his chair and was fast asleep.

"He has succumbed even quicker than I expected," said Carne to himself as he bent over the prostrate figure and listened to his even breathing. "It is, perhaps, just as well that this drug is not known in England. At any rate, on this occasion it has answered my purpose most admirably."

At five minutes before seven o'clock a hearse containing the mortal remains of Mrs. O'Halloran, of Great Chesterton Street, South Kensington, entered the yard of Waterloo Station, accompanied by a hansom cab. A special train was in waiting to convey the party, which consisted of the deceased's brother, a retired Indian officer, and her cousin, the vicar of a Somersetshire parish, to Southampton, where a steam yacht would transport them to Guernsey, in which place the remains were to be interred beside those of her late husband.

"I think we may congratulate ourselves, Belton, on having carried it out most successfully," said Carne when the coffin had been carried on board the yacht and placed in the saloon. "As soon as we are under weigh we'll have this lid off and get the poor old gentleman out. He has had a good spell of it in there, but he may congratulate himself that the ventilating arrangements of his temporary home were so perfectly attended to. Otherwise I should have trembled for the result."

A few hours later, having helped his guest to recover consciousness, and having seen him safely locked up in a cabin on board, the yacht put in at a little seaport town some thirty or forty miles from Southampton Water, and landed two men in time to catch the midnight express to London. The following afternoon they rejoined the yacht a hundred miles or so further down the coast. When they were once more out at sea Carne called the skipper to his cabin.

"How has your prisoner conducted himself during our absence?" he asked. "Has he given any trouble?"

"Not a bit," replied the man. "The poor old buffer's been too sick to make a row. He sent away his breakfast and his lunch untouched. The only thing he seems to care about is champagne, and that he drinks by the bottle full. I never saw a better man at his bottle in all my life."

"A little sickness will do him no harm; he'll have a better appetite when he gets on dry land again," said Carne. "His time is pretty well up now, and as soon as it is dark to-night we'll put him ashore. Let me know when you sight the place."

"Very good, sir," replied the skipper, and immediately he returned to the deck again.

It was well after ten o'clock that evening when Simon Carne, still attired as a respectable Church of England clergyman, unlocked the door and entered his prisoner's cabin.

"You will be glad to hear, my lord," he said, "that your term of imprisonment has at last come to an end. You had better get up and dress, for a boat will be alongside in twenty minutes to take you ashore."

The unfortunate gentleman needed no second bidding. Ill as he had hitherto been, he seemed to derive new life from the other's words. At any rate, he sprang out of his bunk, and set to work to dress with feverish energy. All the time Carne sat and watched him with an amused smile upon his face. So soon as he was ready, and the captain had knocked at the door, he was conducted to the deck and ordered to descend into a shore boat, which had come off in answer to a signal, and was now lying alongside in readiness.

Carne and Belton leant over the bulwarks to watch him depart.

"Good-bye, my lord," cried the former, as the boat moved away. "It has been a sincere pleasure to me to entertain you, and I only hope that, in return, you have enjoyed your little excursion. You might give my respectful compliments to the members of the Canary Island Relief Fund, and tell them that there is at least one person on board this yacht who appreciates their kindly efforts."

Then his lordship stood up, and shook his fist at the yacht until it had faded away, and could no longer be seen owing to the darkness. Presently Carne turned to Belton.

"So much for the Most Noble the Marquis of Laverstock," he said, "and the Canary Island Relief Fund. Now, let us be off to town. To-morrow I must be Simon Carne once more."

Next morning Simon Carne rose from his couch, in his luxurious bedroom, a little later than usual. He knew he should be tired, and had instructed Belton not to come in until he rang his bell. When the latter appeared he bade him bring in the morning papers. He found what he wanted in the first he opened, on the middle page, headed with three lines of large type:

GIGANTIC SWINDLE.
THE MARQUIS OF LAVERSTOCK ABDUCTED.
THE CANARY ISLAND RELIEF FUND STOLEN.

"This looks quite interesting," said Carne, as he folded the paper in order to be able the better to read the account. "As I know something of the case I shall be interested to see what they have to say about it. Let me see."

The newspaper version ran as follows:

"Of all the series of extraordinary crimes which it has been our unfortunate duty to chronicle during this year of great rejoicing, it is doubtful whether a more impudent robbery has been perpetrated than that which we have to place before our readers this morning. As every one is well aware, a large fund has been collected from all classes for the relief of the sufferers by the recent Canary Island earthquake. On the day before the robbery took place this fund amounted to no less a sum than one hundred thousand pounds, and to-morrow it was the intention of the committee, under the presidency of the Most Noble the Marquis of Laverstock, to proceed to the seat of the disaster, taking with them the entire amount of the sum raised in English gold. Unfortunately for the success of this scheme, his lordship was the recipient, two days ago, of a letter from a person purporting to reside in Great Chesterton Street, South Kensington. She signed herself Janet O'Halloran, and offered to add a sum of ten thousand pounds to the amount already collected, provided the Marquis would call and collect her cheque personally. The excuse given for this extraordinary stipulation was that she wished to convey to him her thanks for the trouble he had taken.

"Accordingly, feeling that he had no right to allow such a chance to slip, his lordship visited the house. He was received in the drawing-room by a man dressed in the garb of a clergyman, who, assisted by a military-looking individual, presently clapped a revolver to his head and demanded, under the threat of all sorts of penalties, that he should give up to him the cheque drawn upon the Bank, and which it was the Marquis's intention to have cashed the following morning. Not satisfied with this assurance, he was also made to write an order to the banking authorities authorising them to pay over the money to the bearer, who was a trusted agent, while at the same time he was to supply them with his signet ring, which, as had already been arranged, would prove that the messengers were genuine and what they pretended to be. Next he was ordered to drink a powerful opiate, and after that his lordship remembers nothing more until he woke to find himself on board a small yacht in mid-channel. Despite the agony he was suffering, he was detained on board this piratical craft until late last night, when he was set ashore at a small village within a few miles of Plymouth. Such is his lordship's story. The sequel to the picture is as follows.

"Soon after the Bank was opened yesterday, a respectable-looking individual, accompanied by three others, who were introduced to the manager as private detectives, put in an appearance and presented the Relief Fund's cheque at the counter. In reply to inquiries the letter written by the Marquis was produced, and the signet ring shown. Never for a moment doubting that these were the messengers the Bank had all along been told to expect, the money was handed over and placed in a handsome private omnibus which was waiting outside. It was not until late last night, when a telegram was received from the Marquis of Laverstock from Plymouth, that the nature of the gigantic fraud which had been perpetrated was discovered. The police authorities were immediately communicated with and the matter placed in their hands. Unfortunately, however, so many hours had been allowed to elapse that it was extremely difficult to obtain any clue that might ultimately lead to the identification of the parties concerned in the fraud. So far the case bids fair to rank with those other mysterious robberies which, during the last few months, have shocked and puzzled all England."

"I regard that as a remarkably able exposition of the case," said Carne to himself with a smile as he laid the paper down, "but what an account the man would be able to write if only he could know what is in my safe upstairs!"

That afternoon he attended a committee meeting of the fund at Weltershall House. The unfortunate nobleman whose unpleasant experience has founded the subject of this story was present. Carne was among the first to offer him an expression of sympathy.

"I don't know that I ever heard of a more outrageous case," he said. "I only hope that the scoundrels may be soon brought to justice."

"In the meantime what about the poor people we intended to help?" asked Lady Weltershall.

"They shall not lose," replied Lord Laverstock. "I shall refund the entire amount myself."

"No, no, my lord; that would be manifestly unfair," said Simon Carne. "We are all trustees of the fund, and what happened is as much our fault as yours. If nine other people will do the same I am prepared to contribute a sum of ten thousand pounds towards the fund."

"I will follow your example," said the Marquis.

"I also," continued Lord Amberley.

By nightfall seven other gentlemen had done the same, and, as Simon Carne said as he totaled the amounts: "By this means the Canary Islanders will not be losers after all."

AN IMPERIAL FINALE

OF ALL THE functions that ornament the calendar of the English
social and sporting year, surely the Cowes week may claim to rank
as one of the greatest, or at least the most enjoyable. So thought
Simon Carne as he sat on the deck of Lord Tremorden's yacht,
anchored off the mouth of the Medina River, smoking his cigarette
and whispering soft nothings into the little shell-like ear of Lady Mabel
Madderley, the lady of all others who had won the right to be considered the beauty of the past season. It was a perfect afternoon, and, as
if to fill his flagon of enjoyment to the very brim, he had won the
Queen's Cup with his yacht, *The Unknown Quantity*, only half an
hour before. Small wonder, therefore, that he was contented with
his lot in life, and his good fortune of that afternoon in particular.

The tiny harbour was crowded with shipping of all sorts, shapes,
and sizes, including the guardship, his Imperial Majesty the Emperor of Westphalia's yacht the *Hohenszrallas*, the English Royal
yachts, steam yachts, schooners, cutters, and all the various craft
taking part in England's greatest water carnival. Steam launches
darted hither and thither, smartly equipped gigs conveyed gaily-
dressed parties from vessel to vessel, while, ashore, the little town
itself was alive with bunting, and echoed to the strains of almost
continuous music.

"Surely you ought to consider yourself a very happy man, Mr.
Carne," said Lady Mabel Madderley, with a smile, in reply to a
speech of the other's. "You won the Derby in June, and to-day you
have appropriated the Queen's Cup."

"If such things constitute happiness, I suppose I must be in the seventh heaven of delight," answered Carne, as he took another cigarette from his case and lit it. "All the same, I am insatiable enough to desire still greater fortune. When one has set one's heart upon winning something, beside which the Derby and the Queen's Cup are items scarcely worth considering, one is rather apt to feel that fortune has still much to give."

"I am afraid I do not quite grasp your meaning," she said. But there was a look in her face that told him that, if she did not understand, she could at least make a very good guess. According to the world's reckoning, he was quite the best fish then swimming in the matrimonial pond, and some people, for the past few weeks, had even gone so far as to say that she had hooked him. It could not be denied that he had been paying her unmistakable attention of late.

What answer he would have vouchsafed to her speech it is impossible to say, for at that moment their host came along the deck towards them. He carried a note in his hand.

"I have just received a message to say that his Imperial Majesty is going to honour us with a visit," he said, when he reached them. "If I mistake not, that is his launch coming towards us now."

Lady Mabel and Simon Carne rose and accompanied him to the starboard bulwarks. A smart white launch, with the Westphalian flag flying at her stern, had left the Royal yacht and was steaming quickly towards them. A few minutes later it had reached the companion ladder, and Lord Tremorden had descended to welcome his Royal guest. When they reached the deck together, his Majesty shook hands with Lady Tremorden, and afterwards with Lady Mabel and Simon Carne.

"I must congratulate you most heartily, Mr. Carne," he said, "on your victory to-day. You gave us an excellent race, and though I had the misfortune to be beaten by thirty seconds, still I have the satisfaction of knowing that the winner was a better boat in every way than my own."

"Your Majesty adds to the sweets of victory by your generous acceptance of defeat," Carne replied. "But I must confess that I owe my success in no way to my own ability. The boat was chosen for me by another, and I have not even the satisfaction of saying that I sailed her myself."

"Nevertheless she is your property, and you will go down to posterity famous in yachting annals as the winner of the Queen's Cup in this justly celebrated year."

With this compliment his Majesty turned to his hostess and entered into conversation with her, leaving his aide-de-camp free to discuss the events of the day with Lady Mabel. When he took his departure half an hour later, Carne also bade his friends good-bye, and, descending to his boat, was rowed away to his own beautiful steam yacht, which was anchored a few cables' length away from the Imperial craft. He was to dine on board the latter vessel that evening.

On gaining the deck he was met by Belton, his valet, who carried a telegram in his hand. As soon as he received it, Carne opened it and glanced at the contents, without, however, betraying very much interest.

An instant later the expression upon his face changed like magic. Still holding the message in his hand, he turned to Belton.

"Come below," he said quickly. "There is news enough here to give us something to think of for hours to come."

Reaching the saloon, which was decorated with all the daintiness of the upholsterer's art, he led the way to the cabin he had arranged as a study. Having entered it, he shut and locked the door.

"It's all up, Belton," he said. "The comedy has lasted long enough, and now it only remains for us to speak the tag, and after that to ring the curtain down as speedily as may be."

"I am afraid, sir, I do not quite take your meaning," said Belton. "Would you mind telling me what has happened?"

"I can do that in a very few words," the other answered. "This cablegram is from Trincomalee Liz, and was dispatched from Bombay yesterday. Read it for yourself."

He handed the paper to his servant, who read it carefully, aloud:

To Carne, Porchester House, Park Lane, London.—Bradfield left fortnight since. Have ascertained that you are the object.

Trincomalee.

"This is very serious, sir," said the other, when he had finished.

"As you say, it is very serious indeed," Carne replied. "Bradfield thinks he has caught me at last, I suppose; but he seems to forget that it is possible for me to be as clever as himself. Let me look at the message again. Left a fortnight ago, did he? Then I've still a little respite. By Jove, if that's the case, I'll see that I make the most of it."

"But surely, sir, you will leave at once," said Belton quickly. "If this man, who has been after us so long, is now more than half way to England, coming with the deliberate intention of running you to earth, surely, sir, you'll see the advisability of making your escape while you have time."

Carne smiled indulgently.

"Of course I shall escape, my good Belton," he said. "You have never known me neglect to take proper precautions yet; but before I go I must do one more piece of business. It must be something by the light of which all I have hitherto accomplished will look like nothing. Something really great, that will make England open its eyes as it has not done yet."

Belton stared at him, this time in undisguised amazement.

"Do you mean to tell me, sir," he said with the freedom of a privileged servant, "that you intend to run another risk, when the only man who knows sufficient of your career to bring you to book is certain to be in England in less than a fortnight? I cannot believe that you would be so foolish, sir. I beg of you to think what you are doing."

Carne, however, paid but small attention to his servant's intreaties.

"The difficulty," he said to himself, speaking his thoughts aloud, "is to understand quite what to do. I seem to have used up all my

big chances. However, I'll think it over, and it will be strange if I
don't hit upon something. In the meantime, Belton, you had better see that preparations are made for leaving England on Friday
next. Tell the skipper to have everything ready. We shall have done
our work by that time; then hey for the open sea and freedom from
the trammels of a society life once more. You might drop a hint or
two to certain people that I am going, but be more than careful
what you say. Write to the agents about Porchester House, and
attend to all the other necessary details. You may leave me now."

Belton bowed, and left the cabin without another word. He
knew his master sufficiently well to feel certain that neither
intreaties nor expostulations would make him abandon the course
he had mapped out for himself. That being so, he bowed to the
inevitable with a grace which had now become a habit to him.

When he was alone, Carne once more sat for upwards of an hour
in earnest thought. He then ordered his gig, and, when it was ready,
set out for the shore. Making his way to the telegraph office, he
dispatched a message which at any other, and less busy, time,
would have caused the operator some astonishment. It was addressed to a Mahommedan dealer in precious stones in Bombay,
and contained only two words in addition to the signature. They
were:

"Leaving—come."

He knew that they would reach the person for whom they were
intended, and that she would understand their meaning and act
accordingly.

The dinner that night on board the Imperial yacht *Hohenszrallas* was a gorgeous affair in every sense of the word. All the principal yacht owners were present, and, at the conclusion of the banquet, Carne's health, as winner of the great event of the regatta,
was proposed by the Emperor himself, and drunk amid enthusiastic applause. It was a proud moment for the individual in question, but he bore his honours with that quiet dignity that had stood
him in such good stead on so many similar occasions. In his speech
he referred to his approaching departure from England, and

this, the first inkling of such news, came upon his audience like a thunder-clap. When they had taken leave of his Majesty soon after midnight, and were standing on deck, waiting for their respective boats to draw up to the accommodation ladder, Lord Orpington made his way to where Simon Carne was standing.

"Is it really true that you intend leaving us so soon?" he asked.

"Quite true, unfortunately," Carne replied. "I had hoped to have remained longer, but circumstances over which I have no control make it imperative that I should return to India without delay. Business that exercises a vital influence upon my fortunes compels me. I am therefore obliged to leave without fail on Friday next. I have given orders to that effect this afternoon."

"I am extremely sorry to hear it, that's all I can say," said Lord Amberley, who had just come up. "I assure you we shall all miss you very much indeed."

"You have all been extremely kind," said Carne, "and I have to thank you for an exceedingly pleasant time. But, there, let us postpone consideration of the matter for as long as possible. I think this is my boat. Won't you let me take you as far as your own yacht?"

"Many thanks, but I don't think we need trouble you," said Lord Orpington. "I see my gig is just behind yours."

"In that case, good-night," said Carne. "I shall see you as arranged, to-morrow morning, I suppose?"

"At eleven," said Lord Amberley. "We'll call for you and go ashore together. Goodnight."

By the time Carne had reached his yacht he had made up his mind. He had also hit upon a scheme, the daring of which almost frightened himself. If only he could bring it off, he told himself, it would be indeed a fitting climax to all he had accomplished since he had arrived in England. Retiring to his cabin, he allowed Belton to assist him in his preparations for the night almost without speaking. It was not until the other was about to leave the cabin that he broached the subject that was occupying his mind to the exclusion of all else.

"Belton," he said, "I have decided upon the greatest scheme that has come into my mind yet. If Simon Carne is going to say farewell to the English people on Friday next, and it succeeds, he will leave them a legacy to think about for some time after he has gone."

"You are surely not going to attempt anything further, sir," said Belton in alarm. "I *did* hope, sir, that you would have listened to my intreaties this afternoon."

"It was impossible for me to do so," said Carne. "I am afraid, Belton, you are a little lacking in ambition. I have noticed that on the last three occasions you have endeavoured to dissuade me from my endeavours to promote the healthy excitement of the English reading public. On this occasion fortunately I am able to withstand you. To-morrow morning you will commence preparations for the biggest piece of work to which I have yet put my hand."

"If you have set your mind upon doing it, sir, I am quite aware that it is hopeless for me to say anything," said Belton resignedly. "May I know, however, what it is going to be?"

Carne paused for a moment before he replied.

"I happen to know that the Emperor of Westphalia, whose friendship I have the honour to claim," he said, "has a magnificent collection of gold plate on board his yacht. It is my intention, if possible, to become the possessor of it."

"Surely that will be impossible, sir," said Belton. "Clever as you undoubtedly are in arranging these things, I do not see how you can do it. A ship at the best of times is such a public place, and they will be certain to guard it very closely."

"I must confess that at first glance I do not quite see how it is to be managed, but I have a scheme in my head which I think may possibly enable me to effect my purpose. At any rate, I shall be able to tell you more about it to-morrow. First, let us try a little experiment."

As he spoke he seated himself at his dressing-table, and bade Belton bring him a box which had hitherto been standing in a corner. When he opened it, it proved to be a pretty little cedar-wood affair divided into a number of small compartments, each of which contained *crêpe* hair of a different colour. Selecting a small portion from one particular compartment, he unraveled it until he had obtained the length he wanted, and then with dexterous fingers constructed a moustache, which he attached with spirit gum to his upper lip. Two or three twirls gave it the necessary curl, then with a pair of ivory-backed brushes taken from the dressing-table he brushed his hair back in a peculiar manner, placed a hat of uncommon shape upon his head, took a heavy boat cloak from a cupboard near at hand, threw it round his shoulders, and, assuming an almost defiant expression, faced Belton, and desired him to tell him whom he resembled.

Familiar as he was with his master's marvelous power of disguise and his extraordinary faculty of imitation, the latter could not refrain from expressing his astonishment.

"His Imperial Majesty the Emperor of Westphalia," he said. "The likeness is perfect."

"Good," said Carne. "From that exhibition you will gather something of my plan. To-morrow evening, as you are aware, I am invited to meet his Majesty, who is to dine ashore accompanied by his aide-de-camp, Count Von Walzburg. Here is the latter's photograph. He possesses, as you know, a very decided personality, which is all in our favour. Study it carefully."

So saying, he took from a drawer a photograph, which he propped against the looking-glass on the dressing-table before him. It represented a tall, military-looking individual, with bristling eyebrows, a large nose, a heavy grey moustache, and hair of the same colour. Belton examined it carefully.

"I can only suppose, sir," he said, "that, as you are telling me this, you intend me to represent Count Von Walzburg."

"Exactly," said Carne. "That is my intention. It should not be at all difficult. The Count is just your height and build. You will only need the moustache, the eyebrows, the grey hair, and the large nose, to look the part exactly. To-morrow will be a dark night, and, if only I can control circumstances sufficiently to obtain the chance I want, detection, in the first part of our scheme at any rate, should be most unlikely, if not almost impossible."

"You'll excuse my saying so, I hope, sir," said Belton, "but it seems a very risky game to play when we have done so well up to the present."

"You must admit that the glory will be the greater, my friend, if we succeed."

"But surely, sir, as I said just now, they keep the plate, you mention in a secure place, and have it properly guarded."

"I have made the fullest inquiries, you maybe sure. It is kept in a safe in the chief steward's cabin, and, while it is on board, a sentry is always on duty at the door. Yes, all things considered, I should say it is kept in a remarkably secure place."

"Then, sir, I'm still at a loss to see how you are going to obtain possession of it."

Carne smiled indulgently. It pleased him to see how perplexed his servant was.

"In the simplest manner possible," he said, "provided always that I can get on board the yacht without my identity being questioned. The manner in which we are to leave the vessel will be rather more dangerous, but not sufficiently so to cause us any great uneasiness. You are a good swimmer, I know, so that a hundred yards should not hurt you. You must also have a number of stout canvas sacks, say six, prepared, and securely attached to each the same number of strong lines; the latter must be fifty fathoms long, and have at the end of each a stout swivel hook. The rest is only, a matter of detail. Now, what have you arranged with regard to matters in town?"

"I have fulfilled your instructions, sir, to the letter," said Belton. "I have communicated with the agents who act for the owner of Porchester House. I have caused an advertisement to be inserted in all the papers to-morrow morning to the effect that the renowned detective, Klimo, will be unable to meet his clients for at least a month, owing to the fact that he has accepted an important engagement upon the Continent, which will take him from home for that length of time. I have negotiated the sale of the various horses you have in training, and I have also arranged for the disposal of the animals and carriages you have now in use in London. Ram Gafur and the other native servants at Porchester House will come down by the midday train to-morrow, but before they do so, they will fulfill your instructions and repair the hole in the wall between the two houses. I cannot think of any more, sir."

"You have succeeded admirably, my dear Belton," said Carne, "and I am very pleased. To-morrow you had better see that a paragraph is inserted in all the daily papers announcing the fact that it is my intention to leave England for India immediately, on important private business. I think that will do for tonight."

Belton tidied the cabin, and, having done so, bade his master good-night. It was plain that he was exceedingly nervous about the success of the enterprise upon which Carne was embarking so confidently. The latter, on the other hand, retired to rest and slept as peacefully as if he had not a care or an anxiety upon his mind.

Next morning he was up by sunrise, and, by the time his friends Lords Orpington and Amberley were thinking about breakfast, had put the finishing touches to the scheme which was to bring his career in England to such a fitting termination.

According to the arrangement entered into on the previous day, his friends called for him at eleven o'clock, when they went ashore together. It was a lovely morning, and Carne was in the highest spirits. They visited the Castle together, made some purchases in the town, and then went off to lunch on board Lord Orpington's yacht. It was well-nigh three o'clock before Carne bade his host and hostess farewell, and descended the gangway in order to return to his own vessel. A brisk sea was running, and for this reason to step into the boat was an exceedingly difficult, if not a dangerous, matter. Either he miscalculated his distance, or he must have jumped at the wrong moment; at any rate, he missed his footing, and fell heavily on to the bottom. Scarcely a second, however, had elapsed before his coxswain had sprung to his assistance, and had lifted him up on to the seat in the stern. It was then discovered that he had been unfortunate enough to once more give a nasty twist to the ankle which had brought him to such grief when he had been staying at Greenthorpe Park on the occasion of the famous wedding.

"My dear fellow, I am so sorry," said Lord Orpington, who had witnessed the accident. "Won't you come on board again? If you can't walk up the ladder we can easily hoist you over the side."

"Many thanks," replied Carne, "but I think I can manage to get back to my own boat. It is better I should do so. My man has had experience of my little ailments, and knows exactly what is best to be done under such circumstances; but it is a terrible nuisance, all the same. I'm afraid it will be impossible for me now to be present at his Royal Highness's dinner this evening, and I have been looking forward to it so much."

"We shall all be exceedingly sorry," said Lord Amberley. "I shall come across in the afternoon to see how you are."

"You are very kind," said Carne, "and I shall be immensely glad to see you if you can spare the time."

With that he gave the signal to his men to push off. By the time he reached his own yacht his foot was so painful that it was necessary for him to be lifted on board—a circumstance which was duly noticed by the occupants of all the surrounding yachts, who had brought their glasses to bear upon him. Once below in his saloon, he was placed in a comfortable chair and left to Helton's careful attention.

"I trust you have not hurt yourself very much, sir," said that faithful individual, who, however, could not prevent a look of satisfaction coming into his face, which seemed to say that he was not ill-pleased that his master would, after all, be prevented from carrying out the hazardous scheme he had proposed to him the previous evening.

In reply, Carne sprang to his feet without showing a trace of lameness.

"My dear Belton, how peculiarly dense you are to-day," he said, with a smile, as he noticed the other's amazement. "Cannot you see that I have only been acting as you yourself wished I should do early this morning—namely, taking precautions? Surely you must see that, if I am laid up on board my yacht with a sprained ankle, society will say that is quite impossible for me to be doing any mischief elsewhere. Now, tell me, is everything prepared for tonight?"

"Everything, sir," Belton replied. "The dresses and wigs are ready. The canvas sacks, and the lines to which the spring hooks are attached, are in your cabin awaiting your inspection. As far as I can see, everything is prepared, and I hope will meet with your satisfaction."

"If you are as careful as usual, I feel sure it will," said Carne. "Now get some bandages and make this foot of mine up into as artistic a bundle as you possibly can. After that help me on deck and prop me up in a chair. As soon as my accident gets known there will be certain to be shoals of callers on board, and I must play my part as carefully as possible."

As Carne had predicted, this proved to be true. From half-past three until well after six o'clock a succession of boats drew up at his accommodation ladder, and the sufferer on deck was the recipient of as much attention as would have flattered the vainest of men. He had been careful to send a letter of apology to the illustrious individual who was to have been his host, expressing his sincere regrets that the accident which had so unfortunately befallen him would prevent the possibility of his being able to be present at the dinner he was giving that evening.

Day closed in and found the sky covered with heavy clouds. Towards eight o'clock a violent storm of rain fell, and when Carne heard it beating upon the deck above his cabin, and reflected that in consequence the night would in all probability be dark, he felt that his lucky star was indeed in the ascendant.

At half-past eight he retired to his cabin with Belton, in order to prepare for the events of the evening. Never before had he paid such careful attention to his make-up. He knew that on this occasion the least carelessness might lead to detection, and he had no desire that his last and greatest exploit should prove his undoing.

It was half-past nine before he and his servant had dressed and were ready to set off. Then, placing broad-brimmed hats upon their heads, and carrying a portmanteau containing the cloaks and headgear which they were to wear later in the evening, they went on deck and descended into the dinghy which was waiting for them alongside. In something under a quarter of an hour they had been put ashore in a secluded spot, had changed their costumes, and were walking boldly down beside the water towards the steps where they could see the Imperial launch still waiting. Her crew were lolling about, joking and laughing, secure in the knowledge that it would be some hours at least before their Sovereign would be likely to require their services again.

Their astonishment, therefore, may well be imagined when they saw approaching them the two men whom they had only half an hour before brought ashore. Stepping in and taking his seat under the shelter, his Majesty ordered them to convey him back to the yacht with all speed. The accent and voice were perfect, and it never for an instant struck any one on board the boat that a deception was being practiced. Carne, however, was aware that this was only a preliminary; the most dangerous portion of the business was yet to come.

On reaching the yacht, he sprang out on the ladder, followed by his aide-de-camp, Von Walzburg, and mounted the steps. His disguise must have been perfect indeed, for when he reached the deck he found himself face to face with the first lieutenant, who, on seeing him, saluted respectfully. For a moment Carne's presence of mind almost deserted him; then, seeing that he was not discovered, he determined upon a bold piece of bluff. Returning the officer's salute with just the air he had seen the Emperor use, he led him to suppose that he had important reasons for coming on board so soon, and, as if to back this assertion up, bade him send the chief steward to his cabin, and at the same time have the sentry removed from his door and placed at the end of the large saloon, with instructions to allow no one to pass until he was communicated with again.

The officer saluted and went off on his errand, while Carne, signing to Belton to follow him, made his way down the companion ladder to the Royal cabins. To both the next few minutes seemed like hours. Reaching the Imperial state room, they entered it and closed the door behind. Provided the sentry obeyed his orders, which there was no reason to doubt he would do, and the Emperor himself did not return until they were safely off the vessel again, there seemed every probability of their being able to carry out their scheme without a hitch.

"Put those bags under the table, and unwind the lines and place them in the gallery outside the window. They won't be seen there," said Carne to Belton, who was watching him from the doorway.

"Then stand by, for in a few minutes the chief steward will be here. As soon as he enters you must manage to get between him and the door, and, while I am engaging him in conversation, spring on him, clutch him by the throat, and hold him until I can force this gag into his mouth. After that we shall be safe for some time at least, for not a soul will come this way until they discover their mistake. It seems to me we ought to thank our stars that the chief steward's cabin was placed in such a convenient position. But hush, here comes the individual we want. Be ready to collar him as soon as I hold up my hand. If he makes a sound we are lost."

He had scarcely spoken before there was a knock at the door. When it opened, the chief steward entered the cabin, closing the door behind him.

"Schmidt," said his Majesty, who was standing at the further end of the cabin, "I have sent for you in order that I may question you on a matter of the utmost importance. Draw nearer."

The man came forward as he was ordered, and, having done so, looked his master full and fair in the face. Something he saw there seemed to stagger him. He glanced at him a second time, and was immediately confirmed in his belief.

"You are not the Emperor," he cried. "There is some treachery in this. I shall call for assistance."

He had half turned, and was about to give the alarm, when Carne held up his hand, and Belton, who had been creeping stealthily up behind him, threw himself upon him and had clutched him by the throat before he could utter a sound. The fictitious Emperor immediately produced a cleverly constructed gag and forced it into the terrified man's mouth, who in another second was lying upon the floor bound hand and foot.

"There, my friend," said Carne quietly, as he rose to his feet a few moments later, "I don't think you will give us any further trouble. Let me just see that those straps are tight enough, and then we'll place you on this settee, and afterwards get to business with all possible dispatch."

Having satisfied himself on these points, he signed to Belton, and between them they placed the man upon the couch.

"Let me see, I think, if I remember rightly, you carry the key of the safe in this pocket."

So saying, he turned the man's pocket inside out and appropriated the bunch of keys he found therein. Choosing one from it, he gave a final look at the bonds which secured the prostrate figure, and then turned to Belton.

"I think he'll do," he said. "Now for business. Bring the bags, and come with me."

So saying, he crossed the cabin, and, having assured himself that there was no one about to pry upon them, passed along the luxuriously carpeted alley way until he arrived at the door of the cabin, assigned to the use of the chief steward, and in which was the safe containing the magnificent gold plate, the obtaining of which was the reason of his being there. To his surprise and chagrin, the door was closed and locked. In his plans he had omitted to allow for this contingency. In all probability, however, the key was in the man's pocket, so, turning to Belton, he bade him return to the state room and bring him the keys he had thrown upon the table.

The latter did as he was ordered, and, when he had disappeared, Carne stood alone in the alley way waiting and listening to the various noises of the great vessel. On the deck overhead he could hear some one tramping heavily up and down, and then, in an interval of silence, the sound of pouring rain. Good reason as he had to be anxious, he could not help smiling as he thought of the incongruity of his position. He wondered what his aristocratic friends would say if he were captured and his story came to light. In his time he had impersonated a good many people, but never before had he had the honour of occupying such an exalted station. This was the last and most daring of all his adventures.

Minutes went by, and as Belton did not return, Carne found himself growing nervous. What could have become of him? He was in the act of going in search of him, when he appeared carrying in his hand the bunch of keys for which he had been sent. His master seized them eagerly.

"Why have you been so long?" he asked in a whisper. "I began to think something had gone wrong with you."

"I stayed to make our friend secure," the other answered. "He had well-nigh managed to get one of his hands free. Had he done so, he would have had the gag out of his mouth in no time, and have given the alarm. Then we should have been caught like rats in a trap."

"Are you quite sure he is secure now?" asked Carne anxiously.

"Quite," replied Belton. "I took good care of that."

"In that case we had better get to work on the safe without further delay. We have wasted too much time already, and every moment is an added danger."

Without more ado, Carne placed the most likely key in the lock and turned it. The bolt shot back, and the treasure chamber lay at his mercy.

The cabin was not a large one, but it was plain that every precaution had been taken to render it secure. The large safe which contained the Imperial plate, and which it was Carne's intention to rifle, occupied one entire side. It was of the latest design, and when Carne saw it he had to confess to himself that, expert craftsman as he was, it was one that would have required all his time and skill to open.

With the master key, however, it was the work of only a few seconds. The key was turned, the lever depressed, and then, with a slight pull, the heavy door swung forward. This done, it was seen that the interior was full to overflowing. Gold and silver plate of all sorts and descriptions, inclosed in bags of wash-leather and green baize, were neatly arranged inside. It was a haul such as even Carne had never had at his mercy before, and, now that he had got it, he was determined to make the most of it.

"Come, Belton," he said, "get these things out as quickly as possible and lay them on the floor. We can only carry away a certain portion of the plunder, so let us make sure that that portion is the best."

A few moments later the entire cabin was strewn with salvers, goblets, bowls, epergnes, gold and silver dishes, plates, cups, knives, forks, and almost every example of the goldsmith's art. In his choice Carne was not guided by what was handsomest or most delicate in workmanship or shape. Weight was his only standard. Silver he discarded altogether, for it was of less than no account. In something under ten minutes he had made his selection, and the stout canvas bags they had brought with them for that purpose were full to their utmost holding capacity.

"We can carry no more," said Carne to his faithful retainer, as they made the mouth of the last bag secure. "Pick up yours, and let us get back to the Emperor's state room."

Having locked the door of the cabin, they returned to the place whence they had started. There they found the unfortunate steward lying just as they had left him on the settee. Placing the bags he carried upon the ground, Carne crossed to him, and, before doing anything else, carefully examined the bonds with which he was secured.

Having done this, he went to the stern windows, and, throwing one open, stepped into the gallery outside. Fortunately for what he intended to do, it was still raining heavily, and in consequence the night was as dark as the most consummate conspirator could have desired. Returning to the room, he bade Belton help him carry the bags into the gallery, and, when this had been done, made fast the swivel hooks to the rings in the mouth of each.

"Take up your bags as quietly as possible," he said, "and lower them one by one into the water, but take care that they don't get entangled in the propeller. When you've done that, slip the rings at the other end of the lines through your belt, and buckle the latter tightly."

Belton did as he was ordered, and in a few moments the six bags were lying at the bottom of the sea.

"Now off with these wigs and things, and say when you're ready for a swim."

Their disguises having been discarded and thrown overboard, Carne and Belton clambered over the rails of the gallery and lowered themselves until their feet touched the water. Next moment they had both let go, and were swimming in the direction of Carne's own yacht.

It was at this period of their adventure that the darkness proved of such real service to them. By the time they had swum half a dozen strokes it would have needed a sharp pair of eyes to distinguish them as they rose and fell among the foam-crested waves. If, however, the storm had done them a good turn in saving them from notice, it came within an ace of doing them an ill service in another direction. Good swimmers though both Carne and Belton were, and they had proved it to each other's satisfaction in the seas of almost every known quarter of the globe, they soon found that it took all their strength to make headway now. By the time they reached their own craft, they were both completely exhausted. As Belton declared afterwards, he felt as if he could not have managed another twenty strokes even had his life depended on it.

At last, however, they reached the yacht's stern and clutched at the rope ladder which Carne had himself placed there before he had set out on the evening's excursion. In less time than it takes to tell, he had mounted it and gained the deck, followed by his faithful servant. They presented a sorry spectacle as they stood side by side at the taffrail, the water dripping from their clothes and pattering upon the deck.

"Thank goodness we are here at last," said Carne, as soon as he had recovered his breath sufficiently to speak. "Now slip off your belt, and hang it over this cleat with mine."

Belton did as he was directed, and then followed his master to the saloon companion ladder. Once below, they changed their clothes as quickly as possible, and having donned mackintoshes, returned to the deck, where it was still raining hard.

"Now," said Carne, "for the last and most important part of our evening's work. Let us hope the lines will prove equal to the demands we are about to make upon them."

As he said this, he took one of the belts from the cleat upon which he had placed it, and, having detached a line, began to pull it in, Belton following his example with another. Their hopes that they would prove equal to the confidence placed in them proved well founded, for, in something less than a quarter of an hour, the six bags, containing the Emperor of Westphalia's magnificent gold plate, were lying upon the deck, ready to be carried below and stowed away in the secret place in which Carne had arranged to hide his treasure.

"Now, Belton," said Carne, as he pushed the panel back into its place, and pressed the secret spring that locked it, "I hope you're satisfied with what we have done. We've made a splendid haul, and you shall have your share of it. In the meantime, just get me to bed as quickly as you can, for I'm dead tired. When you've done so, be off to your own. To-morrow morning you will have to go up to town to arrange with the bank authorities about my account."

Belton did as he was ordered, and half an hour later his master was safely in bed and asleep.

It was late next morning when he woke. He had scarcely breakfasted before the Earl of Amberley and Lord Orpington made their appearance over the side. To carry out the part he had arranged to play, he received them seated in his deck chair, his swaddled up right foot reclining on a cushion before him. On seeing his guests, he made as if he would rise, but they begged him to remain seated.

"I hope your ankle is better this morning," said Lord Orpington politely, as he took a chair beside his friend.

"Much better, thank you," Carne replied. "It was not nearly so serious as I feared. I hope to be able to hobble about a little this afternoon. And now tell me the news, if there is any."

"Do you mean to say that you have not heard the great news?" asked Lord Amberley, in a tone of astonishment.

"I have heard nothing," Carne replied. "Remember, I have not been ashore this morning, and I have been so busily engaged with the preparations for my departure tomorrow that I have not had time to look at my papers. Pray what is this news of which you speak with such bated breath?"

"Listen, and I'll tell you," Lord Orpington answered. "As you are aware, last night his Imperial Majesty the Emperor of Westphalia dined ashore, taking with him his aide-de-camp, Count Von Walzburg. They had not been gone from the launch more than half an hour when, to all intents and purposes, they reappeared, and the Emperor, who seemed much perturbed about something, gave the order to return to the yacht with all possible speed. It was very dark and raining hard at the time, and whoever the men may have been who did the thing, they were, at any rate, past masters in the art of disguise.

"Reaching the yacht, their arrival gave rise to no suspicion, for the officers are accustomed, as you know, to his Majesty's rapid comings and goings. The first lieutenant met them at the gang-way, and declares that he had no sort of doubt but that it was his Sovereign. Face, voice, and manner were alike perfect. From his Majesty's behaviour he surmised that there was some sort of trouble brewing for somebody, and, as if to carry this impression still further, the Emperor bade him send the chief steward to him at once, and, at the same time, place the sentry, who had hitherto been guarding the treasure chamber, at the end of the great saloon, with instructions to allow no one to pass him, on any pretext whatever, until the chief steward had been examined and the Emperor himself gave permission. Then he went below to his cabin.

"Soon after this the steward arrived, and was admitted. Something seems to have excited the latter's suspicions, however, and he was about to give the alarm when he was seized from behind, thrown upon the floor, and afterwards gagged and bound. It soon became apparent what object the rascals had in view. They had caused the sentry at the door of the treasure chamber to be removed and placed where not only he could not hinder them in their work, but would prevent them from being disturbed. Having obtained the key of the room and safe from the chief steward's pocket, they set off to the cabin, ransacked it completely, and stole all that was heaviest and most valuable of his Majesty's wonderful plate from the safe."

"Good gracious!" said Carne. "I never heard of such a thing. Surely it's the most impudent robbery that has taken place for many years past. To represent the Emperor of Westphalia and his aide-de-camp so closely that they could deceive even the officers of his own yacht, and to take a sentry off one post and place him in such a position as to protect them while at their own nefarious work, seems to me the very height of audacity. But how did they get their booty and themselves away again? Gold plate, under the most favourable circumstances, is by no means an easy thing to carry."

As he asked this question, Carne lit another cigar with a hand as steady as a rock.

"They must have escaped in a boat that, it is supposed, was lying under the shelter of the stern gallery," replied Lord Amberley.

"And is the chief steward able to furnish the police with no clue as to their identity?"

"None whatever," replied Orpington. "He opines to the belief, however, that they are Frenchmen. One of them, the man who impersonated the Emperor, seems to have uttered an exclamation in that tongue."

"And when was the robbery discovered?"

"Only when the real Emperor returned to the vessel shortly after midnight. There was no launch to meet him, and he had to get Tremorden to take him off. You can easily imagine the surprise his arrival occasioned. It was intensified when they went below to find his Majesty's cabin turned upside down, the chief steward lying bound and gagged upon the sofa, and all that was most valuable of the gold plate missing."

"What an extraordinary story!"

"And now, having told you the news with which the place is ringing, we must be off about our business," said Orpington. "Is it quite certain that you are going to leave us to-morrow?"

"Quite, I am sorry to say," answered Carne. "I am going to ask as many of my friends as possible to do me the honour of lunching with me at one o'clock, and at five I shall weigh anchor and bid England good-bye. I shall have the pleasure of your company, I hope."

"I shall have much pleasure," said Orpington.

"And I also," replied Amberley.

"Then good-bye for the present. It's just possible I may see you again during the afternoon."

The luncheon next day was as brilliant a social gathering as the most fastidious in such matters could have desired. Every one then in Cowes who had any claim to distinction was present, and several had undertaken the journey from town in order to say farewell to one who had made himself so popular during his brief stay in England. When Carne rose to reply to the toast of his health, proposed by the Prime Minister, it was observable that he was genuinely moved, as, indeed, were most of his hearers.

For the remainder of the afternoon his yacht's deck was crowded with his friends, all of whom expressed the hope that it might not be very long before he was amongst them once more.

To these kind speeches Carne invariably offered a smiling reply.

"I also trust it will not be long," he answered. "I have enjoyed my visit immensely, and you may be sure I shall never forget it as long as I live."

An hour later the anchor was weighed, and his yacht was steaming out of the harbour amid a scene of intense enthusiasm. As the Prime Minister had that afternoon informed him, in the public interest, the excitement of his departure was dividing the honours with the burglary of the Emperor of Westphalia's gold plate.

Carne stood beside his captain on the bridge, watching the little fleet of yachts until his eyes could no longer distinguish them. Then he turned to Belton, who had just joined him, and, placing his hand upon his shoulder, said:

"So much for our life in England, Belton, my friend. It has been glorious fun, and no one can deny that from a business point of view it has been eminently satisfactory. You, at least, should have no regrets."

"None whatever," answered Belton. "But I must confess I should like to know what they will say when the truth comes out."

Carne smiled sweetly as he answered:

"I think they'll say that, all things considered, I have won the right to call myself 'A Prince of Swindlers.'"

Coachwhip Publications

CoachwhipBooks.com

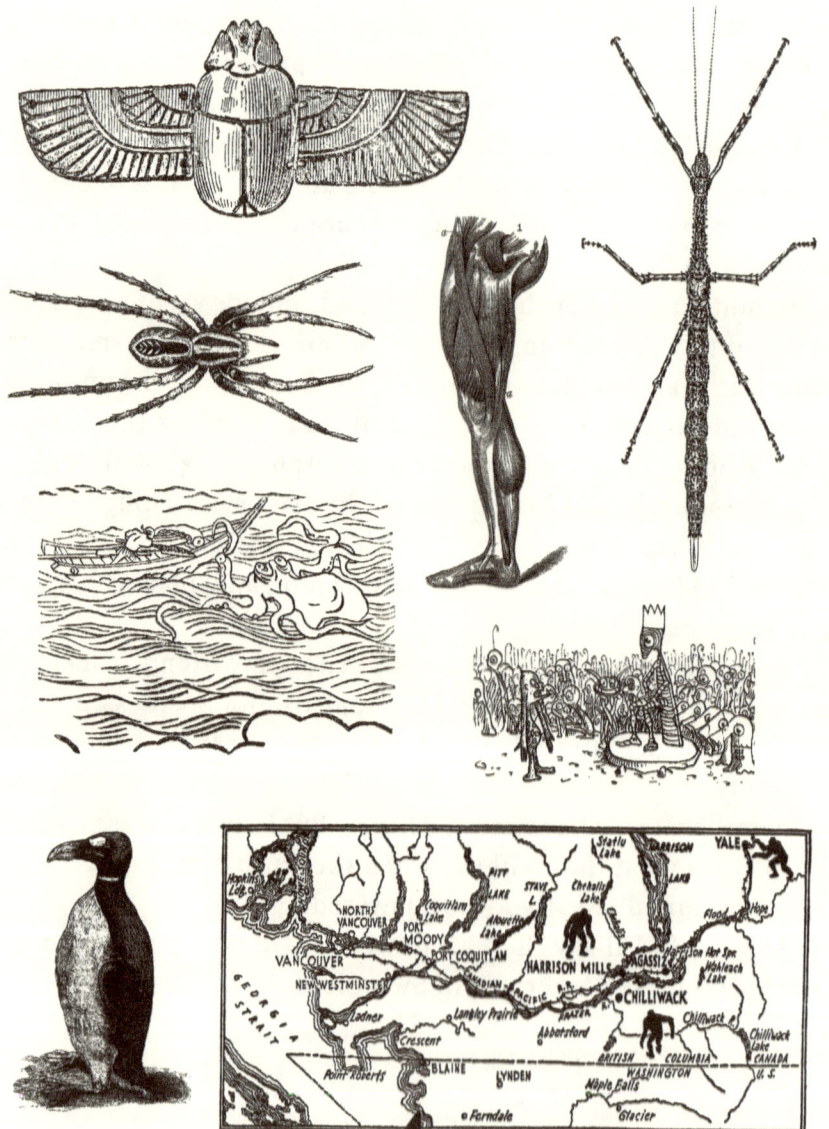

COACHWHIP PUBLICATIONS

ALSO AVAILABLE

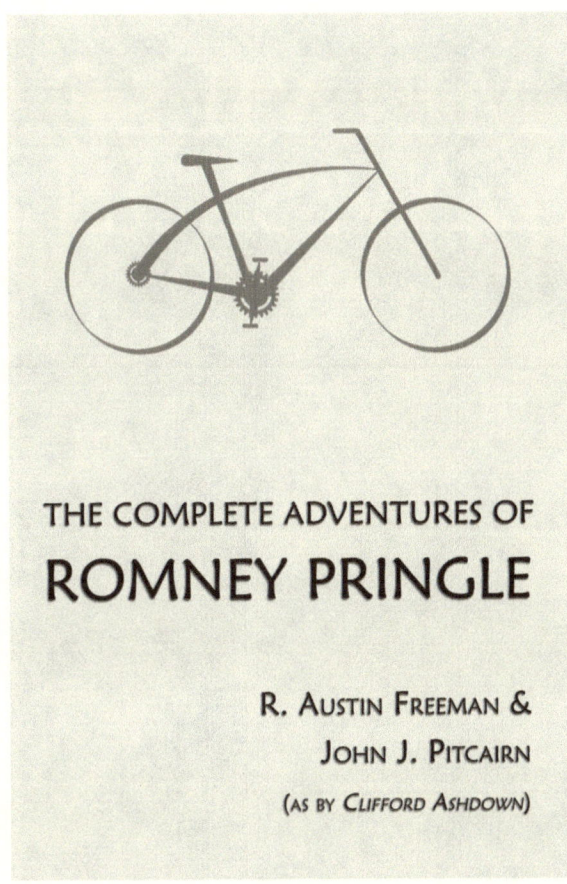

THE COMPLETE ADVENTURES OF

ROMNEY PRINGLE

R. AUSTIN FREEMAN &
JOHN J. PITCAIRN

(AS BY CLIFFORD ASHDOWN)

The Complete Adventures of Romney Pringle
R. Austin Freeman & John J. Pitcairn

ISBN 1-61646-090-3

COACHWHIP PUBLICATIONS

ALSO AVAILABLE

The Legal Exploits of Randolph Mason
Melville Davisson Post

ISBN 1-61646-061-X

COACHWHIP PUBLICATIONS

ALSO AVAILABLE

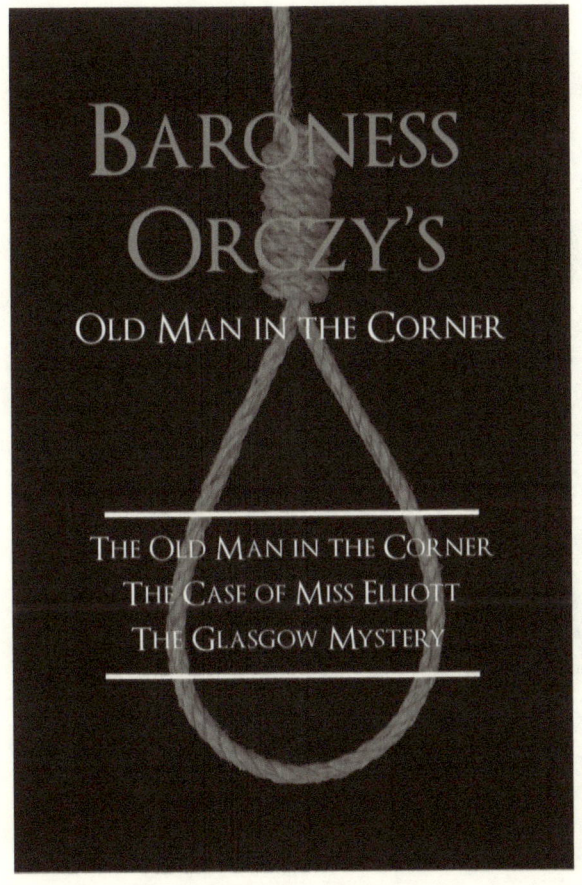

Old Man in the Corner
Baroness Orczy

ISBN 1-61646-015-6

COACHWHIP PUBLICATIONS

ALSO AVAILABLE

12 Cases for Max Carrados
Ernest Bramah

ISBN 1-61646-018-0

COACHWHIP PUBLICATIONS

ALSO AVAILABLE

NOVEMBER JOE

DETECTIVE OF THE WOODS

H. HESKETH-PRICHARD

November Joe: Detective of the Woods
H. Hesketh-Prichard

ISBN 1-61646-013-X

www.ingramcontent.com/pod-product-compliance
Lightning Source LLC
Chambersburg PA
CBHW031033030726
47497CB00004B/1120

* 9 7 8 1 6 1 6 4 6 1 4 0 9 *